PENGUIN BOOKS

A MARKET FOR MURDER

Anjana Rai Chaudhuri was born in Kolkata, India, and obtained a PhD in Chemistry from the United States. She lived in America for six years, married her Singaporean husband there, finally settling in Singapore. Anjana worked for many years as a research scientist in premier universities (including the University of Oxford, UK) and is the author of a science book chapter, fourteen research papers and review articles published in prestigious chemistry journals. Anjana's love of English Literature led to a BA in English Language and Literature from the Singapore University of Social Sciences in 2012. She is a double gold medal winner, for her master's in chemistry and BA in Literature, respectively. Motivated by her husband's diagnosis of chronic leukaemia, Anjana became a founder/moderator of cancer patient support groups, volunteering at the Singapore General Hospital, which led to the hospital awarding her an inspirational caregiver award. Her work with cancer patients led to two publications, one in the prestigious *British Medical Journal*. Anjana is the author of three works of fiction. Her first novel, a historical romance, *The Scent of Frangipani*, was published in 2019 by Monsoon Books, UK.

Also by Anjana Rai Chaudhuri

A Time for Murder, Penguin Random House SEA, 2021
A Taste for Murder, Penguin Random House SEA, 2022

A Market for Murder

A Das Sisters Mystery

Anjana Rai Chaudhuri

PENGUIN BOOKS

An imprint of Penguin Random House

PENGUIN BOOKS

USA | Canada | UK | Ireland | Australia
New Zealand | India | South Africa | China | Southeast Asia

Penguin Books is part of the Penguin Random House group of companies
whose addresses can be found at global.penguinrandomhouse.com

Published by Penguin Random House SEA Pte Ltd
9, Changi South Street 3, Level 08-01,
Singapore 486361

Penguin
Random House
SEA

First published in Penguin Books by Penguin Random House SEA 2022

ISBN 9789814954303

Typeset in Garamond by MAP Systems, Bangalore, India

www.penguin.sg

Contents

Saturday, 15 January 2011

Mount Hehuan, Taiwan

Prologue

Industrialist, Ronnie Lee, leant back in his seat and gazed out of the aircraft window. His private plane was flying over mountain ranges on its way from Taipei to Taichung. Wispy mushroom clouds floated by, playing hide-and-seek with the sun. *Light and shade, joy and sorrow, one defined the other.* Except when one was in a nightmare and hurtling down a dark tunnel without the promise of light. *His life with Alice.* Ronnie took a sip from the wine glass resting on the pull-out tray in front.

His business trip to Taiwan had panned out well and there were still a few days left before returning to Singapore. He planned on spending them in Taichung while sewing up the deal enabling his businesses to remain afloat for a few more months. His business partner had promised to take him skiing on Mount Hehuan and he was looking forward to that. Images of alpine holidays taken with his late first wife, Natalie, and his two children, Alan and Linda, flashed through his mind. He sighed. That had been the good life, fractured by illness and the worst mistake he ever made. *A mistake called Alice.*

Thoughts of his second wife filled him with anger. To cuckold him with his own golfing buddy, Nelson Ong—her daring and his humiliation. And Alice was continuing the affair—it was now six years running. While he wanted a divorce, thoughts of Etienne, his son with Alice, made him pause. Etienne was immature and slow of learning. He still needed a father's guiding hand. So, Ronnie had done the next best thing. In his last will and testament, he disinherited Alice. At least, he would have the satisfaction of knowing that after he died, Alice would not have access to 39, Primrose Crescent, the bungalow she loved, but which he had built with his hard-earned money.

His thoughts dwelled on his older children. He worried about both. Alan was unmarried and unsettled in life. Selena had been the love of Alan's life and her death in a car crash had left him shattered. Ronnie had pleaded with his son to move on, but to no avail. Linda was married to a man who was after her fortune. He decided to have a talk with her when he was back in Singapore. Linda deserved better in life.

The plane lurched sharply, the wine glass on the tray rattled ominously, and Ronnie reached for his seatbelt.

Rosvinder Rosie Kaur, the pilot of Ronnie's plane, looked forward to landing in Taichung soon. The cockpit afforded a beautiful view of rugged mountains capped with snow. The weather was good, the flight had been smooth. Her elder daughter, Nina, was going through a particularly difficult and defiant adolescent phase and Rosie needed to call her in Singapore from her Taichung hotel. Pradeep, Nina's father, struggled to manage her tantrums. Nina, belligerent and unhappy with the world was so different from placid Rina, three years younger. Rosie hoped Nina would soon leave this rebellious phase behind.

Pradeep was up for tenure at the Pelangi University of Engineering and Social Sciences and Rosie's lips lifted in a smile. He was sure to get it. Her mind dwelled on their student days at Temasek University and their gang of three, Pradeep, herself, and Alan Lee, the son of her employer and whose plane she was flying. In her second year of Electrical Engineering, she had dropped out, intent on learning to fly. Her father had been a pilot and Rosie yearned to emulate him. Pradeep had not batted an eyelash and continued courting her and they had married as soon as he obtained his doctorate degree. By that time, Rosie was flying commercial planes and loving it.

Rosie blinked. Was the flight display unit flickering? No, she rubbed her eyes. All the flight parameters were stable and in fifteen minutes they would be landing in Taichung. She checked the altimeter readings, they were fine, the plane was flying over the mountain range at a steady altitude.

Rosie's mind harked back to the past. Her marital bliss had been complete when the two girls arrived and with the help of a maid, Rosie was still clocking in the hours needed to hold on to her commercial pilot's licence while at the same time taking care of her home. Life was flowing smoothly until that night in Hong Kong. Why had she taken the vodka offered by a colleague knowing she was flying in a few hours and what had made her take more?

She was still lucid before the flight from Hong Kong to Singapore, with only a slight headache. Unfortunately, her co-pilot was John Wang, one of the most disliked captains among the flight crew. One error on her part, and the plane had gone into a minor stall, hastily corrected by the captain, who had been taking a toilet break and had rushed back to the cockpit. Looking at her suspiciously, he had edged towards her and smelt liquor on her breath. That had been the end of her commercial flying career and dreams.

Rosie sighed. Grounded at home, she had taken her frustrations out on her elder daughter and now her guilty conscience blamed herself for Nina's rebellious streak. At her wit's end, hating being a housewife after flying the skies, she had even contemplated divorce when Pradeep, tired of her whining, stopped speaking to her. It was then their college friend, Alan Lee, visited their home with his father, searching for a pilot to fly Ronnie's private plane. That was more than five years ago and while her salary was not on par with what she earned before, there was no greater joy for a pilot than flying the skies.

Rosie stiffened. Why were the mountain peaks so close? She glanced at the altimeter and caught it blinking before the whole flight display unit went blank.

'The display unit has gone blank! It's not reading anything!' Rosie cried out as she frantically pulled the yoke back to force the nose of the plane upward in a desperate attempt to climb over the mountain range.

But it was too late. The last scene Rosie saw before her death was the mountain rushing towards her.

MURDER IN BALI

Wednesday, 15 May 2013

Bali, Indonesia

1

Lily Das looked at her reflection in the hotel room mirror. Her close-cropped hair was a black sheen framing a face radiant from the makeup she had applied. Foundation and powder blunted the sharpness of her long nose. She carefully applied a shocking pink lipstick to her thin lips. There was a grunt from the bed of the lanai and Lily directed a sly smile at her sister, Dolly, lounging on a twin bed.

'You're forty-seven years old, Lily,' scolded her fifty-five-year-old sister. 'Can't you find a nude shade of lipstick? Shocking pink at your age looks like a bad joke! And your lipstick has smeared, do put your contact lenses on when you are applying make-up.' She gave Lily a quick smile. 'Good to see you dressing up and enjoying yourself, though. You needed a break. Little Molly is sweet, but she has taken a lot out of you. You've lost weight, Lil.'

At the mention of her infant daughter, Lily smiled happily. 'Oh, I didn't mind the sleepless nights and giving up work to take care of Moll. And Frankie helped. He forgot his OCD and rushed in through the connecting door from his studio apartment every time he heard Molly crying in the night. This baby has worked wonders for our marriage.' Her eyes softened with love. 'When Frankie looks at Molly with so much love, I feel like crying!' She began putting on her contact lenses.

Dolly smiled, her eyes lighting up. 'It's true, you and Frankie look like newly-weds nowadays. What a relief! I once thought his OCD would end your marriage. And then his therapist had a brainwave.' She thought back to the therapist's advice of Lily and Frankie living in separate apartments for Frankie's OCD to remain confined to his own space without affecting Lily.

Looking in the mirror, Lily dabbed her lips with a tissue that she grabbed from a box on the dressing table. 'It was Frankie's idea for me to take this break in Bali. I just hope the new café I've opened in our condo complex will do as well as my first venture there. Vernon and Angie are putting in a lot of hard work. With Ashikin sharing the lease with me, I don't feel as tense as before. Girlie is a second mother to Molly, and she is in good hands while I'm here.'

Dolly nodded at the mention of their mother's domestic helper. 'Girlie works hard. Mummy is getting frail and needs more attention. And then she has little Molly to look after and little Ben, too.'

Lily laughed. 'Ben is the spitting image of Vernon and will grow up to be as troublesome. Yes, Angie leaves Ben with Girlie. Mummy's condo unit at Silver Springs is like a mini nursery.' Lily patted her hair, looked in the mirror at the blue eye shadow lining her eyes, matching the sky-blue dress she wore, nodded at her reflection, satisfied, and turned to her sister. 'I just wish Mummy would stop calling Molly "Silly". It's getting on my nerves.'

Dolly laughed loudly. 'Mummy says "Silly" rhymes better with "Lily" than "Molly" and that "Molly" would have been a more appropriate name for my daughter if I had one. Rhymes with "Dolly". You could've named her "Milly" and saved all this hassle.'

Lily shook her head. 'Nicknames stick, though. And I don't want Molly to be bullied by her classmates, later.' Lily came and sat on her bed. 'I'm sorry Joey couldn't join us.'

Dolly shrugged. 'He's away overseas most days of the month. Now that he is his own boss and runs a full-fledged PI agency, I thought he could get his minions to do overseas assignments. But that hasn't happened yet. I'm not lonely with Ash in the house.' Her eyes softened as she mentioned her son.

'And his girlfriend, Amita is there, too,' Lily quipped mischievously.

'You know they are both in the physics programme at Temasek U. They study together! But yes, they are very much in love.' Dolly smiled, indulgently.

Lily looked at her watch. 'Dolly, I'm hungry. You haven't even taken a shower yet! Hurry up! I want to have dinner.'

Dolly smiled at Lily, nodded, got up from the bed and walked to the bathroom. She was still beautiful with good skin, a great figure and regular features. Her job at the Singapore Criminal Investigation Department entailed gruelling hours but Dolly did not mind as she loved her work. Her second husband, Eurasian, Joey Pestana, got along well with her son, Ash, from her first marriage. Ash and Joey had grown so close that sometimes Dolly felt like an outsider.

Lily went outside the lanai and sat on one of the chairs in their small, private courtyard. She looked out over the wide expanse of a green lawn at the Indian Ocean, wild and stormy, foamy waves crashing on to Seminyak Beach. The roar of the ocean resounded in her ears and the setting sun coloured the waters a rippling gold. Bali was beautiful.

Lily sighed. She had come so far from those dark days after her first husband Joy's funeral. Although an arranged marriage, Lily had fallen deeply in love with Joy after the nuptials, the only shadow in their blissful union being her repeated miscarriages. She had been devastated when Joy was diagnosed with Stage IV cancer and died a few months after his diagnosis.

Her widowed mother, Uma, had plucked her out of despair and pushed her to make her home with her at Silver Springs Condominium in Holland Avenue in Singapore. Lily's interests were cooking and reading murder mysteries, in that order. When the lease of a shop on the ground floor of her condo became available a few years ago, Lily had opened a minimart selling groceries and necessities. She hired a Chinese lad, Vernon, who shared her interest in whipping up culinary delights and partitioned her minimart into a café, which she ran with Vernon's help.

Starting out small, the café, Lily's Kitchen, had become a huge success earning Lily enough profit to close the minimart and expand the café. Two years ago, she had graduated to running a stall at the science canteen of Temasek University after her marriage to a Eurasian, Frankie Kennedy. Then, Frankie and Lily adopted a little girl from India whom they named Molly. Frankie bought two studio units for them at Silver Springs Condo and Lily gave up work to take care of Molly. With Molly a little older now and Girlie taking care of her, Lily could work again. She opened a café at Block C of the condo complex, taking on her Malay friend, Ashikin, as partner. The café, selling Indian and Malay food, was popular in the complex, garnering Lily a good income. Lily smiled. Life was good.

Lily got to her feet and walked across the lawn towards the beach and the ocean. Surfers were returning from the waters, shouting exuberantly to one another, a lone figure rode a horse across the beach while children still played in the sand under the watchful eyes of their parents. Lily stood on the beach watching the sun dip into the horizon.

She had brought with her the latest murder mystery by Louise Penny and was half-way through the book. Lily smiled. Her involvement with real-life murder mysteries had been far more thrilling than what she read in books and for that, she had to thank her police superintendent sister, Dolly.

As she walked back to the lanai, Lily cast her mind back four years ago to the time when an Indian woman had fallen to her death in her condominium complex. What appeared to be a suicide turned out to be a murder and two more killings followed. Dolly had headed the investigation and Lily blushed when she thought of the praise heaped on her for supplying the critical insight that cracked the case. It was during that time, her neighbour, lawyer, Frankie Kennedy, started handling Dolly's divorce case and had fallen in love with Lily.

Lily sat down on the bench in front of the lanai. She thought back to the time she had been in danger of losing her business licence while running the stall in Temasek University when a customer had died after eating her food. With Dolly's help, she discovered the man had been murdered. Working together, the sisters successfully put the cunning killer under lock and key.

'Well, I'm ready if you are.'

Lily turned around at her sister's voice and smiled appreciatively. Dolly looked beautiful in a black and white pantsuit and costume jewellery. Dolly had always been the pretty one, Lily thought ruefully, as she rose from the bench, tried to tuck in her tummy and walk straight.

* * *

The hotel restaurant, The Sea-Shell Café, boasted an oceanfront view and a warm, inviting ambience. The hotel manager, an Englishman named Mark Latham, stood outside the entrance, a pinched expression on his face. He nodded curtly at the sisters and looked on as a waitress showed them to their table.

'We have a Balinese dance performance of the Ramayana at 8.30 p.m.,' the cheerful waitress said as she seated the sisters. 'I am Darti, and I will be your hostess tonight. Our specials are the Indian chicken curry set and the western grilled sea bass set. Our soup of the day is chicken vegetable soup.' The waitress placed two menus on the table and smiled.

'Oh, we'll watch the Balinese dance for sure!' Lily exclaimed. 'Where is the performance going to take place?'

The waitress smiled, showing pearly white teeth in a round, comely face. She pointed towards an open space next to the restaurant. 'At the amphitheatre, madam. Maybe you can have your coffee there when the dance begins?' She nodded and glided away to the next table.

Lily perused the menu. 'Well, a sparse menu, overall. I think I will order the roasted spring chicken with trimmings.'

'It won't fill you up,' Dolly admonished. 'Order the Indian curry set, it comes with rice,' she advised her sister.

They both ordered the curry set and sat back to enjoy the sea breeze. The sun had set, and the beach looked dark and ominous, but they could still see the white crests of the waves and hear the thundering sound as they rammed into the shore.

Dolly felt a certain peace stealing over her. The last year had been relatively stress-free at work after the threat of being retrenched by her previous supervisor, Superintendent Siti Abdullah, had dissipated when the latter was transferred out of the department. Her replacement, Superintendent Geraldine Ang, while being a hard taskmaster, was fair and more pleasant to her subordinates. However, stress at her workplace had been replaced by an underlying tension in her marriage. Joey spent far too much time abroad and Dolly could not help wondering if he had a mistress in Malacca, where he spent a week every month. Her first husband's infidelity during their marriage made Dolly overly suspicious.

Joey had been her Junior College classmate and she had met him again when he had assisted her as a private investigator during her divorce from Dr Pritam Singh, her first husband. After three months of dating, they had quickly married, both being in their fifties and thinking they should make the most of their time together. Why did Joey go off to Malacca at least once a month? Dolly smiled at the waitress as she placed two plates of curry and rice on the table. As she started eating, Dolly's thoughts dwelled on her son.

Dolly had married her first husband Pritam Singh for love and that love had lasted a long time, producing its fruit and the apple of her eyes, her son, Ashok. The interfaith marriage, Dolly being an Indian Hindu and Pritam being an Indian Sikh had been peaceful after Dolly readily agreed to Ashok being raised according to the Sikh faith. That had been a blessing in disguise as Ash was in love with Amita Singh, a Sikh girl and his religious affiliation helped Amita's parents accept him as a future groom.

Lily frowned at the chicken curry, trying to determine the alien spices used. She flicked a glance at her sister and said, 'I'm sure Joey is deeply in love with you, Doll. You should look at his eyes when they are on you. Girlie would describe the look as "gooey".' She had read her sister's mind.

The sisters laughed, concentrating on their food. They did not notice a slim, middle-aged Chinese man looking speculatively at them from a neighbouring table.

2

Forty-nine-year-old Alan Lee dressed for dinner in his ocean-view villa at the Beachcombers Hotel in Seminyak. Having arrived from Singapore in the morning, he had just returned from visiting the temple at Tanah Lot. Now he was ready for the real work on hand, the reason for visiting Bali. To find out more about the counterfeit computer chip crime syndicate. Soon he would visit the bar connected to one of the syndicate masterminds, to find out if there was a computer chip recycling assembly factory here in Bali.

He was committed to avenging his father's death and saving his deceased friend, Rosvinder Kaur's reputation. He disbelieved the official verdict that his father's private plane had crashed due to an error on the part of the pilot, his friend, Rosvinder. Instead, Alan believed his father's plane had crashed due to counterfeit chips in the flight display unit causing the plane to malfunction.

Alan remembered Rosvinder's husband and his buddy, Pradeep's face, etched with shock and sorrow when the year-long investigation into his father's plane crash deemed the cause as pilot error. While not a legal requirement, Ronnie Lee had fitted his light private aircraft with black boxes for safety. But the plane had crashed into the jungles of a Taiwanese mountain and neither the cockpit voice recorder nor the flight data recorder could be found. What the investigators uncovered instead was Rosvinder Kaur's flying history and that she had once been drunk while flying a commercial aeroplane, resulting in the loss of her commercial flying licence. The investigators had single-mindedly focused on the pilot's history, ignoring other possible causes of the crash.

Alan, with his stepbrother, Etienne, had flown to Taichung in Taiwan in January 2012, and his plea to reopen the investigation had fallen on deaf ears. What Alan did with the ample money his deceased father left, was pay a team of natives to thoroughly search the crash area. Six months into their search, the natives found the cockpit voice recorder and Alan flew to Taiwan and brought it back with him. He knew a friend at the Transport Safety Investigation Bureau and with his help had downloaded the data from the recorder. Alan heard the words Rosie screamed a second before the crash.

Why had the flight display unit gone blank? Before it did so, was it giving erroneous readings so that Rosie took pre-emptive action too late? Alan knew his father had bought a new flight display unit three months before the crash when he had the whole cockpit refurbished. Alan talked to Donald Quek, his father's technician, who took care of the plane, but found him surly and uncooperative.

'The pilot is your college mate, you're trying to clear her name and blame me, is it?' Quek asked Alan, his face red. 'Nothing was wrong with the plane.'

The trail appeared to have fizzled out, then unexpectedly blazed back to life when, one day, his subordinate at work, Lionel Chu, entered his office, looking worried.

'Alan, Lexco has sent back some dies that have failed in the field. They are upset and I immediately ordered our Failure Analysis Lab to find out why the dies failed.'

'*What?*' Alan's face lost colour. In all his years as Manager of Yield Engineering at Waferworld, the second largest semiconductor wafer foundry in the world, Lexco, one of their most valued customers, had never returned failed dies. Losing Lexco's custom would be a major business setback for Waferworld.

Lionel's face was puzzled. 'The reliability parametric checks are failing on all the dies.'

Alan frowned. 'How can that be? The turnkey company packaged the dies so they must have passed the reliability checks we devised for them.'

Waferworld did not test and package its dies, instead hired a turnkey company to do the job. It was the turnkey company's responsibility to test the dies and bin them out, package the ones that passed the tests and met the specs, and discard the faulty dies. A chat with the turnkey company manager in charge of testing and packaging Waferworld dies had been unfruitful with the manager insisting that all packaged dies had passed the reliability test. Then, how had faulty dies entered the supply chain? And as an employee of Waferworld, Alan knew the dies in question had been manufactured for airplane parts.

It was at this point Alan began wondering about substandard chips sold on the black market. Being a manager in a foundry that manufactured Integrated Circuit chips, Alan had always been aware of the counterfeit chip black market. Research from journals and the internet revealed the counterfeit chip market generated billions of dollars in revenue and was growing as years passed. Did his father's plane have a new flight display unit fitted with counterfeit chips? He knew Ronnie Lee wanted to cut costs and told his technician to refurbish the plane cheap so perhaps Donald Quek had bought low-cost parts and those had a high likelihood of using counterfeit materials.

When he talked to Donald again and learnt that his father's plane had been fitted with parts and chips from a new Singapore broker, Alan was fairly sure the broker was selling counterfeit parts and chips. The fact that the broker had shut down his Singapore business soon after the crash, further cemented Alan's belief that the flight display unit in his father's plane had faulty chips.

At the same time, Alan suspected the turnkey company serving Waferworld of being corrupt and a source of faulty die supply by not discarding failed dies, instead selling them on the black market. It was entirely probable, Alan thought, that this thriving counterfeit chip black market in Singapore had supplied the broker of the plane spare parts company his father used, with faulty chips for his private plane.

Before he could inform the police, Alan knew he had to gather more evidence and he did so surreptitiously with Lionel's help. He had Lionel cultivate a mole inside the turnkey company and the mole was slowly gathering evidence pointing to the source of corruption there. The mole had been able to steal some of the dies that had failed specifications and should have been discarded but kept aside, and Alan had sent them for ABI Sentry testing for counterfeit chips. The results came back positive, and Alan had stored the data on a mobile hard disk as evidence to show the police when he was ready.

The mole also identified the corrupt employee in the turnkey company. Alan suspected the employee was working for a counterfeit chip syndicate. The trail to discover the identity of one of the syndicate masterminds had led Alan to Bali, though he was sure the main person heading the counterfeit chip syndicate worked out of Singapore.

Alan walked over to the mirror and began brushing his hair. He hoped the Bali trip would allow him to gather hard evidence against the syndicate, such as a factory assembling counterfeit chip parts and repackaging them for the black market. That was what the mole had overheard the corrupt employee say on the phone. It made sense to have an assembly factory in Bali where the law sometimes turned a blind eye, than have one in Singapore. He had to find evidence fast to thwart his stepmother from initiating a civil suit in the courts against Rosie's estate for Ronnie's wrongful death. He wanted to make his stepmother understand the plane had crashed due to faulty parts.

As soon as the official investigation into his father's plane crash cited pilot error as the cause, Alan's stepmother, Alice Lee, furious at being disinherited from the family property, decided to sue the pilot, Rosvinder Kaur's estate for negligence to gain compensation for the wrongful death of her husband. Alice decided she would financially benefit from her husband's death. If she did not get the house, at least, she would win a large amount of money in compensation for his death.

So far, Alan's veiled hints that he would evict his stepmother from his bungalow if she initiated civil court proceedings against Rosie's estate, had worked. Alice Lee was hesitant to initiate the civil suit. She loved her husband's bungalow too much to leave it. But Alan knew the ploy would not work for much longer. He had decided to evict Alice from his bungalow to sell it as he wished to set up a foundation for kidney dialysis patients in his mother's memory and he needed funds. He knew as soon as he gave his stepmother an eviction notice, Alice would go ahead with initiating the civil suit against Rosie's estate.

Alan sprayed some cologne on his neck in front of the dressing table mirror. He was prepared for the civil suit. He had already decided to have his lawyer represent Pradeep and Rosie's estate. Alan felt his lawyer could win the civil suit and save Rosvinder's reputation and Pradeep from bankruptcy if Alan could find enough evidence of counterfeit chips being sold in the Singapore black market. Alan was sure the evidences from the cockpit voice recorder and of counterfeit chips sold on the black market in Singapore would tilt the balance in court in favour of the airplane malfunctioning.

When he returned to Singapore, Alan planned to have his lawyer, Jonas Ellis, take up the case on Pradeep's behalf. If Jonas agreed, Alan would bring him up to speed on the evidences he had found so far on the counterfeit chip Singapore market.

He had kept the mobile hard disk with all the evidence he had gathered on the faulty dies in a safe place. It had enough incriminating evidence to nail at least one of the crime syndicate members. Lionel wanted Alan to give him the hard disk for safekeeping, but Alan demurred. Lionel had been acting strangely and Alan had become apprehensive of Lionel betraying his trust.

Alan sighed and glanced at his watch. It was getting late, and he needed to stake out the Nightowl Bar. He went to the table by the window, logged off his laptop, closed the screen and walked out of the villa.

He felt uneasy as he walked in the hotel grounds. The lanais and villas were spread over a large area with vegetation everywhere, he felt eyes watching him all the time. He was no fool. With the millions generated from selling faulty chips, the masterminds behind the syndicate would stop at nothing to ensure their path to profits remained intact. If they knew he was on their tail, they would kill him. He smiled ruefully at his imagination, shrugged, and reached the hotel restaurant.

* * *

Alan was eating his sea bass dinner when he saw a couple of women two tables away. He frowned; he knew them from somewhere. He had even talked to them. Suddenly, he smiled. Now, he remembered. His sister, Linda, had introduced him to them at a food stall at the Silver Springs Condo complex where she lived. In fact, the chubbier of the two ladies had been Linda's classmate from school and ran the food stall. Now, what was the name of the food stall?

He shook his head. No, he could not remember that. But he recalled that Linda's classmate's sister was a police inspector. What *were* their names? One was named after a flower? After a minute of intense concentration, his face cleared. Lily Das was the name of Linda's classmate, and her sister was called Dolly. Dolly was the police inspector. Well, it was a small world, Alan thought. Seeing a Singapore police inspector sitting only yards away from him just when he was becoming afraid of sleuthing a Singapore crime syndicate on his own. He quickly finished his food and paid up. He got up and casually approached the table where the Das sisters were eating their desserts.

'Madam Lily Das, do you remember me? I'm Linda Lee's brother, Alan. Linda Lee, your schoolmate? She lives in the same condo complex as you. We met one day at your café at the Silver Springs Condo, and I was introduced to you, too, Inspector Das.'

Comprehension dawned on Lily's face while Dolly looked puzzled. 'Yes, yes, your nephew and niece, Duleep, and Natasha are regular customers!' Lily turned to her sister. 'You met Mr Lee once at the café, Doll, remember Ronnie Lee's son?' She turned back to Alan and smiled. 'My sister is Assistant Superintendent now,' she announced, proudly.

Dolly was nodding. 'Ah, yes. We met a long time ago. We are sorry about your father's death in an airplane crash, he was a great philanthropist.'

'Thank you. Yes, my father was a compassionate man. May I join you for dessert?' Alan asked.

'Of course!' Lily said. 'Please have a seat.'

When Darti hovered near their table, Alan said, 'One scoop of vanilla ice-cream will do for me.'

3

Lights had come on in front of the restaurant, throwing into focus the crater of the amphitheatre where the Balinese dance was going to take place. The Das sisters sat at their table inside the restaurant with Alan Lee, conversing about Linda and her children.

During a lull in the conversation, Alan burst out, 'ASP Das, I know I am out of order, but I need your advice on an issue.'

His apologetic voice elicited a wry smile from Dolly. 'What's the problem?'

'Are you aware of any counterfeit computer chip syndicate operating out of Singapore?'

Taken by surprise, Dolly sat up straight while Lily hiccupped over her chocolate cake.

Dolly said, 'You mean fake computer chips? What is the basis of your suspicion that such a syndicate exists in Singapore?' She cut a slice of the chocolate cake on her plate and popped it into her mouth.

Alan Lee smiled at Darti as she placed a bowl of ice-cream on his placemat. He turned to Dolly. 'I'm a manager at Waferworld, a computer chip manufacturer, we have our plant in Woodlands. I've been noticing suspicious activities from one of our turnkey suppliers. Chips manufactured at Waferworld are being sold on the black market. Last year, one of our customers reported dies that had failed in the field and when I examined the dies, I noticed they were Waferworld dies that were faulty and should have been discarded by the turnkey company.'

'Turnkey company?' Dolly raised her brows.

Patiently, Alan explained the function of a turnkey company and continued, 'One of our turnkey companies is recycling faulty dies and selling them on the black market to distributors and suppliers. Seeing it is a Waferworld die, customers would buy it and then in a short time, the dies would fail.'

Dolly said thoughtfully, 'And the black market syndicate would charge the same price for the die as Waferworld? Without having to manufacture it. And there are many dies we are talking about.'

Alan Lee nodded. 'They would charge cheaper, but the main point is that they would be making profit without manufacturing the dies. Counterfeit chip industries are worth millions of dollars. They would be selling Waferworld's name and then when too many such chips on the black market eventually fail, which is a cert, it would give Waferworld a bad reputation. The faulty dies leak current, ASP Das, and they would fail after a while, but without a warranty, the customer has no hope of getting a replacement.'

Alan ate some of his ice-cream and said, 'I managed to obtain some of the faulty dies from the turnkey company. They should have been discarded but had been set aside, presumably for the black market. I ran some tests on these dies and they are faulty. I've collected all the data and stored them on a hard disk. With the help of my subordinate at work, Lionel Chu, I've placed a mole in the turnkey company. It was he who gave us the faulty dies I sent for testing. I have reason to believe the crime syndicate operates out of Singapore, and one of its masterminds is here in Bali. When I have more evidence, I would like to present them to you, ASP Das.'

Dolly looked alarmed. 'Don't investigate the syndicate on your own, Mr Lee. Leave it to the police. These syndicates can be dangerous. They operate a lucrative business stealing computer chips and would eliminate anyone who is about to blow the whistle. I strongly suggest you report your findings to us as soon as possible. We have a branch at CID looking into crime syndicates, ASP Brendan Gan heads the branch.'

Alan finished the last of his ice-cream and smiled. 'Yes, I will do that, ASP Das.' He looked at his watch.

'We were sorry to hear about your father's death. I believe his private plane crashed.' Lily's eyes were curious.

Alan Lee's eyes gleamed. 'I think my father's plane crash is also connected to a faulty chip though the pilot was blamed for the crash. I had men retrieve the cockpit voice recorder and the pilot had screamed that the flight display unit had gone blank seconds before the crash. My father's plane had been fitted with a new flight display unit and it would only malfunction if the chips inside were counterfeit. But, of course, the display unit was smashed up in the crash so there will never be any proof to back my suspicions. All I can do is prove the existence of the crime syndicate from the faulty Waferworld dies and help the police break up the syndicate. A Singapore broker sold parts for my father's plane, it crashed, faulty dies are appearing in our Singapore supply chain and a Singapore turnkey company is selling faulty dies.'

Alan Lee looked at his watch again and got to his feet. 'I need to go. I will see you soon in Singapore then, ASP Das, at CID HQ. Please introduce me to ASP Gan and I will give him all the evidence I have gathered. Madam Lily, I will be sure to sample one of your curries the next time I visit my sister. Goodbye.' Alan Lee placed some money near his bowl, nodded pleasantly and left the table.

'He seems to have counterfeit chips on his brain,' Lily observed while finishing the last of her chocolate cake.

'On the other hand, his interest in the syndicate if one exists, may be personal. He works with computer chips, and he suspects his father's plane crash stemmed from faulty chips. Well, I'm sure he'll talk to Brendan Gan soon. This is not my department.' Dolly had finished her dessert and was leaning thoughtfully back in her chair.

Cymbals clanged nearby and the waitress, Darti, came to their table with the bill. 'The Ramayana dance is about to start, ladies,' she said. 'Shall I serve you coffee at the amphitheatre?'

Dolly signed the bill and nodded enthusiastically. 'Yes, please, two coffees with cream and sugar.'

The two sisters exited the restaurant and walked the short distance to the amphitheatre. There was a crater with stone seats and at the bottom was a round stage. A small band of musicians were seated around the stage, strumming their instruments. The sisters looked with interest at the different instruments. They chose to seat themselves at a table with chairs outside the crater but with a good view of the stage.

They were enthralled by the Balinese dance. While knowing the story of the Ramayana and having no trouble following the drama, the sisters thought the dancing itself was different from the Indian style of dancing they were accustomed to watching. While not as intricate as Indian dancing, the Balinese dancing was graceful with many more head and face movements and colourful costumes. They settled themselves on their chairs with cups of coffees as the two-hour long recital started to gain momentum.

4

Alan Lee felt the hairs on the back of his neck prickle with tension as he sat on a stool at the bar counter of the Nightowl Bar. Was this the right place Lionel's mole had fingered? The mole had overheard a conversation on the phone about this bar and a counterfeit chip recycling factory presumably run by its owner. The pub seemed normal, crowded, all the booths by the windows were occupied with a smattering of people at the bar. Alan nursed his malt whiskey and looked around.

He quickly turned his head away from the mean-looking bald bouncer at the door. The man seemed to be staring at him. A waiter was hovering at his elbow and Alan looked at him, inquiringly.

Squinting heavily, the waiter said, 'Some finger food, sir? Chicken kebab?'

Alan saw the waiter eyeing his Rolex watch and said, cryptically, 'Okay, a plate of that will do.' Would the waiter know whether a computer chip recycling factory existed in Bali? He looked the friendliest of the Nightowl Bar staff. Alan decided to take the plunge. He turned to the waiter and asked, 'Do you know of any chip factory in Bali, you know, that makes computer chips?'

The waiter dropped the empty glass he was holding, and it broke into smithereens on the floor. At once, a well-built man wearing gold chains came to the counter.

The proprietor's eyes flashed as he scolded the waiter in the native tongue.

Alan said, hurriedly. 'I'll pay for the damages, put it on my bill. I nudged his elbow.'

The proprietor looked closely at Alan and nodded, nonchalantly. 'If you say so, sir. Did you order finger food?'

'Yes, a plate of chicken kebab.' Alan looked at the waiter, wanting to catch his eye and have a conversation later, but the waiter dashed away to get the broom and dustpan to sweep up the glass. As the proprietor stood by for the entire duration of the sweeping up process, Alan did not have the opportunity to talk to the waiter.

His plate of kebabs arrived, and Alan found the food quite tasty. Halfway through his meal, he looked around and saw the cock-eyed waiter conversing with the bouncer at the door. His heart thudded as the bouncer continued staring at him.

Quickly finishing his finger food and downing the rest of his whiskey, Alan rose from the stool, placed some money on the counter and made for the door. The bouncer and the waiter were nowhere in sight and Alan stepped out of the pub into the cool night. He felt nervous. Why had the bouncer been staring at him? A breeze was blowing in from the sea and Alan shivered.

The Beachcombers Hotel car was waiting for him outside and Alan gratefully stepped into the car. As the driver started the engine, a motorcycle revved up nearby and through the back of the car, Alan saw the bouncer and the waiter from the pub sitting on the bike. They were looking straight at his car.

'Drive me to the hotel quickly, please,' he said to the driver, who nodded.

Halfway to the hotel, turning in his seat to gaze out of the back of the car, Alan found the motorcycle was no longer following them. He heaved a sigh of relief and chided himself for morbid fancies. But one could never tell. The waiter had become nervous on being questioned about the chip factory. He sighed. His journey had been fruitless tonight and he decided to visit the pub again the next day.

The car left him at the entrance to the hotel lobby. Alan glanced at his watch. It was nearly 11 p.m. Walking to the lobby, he stopped, startled. A face vanished behind a potted plant near the door, and he could have sworn it was the face of the Nightowl Bar waiter. Alan walked on and nervously greeted the receptionist who told him to take a seat in the lobby until the buggy driver arrived to take him to his villa. Seated on a padded sofa, Alan looked over his shoulder, glancing at the row of potted plants. There was no one there.

In five minutes, a smiling Indonesian man entered the lobby, greeted him, and told him his buggy was ready. Thankfully, Alan followed the man and seated himself in the backseat of the buggy. Soon, the buggy was lumbering along the ill-lit path enclosed on both sides by vegetation.

'I am Sulaiman, sir,' the buggy driver, said, engagingly. 'You have good day today, sir?'

Alan smiled and told the driver about his visit to the Tanah Lot temple. Soon, they were having an animated conversation, the driver enthusiastically telling Alan of his brother-in-law, who was one of the caretakers of the temple.

Alan looked out as the buggy rolled to a stop.

'Your villa, sir. Have a good night, sir.'

Alan alighted from the buggy, took out his wallet from his trouser pocket, and extracted some rupiah from it. The dim light from the streetlamp shone on Alan's Rolex watch, making it shine.

'Thank you, sir.' Sulaiman gratefully accepted his tip, started his buggy, turned it around and made for the road back to the hotel lobby.

Driving at a slow pace, Sulaiman frowned when he heard a cry from the direction of Villa 22, Alan Lee's villa. He quickly turned the buggy around and drove noiselessly towards the villa. He stopped the buggy and looked in disbelief at Alan Lee lying near Villa 22's gate and a man going through his pockets.

Without hesitation, Sulaiman leapt down from the buggy and ran towards the man. 'Hey, what are you doing?'

The man looked up and Sulaiman gasped as he recognized the robber. Before he could say anything else, the man ran towards him, and Sulaiman could see the glint of a knife in the man's hand. He wrestled with the man, trying to shake the knife off. But the man was too strong for Sulaiman. Grasping Sulaiman with one strong hand, the killer plunged the knife into the buggy driver.

Sulaiman opened his mouth to scream as he felt a sharp pain near his heart. The man placed his strong hands over Sulaiman's mouth and as the buggy driver began to slump, the man lowered him to the ground. Soon, Sulaiman's sightless eyes were staring at the night sky.

The assailant was about to pull the *kukri* out of Sulaiman when he heard voices in the air. The man disappeared into the undergrowth.

* * *

The Ramayana recital ended with a clang of cymbals, the dancers trooped off the stage, and the musicians began putting away their instruments.

Dolly sipped the last of her second cup of coffee. 'Watching this beautiful, Balinese open-air recital of an age-old Indian classic with the waves of the Indian Ocean thundering in the background, it's a wonderful experience to cherish all our lives.'

'I will never forget this experience,' Lily agreed, enjoying the cool breeze from the ocean. The sisters rose from their table and made their way to the restaurant entrance.

'Let's call for a buggy,' Lily said, 'my feet are killing me. We walked a long time in Seminyak today.'

'Okay,' Dolly agreed. 'It would be good to have an early night; we have to pack and fly back tomorrow.' She glanced at her watch. 'It's 11.15 p.m.! How time flies when you're watching an engrossing show.'

The manager, Mark Latham, was at the restaurant entrance. 'There are no buggies available now,' he said, uncompromisingly. He was a tall individual with sandy hair and moustache, small watery blue eyes, and a sharp nose.

Lily bristled. 'We can wait,' she said.

'Never mind, it's not a long walk,' Dolly soothed.

'I don't like that manager,' Lily said as the sisters started walking along the paved, dimly lit path flanked on either side by vegetation through which the lights of lanais and villas twinkled.

'Let's keep to the road used by the buggies, it's so dark,' Dolly said.

The sisters walked along a narrow road, better lighted than the pathways. Around them crickets chirped, the roar of the ocean was muted, and the slight mist lent an air of mystery and eeriness. On the side of the road, in front of the dim silhouette of a villa, a buggy was parked.

'There's a buggy!' Lily protested. 'The driver must have nodded off. *What?*'

Her sister had uttered an exclamation and was hurrying towards the villa. 'There's someone lying near the gate,' Dolly cried.

'Maybe some laundry left outside,' Lily said, fighting hard to keep pace with her sister.

Dolly arrived at the villa gate and exclaimed loudly. Lily nearly ran the rest of the way and joined her sister. She looked at the ground and gasped. There were two men lying on the ground about five feet apart. A knife was sticking out of the chest of the man nearest to the road. Dolly knelt by that body, feeling for the pulse. Lily ran to the other body, looked at the face of the prone man on the ground and screamed.

When her sister looked up, Lily pointed a shaking finger at the man by the gate and cried, 'It's Alan Lee, Doll! And he looks dead.'

Dolly rose from the side of the first man and ran to Alan Lee's body. She knelt by it and felt for the man's pulse. Slowly, she shook her head. Blood soaked the front of Alan Lee's shirt, and his eyes were half-open.

Dolly rose from the ground and told her sister, 'Go back to the restaurant, that is nearer to us than the lobby. Raise the alarm, Lil! This is a double murder and a crime scene. Ask for an ambulance as well, I am no doctor, but I think both these men are dead. Get going, Lily!'

Lily ran down the road towards the restaurant while ASP Dolly Das guarded the crime scene.

* * *

Lily stood away from the gate of Villa 22, watching the paramedics checking for life in the bodies of Alan Lee and the other man, presumably the buggy driver. Dolly stood next to the buggy, flanked by the hotel manager, Mark Latham, his face white and pinched. There was the sound of a distant siren and Lily deduced the Bali police were arriving. The loud chirping of crickets seemed incongruous, like someone blowing a trumpet at a funeral. The lights on the path were dim and the shadows cast by the bystanders lent a ghostly aspect to the crime scene.

Lily felt someone breathing down her neck and turned sharply around. An Indonesian man in his twenties with a prominent squint stepped hurriedly back. As Lily gazed at him, he asked in a frightened voice:

'Is Sulaiman dead?'

'Who is Sulaiman?' Lily queried.

The man informed her in a hushed voice Sulaiman was the man lying next to the buggy and he was a buggy driver from the hotel. He was also his childhood friend, and they hailed from the same village near Mount Batur.

'I am sorry for your loss. Do you work at the hotel?' Lily asked, kindly.

'What are you doing here, Ananda?' The words were spoken sharply in the Indonesian language.

Lily turned fully around to see the waitress, Darti, looking at the man, fire shooting from her eyes. The man glared at Darti and began to rapidly walk away. Soon he was swallowed up by the darkness. Darti looked at the people around the gate and then at Lily.

'That's my brother, Ananda. What happened here? I heard the receptionist say there was a killing?'

Lily nodded. 'The buggy driver and a guest have been killed. The police should be on their way.'

As she spoke, a posse of Criminal Investigation Agency detectives strode down the narrow path and the crowd around the buggy parted to allow them entry. A rotund, short man with a moustache was leading them.

'The Bareskrim come,' Darti whispered.

'Bareskrim?'

Darti collected herself. 'The police who catch killers. Criminal Investigation Agency?'

Lily nodded and said, 'You speak good English, Darti.'

Darti's lips lifted in a shy smile. 'I stay with my auntie in Jakarta and study in mission school. She is Christian.'

Lily nodded. Dolly was making her way out of the thinning crowd around the bodies as officers requested people return to their rooms and leave the police in charge.

'We'll return to our lanai, Lily,' Dolly said. 'The Bali CIA is here, and we should let them conduct their investigation.'

* * *

Back at their lanai, Dolly sat thoughtfully in the lounge area while Lily made coffee for them. She thanked her sister when Lily placed steaming cups on the coffee table in front of the sofas.

Lily sat down and looked speculatively at her sister. 'Do you think Alan Lee was murdered by the counterfeit computer chip syndicate he mentioned?'

'He shouldn't have been sleuthing on his own. These organizations are dangerous.' Dolly's voice was sad. She took a sip of her coffee. 'I don't know, really. It could be a robbery. I noticed Alan Lee was wearing a gold Rolex watch at dinner and I didn't see that watch on his wrist just now. The police will investigate, find out if his valuables were stolen.'

'Maybe the syndicate had thugs kill him.' Lily's imagination was running wild as she searched her memory for a similar plot among the crime novels she had read. She took a long sip of her coffee, burnt her tongue and grimaced.

The phone on the table near Dolly rang. Dolly picked up the receiver. Her eyes widened, and Lily raised her eyebrows, questioningly. She listened to her sister's side of the conversation.

'Yes, sir. Certainly, sir. I will hold the line.'

Dolly covered the landline phone mouthpiece and whispered to Lily, 'My big boss, Deputy Assistant Commissioner John Nathan is on the phone. He is connecting me to Lester Chong, Singapore's Junior Minister of Transport.'

'Wow,' Lily breathed.

Dolly spoke for five minutes on the phone, was connected back to her boss, heard his instructions, and then slowly placed the receiver back in its cradle.

'What? What?' Lily demanded.

Dolly sighed and lifted her cooling cup of coffee to her lips. 'Alan Lee was Lester Chong's maternal cousin. Alan's mother and Lester's father were siblings. Alan's maternal grandmother is alive and is devastated by her grandson's death. The Bali CIA informed Lester Chong about Alan's murder half an hour ago as Alan had listed Lester as his emergency contact on the hotel register. Lester Chong has requested me to stay on in Bali and help the Bali police with their investigations and DAC Nathan endorsed the request. The Bali inspector in charge of the investigation into Alan Lee's death will meet me tomorrow morning.'

'I will stay on as well.' Lily gulped down her coffee, her eyes starry.

'No, Lily! Mummy hasn't been well.' Dolly's eyes became misty. 'Two years ago, the doctor said her Parkinson's Disease will progress slowly. It's full-fledged now. Do you see how her hands shake? She can't carry Molly and that breaks her heart. Girlie must do most things for her. Mummy perks up when she sees us, and she was looking forward to having us back. And she has her check-up with the neurologist later in the week. You need to take her to the hospital. I don't know how long I'll be here.'

Lily looked disappointed but nodded. 'Mummy has terrible pain in her legs at night and Girlie gives her massages. Okay, Doll, I'll return to Singapore.'

Dolly noted Lily's crestfallen look and asked, 'Alan Lee's sister lives at Silver Springs, right? You can have a casual conversation with her in case there is a personal angle to Alan Lee's murder.'

Lily's face brightened. She could sleuth around in Singapore while Dolly was busy on the Bali front. 'Linda Lee lives two doors away from Mummy's unit. I'll have a chat with her then.'

Dolly said, 'I feel a certain obligation to Alan to investigate his murder as he confided his suspicions of the syndicate to me. I think it's either a robbery gone wrong, or the syndicate ordered a hit on him.'

'I wonder if Girlie knows the helper who works in Linda's condo unit. I have seen a helper there.' Without waiting for Dolly's response, Lily snatched her mobile phone and keyed in the numbers for home.

While Lily talked on the phone, Dolly went to the window and peeped through the curtains. The window had an unobstructed view of Villa 22 opposite. Staff and the manager were still standing around, but there were more detectives present than before, and from their apparel, Dolly deduced they were the forensic team. A siren blared, and she saw the white of the ambulance penetrate the darkness. The bodies would soon depart for the morgue. Dolly turned around at Lily's voice.

'Linda Lee's helper is called Lestriani, an Indonesian. Girlie has talked to her a few times and the maid speaks English. Girlie will try to extract information out of her about the family. What's going on outside?'

'I think the forensic team is done, and the bodies will depart for the morgue soon.'

'Poor Alan Lee. He seemed a nice man.'

With that epitaph from Lily, the sisters ordered apple pies from room service and settled on their beds to watch a movie on the big TV facing them. While the movie flickered on the screen, the image of Alan Lee's bloodied body lying in front of his villa gate, refused to leave the minds of the Das sisters.

Thursday, 16 May 2013

Bali, Indonesia

5

Lily gazed at the Indian Ocean lit by the rising sun and watched the activity on the beach from the confines of The Sea-Shell Café where she was having breakfast with Dolly. Darti, looking frightened and harassed, brought Lily another guest's breakfast and when spoken to sharply by the manager, Mark Latham, burst into tears and rushed away.

'I must apologize for the service today,' the British manager said, his lips pursed. 'The double murders have upset the staff. Your breakfast order will soon be here. May I know if you are scheduled to leave this morning as per your itinerary?' For a moment, the mask slipped, and the Briton's face was intensely curious.

Dolly spoke, after sipping her orange juice. 'I'm afraid I must stay on for a while. I work for the Singapore CID and the Singapore government has asked me to assist in the investigation into the murder of Alan Lee, the man who was killed here last night. He was a Singapore national. I am soon to meet with the CIA officer from Bali in charge of the investigation.'

Mark Latham frowned, his blue eyes glowing with curiosity. 'But Mr Lee's murder was obviously a robbery gone wrong,' he said. 'His gold watch, mobile phone, and wallet are missing. I am sure the Bali CIA will soon catch the robber.'

'How do you know about the missing items, Mr Latham?' Dolly asked, pleasantly.

'Well, the Bali police are not very discreet and everyone in Bali is related to everyone else in some way or another so gossip spreads. Some policemen told our staff of the missing items,' Mark Latham said, apologetically. 'Surely, the motivation was robbery, why, the buggy driver, Sulaiman, was killed as well.' The sun beat on Latham's face, accentuating the lines and wrinkles.

Dolly finished her orange juice and looked curiously at the ham and chicken cold cuts Lily was being served. They looked dry and unappetizing. She looked up at Latham. 'You mean Sulaiman was murdered because he could finger the robber and killer? Someone he knew. Maybe one of the staff. Sulaiman had been with you long?'

'No, not long. He joined our staff about six months ago and was a good worker. He comes from a poor family living in a village near Mount Batur. Our staff are strictly vetted, we don't hire criminals,' Latham added, indignantly.

'Greed for money is an unpredictable emotion. It can make honest men thieves. Are there any CCTV cameras on the premises?' Dolly looked unenthusiastically at the soggy breakfast of runny eggs and blackened bacon being served to her by a sombre waiter.

'Two in the lobby and one outside the gift shop. I will leave you to your breakfast then, ma'am.' Mark Latham nodded and moved away.

'What awful food today,' Lily opined, chewing on a tough piece of meat. 'Everyone is frightened.'

Dolly soon gave up on her eggs and bacon and munched desultorily on a croissant. She looked up and saw a rotund, short Indonesian man with a beaming smile and luxuriant black moustache, making his way to their table.

He stopped by the table and said, 'I am Inspector Harjono of Bali CIA.' He looked from Dolly to Lily. 'ASP Das?'

Dolly rose from her seat and warmly shook the inspector's hand. 'I am ASP Das. This is my sister, Lily, we were on holiday here. Lil, I'll see you soon at the lanai. Have a seat, Inspector.'

'Harjono, please call me Harjono,' wheezed the jolly inspector, nodding pleasantly to Lily. 'Welcome to Bali, ladies. Sorry your holiday interrupted by tragedy.'

After Lily had left, Harjono said, 'The manager of Beachcombers Hotel— he is British, Mr Mark Latham. He is worried the murders, ah, it will affect business, so he says do not harass staff. He is—what you call—stick-in-the-mud.' Harjono giggled pleasurably at his command of English. Darti served a cup of coffee to Harjono and gave him a tentative smile.

Dolly finished her breakfast and looked at Harjono, who was eyeing the nasi lemak breakfast of a Chinese guest at the next table. 'Are you hungry, Harjono? Some breakfast for you?'

'Oh, no, no!' Harjono giggled. 'My wife runs a restaurant and I breakfast like a king, eh? I was checking quality of nasi lemak. This hotel, British, eh? Not make good nasi lemak, I think.'

Dolly smiled at Darti placing a basket of croissants on the table and turned to Harjono. She quite liked the jolly inspector. 'My sister and I met Alan Lee last night,' she told Harjono and watched his face light up. 'We were having dinner and he invited himself over. Alan told me he was trying to uncover a counterfeit computer chip syndicate operating out of Singapore. He may have been in Bali on their trail.'

Harjono was having trouble following Dolly's words but latched on to the word 'chips'. 'Computer chips, huh? Fake? Sold on the black market. You mean phones?'

'I think it is the chips, themselves. The chips are inside the phones, computers, and electronic devices. We must find out more, but maybe Alan Lee was killed by the black market syndicate. Were Alan Lee's valuables stolen? If so, this could also be a simple robbery and murder.'

Harjono looked doubtful. 'We were told by the waiters Alan Lee wore a gold watch. That is missing. His mobile phone and wallet also. But madam, in Bali, sure, there are thieves. They steal, not kill to steal. If his villa robbed, I understand. But to kill to steal, and two killings. And one an Indonesian. Brother kill brother, just like that.' Harjono shook his head. 'I don't think so, ASP Das.'

'Any help from the forensic team in fingering the murderer?' Dolly smiled at Darti pouring her fresh coffee.

Harjono munched a croissant and said, 'Yes, yes, ASP Das. The knife used for the killings is a kukri and already go for fingerprinting. Also, the buggy driver put up a fight, ASP Das.'

'Any defensive wounds?' Dolly's face shone with a timbre of excitement.

Harjono nodded, enthusiastically. 'Skin under Sulaiman's fingernails. From murderer. We send for DNA analysis, ASP Das. We send here to a DNA laboratory, but our top lab is in Jakarta, you know. We send sample there early this morning. But results will take time.'

The concierge's assistant, Abdul, was making his way to the table. He smiled broadly at Harjono.

Harjono got to his feet and thumped Abdul on the back and said some warm words in their language. He said to Dolly in English, 'Abdul is my nephew, his mother my cousin, you know?' He giggled and sat down again.

Abdul joined his hands together and greeted Dolly in the traditional way.

'Do you know where Alan Lee went after dinner last night?' Dolly asked Abdul.

The concierge's assistant nodded, looking askance at his uncle. 'He wanted to go to the Nightowl Bar in Seminyak and I called for a car to take him there.' Dolly noted that Abdul spoke more fluently than his uncle.

'Nightowl! Hadyanto's place?' Harjono squeaked in alarm.

'Yes, Uncle. But he did return from there and asked for a buggy to take him to his villa, so nothing happened there,' Abdul replied, looking worried.

'Nightowl Bar is a pub owned by a scoundrel, Hadyanto. Bad reputation, you know,' Harjono explained to Dolly. 'We have our eye on him for months. His criminal gang is into thieving, maybe more. His bouncer, Ramdin, he is hatchet man, haha!' Harjono could not suppress a giggle. He sobered up on seeing Dolly's stern look and said, 'What was Mr Lee doing there? Hadyanto can kill somebody for money. Or gold watch. Easily,' he added, knowingly.

'We should interview Hadyanto,' Dolly decided. She turned to Abdul. 'Is it possible for us to see the CCTV footage of the lobby at the time Alan Lee left for the Nightowl Bar and when he returned?'

'Sure, madam. I ask Lakshmana, the security guard, to bring the tapes to you, after I take Mr Latham's permission.'

'We go to security guard and view the tapes at his office, Abdul,' Harjono said, peremptorily.

'Yes, Uncle.' Abdul frowned and cleared his throat. 'Just before he left for Nightowl Bar last night, Alan Lee gave me a letter to post. I slide letter into post box outside hotel.'

'Can you remember to whom it was addressed?' Dolly asked, sitting up, alert. In the light of Alan's murder and his conversation with Dolly about the crime syndicate, the letter could hold important information, she thought.

When Abdul shook his head, Dolly said, 'When is the post collected from the mailbox in front of the hotel?' She looked at Harjono. 'Maybe the letter is still there? Can you check, Inspector?'

Harjono nodded. 'I have some men at the gate, I call them, madam.' He took out his mobile phone from his pocket and dialled, furiously. Harjono spoke to his men in his native tongue, the urgency in his voice apparent. Abdul gave Dolly a smile and walked away.

Darti arrived with the coffee jug and refilled their cups. Sipping his coffee, Harjono told Dolly about the Bali forensic laboratory and the morgue where the bodies would soon be examined by the pathologist. After fifteen minutes, Harjono's mobile rang, and he eagerly snatched up his phone. He listened to the caller at the other end, and his face fell.

After switching off his mobile, he looked at Dolly. 'The post is collected early, madam, at 8.00 a.m. No luck there. The letter is on its way out of Bali.'

Dolly looked disappointed. After discussing with Harjono his investigation plan, she rose from her chair and said, 'Harjono, I need to go to my lanai to see my sister off. She is returning to Singapore by the afternoon flight. Can I meet you later at the security guard's office to view the tapes from last night?'

Harjono nodded, getting up from his chair. 'We meet there at 3 p.m., madam. I need to visit the morgue and be there when the autopsies start. The pathologist will be working on Mr Alan Lee first. See you, soon, madam. I hope your sister has a safe flight home.'

Dolly found Lily sitting on the bed of the lanai, grumpily watching television, her suitcase packed and left by the door.

'Harjono and I have found out where Alan went after he left us last night. He went to a disreputable pub, and I am wondering whether the owner of the pub has a connection to the crime syndicate. We will interview him. Have a safe flight, Lil, and give Mummy a kiss from me, and Molly, too.'

'Do give me updates on the phone, Doll.'

The phone rang, informing Lily a buggy was at the door to take her to the lobby, where a car waited to take her to the airport. The sisters embraced, and Dolly waved until Lily's buggy was a speck in the distance.

Singapore

Girlie, Uma Das's helper, peeped into the old lady's bedroom and sighed with relief on hearing eighty-two-year-old Uma, snoring gently. It was 2.30 p.m. Girlie picked up the old lady's mobile phone from the desk by the window and placed it near her hands on the bed. She left the bedroom, snatched up the house keys, and let herself out of the condo unit.

Girlie had been working for Uma for four years, supporting her daughter in the Philippines after her husband, a hard-drinking sailor, had mortgaged their house in Cebu. He now worked at a shipyard, but Girlie continually worried about his alcohol consumption and gambling habits.

Girlie was short with a round face, large eyes, and curly hair. She had been thrilled to help Lily and Dolly solve several murders and loved being a member of Lily's amateur sleuthing team.

Her heart had beaten with excitement when the phone rang last night and Lily told her she needed her help in solving the murder of a gentleman called Alan Lee, whose sister, Linda, lived on their floor. When Lily asked if Girlie knew their maid, Girlie demurred. While she knew the Indonesian maid, Lestriani, as a nodding acquaintance, she had not spoken to her at great length. That could be remedied, Girlie thought, and told Lily she knew Lestriani and would speak to her.

Girlie made her way to the children's playground in the condominium complex and looked around. Several children were playing near the seesaws, jungle gyms and swings and their nannies pooled around a bench, chatting, and laughing with each other. Girlie's searching eyes found a petite figure, sitting alone on a bench, watching the merry-go-round where a young Sikh boy in a *patka* was whooping with merriment.

Girlie walked determinedly towards the Indonesian maid and stood smiling at her. 'Hi, Lestriani,' she said.

The Indonesian maid glanced up in surprise, then her lips lifted in a smile. She had a round face and large soulful eyes. 'Hi, Girlie.'

'Can I sit?' Without waiting for a reply, Girlie seated herself next to the other maid. 'You here on Thursday? The children back from school already?'

Tears pooled in Lestriani's eyes. The Indonesian maid nodded in the direction of the Sikh boy. 'No. They stay home today, their uncle die. I bring Duleep away from flat. His mother crying and crying. Cannot tell children bad news.'

'What's wrong?'

Lestriani told Girlie that the children's uncle, Alan Lee, was robbed and killed while holidaying in Bali. She went on to tell Girlie how generous Alan had been, always giving her money during Chinese New Year to send home to her family. 'I got four children in Indonesia. You?' Lestriani's eyes glistened.

'One.'

'Husband?'

'Yes, have. Drink and gamble.' Girlie shrugged.

Lestriani shifted nearer to Girlie on the bench. 'Same,' she whispered.

'Your ma'am friendly with her brother?' Girlie steered the conversation towards the work on hand.

'Yes, yes. Alan Sir play chess with children, and they visit his big house.'

'Big house?' Girlie interjected the right note of wonder in her voice to enable Lestriani to expand on her information.

Lestriani, animatedly, told Girlie about Alan Lee's large two-storey bungalow and that his father had been a big businessman. Her lips twisted into a grimace. 'But they not happy.'

'Why?'

Lestriani told Girlie about Ronnie Lee's first wife dying from an illness and how his second wife, daughter of a former cabinet minister, hated her stepchildren. Lestriani whispered in Girlie's ears that Alice Lee, the stepmother, wanted her late husband's bungalow for herself and refused to leave the house when Ronnie Lee died. Alan, Ronnie's heir, was too kind to kick his stepmother out, Lestriani said, but recently she heard he had engaged a lawyer to start eviction proceedings. 'I don't know what happen now with Alan Sir dead,' Lestriani concluded, her eyes glistening with a few more tears. She continued, 'Her son nice.'

'Whose son? Alice Lee?'

Lestriani nodded. She said, slowly, in halting English, 'Ronnie and Alice have one son, Etienne Sir. Natasha and Duleep love their uncle Etienne. Ma'am love both her brothers, own brother, and stepbrother. But stepma bring trouble in family.'

'Natasha and Duleep are the two children you look after?' Girlie was trying to place everyone in her mind and prepare her report to Lily who was arriving in Singapore in the evening.

'Yes, see, Duleep playing near the swing. He is in Primary Three. Natasha is in Primary Five. We get news of Alan Sir's death last night. Ma'am keep children home.'

'And their father?'

'Patrick Sir. He Sikh. Duleep and Natasha, they visit Gurdwara every Sunday,' Lestriani said.

A little boy with a fair face and red cheeks ran up to the two domestic helpers, his eyes sparkling. 'I'm hungry!' Duleep announced.

Lestriani got up from the bench and said, 'We go home now, Duleep.' She smilingly nodded a farewell to Girlie.

Girlie watched Lestriani walk away. She had enough information on Alan Lee's family for one day. She would tell Lily about Alice, the villain of the Lee family and casually wondered if Alice Lee had anything to do with her stepson's murder.

6

Bali, Indonesia

ASP Das and Inspector Harjono crowded into a small office at the back of the hotel with a window overlooking a garden. Three CCTV monitors occupied a large table by the window. The monitors displayed the main door, the hotel lobby, and the entrance to the gift shop. A digital video recorder was placed next to the monitors.

Lakshmana, the security guard, was a bald, round-faced smiling man. He seated the two police officers in comfortable padded chairs, used the computer keyboards to retrieve last night's footages and displayed them on the monitor screens. He fast-forwarded the video recordings of the CCTV cameras of the lobby and door to the time of Alan Lee's departure for the Nightowl Bar.

Dolly looked keenly at the monitors. The time on the footages read 8.30 p.m. and the foyer video showed receptionists sitting at their desks. An American couple was checking out at one desk with the man wildly gesticulating and the receptionist's smile getting thinner and thinner. Mark Latham strode into the screen and immediately the guest stopped waving about and turned to speak to the hotel manager. Alan Lee sauntered in from the door leading to the villas.

Dolly coughed. Harjono seemed more interested in the altercation between the guest and the hotel manager, but looked around and followed Dolly's finger, pointing to Lee on the screen.

Harjono's eyes lit up. 'Ah, murdered man!'

Onscreen, Alan Lee made his way to the concierge's desk, and the police officers saw him give Abdul an envelope. He stood chatting with Abdul, before the assistant concierge smilingly led the way to the main door leading to the carpark. Alan followed Abdul out of the lobby. Dolly noticed with interest that Mark Latham had stopped talking to the American hotel guest and was looking after the retreating figures of Alan and Abdul. The main door camera showed Abdul seeing Alan Lee into a car waiting at the kerb and giving a wave as the car revved up and drove away. Lakshmana paused the footages on the monitors.

'Alan Lee leaves for Nightowl Bar. Nothing suspicious,' Harjono observed.

'Wait,' Dolly was frowning. 'Harjono, the lobby has three doors, one leading to the carpark, one to the restaurant and one to the villas and lanais. Note Alan Lee entered through the door from the villas and not from the restaurant. He left us in the restaurant around 8 p.m. and he is at the lobby at 8.30 p.m. Could it be he went back to his villa to write the letter he wanted Abdul to post? Anyway, let's fast forward to the time of Alan Lee's return to the hotel.'

Lakshmana fast forwarded the tapes to around 10.45 p.m. Dolly and Harjono leant forward as the monitors displayed the footages of the lobby and main door late at night.

The hotel lobby looked deserted with only two male receptionists manning two desks. The door camera captured a car parking outside the lobby and Alan Lee alighting from it. He walked towards the lobby door, stopped and stared at the potted plants lining the way to the door, then walked on. The foyer camera then captured Alan Lee walking towards one of the reception desks. The receptionist pointed him to a chair, Lee nodded and sat on the chair. He looked over his shoulder and the camera captured his tense face.

'He looks worried, eh?' Harjono opined.

Dolly nodded. Alan repeatedly ran his hands through his hair and kept looking over his shoulder.

'Wait! Who is that?' Harjono squeaked, loudly.

The main door camera had captured a shadowy figure lurking behind a potted plant outside the lobby, near the door. The man disappeared as a buggy stopped outside the door and a man in Indonesian garb got out.

The young buggy driver walked towards the door and the foyer camera captured him entering the lobby and bending to speak a few words to Alan Lee. Alan Lee got to his feet, said a few words to the receptionist and followed the buggy driver out of the lobby. The door camera captured Alan Lee and the driver getting into the buggy and the buggy driving away.

'Sulaiman,' Lakshmana said in a small voice.

After the buggy left, the door camera captured a figure emerging from behind a potted plant and sauntering in through the door. The foyer camera captured him as a young man wearing jeans, a dark T-shirt and with a sulky expression on his face. Both Harjono and Lakshmana uttered exclamations.

'Do you know this man?' Dolly demanded.

Harjono nodded, grimly. 'He is Ananda, a thief, and a member of Hadyanto's gang. He is also sister to hotel waitress, Darti.'

Dolly opined, 'Let's see what he does.'

The foyer camera captured Ananda sitting on a chair in front of the receptionist. They began chatting and after five minutes, a cup of coffee was delivered to the table and Ananda began sipping the beverage. The receptionist began leafing through documents on his desk.

Dolly said, 'This fellow, Ananda, did not follow the buggy, but is chatting with the receptionist.'

'Receptionist name is Jamal. Work here long time,' offered Lakshmana.

Harjono nodded. 'We will talk to receptionist.' He turned to Dolly. 'Ananda, no business at this hotel. Very suspicious.'

Around 11.30 p.m., the foyer camera showed a man running into the lobby, gesticulating wildly and both the receptionist and Ananda leapt to their feet. Ananda ran to the door leading to the villas.

'The murder is discovered,' Harjono said, gloomily, 'and Ananda have alibi, yes, talk all the time to receptionist so not killer.'

The security guard tapped a key and the footages on the monitors froze.

'We must interview Ananda,' Dolly said to Harjono. 'He may have been an accomplice and allowed the murderer in through the gate. Where did he go afterwards? Was he sent to steal items from Alan Lee's villa? I am sure you have checked out the villa, Harjono.'

Harjono sighed. 'Yes, madam. Villa look okay. We go talk to Ananda, he will be at Hadyanto's pub.' Harjono turned to the security guard and said in his native tongue, 'Lakshmana, I need you to make me a digital copy of the footage and send it to me, it is evidence, you understand?' He turned back to Dolly. 'Please to come, madam.'

Harjono led the way out of the security guard's office. Dolly stopped to thank the smiling security guard before she followed Harjono out.

Dolly said, 'Should we talk to the manager, Mark Latham about the security guard at the gate? Maybe the manager can call the guard to talk to us. He allowed in Ananda and can tell us if he was accompanied into the grounds by anyone else.'

They found Mark Latham in a small office off the lobby. When everyone was seated, Dolly posed her question to the manager who sadly shook his head. 'Aditya was the gate security guard last night. He called me after 11 p.m. and said his mother had taken ill at his village. He left immediately and it took me a while to rouse one of the other guards.' Latham frowned. 'The main gate may have been left unmanned for half an hour or so.'

'Aditya may have allowed in unauthorized people,' Dolly said, sharply. 'His address?'

'No address as such, madam.' Mark Latham's watery blue eyes blinked. 'Just the name of a village.' He rattled off the name to Harjono, who nodded.

'Ananda, the waitress, Darti's brother, was seen on the premises late at night, at the time of the murder. Does he have any business here?' Dolly noted with interest the colour fade from Latham's face.

The manager said, 'He comes sometimes to see his sister home, especially if it's very late at night.'

'So the security guards would let him in, no questions asked?' Dolly raised an eyebrow.

When Latham nodded, Dolly thanked the manager and followed Harjono out of the office.

The officers made their way to the car to take them to the Nightowl Bar.

The police car with Harjono and Dolly travelled towards eastern Seminyak. Harjono sat in the front seat busily making notes on his tablet, uttering a few squeaks now and then. Dolly looked at the blue of the ocean and the silhouettes of ships at anchor. Several sailboats criss-crossed the waters while swimmers bobbed about in the sea. The beach glinted gold-white in the late afternoon sun. Soon, the crowded beachside receded as the road twisted and turned, snaking upwards. Habitations became fewer, a small house with a courtyard here, a mud hut there.

Harjono broke the silence in the car. 'We soon catch the killer, madam,' he said, confidently. 'The knife used is a kukri, Nepalese weapon. I already tell my men to send word to the Nepalese community here to ask if anyone borrow kukri. Small Nepalese community here, madam.

Also, our fingerprint team is working on the weapon used to kill. We get answer soon.'

Dolly nodded. 'It's the DNA from the skin underneath Sulaiman's fingernails that will nail the killer, Harjono. What kind of criminal activities is Hadyanto involved in?'

Harjono turned to her. 'His gang steal from tourists, we catch them many times. Recently, we hear he go to Shenzhen for business. Also, we hear he have a factory near Pujung. But we cannot get warrant yet to search Pujung factory. Hadyanto very clever, we cannot find out what he does.'

Suddenly, the road turned and dipped down. The beach was visible again on one side and a narrow strip of garishly lit restaurants and pubs appeared on the other. The Nightowl Bar was lit up in pink neon lights. The driver parked the car and Harjono and Dolly went into the pub.

It was a small wood-beamed establishment designed to mimic a British pub. There was a chrome counter with glasses hanging from the ceiling and liquor and beer taps. A broad, muscular Indonesian man wearing a sleeveless singlet to best display a variety of tattoos on both arms, lumbered towards them. He wore navy jeans, and gold necklaces and bracelets. His eyes were hostile behind hooded lids and Dolly thought he resembled a vulture. He twirled his moustache as he faced Harjono.

Harjono's eyes glittered and narrowed as he looked coldly at the man in front. He said in a sharp voice in the native tongue, 'Hadyanto, we want to speak to Ananda, he works for you as a waiter.'

'Ananda has left my service.' Hadyanto shot back.

'Why?' Harjono asked, sharply.

'He had a fight with Ramdin. He owed Ramdin money for gambling and refused to pay. So, Ramdin hit him, Ananda left.' Hadyanto looked inquiringly at Dolly.

Harjono introduced Dolly to Hadyanto and told her briefly what Hadyanto had said about Ananda. He continued in a hard voice to Hadyanto, 'A Singapore tourist was murdered at Beachcombers Hotel yesterday. His name was Alan Lee. He came to your pub last night, Hadyanto. You remember? Why did he come here?'

Hadyanto said. 'I don't know any Lee, so many people come to my pub to eat and drink, I don't keep tabs.'

'Call Ramdin, he may remember,' Harjono ordered.

'Ramdin went back to his village,' Hadyanto said. 'Helping with preparations for his brother's wedding. I am short-staffed, as you can see. Got to serve customers myself.'

Dolly looked around the pub. It had four booths by the windows and a dozen tables and chairs. The décor was basic but cosy. The ocean could be seen outside the windows, the white froth of waves breaking against the sandy beach. When Harjono translated his conversation with Hadyanto to Dolly, she looked candidly at the pub owner.

'It is suspicious that two of your men have disappeared after two men were killed at Beachcombers Hotel,' Dolly said. 'Ananda was seen in the hotel grounds at the time of the murder.'

Hadyanto shrugged his broad shoulders and replied in English, 'Staff go back home, it is normal.'

Harjono said, 'Hadyanto, we know you have a factory near Pujung. What do you sell?'

Hadyanto's eyes narrowed and glittered. He shrugged his shoulders. 'I don't know what you are talking about, Inspector.' He nodded to a tourist couple who had entered the pub and seated themselves at the bar counter. 'I need to get back to work.'

In the car, going back to the hotel, Harjono told Dolly about Ramdin, the bouncer at the Nightowl Bar, feared for his muscle and temper. 'Why would Lee want to visit a no-good pub?' Harjono mused in the car.

'The pub may have a connection to the counterfeit chip syndicate. Maybe he arranged to meet someone?' Dolly observed. 'We must track down Ananda. Do you know where he lives?'

'We can find out from his sister, Darti,' Harjono said, grimly. 'We will also interview Jamal, the receptionist Ananda was talking to at hotel last night. I need to phone pathologist about Sulaiman's post-mortem. Maybe you have a cup of tea at the hotel and wait for me, ASP Das?'

After drinking tea and munching on a croissant, Dolly met Harjono in a small office off the lobby where the police could conduct private interviews. Jamal was a tall young man with a pleasant face and big wide eyes. He placed his hands together in greeting before seating himself.

Harjono showed Ananda's photo to Jamal. 'Know him?'

Jamal looked at the photo and readily nodded. 'He is Ananda, Darti's brother. He comes sometimes to the hotel to visit his sister.' The receptionist spoke fluent English.

'What about last night? Did you see him?' Dolly leant forward, eagerly.

Jamal was nodding. 'Yes, he was at the reception desk last night. He came over and asked if Darti was at the hotel. I told him I don't know. He saw the cup of coffee on my table and asked for a coffee. What to do? We all like Darti, except Ananda is a thief. I ordered a coffee from Room Service for

Ananda, and he sat with me chatting until we heard of the murder. Then I ran out with the other staff. I did not see Ananda after that.'

Dolly said with resignation, 'Ananda was with you chatting from what time?'

'After eleven, madam. Mr Alan Lee had just left with Sulaiman in the buggy.'

'Right after the two left?' Harjono's face was purple with excitement. 'Jamal, try to remember, this is important.'

'Yes, Inspector, I *do* remember, it was right after Mr Lee left with Sulaiman,' Jamal insisted.

'You say Ananda comes to visit his sister?' Dolly queried. 'So, the guard at the gate would allow him in? Even late at night?'

Jamal nodded. 'Sometimes he takes Darti home from the hotel if she works too late. The roads are not safe for ladies at night. Ananda also comes to see Mr Latham, our part-time hotel manager.'

'Wait,' Dolly said. 'Why do you say part-time hotel manager? Doesn't he work at Beachcombers full-time?'

Jamal was voluble. 'No, madam. Mr Latham is away half of the month. He has a bungalow in Ubud, and he stays there or visits China. Mr Latham runs a business, and he sells products in China. That is why we have our second manager, Mr Shaw.'

'What kind of business?' Dolly asked, sharply and sighed when Jamal shook his head. 'Why would Ananda visit Mark Latham?'

'For business. Ananda works part-time in Mr Latham's factory.' Jamal's eyes were wide.

'Where is the factory? What does it make?' Harjono asked brusquely, but Jamal again shook his head.

After Jamal had left, Harjono looked at Dolly. 'Mr Latham highly suspicious. We go see him, yes?'

But Mark Latham had left the hotel. A brown-haired, blue-eyed man sat in the manager's office reading a newspaper. He introduced himself as Jeremy Shaw.

'Mark is here for the first half of the month and I for the second,' Shaw said, readily. 'He was supposed to leave for his Ubud bungalow last night but stayed on till late afternoon today because of the murder. The staff are nervous, and he wanted to calm them.' He readily gave Latham's Ubud address.

'We understand Mark Latham has business interests here and in China. Do you know what kind of business it is?' Dolly said.

Jeremy Shaw shook his head. 'I'm afraid I have no idea. Mark is reticent and secretive, but he is a good trainer. I am learning a lot from him. He was not always a hotel manager. I think he worked as an engineer before he joined the hospitality business.'

As the police officers walked to Dolly's lanai, she looked at Harjono. 'Both Hadyanto and Latham seem to run a factory with connections to China. Could it be the same factory? I wonder if Latham is a criminal. Would it be possible to find Hadyanto's factory?'

Harjono nodded. 'Yes, near Pujung. I do my best, ASP Das.'

The sun was dipping down into the horizon. Harjono apologetically glanced at his watch.

'We've had a long day,' Dolly agreed. 'We'll see Mark Latham tomorrow and hopefully we can locate Ananda and the Pujung factory.'

In her lanai, Dolly took a shower and ordered Bombay Pizza from the in-room dining menu. After a call to her sister's mobile went unanswered, Dolly settled on the bed to watch a Hindi movie on television.

Friday, 17 May 2013

Bali, Indonesia

7

After breakfasting at The Sea-Shell Café, Dolly went back to her lanai to freshen up before Harjono arrived to pick her up in the squad car to go to Mark Latham's bungalow in Ubud. The landline in her room rang and it was Lily at the other end of the phone. After inquiries and updates on their mother's health had concluded, Lily related to her sister the information about Alan Lee's family Girlie had dug up.

'Hm,' Dolly said into the phone. 'Alice Lee was disinherited, and she refuses to leave her stepson's bungalow and Alan was going to evict her with the help of his lawyer. That is useful to know though a weak motive to kill Lee. Good work from Girlie.'

Lily squeaked eagerly from the other end of the line, 'I could visit Linda Lee to know more about Alice Lee.'

Dolly's voice was sharp. 'Lil, the family is recently bereaved so now may not be the best time to drop by. Maybe later. I still think the perpetrators are the counterfeit chip crime syndicate. We had a breakthrough here. From the lobby CCTV, we saw someone lurking there when Alan returned from his evening trip and before he took the buggy. This fellow had no business there. His name is Ananda, and he is the loafer brother of the waitress, Darti. *What?*'

Lily was squeaking loudly on the phone. 'He was among the onlookers gathered around the bodies that night. He was right behind me. He had a frightened look on his face and asked me if the buggy driver was dead. He said they hailed from the same village.'

'Oh, so he was at the crime scene. How do you know it was Ananda?'

'Darti arrived and scolded him and he ran away. Darti told me he was her brother,' Lily replied.

'This is useful information, Lily. I hope Harjono gets hold of Ananda soon, he may hold the key to Lee's murder. Though it seems he had an alibi, he was chatting with the receptionist when the murders were committed. He could be an accomplice to the murder, though, bringing the murderer in through the hotel gate. The security guards know Ananda, as he is Darti's brother. Alan Lee's Rolex watch is still missing. So, we can't rule robbery out as a motive. But why kill Sulaiman? Maybe Alan Lee cried out when stabbed and Sulaiman heard the cry and reversed the buggy and came on the scene. The killer was someone he knew. Well, let's hope the forensic team here come up with some answers regarding the identity of the killer. Take care, Lil.'

After Lily had rung off, Dolly sat in the shaded courtyard of her lanai, sipping a latte, and wondering why the Indonesian inspector was late, it was nearly 10 a.m. Five minutes later, a dishevelled Harjono approached along the gravelled path to the lanai, a harassed look on his face.

'Good news and bad news,' Harjono announced. When Dolly pointed to the opposite chair, he gratefully sank down in it. 'Last night, I receive a phone call from a Nepalese guard working at a hotel in Ubud. His name is Bhaskar Thapa. Bhaskar is Ramdin's friend. Madam, you remember Ramdin, the bouncer from the Nightowl Bar? A few days ago, Ramdin ask Bhaskar to lend him his kukri to chop wood in his village. One of my men bring Bhaskar to our HQ to look at the kukri used to kill Alan Lee and Sulaiman. Bhaskar identify the kukri as the one he give to Ramdin. It had his initials carved on the handle.'

'So, Ramdin may be the killer!' Dolly's voice was excited. 'You need to find him, Harjono!'

Harjono sighed sadly. 'We did find him, madam. A fisherman phone us. A body is floating in water near Kuta Beach. When we arrive, we find a knife sticking out of the back of the body. When we turn body over, it is Ramdin! Someone killed him.'

'Killed to stop him from talking.' Dolly sighed, heavily. 'Is Ramdin Lee's killer or did he lend the kukri to someone else?'

Harjono was nodding. 'We know soon, madam. The fingerprints team is ready with results soon. They have Ramdin's print from morgue and they compare to prints on kukri. The forensic lab here will have results by tomorrow, madam, on the DNA found under Sulaiman's fingernails.'

Dolly nodded. 'Even if Ramdin's fingerprints are on the kukri, it does not conclusively prove he is the killer. He may have lent someone the knife. Are your men searching Ramdin's house?'

Harjono inclined his head. 'Yes, madam. Ramdin live with another waiter in small shack in Uluwatu. We raid shack.' He nodded at his mobile phone. 'My men call me, madam, if they find gold watch.'

Dolly raised an eyebrow. 'You said you had good news. What is it?'

Harjono gave a satisfied sigh before grinning from ear to ear. 'This morning, my men catch Darti's brother, Ananda. He was stealing watermelons from a field and the owner phone my men. He is in custody, and you can interview him at headquarters. He has a lot of explaining to do, yes?'

'We didn't see anyone else in the CCTV footage, Ananda was hiding behind the potted plant at the lobby door and then talking to the receptionist. Since Ananda worked in the same pub as Ramdin, it is likely Ananda is an accomplice, he may have brought Ramdin in through the gate. The security guard would know Ananda. Have your officers found him?'

Harjono raised his bushy eyebrows. 'The security guard? We are still looking for him, madam. Aditya disappear from the time of murder. We go interview Ananda, madam.'

Soon the squad car was making its way to CIA HQ in Bali.

* * *

Harjono's office was a small cubby hole with a tiny desk and an old computer, Harjono preferring to work from his electronic tablet. The Indonesian inspector ordered some snacks and tea and after eating, Harjono accompanied Dolly to a small interview room with a uniformed police constable posted at the door.

Sunlight spilled in through the window of the room. At a table sat a young man in dirty jeans and T-shirt, a stubble of hair on his chin. He had a squint in his eye and Dolly was not sure where he was looking most of the time.

Harjono glanced at Dolly and the Singaporean superintendent nodded, accepting the mantle of chief interviewer. The officers seated themselves opposite Ananda.

'Your name is Ananda Kusni.' Dolly glanced at the notes in front of her. 'You work as a waiter at the Nightowl?'

The prisoner looked sullen and shook his head. In halting English, he claimed Ramdin had mocked him for getting too many tips. He pushed Ramdin, a fight broke out and Hadyanto sacked Ananda.

'You were fired for being good at your job?' Dolly's voice held the right note of incredulity to induce a flush on the young man's face.

'Hadyanto said the fight was about money you owed Ramdin,' Harjono cut in, speaking in the native tongue.

Ananda began chewing his nails.

Dolly said sharply, 'What were you doing at Beachcombers Hotel Wednesday night when two men were killed? Around 11 p.m.? Why were you there?'

For a moment, naked fear flashed in the young man's eyes, and he stopped chewing his nails. 'Darti work late, I come to take her home,' Ananda said, softly.

Harjono glared at Ananda and fired off a spate of words that Dolly could not follow. He threateningly sliced the air in front of his own throat. He turned to Dolly and said, 'I tell him we hang him for murder.'

'I kill nobody!' Ananda squeaked. 'I talk to Jamal all the time. Ask him!'

'Who did you bring with you to the hotel that night?' Dolly asked in a deceptively casual voice.

Harjono again sliced the air in front of his throat.

After some hesitation, Ananda narrated to Harjono in his native tongue what happened that night. Ramdin had paid both Ananda and Aditya, the security guard, a large sum of money to be let in through the hotel gate and to keep silent about his presence. Ramdin wanted to steal Alan Lee's gold Rolex watch and wanted Ananda to give him directions to Alan Lee's villa. Ananda thought Ramdin would steal the watch from inside the villa when Lee was asleep. He wanted to accompany Ramdin and act as a look-out, but Ramdin refused the offer and told him to wait in the lobby. After the burglary, they were then to spend the night at Ramdin's Uluwatu shack and leave the next morning to try to sell the watch for a lot of money. When Ananda heard about the murders, he went home and next day at the pub, asked Ramdin for more money to keep his mouth shut. It was at this point, Ramdin hit him and Hadyanto sacked him.

'Trying blackmail, eh?' Harjono sneered. 'You are a shame to your family!'

For a moment, regret washed over Ananda's face, and he lowered his eyes. He looked up at Dolly and said, 'I did not kill anybody, Sulaiman my friend.' He turned desperately to Harjono and added, 'I did not know Ramdin enter the hotel to kill people. Please believe me, Inspector.'

'What did you do after the murders were discovered?' Harjono asked.

Ananda said he looked for Ramdin but could not find him. He said he hung around the villa hoping Sulaiman was still alive. But Darti arrived and scolded him for being on the premises. Ananda went into a long tirade against his sister, whom he thought was pretentious just because she was a little more educated than the rest of her siblings.

After translating for Dolly, Harjono said, 'Ramdin was killed, his body found at Kuta Beach this morning, knife stuck in his back.' Harjono nodded at Ananda, knowingly.

Ananda emitted a howl. 'They kill me, too! I know too much. Please keep me in jail, Inspector.'

'Who are "they" and what do you know?' Dolly asked.

Ananda hesitated, then remembered Ramdin's fate. He seemed to make up his mind to turn informant and get police protection. He told Harjono he worked part-time for Latham, the Beachcombers Hotel manager, in a factory he owned with Hadyanto, near Pujung. The factory was hidden deep inside the jungle, to keep it out of sight. According to Ananda, the factory remodelled faulty computer chips for Latham to sell them to a company in China.

When Harjono translated Ananda's words, Dolly sighed. It was all falling into place. 'Yes, these are called counterfeit chips and they are sold on the black market. What were your duties?'

Ananda told Harjono he supervised low-paid workers to remove faulty dies from packages, re-mark, and re-package them. When Harjono translated his words for Dolly's benefit, Ananda added in English, 'Hadyanto my boss, but Latham big boss.'

'What was your salary?' Dolly asked, quizzically.

When Ananda told them, Harjono whistled. 'Pay you a lot of hush money, eh? So, where is this factory near Pujung? You take us there, Ananda!'

* * *

The drive to Pujung was tense and once they got out of the car, they had to trample through dense undergrowth to reach a long low building hidden behind a crop of trees. A squad car of Harjono's officers had accompanied them and Harjono ordered his men to search the factory. To the dismay of the police officers, the building was deserted and showed no signs of it ever being occupied.

'Wiped clean,' Harjono sighed. 'No trace of fake chips or anything else.' He looked hopefully at his officers who were searching for clues in the rest of the building, but they shook their heads.

'You sure you bring us to right place, Ananda?' Harjono said, threateningly.

'Yes, they have all gone, Inspector.' Ananda giggled and sobered up when Harjono fixed a gimlet eye on him.

Harjono went outside to call his officers to raid the Nightowl Bar and Latham's bungalow and bring Hadyanto and Latham in for questioning.

* * *

In the interview room, Harjono asked Ananda, 'You want to end up like Ramdin? If not, you tell us all, Ananda.'

'I don't know more. I just hear Mr Latham talk to *his* boss on phone. His boss live in Singapore.'

Dolly looked thoughtfully at Ananda being led away to the cells. She remembered Alan Lee telling them the crime syndicate operated out of Singapore. It was feasible the syndicate's mastermind lived in Singapore.

Harjono seated Dolly in his office. He picked up the receiver when the phone on his desk rang. A smile spread over his face as he listened to the caller. After putting down the phone, he turned to Dolly. 'That was our fingerprint team, madam. The kukri have Ramdin's prints on it. He is our killer, madam.'

'Unfortunately, he is dead,' Dolly said, waspishly. 'And like I said, what if he lent the knife to someone else? Were there other fingerprints on the kukri?'

Harjono nodded. 'But Ramdin main one, madam.'

'What about the search of Ramdin's house? Has Alan Lee's watch been recovered?'

Harjono nodded and dialled his mobile to connect himself to the officers who were searching Ramdin's house. He listened on the phone, his brows puckered. Thoughtfully, he switched off his mobile and turned to Dolly.

Harjono reported that Ramdin's housemate had disappeared, and the house was empty when his men reached there. A search revealed no gold Rolex watch. Harjono's officers questioned an old neighbour who cleaned and cooked for the men. The old Indonesian woman reported that last night while she was cooking the men their curry and rice, she observed Ramdin showing his housemate a glittering object. In the early morning, when she woke up, she went to sweep the courtyard outside her house. It was still dark. From the light spilling from the open doorway of his house, she saw Ramdin and his housemate leave the house and take the road to Kuta.

'Madam, I think Ramdin show the gold watch to his housemate, eh?' Harjono's eyes were full of conjecture. 'We find name of housemate, Ali Khalil. My men look for him. Possible he kill Ramdin and steal watch.'

The phone rang shrilly and Harjono snatched up the receiver. His face became ashen as he talked to his officers.

'What?' Dolly demanded, noting Harjono tearing at his hair.

'Hadyanto is gone. The Nightowl Bar is closed. The neighbouring eatery said he closed shop last night and told his neighbour he was going overseas. Latham gone too. His native housekeeper said last night he received an overseas call and left for the airport. He never tell her where he was going. All birds fly away, ASP Das, sorry.'

'You should still call the airport and ask Immigration what time the men left.'

Harjono nodded, miserably. 'We did that already. Both men took last night's flights out. Hadyanto was headed for China and Latham for Hong Kong. We are too late, ASP Das.' Harjono's eyes bulged. 'I wonder who knifed Ramdin. His body is in the morgue now and I will ask pathologist for time of death.'

The pathologist informed the officers Ramdin had been killed sometime between midnight and early morning.

'That lets Latham and Hadyanto out,' Harjono pondered.

'And leaves Ananda and Ali Khalil,' finished Dolly, looking keenly at the Indonesian inspector.

Harjono began perspiring. 'I will torture Ananda until he tells me he murdered Ramdin.'

Dolly made soothing noises. 'More likely, it's Ali Khalil who killed Ramdin. The glittering object the old neighbour saw in Ramdin's hands may have been Alan Lee's gold Rolex watch. Again, this is pointing to a robbery except for Hadyanto and Latham running away and Ananda's information about the Pujung factory remodelling computer chips. Ananda could hardly have made that up. And of course, Alan Lee's conversation with me about the crime syndicate is also pointing to Lee's death being a hit by the syndicate. Hadyanto may have had a gang, the workers who recycled the fake chips. He could have paid one of them to kill Ramdin to keep him quiet. For all you know, Ali Khalil could have been one of the factory workers as well, like Ananda, and he was ordered to kill Ramdin. But, yes, you should grill Ananda some more.'

Dolly got to her feet. 'I think it's time I returned to Singapore. You have Ananda in custody and can interrogate him. And your men are searching for Ali Khalil. Please update me on the phone, Harjono. And fax me Ramdin's post-mortem report. If the pathologist has finished with Alan Lee's PM, maybe you can release the body and arrange for me to fly him back to Singapore. Tomorrow afternoon, maybe? We already have a good idea who murdered Alan Lee. Ramdin. And he is dead. But it would be good to pay a visit to Latham's bungalow and look around. Can we do that without a warrant?'

Harjono nodded, dejectedly. 'I get warrant, ASP Das, we will go late morning tomorrow. Do we have enough evidence to ask Interpol to detain Latham and Hadyanto overseas?'

'You have Ananda's testimony about the chip recycling factory. You need to approach your National Central Bureau of Interpol here and ask their help in locating Latham and Hadyanto overseas.'

'Yes, ASP Das. The Sekretariat NCB-Interpol is located in Jakarta. I will email them with Ananda's statement.'

'Since the crime syndicate may be operating from Singapore, I will get in touch with NCB-Interpol in Singapore and ask their help in locating Latham. Alan Lee was killed in Indonesia, but he was a Singapore national. NCB-Interpol in Singapore may be interested in coordinating with other Interpol branches to locate the criminals in this case. But I just have the word of a murdered man and a crook that the syndicate mastermind lives in Singapore. We have a long road ahead of us, Harjono.' Dolly looked morose.

'You will have lunch tomorrow with my wife and me before flight, yes?' And when Dolly smiled, Harjono's face brightened.

Dolly spent the evening having a long chat with her son on the phone. She had an early night after eating a delicious pasta dish from Room Service. Dolly dreamt of dead faces floating in the ocean.

Saturday, 18 May 2013

Bali, Indonesia

8

Dolly sat at The Sea-Shell Café having a breakfast of fried eggs, toast, coffee, and orange juice. She was seated at the edge of the restaurant where the ground sloped down to the beach. The day was gloomy, black clouds lowered over a grim sea, but that did not deter children from building their sandcastles on the beach and riders on horses specked the shoreline. There were fewer boats on the ocean and the surfers were absent.

There was a small cough and Dolly turned around to see the waitress, Darti, standing by the table. She had a coffee jug in her hands, but her usual gracious smile was missing. Her eyes looked red, and Dolly wondered whether she had been weeping.

'I fill up your coffee, madam.' Darti poured coffee into Dolly's cup although it was two-thirds full. She took in Dolly's smile of thanks and lifted her lips wryly. 'Ananda will die in jail, madam. The police here are bad, they beat the prisoners.'

'No, no, I am sure not.' Dolly sipped her hot coffee before biting into a piece of toast liberally spread with marmalade. 'The police think your brother let in the killer Wednesday night. Ananda did not murder Alan Lee and Sulaiman. Jamal vouches for him. But he was working for Hadyanto and Mark Latham, illegal work. Do you know anything about his activities, Darti?'

Darti's face was pale and her eyes misty. 'Ananda dropped out of school, madam. He ran away from home and stole fruits from farms. My father beat him so many times with a cane. But Ananda never learn his lesson. I don't know much because I live with my aunt in Jakarta. After I finish school, I returned to Bali, got job at this hotel. Ananda never stayed home with us. We did not know where he live. He only came home sometimes and gave my mother money. He became friendly with me from last year. Taking me home when I work late shift. I now know it is because he worked for Mr Latham. We all know Hadyanto is a criminal, but Mr Latham? They are saying he has run away from Bali. Is this true, madam?'

Dolly finished her toast and sipped her coffee. 'Yes. Do you know what kind of business Ananda was involved in?'

Darti shook her head and cried, 'Oh please, madam, we hear bad stories of beatings in jail. Inspector Harjono not so bad, but his deputies not nice men. They came last night to search our house. My mother cried and my father is angry and ashamed of Ananda.'

'Do you know a man called Ali Khalil?' Dolly asked.

Darti nodded her head, vigorously. 'Yes, madam. He is Ananda's friend, also wait at tables like my brother. Ananda sometimes stays with him at his shack.'

Dolly was intrigued to see Darti blushing furiously. 'Well, Ali is not at the shack now. Do *you* know him, Darti?'

Darti's eyes dropped, and a shy smile played on her lips. She looked up to say, 'He wanted to court me, madam. But I said no. Anyone from Hadyanto's gang is bad news, madam.'

Dolly nodded. 'You were wise. Do you know where he would go? He is not in the Uluwatu shack.'

Darti was voluble. 'His family lives on Nusa Penida.' On noting the incomprehension on Dolly's face, she explained, 'It is an island you can visit by boat, madam. Not far from Bali Island. Ali's father sells handicrafts at Toyapakeh Market. His family lives in Toyapakeh Village. Ali visits his family every Sunday, madam. You will find him there this Sunday for sure.'

Dolly stored away the information in her head, assured Darti her brother would be treated well in jail and with a relieved but troubled smile on her face, the waitress drifted away.

Dolly sipped her orange juice and looked out at the ocean. A pre-shower breeze nudged some flowers from the nearby tree to the ground. Harjono arrived at the café with the first drops of rain.

The Indonesian inspector looked gloomy. He plonked himself down on the chair opposite Dolly and said, 'My boss is angry I allow Hadyanto, and

Latham slip out of Bali. It happened so fast, madam. Before we could finger the criminals, they were gone.' Harjono confided to Dolly that he was due for promotion and this setback in allowing criminals to escape from Bali would delay the promotion. He gave a heavy sigh before saying, 'Madam, we go now to Mark Latham's bungalow in Ubud. It is probably wiped clean,' he added, gloomily.

Dolly gave Harjono information on Ali Khalil's whereabouts and the Indonesian inspector's face brightened. 'I send my men to Nusa Penida, not far from here, madam.' Harjono got busy on his mobile phone.

There was a heavy downpour and Dolly waited at the lobby entrance for the police car to arrive.

* * *

There were some terraced rice fields on the way to Ubud, but the rain blotted them out. The road was narrow and winding with little factories by the side manufacturing art works. Images of half-formed gods and goddesses lined the roadside, getting wet in the rain. Traffic was slow and, in the car, Harjono outlined his theory of Alan Lee's murder being the result of a robbery gone wrong. He told Dolly that when Alan Lee visited the Nightowl Bar, Ramdin had probably seen the Rolex watch on Alan Lee's wrist and bribed Ananda to let him in through the hotel gate. Ramdin ambushed Alan Lee near his villa, but Lee had retaliated resulting in Ramdin using his kukri. Sulaiman probably heard Lee cry out when stabbed and returned to the villa and Ramdin killed Sulaiman because he could finger him as Lee's killer. After his narration, Harjono sat back, satisfied.

Dolly said, 'There are no defensive marks on Alan Lee, so he was killed, intentionally, and not in a scuffle. I agree Sulaiman was killed because he came on the scene and this time there was a scuffle with Ramdin. I still think Ramdin is a hired killer, he murdered Lee on the orders of the crime syndicate. Being a natural thief, he would take the Rolex watch, anyway. Ananda would not make up the elaborate story of a fake computer chip factory and Alan Lee told me that he was on the trail of a syndicate mastermind. Now I think that was probably Latham. Don't take the easy way out, Harjono, don't drop the case by saying it's a robbery gone wrong. The evidence points in the opposite direction.' She sighed when she saw Harjono's look.

The rain had eased, and they were arriving at a roundabout with many small shops selling a variety of goods. Dolly saw a road sign stating they had arrived in Ubud. From Ubud, they took a narrow road and drove thirty minutes to arrive at some dwellings scattered among terraced rice fields. After the rain, the grass sparkled like diamonds. It was a quiet neighbourhood. The police car stopped at a small wrought iron gate leading to a beautiful garden. A small wooden resort-style bungalow could be seen through tall trees.

'Mark Latham, he lives in style,' Harjono observed. The police officers alighted from the car at the gate and Harjono pushed it open. To their surprise, the gate was unlocked. As they stamped into the muddy yard, a bent old Indonesian man appeared from behind a bed of beautiful roses.

Harjono said a few sentences in their language and the man pointed to a winding path. He looked frightened.

'He is gardener,' Harjono informed Dolly. 'We follow path, we come to house. The housekeeper is called Nona. I tell her on the phone we are coming with search warrant.'

As they spoke, a middle-aged woman appeared in the patio of the house and gave Harjono a nod.

They climbed the few steps to the portico where tables and chairs were liberally placed along with a rattan, moon-shaped swing chair. Pots of plants hung from the ceiling. It was beautiful and pleasant.

'This is Superintendent Das from the Singapore CID, Nona,' Harjono introduced. He pointed to the three officers who had arrived behind them in a police jeep. 'We search house, eh? I tell you I have warrant, Nona.'

Nona shrugged and directed a beaming smile at Dolly. 'Cold drink, madam?' She was dressed in western clothes, but her head was covered with a scarf.

Dolly politely declined and Nona led the way into the house. The patio opened into a beautifully furnished living room filled with expensive artefacts. Balinese paintings hung on the walls. Dolly wondered whether the paintings were authentic.

Dolly turned to Nona. 'Did Mr Latham have an office, a computer, maybe?'

Nona nodded and led the way into the bowels of the house. At the end of a long corridor was a wooden door. Nona pushed it open, and they entered a room flooded with light from windows on all sides. There were bookcases and a big mahogany desk in the middle of the room on which there was a computer and a printer.

'Mr Latham took his laptop with him,' Nona supplied, hanging around in the doorway.

'We look here, you can go now, Nona,' Harjono ordered, and Nona melted away.

Dolly turned the computer on, and it blinked for the password. Dolly turned to Harjono and said, 'It's better if your officers can take out the hard disk from the computer and we do computer forensics with my team in Singapore. I will take the hard disk with me, Harjono. We have good computer forensics there, the officers may be able to retrieve messages, even deleted ones. Maybe those will tell us more about the counterfeit chip scam. I will update you on the findings and fax all results to you. When we are finished, I will send the hard disk back to you.'

Harjono and Dolly sat in the patio while Harjono's men searched the house. This time, Dolly accepted Nona's offer of a cold drink as did Harjono.

Sipping her lemonade, Dolly asked Nona, who was standing near the door to the living room, 'Did Mr Latham have a business and a factory?'

Nona frowned and then nodded. 'He work part-time at hotel only. He spend half the month travelling to China. Yes, some crates arrive at the house and stored at the back.'

'Do you know what kind of factory? What did it make?' Dolly asked.

Nona shook her head. 'I don't know, madam.' She looked at Harjono, who was talking on the phone and ordering his men to search the outhouses and sheds on the property.

'Any visitors to the house, Nona?' Harjono asked her.

Nona talked animatedly for a while and Harjono nodded. He turned to Dolly and said that while there were no visitors, Mark Latham was always talking on the computer and his phone in the study. Nona believed he was talking to people he knew in Singapore as she had heard the name of the country mentioned. Harjono added, 'Probably Skype calls.'

Nona went into another animated narration and Harjono looked excited. He told Dolly, Nona sometimes entered the study during the Skype calls with drinks for Latham. She had seen the face at the other end of the computer and it was that of an Indian woman.

'An Indian woman!' Dolly exclaimed.

Nona could not tell them anything more and in half an hour, Harjono's officers arrived from various parts of the house. One reported that only a few of Latham's clothes were missing and the bedroom was untidy. Latham had left in a great hurry.

Harjono smiled at Dolly. 'Now to come, madam, and have lunch with my wife and me. My officer will reach Latham's hard disk to my house in half an hour. Come, madam, or you are late for your flight home.'

* * *

Harjono's house was located some miles from Seminyak beach, in a remote enclave surrounded by rice paddy fields. Dolly saw farmers working in the fields and bird song filled the air. Peace and tranquillity prevailed in this remote spot. The rain had stopped, and the sun was out.

Harjono's house was a small bungalow with a run-down garden. Two stone lions guarded the archway through which they entered the yard. They went four steps up to a green door and before Harjono could fish for his keys, the door opened to reveal a beautiful, buxom woman dressed in traditional Indonesian clothes with a tudung covering her head. She had large eyes, a pert nose, and a beautiful smile.

Harjono grinned. 'ASP Das, please meet my wife, Aishah. We are married now for fifteen years,' he added, proudly.

'Welcome, welcome,' Aishah gushed, giggling pleasurably. She was as jolly as her husband. 'Harjono tell me everything about you, ASP Das. Thank you for joining us for lunch.'

They trooped into a small living room crammed with antique furniture. But Harjono said, 'We go directly to lunch, Aishah. Madam Dolly has plane to catch.'

They followed Aishah to a small dining room filled with light. It opened into a veranda and a garden blooming with flowers. They sat at a large table which was laid out with western and Indonesian dishes.

'My wife run two restaurants, one in Ubud centre and one near Seminyak. She is a good cook.' Harjono smiled broadly.

Aishah expertly served everyone Indonesian fried rice, chicken rendang, western-style steamed seabass, prawn scampi and a vegetable medley.

Dolly tasted the rendang and exclaimed with pleasure, 'What good food! Aishah, thank you so much for inviting me for lunch.'

They all tucked into their lunch, Harjono eating his food with gusto and beaming around at everyone. It was ten minutes into their lunch that Harjono looked at Dolly.

He told her he had been thinking about the murders and since Lee did not have defensive wounds, it was probable Ramdin was hired to kill Lee. He also agreed with Dolly that Ananda did not have the brains to make up the story of the counterfeit chip recycling factory. 'But, madam, what to do now? Latham and Hadyanto are gone.'

Dolly finished her shrimp scampi and licked her lips. She looked at Harjono. 'You have many loose ends to tie, Harjono. First, you need to find Ali Khalil. Did your men go to Nusa Penida, to his village there?'

Harjono looked gloomily at the vegetables on his plate. His wife noted his look and quickly served him more chicken rendang. Harjono said, 'No, Ali was not at his home in Nusa Penida. But we will find him, madam. We have warrant for his arrest. All my officers are on alert.'

'Any forensic findings from Ramdin's body or clothes?' Dolly smiled at Aishah, who was serving her more shrimp.

Harjono shook his head. 'The knife handle wiped clean, madam. No fingerprints. Our forensic team is processing Ramdin's clothes. No skin underneath fingernail and no other defensive marks on Ramdin. He did not expect to be killed, madam. Someone knife him when his back was turned. But, madam, he had scratches on his hands. Our pathologist say they were a day old. It is possible Ramdin got scratched when fighting with Sulaiman.'

Dolly finished the last of the shrimp and said, 'Yes, that ties in nicely. What about preliminary findings on the killer's DNA from Sulaiman's fingernails?'

Harjono glanced at his watch, nodded, and snatched up his mobile phone. 'I call them, madam, the results are ready by now.'

Harjono dialled a number, spoke some curt words and waited. Soon, a smile spread over his face. He spoke warmly and switched off the phone.

Dolly looked up from the last of the rendang and rice on her plate. She said, 'I take it that it is Ramdin's DNA underneath Sulaiman's fingernails?'

Harjono nodded. 'Yes. Madam, you will now agree that Ramdin killed Sulaiman and Alan Lee.'

Dolly nodded. 'Yes, though do let me know what the Jakarta forensic lab says, okay? Well, at least, I can let our minister know that we have found out who killed his cousin. Though the killer received a different kind of justice than the courts may have offered. The case is far from closed, however. I think Ramdin was paid by someone to kill Alan Lee. Probably the crime syndicate. Mark Latham is a possible member of this syndicate as is Hadyanto.'

Harjono finished his rendang and rice with relish and said, 'I call Sekretariat NCB-Interpol in Jakarta and talk to Supt Ahmed. I have long chat with him. He say no evidence of chip recycling factory. It is hard for him to negotiate with NCB-Interpol in Beijing to locate Latham and Hadyanto. No evidence linking Latham to Lee murder. But he tell me to catch Ali Khalil, get evidence about Ramdin murder and it may be possible for him to apply to Interpol Beijing and try to locate Hadyanto. If Hadyanto order Ramdin murder. Ali Khalil can tell us, yes? Since Alan Lee was a Singapore national, better luck for you to talk to NCB-Interpol at Singapore and try to locate Latham, ASP Das. I try to find Ali Khalil to close the Ramdin murder case.'

Dolly finished eating the vegetables on her plate before saying, 'There is another branch in Singapore CID that investigates crime syndicates, not my branch. I will report to my bosses and see what they say. We will keep in touch by email and phone, Harjono, and keep updating each other.'

There was a wail from inside the house and Aishah hurriedly rose from her chair. Soon, she returned with a cherubic baby in her arms. 'Our son, Mohammed, named after the Prophet,' she said, proudly.

Harjono rose to pinch his baby's cheeks and Mohammed gurgled gleefully.

Aishah said, 'We have four girls and I say enough. But Harjono, he want son and here is Mohammed. He is spoilt by his sisters. I think he will grow up to be proud and having his own way.' She laughed.

'He is a cute baby, Aishah. He reminds me of my little niece, Molly.' Dolly smiled, then glanced at her watch and gave an exclamation.

Harjono said, 'My driver is waiting outside, ASP Das. You will be late for your flight home.'

Dolly got to her feet and thanked Harjono and his wife for their hospitality. At the gate, a policeman was waiting with Mark Latham's computer hard disk, packaged in waterproof wrapping. Dolly slipped the package into her sling bag and got into the car.

She waved to Aishah and Harjono at the gate, the baby clutched in Aishah's arms.

In an hour, Dolly was on the plane, leaning back in her seat and gazing through the window, watching the Indian Ocean speeding by as the plane flew overhead. Soon, she was asleep as the clouds gently rolled by her window. Alan Lee's coffin rattled ominously in the bowels of the aeroplane.

A DEATH IN SINGAPORE

Sunday, 19 May 2013

Singapore

9

It was a bright, sunny morning at the Silver Springs Condo complex. Four towering blocks loomed over the landscaped gardens, swimming and wading pools. The playground resounded with boisterous shouts as children made the most of their Sunday morning. Delicious aromas floated up from Lily's Kitchen, a café situated on the ground floor of Block C. Lily Das was frying pratas while her business partner, Ashikin Ali, stirred a pot of nasi lemak.

Up on the fifteenth floor of Block D, at #15-26, the atmosphere was subdued. Linda Lee, a petite, curly-haired Chinese woman in her late forties, stared at her laptop screen as she lay on the bed in her master bedroom. She could hear murmurs from the kitchen. Her husband, Patrick Singh, was frying omelettes for their children's breakfast.

Linda still could not believe her brother, Alan, was dead. They had met for lunch before he left for Bali, and he had been full of life with plans for setting up a foundation for kidney dialysis patients in their mother's memory. He had wanted her to work at the foundation with him and her heart had rejoiced. He told her he was going to Bali on business and when he returned, he would meet her for a meal at her house and discuss more about the foundation.

The breeze billowed out the window curtains and the sun gently reflected off the glass windowpanes. A robbery gone wrong, Linda thought, glancing outside, and her lips trembled. Her brother was unlucky. She wondered what would happen to the Primrose Crescent bungalow. Alice was still living there although Alan had told her he had instructed his lawyers to evict her. But Alan was dead. And she would have to see to it that Alice was ousted from the bungalow. Her face set resolutely as Patrick Singh, her husband, entered with a tray of toast, omelette, orange juice, and coffee.

'Did the kids manage to eat their breakfast today, Pat? Ever since we told them about Alan, they're bursting into tears in the middle of meals and rushing to their rooms.' Linda sighed. 'They loved their uncle so much.'

Patrick, a tall muscular Indian Sikh with a pink turban on his head, laid the tray over Linda's knees and nodded. 'They ate their meal today without crying. It was good you did not join us. Seeing you makes them blubber.' His voice was strong and vibrant, his large brown eyes sympathetic. 'Duleep, especially, was close to Alan and he woke up yesterday with his eyes red from weeping. Told me Alan had promised to attend the soccer match he is playing in at the end of the month at school. Alan was so involved with the children's activities. They'll miss him terribly.'

Linda's eyes glistened as she nibbled delicately at the coriander and chilli omelette. 'It will take them time to come to terms with Alan's death. Where is Lestriani?'

'She has gone to the market for grocery shopping.' Patrick frowned. 'Her contract is ending this June. Have you offered to renew her contract, Linda?'

'I will speak with the maid. She is a godsend, I agree. But she wants to see her children. We will have to give her home leave if she agrees to renew her contract.'

A curly-haired girl in pigtails stood at the bedroom door.

'Daddy, we'll be late for class.'

'Yes, honey. I'll change quickly and drive you, don't worry.' He left the room.

Linda looked at Natasha, her firstborn, with maternal love and pride. 'Natty, Lestriani has not tied your hair, properly. Come here and I'll do it for you.'

Natasha stood obligingly in front of her mother and soon Duleep joined them. Linda looked at her son, proud tears in her eyes. He was a strapping lad with long hair tied in a bun at the top of his head. He was the apple of her eye, and she could not resist giving him a quick kiss on his cheek after she had finished tying her daughter's hair. Linda's lips set grimly—the Primrose Crescent bungalow was Duleep and Natasha's inheritance and worth fighting for.

She frowned. It had been her decision to send the children to weekend Hindi and Mandarin classes. While Linda encouraged Duleep and Natasha to embrace Patrick's Sikh faith, she still wanted her children to speak and understand Mandarin. But was learning two native languages placing stress on her children?

'Did you finish your Hindi enrichment class homework?' She asked her daughter, tentatively.

'All done, Ma, and the Mandarin homework for tomorrow, too.' Natasha said, enthusiastically, bringing a smile to Linda's face.

After the children left with their father, the telephone rang, it was the maid from the Primrose Crescent bungalow informing her stepbrother, Etienne, wanted to see her regarding Alan's funeral.

'Sir's body has arrived, ma'am,' the maid, Joyce, said in a trembling voice from the bungalow. 'It is in funeral parlour.'

Linda teared up again and after assuring Joyce she would be there, she switched off her mobile phone. She finished her breakfast, dragged herself out of the bed, and into the bathroom to take a shower.

She dressed herself in a black suit and looked at herself in the bedroom mirror. Her eyes were red and puffy, and she quickly opened her make-up kit and began applying eye liner, eye shadow, powder, and lipstick. She heard the key turning in the lock of the main door and soon Lestriani appeared in the doorway.

Linda smiled at her domestic helper. 'Did you get fresh fish?'

Lestriani nodded. 'But so expensive, ma'am. Here is your change.' She came forward and kept the money on the dressing table.

Linda rose from the stool, put the money in her black handbag, hung the bag on her shoulder and said, 'What are we having for lunch?'

'Indonesian fried rice and grilled sea bass with chillies and coriander.'

Linda nodded, sadly. She told her maid that she would be going with Etienne to the funeral parlour to pay their respects to Alan. Then she would eat her lunch at the Primrose Crescent bungalow. She instructed Lestriani to fetch the children back from their enrichment classes at noon and feed them lunch. She would be back by late afternoon.

With tears in her eyes, the maid shut the door after Linda.

* * *

Linda glanced out of the cab window as Pandan Valley came into view. She had grown up here. When she had been ten years old, her father, Ronnie Lee, had built the bungalow at 39, Primrose Crescent. The white two-storey house had two wings separated by the staircase. As a child, Linda had run through the entire house every morning, revelling in the sunlight streaming in through the wide windows bringing with it a scent-laden breeze. While their parents, Ronnie and Natalie, occupied one wing of the house including a big library on the ground floor, Alan and Linda had occupied the first storey of the other wing, the ground floor containing a spacious hall and dining room where Ronnie entertained guests and hosted lavish parties.

As a young boy, Alan had not taken much interest in the inner sanctums, preferring to aid Yusuf, the gardener, grow vegetables in the back garden and flowers in the spacious front garden fronted by a wrought-iron gate and a flame of the forest tree. There had been a small badminton court on one side of the back garden, next to Yusuf's quarters where Alan regularly invited friends to play. Linda had been content to amuse herself on the swing next to the back garden sheds.

Their mother died of kidney disease when Linda was eighteen and Alan twenty. Sadly, their father had already taken Alice Chua as his mistress. As soon as Natalie died, Ronnie married Alice and brought her into the house. Alice had peremptorily taken over the running of 39, Primrose Crescent. Linda, furious at her father's infidelity, hated the stepmother who was only two years older than her.

After Alice's arrival, Linda's swing and Alan's badminton court were swiftly replaced by a wooden deck adjoining the house and jutting into the back garden where Alice held rowdy parties with her high society friends. Now the house had changed so much that Linda felt she was entering someone else's home. She chewed her lips. Her future would soon change. Was she ready for it? Linda nodded, a small blush filling her cheeks. Yes, she was ready to take the big step she had planned for the last year.

The cab stopped in front of huge wrought-iron gates and Linda alighted after paying the fare. She pushed a bell at the side of the gate and soon Yusuf, the gardener appeared, a cap on his grey head and a tearful smile on his face.

Yusuf began wailing how Alan had been like a son to him and recollecting his childhood pranks. And it was in the gardener's arms, those gnarled arms that had swung them as children, that Linda allowed her tears to flow, unabated, as together they mourned Alan.

After some time, Linda gently extricated herself from the gardener's arms and looked towards the house. She turned her head at a thin voice coming from the third-floor window of the adjoining block of flats. It was her childhood friend, Emily.

'Hi Emily!' Linda shouted, warmly. 'How are you, dear?'

Emily shouted back, 'It's good to see you, Linda. I'm fine. So sorry about Alan. He waved to me on his way to the airport just last week. He was a big brother to me, Linda, you know that. I am so shocked. At least now, Selena and Alan are together again.'

Linda nodded, tearing up. They had all been devastated when ten years ago, a car accident paralysed Emily from the waist down. Emily's older sister, Selena, engaged to be married to Alan, had been behind the wheel and tragically died in the car crash. Linda knew Alan visited Emily often to cheer her up and was instrumental in securing her a job where she could work from home.

'I'll come visit you soon, Em,' Linda said, gave a wave and turned towards the house.

10

The white Mercedes-Benz was in the portico with the chauffeur, Samy, polishing its bonnet with a yellow cloth. This meant Linda's stepmother, Alice, was going out. To one of her kitty parties or art exhibitions disguised as social gatherings where exorbitant prices were paid for very ordinary-looking artwork, Linda thought, derisively. She made her way to the front door just as it opened to reveal her stepmother.

Alice Lee, at forty-nine, was slim with dyed jet-black hair, many visits to the plastic surgeon having taken care of facial wrinkles and flabby skin. As a result, her face was smooth and immobile (like the Sphinx, Linda thought), her body ramrod straight with no hint of curves, her smart trouser suit covering her like a sheath (an obelisk, Linda thought). She had thin eyebrows painted to give the impression of perpetually asking a question, full lips accentuated by red, cherry lipstick (with her stepson's body lying in a cold morgue, thought Linda) and mascara enlarging her rather small eyes.

'Ah, Linda.' Alice looked at her stepdaughter as one would gaze at an annoying cockroach in one's path. 'I'm sorry for your loss, girl. I will miss Alan. I was going to telephone you, but Etienne was so upset about Alan that I had to see to him. Please do take Etienne to visit Alan at Singapore Caskets, the one on Lavender Street, your brother is resting there. Lester made all the arrangements for the funeral home. Did he talk with you?' She raised her eyebrows when Linda shook her head. 'Well, he should have talked to you, at least. You are Alan's *sister*, he is only a cousin. And I, of course, am the wicked stepmother.' She gave a thin smile. 'Lester called me this morning and said we were to go on from there, like whether we want to have a wake and funeral service. Of course, I said, it was all up to you and Etienne. I'm nobody here.' A frown crossed Alice's face before it became immobile again.

Linda wondered whether plastic surgery could be used as a mask, hiding emotions as well as wrinkles until a human being resembled a waxwork. She almost thought her stepmother's face would crack like cement if her full lips stretched in a wide smile.

Linda said, 'Etienne and I will first visit Alan and then have a discussion on what we want done.'

'Etienne can't stop crying and he is a grown man.'

'Well, Tien was close to Alan, they were brothers for heaven's sake.' Alice was *so cold*, Linda thought.

'Of course, I'm devastated by Alan's death. We lived in the same house after all,' Alice said, making no move to extend a hand to Linda in commiseration. 'The nature of his death is traumatic for all of us. A murder! That is why Etienne is upset. Who would want to kill Alan?' She peered myopically at her stepdaughter. 'I hear Lester has been involving himself with the investigation. Sending a policeman from Singapore to Bali? Do you think it was a robbery gone wrong, Linda?'

'I don't know!' Linda said, tersely. 'Lester told me ASP Dolly Das of the Singapore CID was vacationing at the same hotel as Alan and that is the reason for asking her to assist the Bali Police. Lester and Alan were close, so Lester's action is unsurprising. I think my grandmother told him to involve himself in the investigation. Granny is fond of us. But I do know one thing— Alan's wake will be held in this house. Alan *owned* this house,' she spat.

Alice's eyebrows shot high into her domed forehead. 'But of course, Alan's wake will be held in this house, if that's what Tien and you want. But you are wrong in saying the house belonged to him. There's a new will— Ronnie made it before his last trip abroad and the house is mine.'

'Don't be delusional, Alice. You've been singing this song for the last two years,' Linda cut in, forcefully. 'Where is this will, by the way? A figment of your imagination, no doubt. Alan was nice enough not to evict you from his house, out of respect for Pa.' She squared her shoulders, not intimidated by the cold glint in Alice's eyes. 'Let me tell you something. The house was Alan's and as his next-of-kin, the house is mine and I have no hesitation in taking you to court to prove that. My children's inheritance is at stake.'

'You do what you like, dear. You seem to forget Etienne is Ronnie's child, too.' Alice's voice was icy. 'Now I really must go. There is a small bazaar in Little India, and the organizers have asked me to cut the ribbon. Now, dear, do see to Etienne's breakfast, the boy has not eaten since yesterday. Pining for Alan isn't going to bring him back.'

Alice daintily walked down the steps leading to the portico where Samy held the car door open for her. Alice seated herself carefully and gave Linda a casual wave.

As the car sped out of the gate, Linda's gaze fell on the nearby shrubs. She caught a sudden movement there. A flash of colour behind a bush. Linda stiffened and jumped as a tall young man wearing horn-rimmed spectacles hesitantly stepped out from behind the rose bush.

'May I help you?' Linda asked, coldly, certain the young man was one of Alice's wards whom she adopted from time to time, a struggling artist or musician on whom Alice periodically lavished funds to further their careers before losing interest.

'Hi,' the man said, hesitantly edging forward. 'My name is Lionel Chu, and I was Alan's colleague at work.'

'Oh, you work at Waferworld?' Linda's voice became friendly. 'I'm Alan's sister, Linda.'

Lionel Chu gave a quick gap-toothed smile before his face saddened. 'Yes, please accept my condolences. Alan was gone too early. I was . . . er . . . wondering if Alan left anything for me? A parcel or package with my name on it?'

'Why would he do that?' Linda asked, sharply.

'Oh, it was work-related,' Lionel said, hurriedly. 'Before he left for Bali, he told me he would leave a parcel for me. Again, please do accept my sincerest condolences.'

As the man began walking away, Linda cried, 'Wait! Alan told me he was going to Bali on a business trip. Did Waferworld send him there? Nobody from the company has contacted us.'

Lionel turned and said evasively, 'He told us at work he was going to Bali on holiday.' The young man nodded and began walking to the gate and was soon out of sight behind the rambutan tree.

Puzzled, Linda entered the mansion and walked up the carpeted stairs to the first floor. Alice had redecorated the house after Natalie Lee's death and Linda had to admit she had done a better job than her own mother, although one could argue that the carpeted corridors lined with wall lamps belonged more in a hotel than a home.

Linda knocked on her stepbrother's door, shouting, 'Tien, it's Sis. Open the door!'

The door swung open and a youth in pyjamas and tee gazed at Linda with red-rimmed eyes. He was broad and muscular with a shock of black hair cut short. He hugged Linda and began crying. Linda led him to his bed and sat him down. Holding his hand, she made soothing noises. After a while, Etienne's sniffles stopped.

'How can Bro be dead?' He moaned. 'He promised we would go to the chess tournament in Jakarta next week.'

Alan had been a junior chess champion and had shared his love for the game with his sister's children. Etienne was slow of intellect, but he compensated for that by his big heart and his love for his siblings. Whenever he could take leave from his work, Alan would go to chess tournaments in the Asia-Pacific region and his stepbrother often accompanied him to cheer him on.

'Now, Tien, you must pull yourself together. Your Ma says you haven't eaten since yesterday.' Linda smoothed Etienne's hair, fondly. 'Alan wouldn't want you to starve because of him. Please do have some breakfast. I'll tell Joyce to make fresh chicken congee, okay?'

Etienne nodded and then whispered, 'Bro was preoccupied for the last six months but he wouldn't tell me why he was so worried.'

'Was it the house?' Linda wondered.

Joyce, the maid, entered, wheeling in a breakfast tray. She had not only prepared congee but also Etienne's favourite—sausages and a soft-boiled egg.

'That will be all, Joyce.' Linda's voice was like a whiplash on seeing Joyce smiling coquettishly at Etienne. Joyce gave Linda a glare and departed, huffily.

Etienne seemed to have recovered his appetite and hungrily ate the food. 'Joyce is a good cook.'

Linda asked, sharply. 'Are you still seeing Della?'

Etienne blushed to the roots of his hair and looked down at the ground. 'Of course, I'm seeing her, Sis. I want to marry her.'

Linda frowned. 'Rubbish! You're too young to get married. This is one topic on which Alice, and I agree, Tien. Della is five years older than you and works as a model. You're mooning over her like a lovesick teenager, and you'll get hurt.'

'I *am* a teenager,' Etienne said, indignantly. 'I'm nineteen. Della loves me, too. We are to be married.'

Linda sighed. 'Della auditions for actress roles in Chinese TV serials. She is so different from you, Tien. She has ambitions to be an actress. You and her come from different worlds. What do you talk about?'

'We see movies together and have fun.' Etienne's face closed up, his eyes becoming unfriendly.

Linda sighed and rose to go to the window. She drew back the heavy brocade curtains, allowing the bright sunlight to filter into the room. She looked down into the garden and was amazed to see Lionel Chu talking to Yusuf, the gardener. She hastily opened the window and shouted:

'What's going on, Uncle Yusuf?'

Lionel Chu and Yusuf both looked up and Lionel beat a hasty retreat and this time Linda saw him walking quickly towards the gate and out of it on to the road. Yusuf cleared his throat and said:

'Mr Lionel was asking me if Mr Alan leave parcel for him.'

'Uncle don't talk to strangers about our family. Why isn't the main gate closed? You should not let strangers into the grounds. Have you seen this man before?'

Yusuf looked discomfited but said strongly with the confidence of an old man who had played with Linda when she had been a child, 'Yes. Mr Lionel was Mr Alan's friend, come here many times. Mr Alan never leave any parcel and I was telling the young man that when you start scolding me.' His voice held layers of indignation.

'Sorry,' Linda said, hastily, and came away from the window.

Etienne had finished his breakfast and looked at his stepsister, shrewdly. 'There's a lot you don't know about our lives since you didn't visit often. You never came to comfort me when we received the news of Bro's murder. You only talked to me on the phone.'

'Well, I'm here now, Tien. Do you know who that young man was?' Linda said, 'Asking if Alan left a parcel for him?'

Etienne nodded. 'That's Lionel. Bro was his mentor at work, and he came over to the house often. Bro was holed up with him many times in his study. I think they were working on a project together.'

Linda said, 'That young man told me Alan had told his colleagues he was going to Bali on holiday. But he told me he was going there on business. What did he tell you, Tien?'

'He said it was a business trip,' Etienne said, readily, 'otherwise I would have gone with him.'

Before she could say anything more, Linda's mobile rang, it was the funeral parlour. She listened for a moment and then uttered an exclamation, switching off the phone.

'Tien, the funeral parlour will close in two hours. We need to go there now. Get dressed quickly. I will be downstairs speaking with Joyce. Alice isn't going to be home any time soon, so I'll ask Joyce to prepare some lunch for us when we return here. Hurry, Tien!'

Etienne rushed to the adjoining bathroom and Linda slowly walked down the stairs. She went along a carpeted corridor connecting the two wings and arrived at a hall. There was the clanging sound of utensils from the door on the far left and Linda walked towards the kitchen.

11

At eighty-two, Uma Das was frail, bent, and occasionally, her right hand shook alarmingly from Parkinson's Disease. After much procrastination, she had her cataracts removed and new lenses inserted in her eyes. With her newly found vision, Uma became her usual feisty self, poking her sharp nose into the affairs of her daughters, and playing with her granddaughter, Molly. She was looking particularly cheerful as she sat on the divan in her living room, gazing at her domestic helper sitting on the floor and feeding Molly her lunch.

'Silly, Silly! Eat your lunch, Silly!' Uma chortled, toothlessly. Her eyes shone with affection as she looked at the curly-haired imp with dusky skin and large dark eyes, who was busy throwing food at Girlie. The domestic helper turned and gave Uma a stern look.

'Ma'am said not to call her "Silly", Auntie, remember? The name will stick in school, she said. Molly, this mashed fish so nice. Eat, eat. Look at little Benny, finished his lunch already and gone to sleep.' She glanced with affection at a small bed where a cherubic Chinese boy of two looked angelic in his sleep. No sign on him now of what a troublemaker he can be, thought Girlie, her eyes alight with love.

Uma glanced at her granddaughter's little paunch and giggled. 'I could call her "Belly",' she said, and smiled at Girlie's full-throated laugh.

After Molly had finished her lunch and had gone to sleep listening to Girlie's lullabies, Uma sat at the dining table waiting for Girlie to serve her lunch. She glanced at the wall clock. It was nearly 1.30 p.m.

'Chicken stew *again*?' Uma grumbled, looking at the soggy mass on her plate.

'You have diabetes, Auntie, no choice. But Ma'am Lily say she will make a new dish for you, Auntie. Vinegar chicken. She say tastes better than chicken stew. She add rosemary and thyme, Auntie. For now, I give you some papaya chutney.'

Girlie doled out a bit of the chutney she had made on to Uma's plate. 'This is not so sweet. You try and tell me how, Auntie. It's a new recipe. If it's good, I ask ma'am to try and if she passes it, she can serve it at her café. She wants to make a good chutney.'

Uma enthusiastically tasted the pickle and licked her lips. 'This is delicious. Some more, Girlie.'

Girlie snatched the bottle of pickle away as Uma stretched her cadaverous hand towards it. 'No, Auntie, just to taste. We have appointment with Dr Heng at 3 p.m., Auntie. She will test your blood sugar. She wants to test two times, one on empty stomach and one on full belly.' Girlie and Uma giggled. 'Today we do the full belly.'

Uma said after chewing a mouthful, 'It's so crowded in the clinic today on account of Dr Heng being closed on Mondays.' She ate for some time and then said, 'Dolly returned from Bali yesterday, Lily said. Why hasn't she called me? That poor man, Alan Lee, killed for his Rolex watch. His sister and Lily went to school together.'

Girlie flitted to the kitchen and came back with a small bowl of sugar-free custard. 'Ma'am Dolly is coming for dinner tonight, Auntie. I make a good Indian meal for the family. I talk to Lestriani, the maid who work for Alan Lee's sister. She say Alan Lee's stepmother bring trouble into family.'

Uma dug into the custard. 'How does that help Dolly's investigation?'

'You never know, Auntie.' Girlie tossed her head. She considered herself a good sleuth. She glanced at the clock. 'Auntie, are you done? We need to go to doctor.'

'Yes, yes. You think custard is any good without sugar? I don't know why you bother making it.'

'Got protein. Good for you, Auntie.' She helped Uma up from her chair and into her bedroom and its adjoining bathroom.

After Uma was settled into a chair at the window, Girlie said, 'I eat my lunch quickly, Auntie, then I dress you and we go to clinic.'

After half an hour, as she dressed Uma in a flowery housecoat, Girlie said, 'I ask Angie to come up from the café, Auntie. Angie should be done at the café, the lunch crowd will have gone. The two sleeping beauties need minding, they can wake up any time.'

Uma chortled and allowed Girlie to brush her thin, wispy hair. Soon, they were ready to go to Dr Susan Heng's clinic in Block C.

As Girlie waited behind Uma's wheelchair at the lift lobby of their floor, the lift doors swung open and a woman in a black suit emerged, her hair dishevelled and with tears in her eyes.

Uma peered sharply at the woman and exclaimed, 'Linda Lee!'

Linda looked at Uma in surprise, then her face cleared. 'Auntie Uma, it's nice to see you. How is Lily?' She cleared her throat, holding the lift door open. 'I'm just coming from the funeral parlour. I went to visit my dead brother, Alan.'

Uma clicked her tongue sympathetically. 'You poor girl. I am so sorry about your brother's death. Taken too young. And look at us, lingering on.' She whispered theatrically, her long nose quivering with curiosity, 'The police think your brother was killed for his Rolex watch. Gold, was it?'

Linda looked surprised. 'Alan's watch was not valuable. It was a replica Rolex. My brother would not wear a real Rolex in Bali. He wasn't that dumb!' She frowned. 'Is that what your daughter, Dolly, thinks? That Alan was killed for the watch?'

'Oh, I don't know,' Uma said, airily, waving her hand, dismissively. 'Dolly never talks about her cases. I haven't even seen her after she returned from Bali. It's an impression I had.' She leant forward, inquisitively. 'Alan never married, eh?'

Linda's eyes shot fire as she said, 'No, and not for any sinister reason, either. He was engaged to be married to a girl called Selena when he was in his thirties. She died in a car accident, and he never got over that. Now, are you satisfied, digging for dirt in my family? Here, I'm not holding the lift door open any more. You can call for it again.' She turned on her heel and left, her shoulders hunched in disgust. The lift door closed.

Uma looked after her angry figure and bit her lips. 'So angry, huh? I was just asking, what?'

'Auntie, it was okay asking about the watch, not okay asking if Mr Alan was married. Too personal and sensitive.' Girlie looked smug, that should stop Uma from making catty comments when she tried to garner information. Girlie went over to press the lift button.

'Anyway, what's a bit of abuse? And from that chit of a girl, I invited to parties at my house. We discovered one important fact which we will tell Dolly when she comes for dinner. The watch wasn't valuable, so odds are Alan was not killed for his valuables. Though, the robber may not have known the watch was a fake and killed him for it. Such a shame if it was that.'

The lift arrived and Girlie pushed Uma's chair in, and they rode down in amiable companionship to the ground floor.

After a delicious meal of pea pulao, lentils cooked with coconut, fried okra, fried eggplant, fish in mustard sauce and a simple chicken curry, the Das family sat around the oval dining table, light from the chandelier reflecting off the cut-glass pudding bowls.

'Girlie makes excellent bread pudding,' Dolly said, licking her lips after swallowing a mouthful of the creamy pudding. She looked relaxed, in a white polka-dotted pant suit, her short hair brushed back and shining. She had slept until noon and was now in a garrulous mood, gearing up for a hectic work week.

Lily smiled at Girlie, who looked guiltily away. Lily sat up. 'What's the matter, Girlie?' She began to frown as Girlie narrated the encounter with Linda Lee. 'Oh dear! Mummy, why did you meddle? I was going to pay a visit to Linda and try to find out about the problems with the stepmother and now she will be hostile when she sees me.' She gazed with dismay at her mother. Uma looked away, pretending not to hear.

'Hm, useful information, though. Harjono and I thought the watch was a gold Rolex. The watch was never found for us to check it.' Dolly scraped the last of her pudding on to her spoon. After eating, she said to Lily, 'Let the dust settle a bit, and then you go visit Linda. We think a crime syndicate ordered the hit and then covered their tracks by silencing Alan's killer, a hired thug called Ramdin. With no good leads, we will have a tough time finding the mastermind of the syndicate who is supposedly living in Singapore. It's like looking for a needle in a haystack. And on top of that, the Bali hotel manager who may be involved with the crime syndicate, has gone into hiding. The best place to start this investigation is to talk to Alan's colleagues at his workplace. They may lead us to the corrupt turnkey company, the source of the counterfeit chips. I will brief Superintendent Ang tomorrow, let's see what she says. We are not looking for a killer here, Alan Lee's killer is dead. We want to identify the members and leaders of the crime syndicate responsible for his murder. This is ASP Brendan Gan's specialty, so I don't know if Supt Ang is going to keep me on the case. The head of the gang in Bali, Hadyanto and another possible member, Mark Latham, have escaped. We need Interpol's help in locating those two.'

'So, you don't really have a murder to solve, Doll.' Seeing Girlie clearing the dishes from the table, Lily rose from her chair and helped her mother into her wheelchair.

'Pack a *tingkat* with Frankie's food, Girlie,' Lily told the domestic helper. 'I'll take it back with me soon. I hope Frankie has been able to sing Molly to sleep. Come, let's go to the living room, Girlie will serve us coffee there.' She began pushing her mother's wheelchair towards the living room.

'Silly Belly,' Uma muttered under her breath and when Lily leant forward inquiringly, she gave her daughter a beaming, toothless smile.

After half an hour, Dolly kissed Uma goodbye and walked with Lily to her studio apartment on the fourteenth floor. Frankie rose from the sofa on seeing them. He looked handsome and relaxed in a singlet and shorts, a soccer match playing on the TV.

After kissing the sleeping Molly and indulging in ten minutes idle chatter with Frankie and Lily, Dolly took her leave. She walked to the carpark, got into her car and drove towards her home in Pasir Ris.

Monday, 20 May 2013

Singapore

12

The day began uneventfully for Lionel Chu. His alarm went off promptly at 5 a.m. as it had been doing for the last five years he had been working as a Senior Engineer at Waferworld Semiconductors. He staggered into the bathroom and looked at his face in the mirror. Grief had etched itself on his face and sleep had failed to erase the mask of pain. What had he done? *Alan was dead.* How would he live with himself now?

His mind meandered to those dark days when death visited his family. He had lost his parents within months of each other. Who knew diabetes would choose a happily married couple to attack and who could imagine the end would come for both so quickly? He had heard diabetics fought a long-drawn-out battle with the disease, but his parents were gone within two years of diagnosis, both from heart failure brought on by their diabetes. He had been twenty-one years old at the time, their only child, and he was shattered.

His comfort had been his paternal grandmother who loved and took care of him and just when he had overcome his grief for his parents, lightning struck again. Lionel looked in the bathroom mirror and scowled. His eyes were bloodshot from last night's gin. He knew he was drinking too much. Lionel splashed water on his face as tears appeared in his eyes.

When the doctor at the polyclinic referred his grandmother to a cardiologist for irregular heart rhythm and the cardiologist recommended a pacemaker be implanted to regulate his grandmother's heartbeat, Lionel had not been unduly worried. The operation was successful and for two months, Lionel's grandmother had felt like a new woman. Then inexplicably one night, she died of heart failure, without warning, without goodbyes. The doctors blamed the pacemaker, saying it likely malfunctioned, resulting in Lionel's grandmother slipping into a coma and dying in her sleep.

Lionel had been devastated and stopped going to work. It had been his manager, Alan Lee, who had come to his house, sat with him for two hours one afternoon when it was raining heavily outside and persuaded him to return to work. *With a vengeance.* For Lionel now had a mission, to bring to justice those responsible for his grandmother's death.

'Lionel,' Alan said, softly, 'you, yourself, showed me the faulty dies the customer returned to our company. They should have been discarded but had been passed by the turnkey company. This is how faulty chips enter the supply chain. The turnkey company may be selling our faulty dies on the black market and making a profit. And you know computer chips are used in aeroplanes and medical devices. If these chips are faulty, there is a chance of fatalities.'

Alan then outlined his theory of why his father's plane had crashed. He believed the plane had been refurbished with cheap parts, containing substandard chips supplied by a new broker. The pilot had cried out that the flight display unit had gone blank seconds before the crash, pointing to the possibility of computer chips inside the unit malfunctioning.

'There is a counterfeit chip syndicate here in Singapore,' Alan said. 'And they are placing faulty chips in our supply chains by selling these to brokers at a lower cost than the original manufacturer.'

'But how does that explain my grandmother's pacemaker malfunctioning?' Lionel asked, his eyes wide.

'Pacemakers are fitted with tiny computer chips that tell the unit how much electric impulse is needed to maintain normal heart rhythm. Your grandma had low pulse rate, right. So, the pacemaker was supposed to send the correct electric impulse to increase her heart rate when it went low. The computer chip inside the pacemaker would analyse the data from her heart and do the needful. If the computer chip was faulty, it would fail after some time and then when your grandma's heartbeat went low, the computer failed to tell the unit to send the correct electric impulse to speed up her heartbeat. This may have led to her death.'

Lionel frowned. 'But the doctors never said it was the chip. All they said was the pacemaker malfunctioned. The manufacturer paid me ample compensation, though.' Lionel remained thoughtful before saying, 'But you are right about our turnkey company. Something is not right there.'

'There's only one way of finding out if faulty chips are being sold on the black market,' Alan said. 'We start watching the turnkey company. You'll agree that someone who steals faulty chips from electronic waste is up to no good. We need to see what is going on in the turnkey company, Lionel. I think I'm right, but we have to get evidence and only then go to the police. But if I am right, Lionel, your time would be better spent avenging your grandma's death than sitting in the house moping.'

Lionel jolted back to the present. Did he have this conversation with Alan only eight months ago? In these months, he had turned into a monster? *Alan was dead. And he had killed him.* He, Lionel, had drifted away from the path of vengeance to the path of greed, and now the tendrils of remorse were tightening their grip on him.

Lionel turned on the shower. The cold onslaught of the water was like balm on his hot, vengeful skin. Alan's kind face and gentle eyes swam in his mind's eye. He began whimpering with pain.

He had turned into an informant, without foreseeing it would lead to murder. He had thought the syndicate would merely scare Alan or offer him a bribe. *Not kill him!* He had underestimated the ruthlessness of the syndicate. He had thought he was being paid to retrieve the incriminating hard disk with evidence of corruption. To make sure Alan did not take it to the authorities. Why did the syndicate have to *kill* Alan?

After his tears dried, came resolution. There was still time to make amends.

He reflected on his request to Alan before he left for Bali to leave the hard disk containing incriminating data on the turnkey company with him. Alan had agreed but had looked at him, strangely. Why? Had Alan suspected him? He had not left any parcel for him at the house. Where was the hard disk which would nail the turnkey company as a key supplier of counterfeit chips? The suspicion that Alan knew of his betrayal hurt him more than the inclination to search for the hard disk for his corrupt employers. For that was what he had become, *an employee of a crime syndicate.*

When he left his apartment and entered the lift of his building, the people there saw a sad, mild-mannered, young man wearing horn-rimmed spectacles. None guessed at the fire of grief and revenge burning in his young heart.

Lionel met Toby Wong for lunch at a small café in Little India. They ordered prata with chicken curry and large steaming mugs of *teh*. The café was popular and crowded with tourists savouring traditional Indian food.

Toby was a short, stocky man of thirty-five with thinning hair and small eyes. A wispy moustache attempted to counter his effeminate looks. He worked for a turnkey company providing testing and packaging services.

After taking a long sip of his tea, Toby said with a frightened look on his face, 'So sorry about Alan. What is the world coming to? One cannot go on a holiday in peace, right?'

A shadow crossed Lionel's face. He dipped his prata in curry, ate for a minute, before saying, 'It's a sad loss for our company and his family.' Lionel gazed bleakly at the bright sunlight outside the windows. *Mine eyes dazzle. He died young.* Lionel's mind meandered into the days when he and Alan had spent long hours discussing the *Duchess of Malfi* together. *So many memories.* They had not only been colleagues, but friends. He was jolted back to the present by Toby's fierce whisper.

'Alan's murder was not on account of what I overheard, was it? He went to Bali for a holiday, right?'

'Right.' Lionel's voice was clipped.

Toby continued eating the prata on his plate. He looked up, his eyes on Lionel's restless ones. 'What's happened to the faulty dies that were set aside by my manager and which I gave you? Did you or Alan send it for testing?'

'Don't worry about that.' Lionel concentrated on finishing the last of his prata.

After a few minutes of relishing his food, Toby glanced up, his gaze measured. 'My next payment is due.'

'You'll get money only if you tell me something of value.' Lionel scowled. 'I've already paid you for the dies you gave us.'

'I told you about Sushila Iyer,' Toby protested. 'She is my direct boss and the woman in charge of the electronic waste at South-East Asia Semiconductor Turnkey Solutions. I've already fingered the corrupt individual for you, Lionel. I'm scared working for her nowadays. When I started asking her questions about the electronic waste of chips used to manufacture Dydo phones, she became aggro. Asked me why I was questioning her like a detective. She's very fierce.' Toby turned his attention back to his meal. He started work on his remaining prata.

'Hmm . . . Dydo phones, huh?' Lionel looked interested. 'You'll only get the next payment after you hack into Sushila's email account. See whom she sends the faulty dies to. She must have a broker here who sells it on the black market.' Lionel finished his meal and started on his tea.

'My fiancée and I are moving into our new apartment in May next year,' Toby whined. 'I need money to pay the renovators. They are so expensive.

Hacking?' Toby squeaked as Lionel's words registered. 'I will be sacked if anyone finds out that I am hacking into company mails!'

'You will get double the money for hacking.' Lionel rose, swallowing the last of his tea. 'We need to know Sushila Iyer's contacts. She's not working by herself for sure. I'll make a move then, Toby. I'll pay the bill at the counter.'

'Wait!' Toby cried. 'I want to pay my respects to Alan. Is there a wake?'

Lionel turned around and his eyes were soft. 'Yes, Toby. His wake is being held at his bungalow in Primrose Crescent. Some of us from Waferworld are going there this evening to pay our respects. You can join us. Meet me at 7.00 p.m. at Waferworld, okay? We'll go to his house from the office.'

Lionel Chu walked along Serangoon Road and turned into Roberts Lane. He took out his mobile phone from his pocket and peered at an address on the screen. Then he began checking out the addresses on either side of the lane. He stopped at a stairwell next to a hairdressing saloon. He peered at the number attached to the wall and climbed up the steep stairs. The steps ended at a landing where there was a small glass door with 'Golden Enterprises—Broker and Seller of Electronic Goods' written on a piece of cardboard above it.

Lionel noted the name down on his phone, climbed down the stairs and exited the building. The sun was shining, and Lionel slowly made his way to the bus-stop.

* * *

Etienne Lee looked with awe at Della Pang. She sat across the table from him in the restaurant inside the National Museum, studying the menu. The mascara on her eyelashes and the nude eyeshadow, both shimmered, while her lotus-bud red lips formed an 'O' as her eyes zeroed in on a menu item.

Her melodious voice tinkled out: 'Mussels! Oh, that would be heavenly, Tien. I will only have that and some white wine.' She raised her rather large eyes from the menu, directing a laser-like beam at her beau. Her tip-tilted nose crinkled up as she smiled at Etienne gazing at her with his mouth open.

'You look good enough to eat, Della,' Etienne breathed.

Della laughed and her musical tinkle attracted a waiter who stood respectfully by with a tablet in his hands. After they had ordered, Della leant back in her chair and looked commiseratively at Etienne. 'I am sorry about Alan, Tien. Really sorry.'

Etienne's eyes hardened. 'He disapproved of us.'

'Everyone does,' Della laughed. 'Why blame just him? People think you are too young to think of marriage and like it or not, there is still a stigma with regards to dating older women. I am five years older than you, pet.'

'What does age matter?' Etienne scoffed. 'Grandad does not know about us, yet.'

Della's eyes flickered. 'Tien, you should give the exclusive dating agreement we have a second thought. You are young and need exposure to more than one woman. I do not mind at all if you date other girls as well.'

Colour rushed into Etienne's face. 'Do you date other men?'

Della grinned. 'Where's the time? I don't have time even for you. A quick mussel feast and I am gone. I have an audition at TVcorp. I am trying out for the part of the heroine's crabby sister in a Chinese historical drama. Will suit me to a tee, I'm sure. And then off to model swimwear at a hotel in Sentosa.' She nodded at the waiter as he placed a dish of succulent mussels on the table. Before helping herself to them, Della took a long sip of her wine.

Etienne's eyes were popping out of his head. 'I wish I could watch you audition for the part and be with you on your photo shoots.'

Della narrowed her eyes and then smiled. She started eating the mussels on her plate. When she had swallowed a mouthful, she said, 'It's all quite boring, really. And so many takes. Well, Tien, now you will be a wealthy beau, won't you? Maybe you can take me to a French restaurant for dinner. Yum, these mussels are good. Why aren't you eating, Tien?'

Etienne reluctantly helped himself to mussels. 'What do you mean about being wealthy?'

'39, Primrose Crescent, Tien. The bungalow. With Alan's death, I'm sure you and your stepsister will inherit it. It is worth five million, at least. Who else would Alan leave the house to? He wasn't married.'

Etienne's face became wooden. 'I don't know. Ma said a lawyer will talk to us next week in Lester's presence about Bro's will.'

Della stiffened. They concentrated on eating the delicious mussels and sipping the wine. It was after she finished the last of her white wine that Della continued, 'Lester Chong, the minister? Alan's maternal cousin? I wonder why he is involved. Is he the executor of Alan's will, I wonder? Anyways, I will be late if I don't get a move on. See you at Cam's party on Saturday? Yeah?' Della rose from the chair and hesitated. 'Alan's wake is being held at your home. Should I pay my respects?'

Etienne looked baffled. 'You didn't know my brother, Della.'

Della gave a small smile. 'I've never been to your house, Tien.'

Etienne said, hastily, 'No need to come on this occasion. I'll invite you, later, when Ma is in a better mood about us.'

Etienne Lee watched his girlfriend disappear beyond the doorway of the restaurant. Such grace, such perfection and a curvaceous tall figure, Etienne mused. The waiter placed the bill gently on the table. Etienne glanced at it and frowned.

'For only mussels and wine?' He demanded and curtly took his credit card out of his wallet when the waiter nodded.

While waiting for the man's return, Etienne fervently hoped Alan had left the bungalow to Linda and him. He needed funds. Although his girlfriend cost him a bundle, he knew with absolute certainty he could not live without her.

* * *

Pradeep Chopra sat in his office at the Pelangi University of Engineering and Social Sciences and fished out from his pocket the legal summons he had received that morning. Alice Lee was holding his dead wife, Rosvinder, responsible for her husband's death and the crash of his private plane. She was initiating a civil suit in the courts against Rosvinder's estate, demanding compensation.

Alan had told him last year after the investigations into the crash deemed Rosvinder at fault, that his stepmother was going to embroil him in a civil suit. Pradeep had begged Alan to deter Alice Lee from doing that as he had very little money and two children to raise. Alan had agreed and initiated a search in Taiwan for the airplane's black boxes, asking his stepmother to wait until the search was over.

Pradeep had been relieved when the cockpit voice recorder had been found and evidence from it pointed to a fault in the plane's display unit. But Alice Lee chose to believe the official verdict of the crash. Pradeep knew it was Alan's veiled threats that kept Alice quiet. But now Alan was dead. So, Alice Lee was taking Pradeep to court.

Alan had told him to be prepared for the civil suit and that he would get his lawyer and evidence to successfully fight the case. An hour ago, Pradeep had called Jonas Ellis, Alan's lawyer, expecting him to be aware and up to speed about representing Rosie's estate against Alice Lee. He was shocked when Jonas said he did not know anything about the case and that Alan had never spoken to him about it or shown him any evidence.

Pradeep buried his head in his hands. Alan had died before he could talk over the evidence he had gathered about the plane crash with Jonas Ellis. And Pradeep did not know what evidence Alan had gathered. He would lose the case and become bankrupt. What was he going to do?

He had already lost his tenure at the university thanks to Alice Lee influencing her father, former cabinet minister, Justin Chua, a member of the university's board of directors, to veto it. He was a mere lecturer in the department now, his dreams of a professorship gone. And now he had to pay a large amount of money to hire a lawyer to defend his wife's estate from Alice Lee's demand of compensation for the death of Ronnie Lee. He would be bankrupt soon and he had two daughters to raise.

Something had to be done. But first, in the evening, he would attend Alan's wake being held at his bungalow. He wanted to pay his respects to his dear friend. Tears clouded his eyes as he remembered their college days together.

* * *

Dolly was seated in Superintendent Geraldine Ang's office on the fifteenth floor of CID HQ. As she flipped through reports, Dolly studied her supervisor of two years. Geraldine Ang, in her fifties, wore a sensible trouser suit and applied little make-up to a pleasant but unremarkable face. Previously, she headed the Bomb and Explosive Branch before transferring to the Special Investigation Section after Supt Siti Abdullah's exit. Dolly had not shared a good professional relationship with Supt Abdullah and had been apprehensive about her relationship with her replacement.

So far, Dolly had found Superintendent Geraldine Ang to be fair, strict, and pleasant. She looked up now from her reports and her lips parted in a smile. 'Thank you for assisting Bali CID, ASP Das. Both DAC Nathan and I are grateful. At least we know the killer's identity, but the masterminds of the counterfeit chips syndicate remain a mystery.'

Supt Ang placed her hands on the table in a steeple and said, 'Ordinarily, we would pass the investigation to the Specialised Crime Division. I have discussed the case with DAC Nathan and with Lester Chong. We all feel this case still falls within Major Crime as there may be a personal angle involved. The dead man was on acrimonious terms with his stepmother and was in the process of evicting her from the family home. We need to explore all lines of inquiry. Alice Lee could have ordered the hit and she does not belong to a crime syndicate. A murder was committed and the person who ordered the killing needs to be brought to trial. Be they a crime syndicate boss or Alice Lee. You need to solve this case, ASP Das. Find out who ordered Alan Lee's murder.'

'We have few resources to sniff out a crime syndicate, ma'am.' Dolly looked worried.

Geraldine Ang's face became impassive. 'The degree of difficulty is there. But don't latch on to one suspect in this case. Investigate Alice Lee thoroughly. Anyone could have hired thugs to kill Alan Lee. Seek help from the Secret Societies Branch of CID, they are highly experienced in dealing with syndicates.'

Dolly was frank. 'Our job would be easier if we bring Mark Latham in for questioning.'

Geraldine Ang nodded. 'Agreed, though this is a bit complicated. While it's true Alan Lee was a Singapore national, his murder was committed in Indonesia. The correct procedure in locating suspected criminals related to his murder would be for NCB-Interpol at Jakarta to liaise with The General Secretariat Interpol HQ at Lyon or NCB-Interpol in Beijing. Interpol China has a sub-bureau in Hong Kong and officers from there could look for Latham. DAC Nathan has talked to Supt Martin Sim from our NCB-Interpol, ASP Das, they have their offices in the International Cooperation Department on Irrawaddy Road. Sim has talked to an officer at The Interpol Global Complex for Innovation on Napier Road. IGCI has criminal intelligence officers from Interpol HQ at Lyon seconded there to head research and innovation teams. Supt Sim consults with a Supt Rachel Kelly who works for Interpol HQ as a criminal intelligence officer in their illicit goods department. Supt Kelly has the authority to initiate an Interpol search for Latham worldwide, if she is satisfied with your evidence against him. My advice is to first talk to Supt Sim and then make an appointment with Supt Kelly and I sincerely hope she helps you locate Mark Latham.'

Back in her office, Dolly buzzed for Charlie. Soon, Inspector Charles Goh waddled in, beaming, his eyes alight behind granny glasses. Charlie had assisted Dolly in all her cases for more than ten years and Dolly did not know how she would cope without him. He was hard-working, loyal, and easy to get along with, the attributes one longed for in a subordinate, Dolly thought.

Without preamble, she updated Charlie on the Alan Lee murder case and what their superiors expected from them.

After an hour of listening carefully and reading Dolly's notes and reports, Charlie sighed. 'This case is a tough one, madam, but we will catch the person who ordered Alan Lee's murder. It seems to me, madam, that the people of interest are Alice Lee and Alan Lee's colleagues at work.'

Dolly smiled. 'Right, Charlie. Our afternoon is full then. I will interview Alice Lee and you go to Waferworld Semiconductors and talk to Alan's colleagues. Talk to Lionel Chu, Alan mentioned him as the colleague who helped him place a mole inside the turnkey company. I'll have a chat with Marty Sim from Interpol regarding locating Latham. Marty and I were sergeants in the same department a long time ago, it will be good catching up with him.'

Charlie nodded as he got to his feet. He was happiest when he was solving crimes with Dolly Das.

13

Dolly parked her car by the kerb on Primrose Crescent, a few yards from number 39, and got out. The neighbourhood was quiet with most of the bungalows hidden behind shady trees. No. 39, was an imposing two-storey bungalow set further away from the road and ringed by tall trees. Dolly pressed the bell at the gate. An old man in a cap shuffled out from behind a hedge and came to the gate. He looked at Dolly inquiringly. Dolly flashed her warrant card and noted the gardener looking apprehensive.

'I have an appointment with Madam Alice,' Dolly said, reassuringly

The gardener opened the gate and Dolly walked in. The gardener nodded at Dolly to follow him and they walked along the path to the porch. She looked around appreciatively at the garden.

'Mr Alan's wake is going on,' the gardener said. 'Many people come last night.' Wiping his eyes with the edge of his shirt, the gardener showed Dolly into Alice Lee's living room.

Dolly sat on a chair, patiently waiting for Alice Lee to keep her appointment. The faint sound of funeral music came from the wake on the other side of the house. She looked around. The room was painted blue and white with matching upholstery on the chairs and sofas. The furniture lent the room a Mediterranean feel.

Dolly was reminded of the trip she had taken with her husband and son to Santorini in Greece a long time ago. She sighed. Pritam Singh was her ex-husband now and married to a Chinese woman, Cheryl, and the proud father of a baby girl. Pritam remained close to their son, Ashok, and Dolly was grateful for that.

She got up from the chair and went to the mantlepiece over the mock fireplace where there were several photo frames. She saw a wedding photo of a younger Alice Lee with her husband, Ronnie, her father, Justin Chua, the cabinet minister, frowning at the camera. There were baby photos of a male child and Dolly deduced those to be that of Alice's son, Etienne. There was a photo of the adult Etienne, a stocky, pleasant-faced boy. Dolly looked closely at a photo of Etienne with his older brother, Alan. Both were laughing together in front of a conference hall, a chess tournament banner in the background. There was a discreet cough.

Dolly quickly turned and saw a thin, willowy woman dressed immaculately in black, looking speculatively at her. Alice Lee motioned Dolly to a chair and seated herself on the sofa.

Dolly said, 'I have some routine questions regarding your stepson's murder, ma'am.' She asked, 'You were close to your stepson?'

Alice flicked a strand of hair behind her ear. She was wearing pearl earrings. 'My son, Etienne, was close to Alan. They went to chess tournaments together. Alan was a champion player and Etienne loved watching his brother play. I am afraid I was not close to Alan and cannot shed any light on his life. Surely, he was killed in Bali for his valuables?' Alice Lee's face was as smooth as silk, her heavily mascaraed eyes flicked curiously over Dolly's face.

'We are still in the early stages of the investigation into Alan Lee's murder,' Dolly said, easily. 'We are interviewing his family and friends to find out if his murder had motives other than robbery. What is your profession, ma'am?'

Alice Lee tittered. 'I don't have one. I guess you could call me a housewife. If you are asking about training, I was sent to boarding school in England at an early age and then on to a finishing school in Switzerland. I have passed my 'O' and 'A' levels. My mother died in a boating accident in France when I was thirteen. She was only thirty-two years old. After passing my 'A' levels, I studied interior design at a prestigious London school. I did not get my diploma because I fell in love with Ronnie Lee when I was twenty. Yes, it caused quite a scandal as his wife, Natalie, was suffering from end-stage kidney disease. My father remarried in 1984. I did not get along with my stepmother, Lydia, so I was only too happy when Ronnie proposed marriage. We got married after Natalie's death. Ronnie was more than twenty years older than me. I gave birth to Etienne ten years after my marriage.

'Linda, my stepdaughter, has never been able to forgive me for dating her father while her mother was alive. She was eighteen and Alan twenty when I entered the house. Yes, ASP Das, I was about the same age as my stepson. Alan was different from Linda. He let bygones be bygones and was always polite and considerate. He accepted his father was madly in love with me. I am sorry to have lost Alan. To get back to your question, Superintendent, I am not qualified as an interior designer, but I have decorated this house and a few houses of my friends. My time with Ronnie was taken up helping him in his business. The rest of my time was spent attending social events and doing charity work. I sit on the board of quite a few NGOs, and I take my roles seriously.'

Dolly noted Alice did not mention raising her son as one of her main duties. 'Do you have connections to any semiconductor businesses?'

Alice's eyebrows disappeared into her hair. 'Semiconductors? You mean chips?'

When Dolly nodded, Alice said, 'No, that was Alan's area of expertise. He worked in the semiconductor industry. I do not know the first thing about wafer fabs!' She laughed.

'What about your boyfriend, Nelson Ong?' Dolly was persistent.

Alice Lee's face closed. 'Nelson? His business is making sauces. Surely you know, Superintendent?'

'Was Alan worried about anything before he left for Bali?'

Alice lifted her lips in a smile. 'As I said before, Superintendent, I was not close to Alan. He kept to himself. This house has two wings. I live in the west wing and Alan lived in the east wing. The east wing of the house has its own dining room though our kitchen is common. I did not see him at meals, and we seldom spoke with each other.'

'39, Primrose Crescent belonged to Alan Lee as per his father's will.' Dolly decided to put the question in the form of a power-laden statement. It had the desired effect.

Alice Lee's face reddened, and her eyes glittered, feverishly. 'Not at all. Ronnie left the house to me in a new will.'

'Has the new will gone for probate?' Dolly inquired, her eyes taking in Alice's rage. Had the intensity of her emotions regarding the house prodded Alice Lee to order her stepson's murder?

'I cannot find it.' Alice shrugged her shoulders.

Dolly recalled her early morning conversation with Lester Chong, the Junior Minister. 'According to Alan's will, which will be executed by Lester

Chong, the house is to be sold and the proceeds divided between your son and Linda Lee's children. Do you intend to contest Alan's will?'

Alice's face had lost colour. 'I will consult my own lawyer about this. Is that all?'

'How did Ronnie Lee die?'

Alice recovered some of her composure. She gazed out of the window, her face holding a timbre of sorrow. 'He was killed when his private plane crashed. The pilot perished as well. I am taking the pilot's husband to court in a civil suit, and I intend to win compensation from the pilot's estate. The pilot had a history of alcoholism. Ronnie knew that, but he hired her anyway on Alan's request as the pilot was Alan's buddy.'

'I believe Alan Lee mounted his own search for the plane's black boxes and the cockpit voice recorder was found.'

Alice flushed. 'Yes, Alan came to me with a ridiculous story of Rosvinder Kaur, the pilot, not being responsible for the crash. Alan said one of the plane parts malfunctioned.' She shrugged. 'I paid no attention to him. He would try to save Rosvinder's reputation, she was his friend.'

'I believe your stepson was friends with the pilot's husband, Pradeep Chopra. He was up for tenure last year for a professorship at Pelangi University, but to everyone's surprise, he was not granted it.'

Alice raised her eyebrows, her face closed. 'Is that so?' She changed the subject. 'You may want to talk to Donald Quek about the plane crash. He is the maintenance technician who looked after Ronnie's plane. He lives near Tengah Airport.'

Dolly noted down the name and address on her tablet. 'Thank you,' she said. She looked at Alice Lee closely. 'Ma'am, did you have cause to wish your stepson harm?'

Two spots of colour appeared on Alice's cheeks. 'That's another way of asking did I have Alan killed. How dare you. No, why should I want Alan dead?'

Dolly was unfazed. 'To gain control of this house. Alan Lee had talked to his lawyer, and you would have been served eviction notices soon, ma'am.'

Alice spluttered, 'Do you know how many millions I'm worth, ASP Das? I could easily buy a better house than this one with my own money. Why would I need to kill for it?'

Dolly said, deceptively, 'Did you know a fellow called Ramdin in Bali?'

Alice looked astounded. 'No. Why?' Her eyes rounded. 'Was he Alan's killer?' Her face was white as she said, 'I did not order my stepson to be killed, ASP Das. I had no cause.'

Dolly inclined her head, then she said, 'I talked to your stepson's lawyer, Mr Ellis, and according to his will, Alan's money is left to trustees to set up a foundation for kidney dialysis patients and to a Ms Emily Gan.'

Alice's eyes glittered and then she nodded. 'I was not aware of the terms of Alan's last will and testament. We are meeting Lester and Jonas later to discuss Alan's will. Alan left money to Emily because of Selena. She lived next door and was Alan's childhood playmate. She and Alan were engaged to be married ten years ago. Unfortunately, Selena died in a car accident. Her sister and mother live next door. Her sister, Emily, was paralysed in the same accident. Anyway, Alan was really devoted to Selena and he has presumably left his money to take care of Emily's needs. He regarded Emily as family. Ronnie, my husband, was sad about Alan not getting over Selena's death and wished Alan could have settled down in life. As for the foundation, that is probably going to be set up in Alan's mother's memory. Alan was devoted to his mother. Natalie Lee was on kidney dialysis for the last two years of her life.'

Dolly nodded and stood up. 'Thank you for your time, ma'am.'

On asking whether she could interview Etienne, Alice gave a nod and took her to the hall. A petite maid was diligently dusting the hallway.

'Joyce, please show ASP Das into the dining room, make her a cup of tea and call Etienne Sir down to see her.'

'Etienne Sir is at Mr Alan's wake in the next wing, madam,' Joyce said. 'Some people are visiting.'

Alice nodded. 'Get him to come here and meet the police, Joyce.'

* * *

The dining hall was cheery, the wide windows overlooking a garden where the Malay gardener was tending to vegetables. Dolly did not have to wait long sipping her tea at the oval dining table. A stocky youth, dressed in black, soon slouched in. Joyce, the maid, gave him a glass of orange juice and a big smile. When the maid had left the room, Etienne gave Dolly a thin smile, his eyes remaining sad.

Dolly motioned him to a seat opposite her and after introducing herself, invited him to talk about his brother, Alan.

Etienne sipped the orange juice and said slowly, 'He was worried about something the past six months. It could have been work-related. We had dinner together on Friday nights at his apartment in the east wing of the house. We usually talked of his chess tournaments, movies, theatre performances and sometimes, we would go out on Fridays for a late-night movie. Recently, though, he seemed preoccupied and when I suggested seeing a movie, he said he was busy. He was out most nights in the past few months.'

Tears glittered in Etienne's eyes. 'Even though he was bored, he took me to see Marvel movies because I'm crazy about them. My brother humoured me. But the best times I've spent were watching him win chess tournaments. He was a champion chess player and I went with him to the tournaments and cheered him on. We were supposed to go to one in Jakarta next week.' Etienne's voice shook.

'Did he have visitors to this house?' Dolly was touched to see the obvious affection Etienne entertained for his stepbrother.

Etienne nodded. 'Lionel Chu visited sometimes. Bro was his mentor at work. I think they were working on a project together. They were always holed up in his study.'

Dolly nodded. 'Alan was close to Linda and her family?'

'He loved the kids and taught them chess. He used to go out for a drink with Pat, Sis's husband, but not lately. Pat, though, came a few times in the evenings the past few weeks to meet Bro here but Bro was out. Yes, Inspector, Bro was close to Sis. He visited her house often for meals. I sometimes went with him as well.'

A shadow fell over Etienne's face. 'Bro and I had a small fight, and we never got to make up.' A solitary tear trickled down his cheek.

'What was that about?'

A defensive note crept into Etienne's voice. 'I love Della Pang and neither Bro nor my mother approved of my relationship. I had words with him over that. He thought she was after my money. Della is five years older than me and a model,' he added in explanation.

Dolly lost interest. She doubted Etienne's personal life had played any part in Alan's murder. 'I met your brother briefly in Bali before he was killed. He said he wasn't happy with the findings of your father's plane crash blaming the pilot. He seemed to think the plane's flight display unit malfunctioned. Do you know anything about this?'

Etienne nodded. 'The Taiwanese authorities blamed Rosie because of her history of alcoholism. Though Bro told me Rosie only had drinks that one time, it's not as if she was an alcoholic. Rosie and her husband, Pradeep, were Bro's friends and came over to our house often. I liked them. Bro used Dad's money to pay natives in Taiwan to search for the plane's black boxes and we were excited when the cockpit voice recorder was found. Bro and I went to

Taiwan to retrieve the recorder and Bro got one of his friends to download the data. Before the plane crashed, Rosie screamed something. Bro thought it meant a fault in the flight display unit caused the plane to crash.'

Etienne went red and would not meet Dolly's eyes. 'Please know I don't support Ma taking Pradeep to court and blaming Rosie for the crash. I tried to talk her out of it, but she wouldn't listen. Bro was trying very hard to find evidence to prove Rosie wasn't responsible for the crash. But Bro is gone, and Ma will make Pradeep bankrupt.' Tears pooled in Etienne's eyes.

Dolly said, 'Your mother and stepbrother got along?'

Etienne looked surprised. 'I guess. They each lived in their own wing of the house, but when they did meet, they were pleasant to each other.'

'Your mother is obsessed with owning this house,' Dolly said, watching Etienne's reaction.

Etienne looked amused. 'I know. She's strange that way. She always thought Papa would leave her the house, but Papa disinherited her when he found out she was seeing Nelson. Ma never got over being left out of Papa's will. So, in her mind, she made up a new will.' Etienne chuckled. 'But Ma is a millionaire in her own right. She could easily buy a more expensive property than this one. I need to go back to Bro's wake,' he said, softly. 'Many of his friends are visiting though most come in the evenings.'

Dolly thanked Etienne and decided to drive over to Tengah Airport to interview Donald Quek, the man who had serviced Ronnie Lee's aeroplane. She was still sure Alan had been killed because he knew too much about counterfeit computer chips and was going to blow the whistle. She wondered if a faulty chip had made Ronnie Lee's plane crash. Even if it were true, there was no evidence.

14

Donald Quek was a tall, balding man with a toothbrush moustache over thick lips. He lived in a small apartment near Tengah Airport and was surprised to see a police superintendent at his door. He invited Dolly in and waved her to a dilapidated sofa, his face curious.

'I read about Alan's murder in the newspaper, and I attended his wake last night,' he said as he sat on a chair. 'I liked him. And Ronnie was nuts about his son. Told me if he did some good in his life, this was it. A cup of tea, ASP Das?'

Dolly shook her head. 'Thanks, no. Alan was dissatisfied with the findings of the investigation into the crash that killed his father.' She looked around. The room was spartan with a sofa set and an old TV.

Donald nodded. 'Yes, even though it was a private plane, the Taiwanese authorities investigated the crash and the investigators blamed the pilot. She had a history of alcohol abuse and flew the plane too low. It crashed into a mountain. Alan was unhappy because the pilot was his buddy and he had recommended her to his father.'

Dolly frowned. 'But surely you know Alan assembled a search team in Taiwan, and they found the cockpit voice recorder last year. The flight display unit of the plane had gone blank, those were the pilot's last words. Doesn't that point to a fault in the plane's hardware or software as a possible cause of the crash?'

Quek's face blanched and a tic appeared near his left eye. 'Alan said he was going to reopen the investigation with the cockpit voice recorder findings but that hasn't happened yet. We met many times. Ronnie was my tennis partner, we were friends. But Alan's tone was angry and his questions intrusive. I resented being blamed for Ronnie's crash.'

'In what way did Alan Lee blame you?'

Quek sighed, the fight draining out of him. 'Alan said I fitted a display unit having a faulty chip. Would I knowingly do that? Sure, we changed the display unit three months before the flight to Taipei. Ronnie had requested a makeover of his plane as some parts were old. I ordered the new plane parts from the company I always use. Alan came nosing around asking for the name of the company. Then he said the spare parts company had a new Singaporean broker for its electronic parts. Did I know that? No, I did not, usually the brokers were from China. He also told me when he went in search of the broker, he found he had closed shop and left Singapore. Alan suspected the chips inside the flight display unit were faulty. "The chips were bought cheap on the black market," he said, and these usually malfunction soon enough. I called up the spare parts company boss to know if he had used a new broker for the chips on that plane, but I found the company had gone bankrupt and been liquidated. ASP Das, I think Alan was just trying to clear the pilot's name. There is no evidence the flight display unit had faulty chips.'

Quek continued, 'What was I to do? Ronnie's businesses were folding up. He told me so himself. He wanted a cheap refurbishment of the plane, so I went for inexpensive parts.'

'I understand Alice Lee has filed a civil suit demanding compensation from the pilot's family.'

Donald Quek flushed. 'Why? Rosvinder Kaur left behind two small children. It is wrong to make the family bankrupt with a lawsuit. I do not support it even though I believe the plane crashed due to pilot error. It's not as though Alice Lee is not stinking rich. Why take money from a family that needs it when you have tons of your own? If you ask me, Alice Lee is one malicious lady. Ronnie was never happy after his second marriage. Alice cheated on him. The two years before he died were the unhappiest, I'd seen Ronnie. I felt sorry for him. A bad marriage is worse than no marriage at all. He couldn't divorce Alice, there was Etienne to consider.'

Dolly talked for five more minutes but did not learn anything new. She thanked Quek and got to her feet.

As she was leaving, Quek said, his voice hoarse, 'I ordered the display unit from the same spare parts company I always used. If they were using cheap counterfeit chips, how is it my fault?'

Dolly was thoughtful as she walked towards her car. His own observation of the turnkey company's operations and his father's plane crash had been instrumental in arousing Alan Lee's interest in counterfeit chip syndicates. The fact he was killed at a hotel where the manager headed a chip recycling factory told its own story. Alan had been right about the existence of a counterfeit chip syndicate. But the trail of the faulty chip in the flight display unit of Ronnie Lee's plane was lost. Dolly hoped Charlie could pin down the turnkey company that had supplied faulty dies to the wafer fab where Alan had worked. That would be a start to learning more of the crime syndicate. She called Charlie, but the line was engaged.

* * *

Old Woodlands Road shone like a glacier from the patina of moisture left by a heavy downpour. The sun was trying to peep out from fluffy grey clouds as Charlie drove towards Woodlands Industrial Park D, where Alan Lee's workplace, Waferworld, was located. Stark, grey buildings with narrow glass windows greeted him as he turned into the drive leading to the carpark. Like a high-security prison, Charlie thought as he parked the car.

At the reception desk, he asked for Lionel Chu, Alan Lee's subordinate. The receptionist showed him into a big meeting room on the ground floor with carafes of ice-water and coffee on the long table and paper cups for those who needed to refresh themselves.

Charlie did not have to wait long. A young man with dishevelled hair and wearing horn-rimmed spectacles entered the room. His eyes were red-rimmed, and his nose twitched with emotion.

'I don't know anything about criminal syndicates!' Lionel looked frightened after Charlie had outlined Alan Lee's interest in the counterfeit computer chip syndicate. 'Alan not only thought a faulty chip crashed his father's plane, but he was also sure a malfunctioning chip in an implanted pacemaker led to my grandmother's death. At least, that part may have been true. My grandmother's doctor mentioned the pacemaker had malfunctioned. As for his father's death, Alan was trying to clear his friend, Rosvinder's name. She was blamed for the crash.'

Charlie pondered, noting the sweat springing up on the young man's forehead. 'So, you know nothing about one of your turnkey companies not discarding faulty dies but instead selling them on the black market?'

Lionel looked terrified, but said, 'Yes, one of our customers reported dies had failed in the field. When we tested those dies, we discovered they were failing a reliability test that should have been performed by the turnkey company. Only the dies passing that test should have been packaged because they met the customer specifications. The faulty dies should have been thrown out.'

'And the name of the turnkey company?'

'South-East Asia Semiconductor Turnkey Solutions, they have their factory and offices at Chai Chee.' Lionel's eyes looked huge behind the horn-rimmed glasses.

Charlie scribbled on his tablet and then said, 'Alan told my superior he had planted a mole in the turnkey company. Would you happen to know anything about that?'

Lionel clutched his hair in a frenzy. 'Alan told me we needed evidence of the turnkey company not throwing away faulty dies. Alan thought the company, itself, was not corrupt, but a person there was. He asked me to find an employee there who would keep an eye out for suspicious activities and help us out.'

'And did you?' Charlie asked, pleasantly.

Lionel sighed. 'Yes, I asked Toby Wong to keep an eye on things. He works in the electronic waste department of the turnkey company.'

'Did he find anything?' On seeing Lionel shake his head, Charlie continued, 'Why did Alan Lee go to Bali?'

Lionel glared. 'For a holiday.'

'No, I don't think so. He told his cousin he went there on business, but when I asked your Human Resources if Waferworld had sent him to Bali, they said no. They said he had applied for holiday leave. Alan had gone to Bali on the trail of the crime syndicate. There was a counterfeit chip factory outside Ubud, and the manager of the hotel Alan was staying in as well as a pub he visited all had connections to this factory. You knew Alan was sniffing out a syndicate because he enlisted your help in roping in a mole. Why are you lying and saying you don't know anything about a syndicate?'

'I have nothing else to say,' Lionel said sullenly.

Lionel Chu had been in Alan's confidence and knew why he had visited Bali. Charlie wondered why the young engineer was keeping information to himself. What secret was he hiding?

* * *

Dolly called Rosvinder Kaur's widower, Pradeep Chopra beforehand to make an appointment at his home. Dolly climbed the stairs of an old walk-up apartment with paint peeling from the walls and pressed the bell outside the door of a third-floor flat. The man who opened the door looked unkempt in shorts and an old tee, his balding hair standing in spikes around his head and his eyes bleary and unfocussed. Dolly wondered whether he had been drinking. She quickly flashed her warrant card and introduced herself. Pradeep Chopra led the way into a cluttered drawing room.

'I am shocked by Alan's death,' Pradeep said, succinctly, after he had cleared junk off the sofa so that Dolly could seat herself. 'He was the only hope I had of warding off Alice Lee's civil suit. She is set to ruin me, ASP Das. It was bad enough Rosie being blamed for the plane crash, but to take us to the cleaners, is a bit too much.'

'Alan Lee found evidence the flight display unit was faulty.'

'Yes, he said the fault may have been in the chips inside the unit. He said he was getting more evidence, but I was sceptical. The supplier who sold the plane parts to Ronnie Lee has gone out of business and was unreachable. So was the broker who sold the parts from a distributor. Alan suspected the chips were generated here in Singapore, but without the broker, there is no lead. I just hoped he would prevail on Alice Lee to withdraw the civil suit but that hasn't happened. I received a summons to appear in court.' Pradeep Chopra's face was red with rage and his eyes glittered feverishly.

'How much compensation is she demanding?' Dolly was sympathetic.

'Two million dollars! I have two children to raise, ASP Das, on my meagre salary.' Pradeep's eyes narrowed. 'Alice Lee not only filed the suit, but she prevailed on her father, former cabinet minister, Justin Chua, to influence the university board members to refuse me tenure as a professor. I am now reduced to the lowly role of a lecturer. Not content with hounding my family, she is ruining me, professionally, as well.'

'Can't you appeal to the university authorities?' Dolly soothed, afraid Pradeep would have a stroke, so red was his face.

'Yes, I have appealed, but do you think I stand a chance against a former cabinet minister? Alice Lee is a mean and vindictive woman and I wish she were dead.'

'Now you don't mean that, Mr Chopra,' Dolly said but there was nothing more she could get out of Pradeep.

As she walked to her car, Dolly thought that if Alice had turned up as a corpse instead of Alan, Pradeep Chopra would be the chief suspect. Dolly sighed. Her last job of the day was a visit to Singapore Interpol and IGCI Interpol and request officers there to mount a search for Mark Latham, the Beachcombers Hotel manager, the only other lead she had on the syndicate.

* * *

Dolly first visited Supt Martin Sim at the ICD building on Irrawaddy Road where NCB-Singapore Interpol was located. As soon as she was shown into his office, Marty Sim's face broke into a wide smile and he told Dolly they would catch up at the canteen. Over cups of tea and curry puffs, Dolly and Marty shared their policing journeys from the time they had parted as sergeants on the same team at Singapore CID. It was half an hour into the conversation when Dolly could interject her request to locate Mark Latham.

Marty, a tall, bespectacled man with a clean-shaven face and a receding hairline, nodded his head at Dolly's request and said, 'Since Alan Lee was murdered in Bali, it's not really within our jurisdiction to locate suspected criminals related to his murder. But we have criminal intelligence officers from The General Secretariat Interpol seconded to the IGCI to lead research teams. They have the power to issue red notices for criminals on the run. I had a chat with Chief Supt Derek Randall who conducts research on cooperation between NCB branches of Interpol and his deputy, Supt Rachel Kelly has offered to take on the Latham case. It will be a part of their research study, Dolly. Supt Kelly is an astute officer in charge of Interpol HQ's department that helps catch criminals selling illicit goods, and counterfeit computer chips would be in that category. Supt Kelly has acted as a consultant in some of our cases and I've found her to be clever and thorough. She is a former Scotland Yard officer and has been with Interpol now for some time. She recently relocated to Singapore from Lyon. She will help you, Dolly. I've talked to her about the case.'

With Marty's words of keeping him updated ringing in her ears, Dolly drove to the IGCI building on Napier Road to keep her 4.30 p.m. appointment with Supt Rachel Kelly. The IGCI building was majestic with dark glass covering its facade and air-conditioners humming inside a glittering lobby. Rachel Kelly's office was on the second floor and a security guard courteously escorted her there.

Brown-haired, blue-eyed Rachel Kelly was quite beautiful, dressed in a black pantsuit with a bejewelled pair of glasses hanging around her neck. She appeared to be around fifty years of age and smiled pleasantly as she greeted Dolly. After seating Dolly and taking her own seat in a swivel chair, Rachel donned her glasses and flipped through some papers on her desk.

When she looked up, her face was puzzled. 'You want us to locate Mark Latham? He has no criminal record in any country he resided in. You want us to arrest him on the testimony of a small-time crook in Bali?' She raised her pencilled eyebrows high above her glasses.

Dolly flushed. 'We have reason to believe Mr Latham was the co-owner of a factory recycling counterfeit chips for the black market. We don't yet know whether he was involved in Alan Lee's murder, but some facts are pointing to it. The hired thug who killed Alan Lee may have worked for Latham in this factory. We want Latham for questioning, so it's not an arrest.'

Supt Kelly's face puckered into stubborn lines. 'Nevertheless. Your informant may be implicating Latham in the murder of Alan Lee to save his own skin. Mark Latham has impeccable qualifications, a Cambridge degree, a long career as an engineer.'

'So, it does seem strange he has switched careers; moving from engineering to hospitality seems rather drastic.' Dolly's voice was as smooth as silk.

'It seems to me you are grasping at straws regarding Mark Latham,' Supt Kelly said in a crisp voice. 'I see from your application that you have no proof of Latham's ownership of the counterfeit chip recycling factory, in fact, we do not even know such a factory exists as the building was empty when you raided it.'

Dolly disliked hearing the trace of amused disdain in the Caucasian woman's voice. 'Are you saying Interpol will not help bring Latham in for questioning in Hong Kong?'

'I am not convinced he is involved in Mr Lee's murder.' Rachel Kelly placed her hands in a steeple on top of her desk and looked coldly at Dolly. 'If you have concrete evidence that he owns an illicit factory, you can re-apply to us to bring him in for questioning. As a consultant on this case, I'm recommending we wait for more evidence linking Latham to counterfeit chips or to Lee's murder.'

'Ma'am, this is a high-profile case. The murdered man was a cousin of one of our ministers. We must use all our resources to find the men who hired a thug to kill Alan Lee,' Dolly said, desperately.

Rachel Kelly's eyes flickered momentarily before sharpening. 'Regardless, ASP Das, my assessment of the situation stands. If you have more evidence, reapply to NCB-Interpol Singapore and Supt Sim will forward the application to me. I'll see what I can do.'

With an abrupt movement, Rachel Kelly rose, and her smile was back in place. 'Have a pleasant day.'

Dolly's face was set as she drove back to headquarters. Ananda may have been a small cog in the machinations of the syndicate, but his evidence of Latham's involvement was sound, Dolly thought. Latham had fled the scene, too, further evidence of his guilt.

Dolly decided to discuss with DAC John Nathan what more she needed to do to get Interpol's help in finding Latham. She stepped on her car accelerator and sped towards the highway on her way home. She wanted to clean her house in preparation for Joey's arrival home the next day.

Tuesday, 21 May 2013

Singapore

15

Looking out of the car window as her chauffeur drove her to the Goodwood Park Hotel, Alice Lee seethed with anger. Her lawyer had just phoned. Alan's will left the bungalow in the care of his maternal cousin, Lester Chong, to sell and divide the proceeds into trust funds for Linda's children and Etienne. Just as ASP Das had said. Alice was sure Lester would soon ask her to leave the house.

The driver parked the car in front of Min Jiang Sichuan Restaurant. A steady drizzle fell from the grey sky and Samy held the car door open, umbrella in hand. He shepherded Alice to the back entrance of the restaurant, the umbrella sheltering her from the rain.

As Alice entered the dining room of the restaurant from the dim interior of the corridor, a grey-haired man of medium height with a salt-and-pepper beard and moustache, rose from a table by the French windows leading to the hotel swimming pool. At sixty, Sauce King, Nelson Ong was still robust with a burgeoning alcohol paunch, rimless glasses lending his face a scholarly look.

His father had started making sauces in the kitchen of his small shanty from recipes handed down by his grandmother and sold the sauces at a small profit to his neighbouring kampong dwellers. By word of mouth, the news of the delicious tastes of Ong Light Soya, Ong Sweet Chilli, Ong Oyster, spread like wildfire, prompting the elder Ong to borrow money to buy a dilapidated factory in Chai Chee.

In five years, this was replaced by a larger modern building and by the time the elder Ong breathed his last, he was the owner of a small empire. His son, Nelson's contribution to the family business was to take the Ong brand to China, Taiwan, Indonesia, and Malaysia and he was among Singapore's well-known millionaires. Not the marrying kind, Nelson made do with a string of beautiful mistresses, the latest of whom was Alice, widow of his golfing partner, Ronnie.

Nelson smiled widely as Alice approached the table. 'Darling! You're late.' He enveloped Alice in an embrace and passionately kissed her red lips.

'Only a bit.' Alice gently disentangled herself and eyed her beau's vibrating mobile phone. 'Hadn't you better take that call? Probably some problem in your ketchup factory in Kuching. I'll order for the both of us.' They sat down at the table.

As Nelson took the call, the hovering waiter, came solicitously forward.

'Oh, a pot of your finest Oolong tea, High Mountain brand if you have it,' Alice said. 'We'll have your dimsum platter for two with a side of Min Jiang noodles for Nelson and a fish congee for me. And oh yes, bring us three orders of mango sago pudding for dessert, it's Nelson's favourite. The noodles now, last time it was too oily, go slow on the grease, okay? Nelson has to watch his cholesterol levels.'

After the waiter had left, Alice found Nelson looking at her with dancing lights in his eyes. 'You look beautiful, Alice, just like a thirty-year-old, who would think that next year you'll be celebrating your fiftieth, eh?'

'No need to remind me of that.' Alice's eyes flashed. 'Alan's will instructs his executor, Lester Chong, to sell 39, Primrose Crescent and divide the proceeds into trust funds for Linda's kids and Etienne. I'll lose my home. Thank you,' she said to the waiter who was pouring out the oolong tea into their teacups.

'39, Primrose Crescent is not your house, pumpkin. Why don't you leave that house? Ronnie bequeathed it to Alan, you know that. You are not hard-up, quite the contrary, your mother's trust fund will buy you a bungalow in District 10. Why put yourself through the hassle of a court case with Lester? He is sure to evict you from 39, Primrose Crescent. Leave before being thrown out, sweetheart.' Nelson took a small sip of his tea. 'Alan's wake is being held at the bungalow?'

Alice nodded. 'In his living room. Etienne and Linda are there most of the time.'

Nelson nodded, soberly. 'I'll be visiting him this evening. I did not know him well, but Ronnie was very proud of Alan.'

Alice glanced unseeingly out of the French windows. The rain had stopped. A child chased a huge plastic ball near the swimming pool. The ball fell into the water and the toddler crept to the pool's edge. As he was about to step into the pool, the safe hands of his parent grabbed him and pulled him back.

Alice, who had been gripping the table edge in tension, relaxed, and sighed. She sipped her tea and said, 'There's something behind all this—I don't think Alan's death is the result of a robbery gone wrong.' After the waiter placed dim sum baskets on the table, she helped herself to pork dumplings and served Nelson prawn dumplings.

Nelson speared a prawn dumpling with his chopstick and popped it into his mouth. After chewing vigorously and appreciating the delicate flavour, he frowned. 'What else could it be but a robbery gone wrong, sweetheart? It's interesting Alan left a trust fund for Linda's children. He did not leave Linda any money?'

Alice laughed. 'Ronnie and Alan never trusted Linda's husband, Patrick Singh. They felt he married Linda for the money she would inherit, so they made sure the money was left to the children. Ronnie always said Linda was silly about Pat, he felt Pat was a gold digger. But when Linda came crying to him, pregnant with Natasha, and said she could not live in a poky flat with Pat's mother any longer, well, Ronnie did buy her a unit at Silver Springs Condo. Ronnie was sure, though, that Patrick was waiting for more money coming to Linda. He told me that.'

Nelson nodded when the waiter offered to serve the noodles into his bowl.

'Yes, Ronnie was a shrewd man, he could sniff out a gold digger.'

They ate in silence before Alice said, 'Etienne's trust fund allows him to draw money out in small amounts pending approval by Lester. He only inherits the lot when he is thirty. What point was Alan making?' She began to eat from the bowl of fish congee the waiter had placed by her plate.

Nelson's eyes held a speculative gleam as he wolfed down the noodles in his bowl. 'Didn't you say Etienne is mooning over a model and aspiring actress much older than him? Maybe Alan sniffed out a gold-digger like his father. Do you want any more pork dumplings, sweetheart?' Nelson was eyeing the dumpling baskets.

'No, no, please do finish them, darling. Della Pang is five years older than Etienne.' Alice said, 'I don't know what's got into my son. He was always a serious boy. I never thought he would be attracted to a model.'

After some time, Alice set the congee aside. Suddenly, she did not feel hungry any more. She worried about her son and his future. She had thought to ask Alan to talk sense into Etienne about breaking up with Della. Now it was too late.

'A bit slow on the uptake, your Etienne.' Nelson sipped his tea and glanced around. The lunch crowd was thinning out.

Alice's lips thinned into a line. 'He passed his 'O' levels, and he doesn't need more education. After finishing his National Service, I will get Papa to hire him as an apprentice in his biscuit factory. He can train to be a manager.' Alice nodded at the waiter placing their mango puddings by their plates.

Nelson's eyebrows rose. 'Really? With Marvin Chua, your stepbrother, as his boss? No love lost between you two and all that, eh?'

Alice's brows knitted together. 'Regardless of his equation with me, Marvin and Etienne get along fine. At twenty-nine, Marvin is nearer Etienne's age than mine. Or you can take Etienne under your wing in one of your sauce factories.'

Nelson smiled and changed the subject. They made small talk about the upcoming wedding of one of their friends and finished their food. Alice ate a little of the mango pudding.

His tablet beeped and Nelson leapt to his feet with relief. 'Important meeting, Alice, afraid I can't stay longer.' He looked at his helping of mango pudding, longingly. 'Maybe you can finish the dessert.'

'Are you crazy? I've got to watch my figure. I'll ask the waitress to pack it along with the rest of my congee. Etienne can have the pudding.' Alice signalled the waitress over and asked her to pack the leftover food.

As a waiter cleared the table, Alice looked around. Nelson was already leaving the restaurant without a backward glance. Alice's eyes narrowed. Why, he had not had the decency to peck her cheek. Nelson was drifting away and the notion he was seeing another woman took hold of Alice's mind. Frowning furiously, she left the restaurant and got into her car.

'Samy, take me to Pa's house.'

Once inside her father's spacious bungalow tucked away behind Stevens Road, Alice made a beeline for the study, taking care to avoid her stepmother, Lydia, sunbathing by the pool. Ten years older than her stepdaughter, Lydia Chua and Alice had never got along. A perfunctory knock, and Alice was inside the study.

The wood-panelled interior, the sight of stacks of books lining the shelves, her father seated behind his mahogany desk smoking a pipe, brought Alice's childhood back to her and she blinked back sudden tears.

'Poppet!' Seventy-three-year-old Justin Chua's voice was warm as he rose from the leather chair behind the desk to envelope his only daughter in his arms. He was a short, burly man with black-framed glasses hiding cunning eyes. As Singapore's Cabinet Minister for Finance, he had ruled the Monetary Authority of Singapore with an iron hand, carefully steering Singapore's financial boat in the stormy global financial sea. He had retired from politics when he had the first of his strokes that left the right side of his body partially paralysed. His recovery had been slow, and he still had trouble moving his right arm and leg. When he ventured out of his house, he used a wheelchair.

'How are you, my angel?' Justin Chua re-seated himself and automatically pushed a plate of biscuits towards his daughter.

He had made his money in the biscuit business, an empire, Marvin, his son with Lydia, now ran. He had been the CEO of Chua's Biscuits, a loving husband, and a doting father, when his first wife, Jean, suddenly died in a boating accident on the French Riviera. He had sent Alice abroad for schooling and with time on his hands, and on a whim, he decided to run for a Member of Parliament seat in the Bukit Timah constituency in 1980. He was more surprised than his cronies when he won the election. Alice had been sixteen at the time and studying in England. Seeing the need for a hostess for the parties he held at his home where politics was the topic of the day, Justin Chua married his beautiful party canvasser, Lydia Ho, and she presented him with his only son, Marvin.

'Bad business about Alan, huh? Lydia and I will pay our respects tonight, Alice. He was a loving brother to Tien.' Justin Chua's eyes swept over his daughter's face as intently as that of a beachcomber hunting for pearls. 'Lester is meddling as usual, I hear, sending the Singapore police to Bali.'

'Pa, in his will, Alan instructed Lester to sell the Primrose Crescent bungalow and divide the sale proceeds between Linda's kids and Etienne,' Alice said without preamble.

'I am glad Tien is a beneficiary of Alan's will. Why don't you leave that house, Alice?' Her father sighed. 'It's not yours and your mother's trust fund has multiplied to millions over the years, you can easily buy a bungalow on prime land. Jean left you a bountiful trust fund which you have never touched.'

'Yes, that's what Nelson said.'

'Ah, Nelson.' Justin Chua coughed. 'Things okay between the two of you?'

'Why do you ask?'

'There's a rumour he's seeing a Eurasian woman.'

'A Eurasian woman!' Alice's voice was shocked.

'Only a rumour,' her father soothed.

Alice looked thoughtful. 'The story *could* be true. I can feel Nelson drifting away from me and I won't let that happen. I might have surveillance on Nelson. Do you know of a good PI, Pa?'

'Be careful about Nelson, he's a hard man when crossed.' Justin Chua drew his brows together. 'Well, there's Philip Wee at People's Park, he can be discreet. Don't be too much of a busybody, Alice.'

Alice nodded and lowered her voice. 'Papa, I will send Etienne here for a few days. Try to talk some sense into him. He is dating a model five years his senior and I believe he is ready to marry her!'

'Marry!' Justin Chua's spectacles slid down his nose. 'He's only nineteen years old. Who is this model? How did he meet her?'

'Her name is Della Pang, and he must have met her at a disco or a party. I don't know! I'm sure Della is stringing him along and wasting his money.'

'Or looking to Etienne inheriting a lot of money,' Justin mused. 'He is your heir, Alice, and your mother's trust funds are worth at least ten million dollars. I wonder if Tien has told Della about Jean's trust funds.'

Alice shrugged. Her thin lips lifted in a smile. 'Well, to get at my mother's money, I would have to die, and I don't intend on doing that for a long time.'

Justin Chua coughed. 'About Rosvinder Kaur's family, Alice. The university denied Dr Pradeep Chopra tenure, let's leave it at that, eh? No need to drag Chopra to court and demand compensation for his wife's mistake. He has two children to raise.'

Alice pursed her lips. 'Chopra has already received a summons for the civil court trial. Rosvinder Kaur's estate must pay me compensation for Ronnie's death. It was the pilot's fault the plane crashed, Pa!'

Justin Chua said shiftily, 'I thought you said Alan had some new evidence from the cockpit voice recorder that exonerated the pilot?'

'Hardly, and Alan is dead now.' Alice's eyes were cold as she rose from her seat.

After promising to send Etienne to his grandfather, Alice ordered Samy to drive her to the People's Park complex in Eu Tong Sen Street where the PI, Phil Wee, had his office. She *had* to find out whether Nelson was seeing another woman.

Wednesday, 22 May 2013

Singapore

16

Lily knocked on Linda Lee's door, a big thermally insulated bag slung over her shoulder. Linda opened the door and looked at Lily in surprise. The time was 12 p.m.

'Linda, how are you? So sorry about Alan's death and sorry I couldn't visit earlier. According to Indian custom, we provide food to a neighbouring house in mourning, so I have brought lunch with me. Your children should be home soon. Duleep loves my chicken biryani.' Lily babbled, smiling tentatively, her eyes curious. She was dressed in a black suit and wore low-heeled shoes.

'Oh!' Linda looked nonplussed. She had just taken a shower and a towel turbaned her hair. 'There is no need. My helper is cooking us lunch.'

'What are friends for? Linda, we went to secondary school together.' As Linda stepped aside from the door, Lily bustled in and put the bag on the dining table set in one corner of the hall. She began taking out the microwavable boxes of food from the bag.

Linda closed the door and came to the table. 'Shouldn't we wait for my children?' She was not accustomed to her lunch hour and home being usurped in this manner. She glowered a little, remembering Uma prying into her family's private affairs, sure that Lily had come to do the same. However, with Lily bringing so much food, she could hardly ask her to leave.

'Yes, of course, Vernon has packed an appetizer box, it's samosas. I thought we could munch on that while waiting for the children. I have got them my chicken nuggets as well.'

Lily located the box of samosas and fished it out. She smiled at Linda. 'Some vegetable samosas, Linda?'

'Thanks, why not? Lestriani can make us some tea. We have Darjeeling. I'm forgetting I'm the hostess. Sit there on the sofa, Lily, I'll join you soon.'

After Linda disappeared into the kitchen, Lily looked around the condo unit. The decor was Indian, right from the wall hangings of Punjabi landscapes to the rich fabric of the Kashmiri carpet on the floor. Bronze potted plants stood in corners interspersed with sculptures imported from India.

Linda arrived with the tea and the two women sat down to their samosas.

'This is delicious,' Linda said, crumbs of pastry forming a crust at the corners of her mouth. 'You really are a good cook, Lily. I remember you excelled in our Home Science class in school. The teacher was always praising your cooking skills. Mrs Ramalingam, wasn't that our Home Science teacher's name?'

'Yes, we called her Rama among ourselves,' Lily giggled and bit into a samosa. 'And do you remember Mrs Chan, the Science teacher? Once she nearly blew up our classroom with a science experiment gone wrong.'

'Yes.' A shadow crossed Linda's face. 'Chan died from kidney disease, later.' She quickly took a sip of tea.

'Oh, so sorry to hear that.' Lily had finished eating one samosa and was eyeing another one in the box. She stretched out her hand and put the samosa on her plate.

Linda had a few tears in her eyes. 'I met Mrs Chan at the dialysis centre my mother was attending. Both had kidney disease, and both died.'

Lily moved nearer to Linda on the sofa and patted her shoulder. 'I'm sorry, Linda. You lost your mom after your 'O' levels?'

'Just. I was eighteen years old when I lost her. One day, Ma called Alan and me to her room and told us the kidney dialysis was not working any more and she did not have long to live. We hugged each other and cried. She made us promise we would look after each other and Pa.' Linda's lips twisted, and her face grew dark. 'Not that we needed to console Pa. Six months after Ma died, he married Alice Chua, the then cabinet minister, Justin Chua's daughter. This was in 1984.'

Lily made soothing noises. 'Yes, yes. Remarrying so soon, not too decent. In our culture, we usually wait one year after bereavement to celebrate any marriages.'

'They were carrying on while Ma was alive!' Linda's face reddened with rage.

'Alice Chua was a beauty in her day, though,' Lily said, egging Linda on.

'If you go for that kind of mannish look,' came Linda's quick rejoinder. 'She fell in love with our bungalow, and set about redecorating the house as soon as she moved in.'

'You don't get along with her,' Lily concluded.

'No and neither did Alan.' Linda's eyes glittered with bad memories. 'I was working at the community library after obtaining a diploma in library science. I started staying out late and returned home when I knew Alice had gone to bed. I married late when I was thirty. I met Pat at a friend's party, and I was glad to get out from under Alice's feet. But I had to suffer Alice for twelve long years.'

Lily looked around the room. 'Your husband is Sikh? I think I've seen him with you sometimes in the complex.'

Linda smiled, stiffly. 'Yes, he has always called himself Patrick from primary school as the Chinese kids couldn't pronounce his name right. I had my children late in life. Natasha, when I was thirty-six and Duleep two years later. Natty is in Primary Five and Duleep is in Primary Three.' Linda's face shone with maternal pride. She said, curiously, 'I've seen you around with a Caucasian man and a small baby.'

Lily nodded. 'I lost my first husband to cancer. Frankie is a Eurasian and we got married only two years ago. Our little Molly is adopted.'

Linda smiled. 'You must bring Molly here for a visit. Natty would love to play with her.'

Lily smiled and felt it was time to turn the conversation to Alice Lee. 'You have a stepbrother?'

Linda's face shone. 'Yes, Etienne. I babysat him and he is a darling. Doing his NS now. I left home when Tien was two. Alice relegated his care to nannies, of course. You can't imagine Alice being a proper mother, can you? She would not let my baby brother disturb her kitty parties, her horse riding, her bridge parties. Poor Tien was raised by helpers. He is such a good boy, though.' Love glimmered in Linda's eyes.

'And Alan stayed on in the house?' Lily inquired, delicately. She had finished her samosa and started on her tea.

'Alan was very different from me.' Linda smiled, sadly, and finished eating the samosa from her plate. 'I'm a firebrand, and my brother was quiet. An introvert, really. We never knew what he was thinking about. Waferworld was his universe, he was climbing the corporate ladder even then. He was

Singapore's Junior Chess Champion and chess tournaments took him all over the world. I don't know, though, if he would have continued living in the house if he had married Selena.'

Lily pricked up her ears. 'He was engaged to be married?'

Linda sighed and a sad light burned in her eyes. 'Yes, ten years ago. Selena Gan was our neighbour. We grew up with Selena and her sister, Emily. Alan dated Selena on and off when we were older, went steady for several years and finally decided to get married.'

Lily's eyes were lit up with interest. 'A long courtship if he had decided to marry when nearly forty.'

Linda nodded. 'Alan was reluctant to marry anyone. When he was young, he had a blood disorder and had to undergo chemotherapy and radiation. It was a few months after our mother died and our father had remarried. The treatment made him infertile and since he could not father children, he did not want to get married. Selena loved him and changed his mind. They had decided to adopt a little child after marriage, just like you, Lily.' Tears shone in Linda's eyes.

'What happened?' Lily asked in a hushed voice.

'Selena loved watching ballets and she and her sister, Emily had gone into town to watch Swan Lake. On their way back home, their car met with an accident. Selena was driving and she died on the spot. Emily was badly injured but slowly recovered. She was paralysed from the waist down. Alan got her a job working from home and he often visited her to cheer her up. Emily and her mother live in a condo unit next to our house.'

'How very sad,' Lily said, softly. Tears glistened in her eyes. 'My first husband, Joy, died of lung cancer in his thirties.' After talking of Joy to a sympathetic Linda, Lily said again, 'Alan must have got along with his stepmother to go on living at the house. Nowadays, single men stay in their own pads.'

Linda's eyes were pinpricks of rage. 'It was Alan's house to live in after Pa's death. Pa willed the house to him. And to think Alice deprived him of his inheritance!'

Lily pricked up her ears and her lips parted in anticipation. She knew most of the story of the Lee family from Girlie via Lestriani, but it was best to hear it directly from Linda. She gulped down the last of her tea and pushed the cup away on the low glass-topped table by her side.

Linda bit savagely into her third samosa. 'More than twenty years into her marriage, Alice started an affair with Pa's golfing partner, Nelson Ong. Pa found out and wrote her out of his will. When Pa died, the will was read, and he had left his money to Alan and trust funds for my children and Etienne. He left the house to Alan, but Alice claimed there was a newer will in which he left the bungalow to her and refused to move out of the house. Alan was too much of a gentleman to kick her out, but I can tell you one thing, he was planning to go to court to claim the bungalow. He had already talked to his lawyer, Jonas Ellis, to start proceedings to evict Alice from 39, Primrose Crescent.'

'His death was lucky for Alice then,' quipped Lily.

'I'm sure the house comes to me now.' Linda looked determined as she sipped her tea. 'I'll start court proceedings against Alice as soon as Alan's will is probated.'

Lily was trying to recollect a piece of information and when she did, she exclaimed, 'I seem to remember that your father did not die naturally. Something in the papers.'

While sipping her tea, Linda told Lily about the plane crash and how the pilot, Rosvinder Kaur was blamed for the crash, based on one incident of flying after taking alcohol. With flashing eyes, she related how Alice Lee was initiating a civil suit against the pilot's estate, asking for compensation for Ronnie's wrongful death. Not only that, Linda said, her lips trembling, Alice had got her father to influence the university board to deny Pradeep Chopra's tenure. Linda stopped to take a deep breath.

Lily's eyes were wide. 'Your stepmother is quite the dragon lady!'

'My brother, if he were alive, would have stopped this civil suit,' Linda said, savagely, and finished the last of her tea.

'My sister was asked to stay back in Bali to help with the investigation into Alan's murder on the request of Lester Chong, the Junior Transport Minister.'

Linda smiled. 'Yes, it was good of your sister to do so. You see, my *lao lao* is alive, and she was upset at Alan's death. Lester is my first cousin, my maternal uncle's son. My grandmother asked Lester to do all he could to find Alan's murderer. Your sister brought back Alan's body last Saturday. His wake is being held at our bungalow. I've been spending a lot of time there greeting the friends who came to pay their respects. His funeral is tomorrow followed by cremation at Mandai. We'll scatter his ashes at sea as he loved to sail there in his younger days.'

She looked inquiringly at Lily. 'Has your sister found out who murdered my brother in Bali? Was it because he wore that Rolex watch? I heard it was stolen. It was a fake and I told your mother that. Such a pity if he was killed for a fake watch.'

Lily coughed. She was not going to reveal details of Dolly's investigation, and that Ramdin had been hired to kill Alan Lee. 'Don't worry, Linda, my sister is a good police officer, she will find Alan's killer.'

There was a commotion at the door and Natasha and Duleep entered, laughing together. They looked at Lily, smiled, and then their eyes swivelled to the boxes of biryani and stayed there.

'Delicious chicken biryani for you, children.' Lily rose and went to the dining table. 'And chicken nuggets, too.'

The children whooped with joy and made for their bedrooms to get changed into home clothes.

'Have lunch with us,' Linda invited.

'No, no, I have been away from my café far too long. Enjoy your lunch and take care. It's been good talking to you, Linda. Once again, sincere condolences on the death of your brother.'

* * *

As she rode the lift down to the ground floor, Lily was thoughtful. She had discovered enough background on Alan Lee's family to keep Dolly focused on a personal angle to the murder. Lily began walking to Block C and her café. Alice Lee hated her stepchildren and Alan's murder stopped her eviction from the bungalow she loved. Alice Lee had a motive to murder Alan. Also, without Alan to deter her, Alice Lee could now initiate a civil suit against the pilot's estate and win compensation. Alice benefited by Alan's death. Could Alice Lee have hired thugs in Bali to get rid of Alan? Stranger things have happened, Lily thought, as she pushed open the glass doors of the café and entered just in time to see her assistant, Vernon, drop a plate of biryani on the floor with a crash.

'You will pay for that plate out of your wages,' Lily snapped.

Vernon sighed and nodded. He looked so dismal that Lily turned away before she felt sorry enough for him to say he need not pay for the broken plate. Her kind heart won over. 'What's wrong, V?' She asked, softly.

Vernon's bad eye squinted from wall to wall. 'Money problems, Mrs D. Angie and I talked it over last night. I work for you double and you let Angie go, Mrs D. I will wash the dishes, man the cash register as well as serve the customers. Angie go and work as housemaid.'

Lily's eyes rounded. 'A maid? You mean she will sweep and mop people's homes?'

Vernon nodded. 'Only way to make good money. She joined a maid agency already, Mrs D. We know you will support us. The money is good and she make more than you pay, Mrs D. The agency give her a house she need to clean every day. The pay is $2000 a month from that one house, Mrs D. With that and other houses, she can make at least 3K a month, easy. More than she can make in retail or even waitressing. So sorry, Mrs D. But I do overtime, not to worry. No need for you to look for hired help.'

Lily's face was sad. She was close to Angie and was sorry to lose her. 'It's all right, V. I do support both of you. I know a baby costs money. Where is Ashikin?'

Vernon said, 'Her little one sick, Mrs D. But Madam A cook all the delicious Malay dishes. Many people buy. I serve them, no worries. I serve you lunch?'

'Pack it for me. I will go home and have it. Don't worry about the future, V, everything will be okay.' She smiled. 'You know I will pay you Angie's wages as well, right? So, you will make more money here at the café.'

Leaving a grateful Vernon behind, Lily walked out of the door and back to Block D and her mother's condo unit, carrying boxes of chicken biryani.

17

Charlie drove along Old Woodlands Road towards Waferworld Semiconductors. Dolly was dissatisfied with the results of his interview with Lionel Chu. She thought Lionel was withholding information and told Charlie to invite him to a session with her at CID HQ.

Charlie was shown into an interview room by a receptionist who informed him that Lionel was on leave, but she would instead get his boss to see him. Instantly, a tall woman wearing thick spectacles, her hair awry, entered like a whirlwind. Charlie stepped back, alarmed.

In a thick voice, Camilla Yong, Member of Technical Staff of Yield Engineering, spoke, 'Chingching said a policeman wanted to see me. Have you come about Lionel?'

'Yes, I understand he is on leave today.'

Camilla said, tearfully, 'You haven't heard, Inspector? A hotel employee telephoned me just now to say Lionel has taken his own life by jumping from Level 24 of the Swiss Hotel. He doesn't have family here. He listed me as emergency contact on the hotel register.'

In a flash, Charlie was out of the door, looking back once at Camilla to say, 'I need to go to the hotel now, is it okay to have a word with you later, Dr Yong?'

'Whatever.' Bursting into tears, Camilla followed him out.

* * *

After phoning Dolly with the news of Lionel's death, Charlie quickly made his way to Raffles City, the mall above which stretched the impressive 226-metre-high Swiss Hotel, one of the tallest buildings in Asia. Parking his car in the spacious carpark, he took the lift to the glittering hotel lobby.

The general manager, a thin wiry man of sixty from Scotland, Rob Bunyon, ushered him to the back of the premises where he had his office.

'Please, do sit down, Inspector Goh.' He ushered Charlie to a comfortable chair and seated himself behind his desk. 'I am sorry this young man, er, Lionel Chu, took his own life. This is our third suicide in two years.' His sad blue eyes blinked from behind round spectacles. 'On account of the height of our hotel, you know, a handful come here to take their own lives. We called the ambulance, the police hotline, and the young man's emergency contact.'

Charlie cleared his throat. 'Lionel Chu was a person of interest in a murder case, so we will be investigating Mr Chu's death. My superior will be here any minute.'

'But he jumped from the small balcony outside his hotel room. It was on Level 24, so his death was instantaneous,' Bunyon said, sadly. 'He was found in a disused lot at the back of the mall that lay below his balcony.'

'Our pathologist and forensic teams will determine the cause of Mr Chu's death,' Charlie said, woodenly. 'When did Mr Chu register at the hotel?'

'Yes, yes, I have all the details.' The manager's voice shook, too many suicides were bad for business. 'Mr Lionel Chu's booking for a one-night stay in a standard room was made two days ago. He arrived yesterday evening and the receptionist checked him into Room 2405.' Bunyon glanced at some notes he had jotted down. 'He checked in at around 6 p.m. and ordered room service dinner and watched movies on TV the whole night. We know since he charged all his expenses to the registered credit card. He ordered a bottle of champagne with his dinner and ordered late night snacks at 11 p.m. He had pre-ordered our American set breakfast for two to be delivered at 8 a.m. this morning.'

'Wait a minute, breakfast for two?' Dolly was being ushered in by a wide-eyed receptionist who was hastily waved away by Bunyon. 'I am Assistant Superintendent Dolly Das of the Singapore CID and in charge of this investigation since Lionel Chu, the dead man, was a person of interest in a murder case.'

After Dolly was seated, Bunyon consulted his notes again. 'Yes, Mr Chu ordered two sets of American breakfasts and he even told Shamsher, our room-service waiter that he was expecting a guest in his room for breakfast.'

'And when was the body found?' Dolly's brain was whirring into action.

'At around 9 a.m.' A sad light flitted into the manager's pale blue eyes. Dolly thought he was visualizing the mangled and smashed up body lying in the disused lot outside. 'Shamsher alerted us. He had gone in with the breakfast trolley at around 8 a.m. and found Lionel Chu alone in the room. Mr Chu told Shamsher to bring the coffee piping hot at 8.45 a.m. When Shamsher entered with the coffee, there was no one in the room and the balcony door was wide open. Shamsher took the lift down and ran to the area under the east-side balconies. The poor young man was lying there on the ground. He fell on to a disused lot near the back of the mall. That is the reason no one else saw the body.'

'Our forensic pathologist is already outside, examining the corpse. When he and the forensic team are done, the ambulance will take the body to the morgue for an autopsy. You must release Mr Chu's room to our forensic officers. The room has not been cleaned, has it?' When Bunyon shook his head, Dolly's voice became brisk. 'Is there CCTV in the corridor outside Room 2405?'

'Yes, there are cameras at the corners of all the hotel corridors.' Bunyon stroked his red moustache thoughtfully. 'There is one other thing.'

'Yes?'

'I asked the receptionist to check into Mr Chu's credit card details and Ms Rosanna, our receptionist, found the room had been booked on a credit card not belonging to Mr Chu. It was a woman's credit card and the room paid for in full.'

'What was the name of the woman?' Charlie squeaked in excitement, his double chins wobbling.

Robert Bunyon glanced back at his notes. 'A Ms Sushila Iyer's credit card had paid for Lionel Chu's stay. I have noted the card number and it is a Citibank Visa credit card.'

Dolly said appreciatively, 'You have made our job easier, thank you. My inspector will obtain the credit card details from you. And if you give him the CCTV tape, we will watch it at HQ and return it to you once we have finished our investigation. We will give you a receipt, of course.'

'Another thing,' Rob Bunyon coughed. 'The hotel guest occupying Room 2406, the room next to that occupied by Mr Chu, has come forward. He was scheduled to leave the hotel today and was checking out when he heard the commotion at the hotel door, saw people rushing out and went with them to Mr Chu's body. I have him in a conference room waiting to be interviewed. He has some information for you.' He pressed the buzzer on his desk.

'Are the rooms connected?' Dolly asked.

'No,' Bunyon replied. 'But the balconies outside the rooms are adjoining.' He looked up as a man in a suit appeared in the doorway. 'Ah, this is one of my managers, Mr Assad. Can you take the police officers to the room where Mr Pak is waiting, Assad?'

The manager nodded and asked the officers to follow him. They walked along carpeted corridors to a room at the other end of the building. The hotel manager opened the door and ushered them into a small conference room where a man was seated at the table.

'I'll be outside if you need me, ASP Das,' Assad said, went out and closed the door behind him.

The police officers seated themselves at the table.

Dolly looked at the man sitting opposite her. The Korean guest was a tall, angular man with small eyes and a pock-marked complexion. He had a habit of swallowing convulsively and his Adam's apple bobbed up and down every time he did that. He had a thick mane of hair and appeared to be about forty years of age. He nodded at the police officers and passed his passport to Dolly.

'Let's see,' Dolly said after glancing at the man's passport. 'You are Pak Kim Chol, a businessman?'

The man spoke in a raspy voice. He told Dolly he was a textile import/ export businessman with shops in Seoul. He often came to Singapore on business and whenever he did, he stayed at the Swiss Hotel.

Dolly nodded. 'What was the duration of your stay?' She took out her mobile phone and took photos of the pages of the businessman's passport. Then, she slid the passport back to him across the table, smiling her thanks.

The man took out a spectacle case from his trouser pocket along with a notebook. He perched the glasses on his nose and turned the pages of his notebook. When he looked up, his bland face had some animation. 'I stay here at this hotel from 18 May to 22 May. I check-out this morning.'

'Now tell us what information you have for us regarding the dead man.'

Pak cleared his throat noisily and launched into an animated narration. That morning, he had risen early to pack his clothes. After taking a shower, at around 8.15 a.m., he went to his balcony to take in the view. Pak gesticulated with his hands as he described a fight taking place in the next balcony between a Chinese man and an Indian woman. 'He was the dead man. They shout so loud.'

'Did you catch any of the conversation?'

Pak said the woman was pointing a finger at the man in a threatening manner and the man talked angrily back at her. 'I hear him say, "I cannot live with this guilt any more. You have spoilt my life. Why did you kill him, for God's sake?" Then the woman say, "You were all right when the money was coming in. Do you want more money?"'

Pak sat back in his chair.

Charlie, who was taking notes, asked, 'Anything more?'

Pak nodded. He said the man became agitated and began shouting loudly. 'He say, "For you, everything is about money. I sent a man to his death, and you are asking me if I want more money. Go away, I don't want to see you ever again." The woman say, "Suit yourself." They both go inside.'

Pak said he then returned to his room, dressed and went down to the lobby to check out. He heard a commotion outside and with other people, rushed out and saw the dead body of his hotel room neighbour. Pak nodded at Dolly, sagely. 'The young man jump from hotel balcony. He was angry and unhappy.'

Dolly said, 'How do you know he took his own life? The woman was still there, right?' Dolly looked at Charlie, who gave an imperceptible nod. They were both thinking Lionel's guest could have pushed him over the balcony.

Pak said, 'Ah, I forget to tell you.' He launched into another narration. He had been curious about the altercation between his neighbours and went out into the balcony sometime after Lionel and his guest had gone inside their room. Pak said he saw Lionel standing alone in the balcony, gazing out into the distance. Pak said the man was crying. 'He say over and over again, "I really can't live with this guilt any more!"'

'And then?' Charlie asked, wondering if Pak had seen Lionel jump to his death.

Pak sighed. The phone rang in his hotel room. It was the hotel manager informing him that a car was waiting outside to take him to the airport. 'I go to the lobby. I did not see the young man jump from balcony. But he was very sad,' Pak said.

'What time did you see the young man standing by himself on his balcony?' Dolly asked, sharply. She was thinking of checking the CCTV camera tape outside Lionel's room and whether the woman guest had left before Lionel came out on the balcony again.

But Pak had only glanced at his watch when he was checking out at the lobby and that was around 9 a.m. Dolly thanked Pak, and asked Charlie to type out a statement for Pak to sign as to what he had seen and heard.

Outside the room, Dolly asked the manager, Assad, to not only get them the CCTV tapes of the hotel corridor outside Lionel Chu's room, but also the hotel lobby CCTV tapes from the timeframe 8-9.30 a.m.

Lionel Chu appeared to have taken bribes from the Indian lady, Dolly thought. If he had taken his own life, remorse was the motive. He had betrayed someone. And that someone had to be Alan Lee as Lionel had asked the lady why they had to kill him. Had Lionel Chu betrayed Alan Lee to the crime syndicate by taking bribes and passing on information and was the Indian lady a member of the syndicate? If so, they could not rule out murder. When the crime syndicate member understood Lionel was regretting giving the syndicate information, he would become a threat to the syndicate, possibly he could inform the police of the syndicate's activities and role in Alan Lee's murder. And so, did the Indian lady push Lionel from the balcony? Would the Indian lady have been able to overpower Lionel? Dolly frowned.

She said to Charlie, 'Ask the forensic team to thoroughly check the balcony of Lionel's room and the clothes he wore. There is a possibility he could have been murdered and if so, the killer could have left traces on the balcony and on Lionel's clothes. Lionel was bent, he took money from the syndicate and informed on Alan Lee. The syndicate member obviously trusted him and so took no precaution not to use her credit card to book him into the hotel. But on the balcony, she got a nasty surprise. Lionel was remorseful of his role in Alan's murder. So, what did this lady do then? Charlie, you take the CCTV tapes back to HQ and contact Citibank about their client's particulars. We need to know all we can about Lionel's visitor. I'll go to the hotel room with the forensic team and then head back to the office. Make sure you talk to the pathologist downstairs before you go, Charlie. Get his impressions of cause of death and more importantly, tell him to look for defensive wounds on the victim, any evidence Lionel was pushed off the balcony by someone.'

18

There had been a sharp downpour and the road glistened as Dolly drove back to CID HQ. She frowned. She was always one step behind in the case. Since he had helped Alan by placing a mole in the turnkey company, Lionel Chu knew about the syndicate and she should have interviewed him herself at CID HQ sooner. And now he was dead, and his secrets had died with him.

At least, they had a credit card and a name for the mysterious lady who had met Lionel for breakfast. She hoped Charlie had got hold of her details from Citibank.

Charlie had not and his face was thunderous as he sat in Dolly's office waiting to update his boss.

'Citibank did not want to give their client's particulars?' Dolly hazarded a guess.

Charlie's face was still purple from the words exchanged with Citibank management. 'There can be so many Sushila Iyers in Singapore,' he said, morosely.

'Send one of our team to Waferworld to ask Human Resources if they employ anyone called Sushila Iyer,' Dolly suggested. 'She could, of course, be a syndicate member, but also a colleague from work. Get Lionel Chu's home address and have our officers search his apartment for any clues. Bring his laptop back to HQ and go through the e-mail messages. Pay a visit to Citibank and mention the Junior Transport Minister, that may open doors. Was his mobile phone on Lionel or in the hotel room?'

'In the hotel room, madam, along with a small carry-on bag with his clothes packed,' Charlie said, sombrely.

'Okay, have Mok go through the mobile phone data and tell him to report on this ASAP.'

After Charlie had left, the phone on Dolly's desk rang. It was DAC Nathan calling her to his office.

Dolly took the lift to her big boss's office on a high floor of CID HQ. She knocked on Nathan's door and entered on hearing his booming, 'Come in!' She found Superintendent Ang already there, seated on one of the guest chairs, her face worried. From behind his desk, DAC John Nathan glowered belligerently. He was a short, rotund, bald man with sharp eyes.

'Sit down, ASP Das,' he said, icily. 'How is it the Junior Minister of Transport's secretary informs me there's been another murder related to the Alan Lee case, and not you, ASP Das?'

Dolly looked thunderstruck. 'Someone must have talked to the press.' Her respect for Rob Bunyon, the Swiss Hotel manager, plummeted considerably.

'I am waiting for your update, ASP Das.'

'Sir, until the forensic team has finished, there is no evidence suggesting Lionel Chu was pushed over the balcony of the hotel by an assailant. It is true he had sat down to breakfast with a guest, and it was a woman since the hotel guest next door saw him arguing with this woman on the balcony.'

'CCTV?' Nathan barked.

'Yes, sir, I was going to go through the footage,' Dolly began.

'Do it NOW, ASP Das, what are you waiting for?' Nathan thundered, his moustache bristling with irritation. 'We are under scrutiny by the ministers. For all you know, this woman may be fleeing the country as we speak. Identify her ASAP. The dead man is the young man who was helping Alan Lee expose the syndicate. A bit lax of you not to grill him earlier. Now, we are unable to get the whole picture.'

Dolly bit her lip in chagrin.

'We want you and Inspector Goh to be quick, ASP Das,' Superintendent Ang agreed, looking tense. 'This is a high-profile case. Alan Lee is the Junior Minister's cousin, and he was knifed and now his colleague falls to his death from a high-rise. We need answers fast. We need to know if the chip syndicate had anything to do with Lionel's death.'

Back in her office, Dolly sat down with a thundery face. 'Junior Minister, Junior Minister,' she muttered and picked up her phone to call Petula Lee.

Constable Petula Lee was young, introspective, and most at home with computers. She had been passed over for promotion several times due to her lack of social skills and ineptitude at working as a team-member. She had been taciturn and rude to her Thai counterparts when she was sent to Bangkok on an international case, so much so that the Thai Deputy Commissioner of Police had sent a written complaint about her to one of the DCPs of Singapore CID.

Her skills in internet surfing, searching, and at times hacking into computers, though, were unparalleled, and had gained her the nickname, 'Techie Pet', and many criminals had been identified and arrested due to her hard work. Soon, a tall, gawky woman of twenty-eight with spiked purple hair entered Dolly's office.

Dolly began to view the CCTV footage of the corridor outside Lionel's hotel room with Petula Lee. The CCTV camera had a good view of the hotel corridor and was mounted very near Lionel's hotel room. In the footage, at around 8.05 a.m., a figure stopped at the room door. The lights in the hotel corridor were dim but Dolly and Petula had no hesitation in identifying the figure as a woman wearing a suit.

'Techie, I need to see her face,' Dolly said, tersely.

'Yes, Boss, not a problem.' Techie Pet rewound the tape to the moment the Indian woman came into view. The woman glanced back for a moment and Techie Pet froze the tape there. They could see a dim face on the footage.

'But the light is not bright, I can't make out her face, can't distinguish her features.' Dolly was distraught, the DAC's voice still ringing stridently in her ears.

'Boss, this is the part I will enhance, filter out noise and background, it will take me around fifteen minutes in my cubicle.' Techie Pet's voice was calm and assured.

'Okay, let's see when the woman leaves.' Dolly looked at the computer screen.

On the CCTV video, at 8.35 a.m., the woman emerged from Lionel's room and began walking away.

'Track her, Techie. We have CCTV tapes from the lobby, see what she does, when she leaves the hotel. The waiter came with the coffee at 8.45 a.m. So, in these ten minutes, Lionel could have gone to the balcony and jumped. Or the woman pushed Lionel over the balcony and was on her way out. We'll have to wait for the forensic team to come up with answers.

'Techie,' Dolly continued, taking out her phone and showing the Korean businessman's passport photo. 'Track this gentleman as well, he was a witness to whatever happened, it's good to know his movements. Make a CCTV time and location profile of both these people from all the tapes given by the hotel for the timeframe 8 to 9.30 a.m. And match them up. Let me know when you're done and I'll come to your cubicle to review the results.'

In an hour, Techie Pet called Dolly to her cubicle. 'Boss,' she said, as soon as Dolly was seated. 'The lobby CCTV does not record the Indian lady guest going out of the hotel main door during the specified time frame.'

'She must have, Techie. Look carefully. Otherwise, where did she go? What about the Korean guest?'

Techie Pet nodded and fast forwarded the tape of the lobby to 9.05 a.m. Dolly saw people rushing to the hotel main door and the businessman was among them.

'The gentleman was at the lobby counter at 8.55 a.m. checking out when the alarm was raised, Boss,' Techie Pet said.

'Okay, did you enhance the image of the lady?'

The constable nodded and placed a glossy photo on the desk.

Dolly stared at the photo of an Indian woman in her thirties with curly hair framing a round face, small kohl-lined eyes, a sharp, hooked nose, and a thin mouth.

Dolly shut her mouth which had been hanging open and looked at Techie Pet. 'How did you doctor this image from that blurry photo, Techie? You sure it's legit?'

'Of course,' Techie Pet said. 'This is the woman who came out of the victim's room at 8.35 a.m., Boss. Shall I send out an APB?'

Dolly nodded, thanked Techie Pet and returned to her cubicle, her brows creased. Where had Lionel's Indian guest gone after leaving his hotel room?

After half an hour, the phone rang, and Charlie's voice was cheerful over the line. 'I visited Citibank and they coughed up details of the credit card without a warrant once I had mentioned the Junior Minister of Transport like you said, madam. The lady in question is a Ms Sushila Iyer, single, age thirty-six, Singapore PR, Indian citizen, lives at Holland Avenue and works at South-East Asia Semiconductor Turnkey Solutions as a manager. We should have no problem finding her. Madam, this turnkey company is the one serving Waferworld and maybe Sushila Iyer is the corrupt employee belonging to the crime syndicate. We need to interview the mole, Toby Wong, he will confirm this.'

After Charlie had rung off, Dolly called the pathologist, Benny Ong, asking him to let her know as soon as possible if Lionel had defensive wounds on him. They had to know whether Lionel had taken his own life, or been murdered.

There was a knock on Dolly's door and both Techie Pet and Corporal Mok entered.

Mok said, 'Madam, there's bad news. We fed the image of the Indian lady outside Lionel Chu's hotel room into the Immigration and Checkpoints database and the officers there just confirmed she boarded a plane an hour ago leaving for Chennai. She's left Singapore, madam.'

'And Boss, we looked more carefully at the CCTV footage of the hotel corridor at 8.35 a.m.,' Techie Pet said. 'When the Indian lady enters Lionel Chu's room, she is coming from one direction, but when she leaves the room, she is walking in the opposite direction.'

'There may be another lift lobby at the other end the corridor,' Dolly suggested. 'And hopefully CCTV cameras there. Go to the Swiss Hotel, Adrian, and take Techie with you. Stake out the corridor and get more CCTV footages to track the Indian lady's movements. I'll talk to DAC Nathan and Supt Ang and see if it's possible to detain Sushila Iyer at Chennai Airport for questioning. It's suspicious that she was the last person to see Lionel alive and she's fled the country. Did she kill Lionel?'

Dolly dialled DAC Nathan's number and updated him on Sushila Iyer's whereabouts. Nathan told her to immediately call Singapore Interpol and have Supt Sim and Supt Kelly in a conference call, along with himself. A phone call from Supt Kelly to NCB-Interpol in New Delhi could have the police there contact Chennai Airport Police to detain Sushila Iyer as soon as her plane landed.

But DAC Nathan was disappointed. Supt Rachel Kelly wanted the request for Iyer's detention at Chennai Airport to go through the proper channels via paperwork and emails.

'Interpol India will not entertain calls even if they are from foreign Interpol officers,' Rachel Kelly said. 'ASP Das, much as I would like to help you, you are again lacking evidence. In this case, evidence of murder. Your forensic team has not concluded Chu was killed, neither has your forensic pathologist. But I do agree Sushila Iyer fled from the country right after a person of interest in the Alan Lee case died. That is suspicious. I recommend the detention and questioning of Iyer. Fax over your request for Iyer's detention at Chennai Airport to Supt Sim and he will forward your faxes and emails to India Interpol. Copy me on all mails, Supt Sim.'

In the evening, there was a tap on Dolly's door and a pleasant-faced, tall Eurasian woman peeped in. Dolly was surprised to see ASP Dolores Diaz of the Serious Sexual Crime Branch.

Dolly stood up, smiling. She liked Dolly Diaz. 'ASP Diaz, what brings you here?'

Dolly Diaz entered the office and handed over an envelope to Dolly Das. 'So sorry, ASP Das. I was on leave for the week and when I returned to the office today, this letter was on my in-tray. It is addressed to you, but the boy who delivers the mails in-house left it on my tray by mistake. The sender never specified the CID department, just your name. So sorry if this was important.'

Dolly looked at the envelope. It was addressed to her from Bali and the sender was the murdered man, Alan Lee. After meeting her and Lily at The Sea-Shell Café, Alan had gone to his villa to write this letter and given it to the assistant concierge, Abdul, to post. It was a letter addressed to her.

Dolly looked up, her eyes shining. 'Thanks, ASP Diaz, we have similar sounding names, eh? Yes, it is an important letter connected with a high-profile case, thanks for reaching it to me.'

ASP Diaz nodded, pleasantly, and left the office. Dolly called Charlie to her office to read the letter together.

Dear ASP Das,

I mentioned I had tested the dies set aside by the turnkey company and all the incriminating results are stored on a mobile hard disk. I have kept the disk safe in an airport locker. I dared not reveal its whereabouts to anyone but you. At Terminal Two of Changi Airport, in Locker No. 5428, you will find the hard disk. If anything happens to me, I leave it to you to bring the criminal syndicate to justice. These greedy syndicates are not only criminal, they take lives and need to be stopped. Sushila Iyer, the electronic waste manager at the turnkey company is the corrupt employee there. Please take the hard disk data to the turnkey company CEO and it will be enough to arrest Sushila Iyer.

Alan Lee

Charlie sat down on the chair opposite Dolly after peering over her shoulder to read the letter. He said, 'Sushila Iyer worked for the turnkey company Alan Lee was investigating, madam. She is the corrupt employee and a syndicate member and the last person to see Lionel alive. Going from the conversation the Korean guest overheard, she may have been bribing Lionel Chu.'

'And killed him when she realized he wasn't loyal to the syndicate any more? Come Charlie, let's go to the airport to retrieve the disk Alan Lee left behind. It's evidence of the turnkey company's corruption.'

Dolly's eyes glinted, sadly. Alan Lee seemed to have had a premonition he would be killed.

* * *

Over dinner at Lily's Kitchen, Dolly filled Lily in on the details of Lionel Chu's death and Alan Lee's letter to her. Lily listened intently and her eyes reflected curiosity.

'So, what was in the hard disk in the airport locker?' Lily's eyes shone; this was better than any fictional mystery she had read.

Dolly ate some roti with mutton rogan josh before answering, 'Alan Lee had sent the dies from the turnkey company to another company that specializes in testing counterfeit chips using the ABI Sentry solution. It's a comprehensive test. All the data from a hundred dies is there. And the testing company concluded the dies were all faulty. They should have been discarded. Instead, they were set aside to be sold on the black market.'

Lily finished her dal and roti and nodded. 'So, the turnkey company is selling the counterfeit chips on the black market and making money.'

Dolly looked at Lily's plate. 'You're not having mutton?'

'Dieting,' Lily said, shortly. 'Dr Heng went on and on about my BMI and being obese.'

Dolly said, 'It's for your own good, Lil. Anyway, the turnkey company had closed for the day when we returned from the airport with the hard disk and had a chance to look at the data. I have an appointment with the top management tomorrow. Sushila Iyer may be the only corrupt employee, not the rest. We'll also talk to the mole, Toby Wong.'

'It seems to me Lionel Chu knew all along about the criminal syndicate selling counterfeit chips,' Lily observed. 'He never said anything when Charlie interviewed him because he knew he had betrayed Alan Lee. He had placed a mole in the turnkey company to nose out the corrupt employee and Sushila found out about Lionel snooping and the syndicate bribed Lionel to spy for them instead. He probably gave information about Alan's movements in Bali to the syndicate, but when Alan was murdered, Lionel was devastated. And killed himself?'

'We cannot rule out murder until the forensic team finishes its investigation,' Dolly said firmly. 'So far, Benny Ong, the pathologist, reported

Lionel did not have any defensive wounds as such. The doctor found it hard to draw his conclusions as the body was pretty smashed up. He said 60 per cent chance of there being no defensive wounds. Lionel would have fought with Sushila if she attempted to push him off the balcony. So, there would be visible defensive wounds. There was no skin under Lionel's fingernails either. No signs of a fight. But more tests are being done.'

Dolly finished the last of her mutton rogan josh. 'Unfortunately, Sushila Iyer has left the country.'

'H'm, Sushila would only flee if she killed Lionel and knew she was caught on CCTV,' Lily mused. She listened carefully as Dolly told her about the evidence of the CCTV tapes outside Lionel's hotel room.

Dolly said, 'Sushila could have left by the hotel's back entrance. My officers are getting more evidence from other CCTV cameras in the hotel. But why didn't she leave by the main door of the hotel? Yes, suspicious.'

'Wait,' Lily said, her brows creased. 'This is the Swiss Hotel. Isn't it connected to Raffles City mall? I remember seeing a lift lobby in the mall that has lifts going directly to the hotel. Maybe Sushila went to the mall?'

'I'll have my officers get footage from the mall.' Dolly nodded. 'But why would she go into the mall after killing Lionel?'

'Maybe she didn't kill Lionel,' Lily mused.

'Then why did she flee?' Dolly demanded.

Lily looked thoughtful. 'Sushila could have fled after she saw Lionel's dead body. Maybe she was in the mall, shopping or having a coffee. People in the mall would be talking of the suicide in the hotel next door. She may have gone to see who died and when she found out it was Lionel, Sushila ran. She knew she had checked him in with her credit card and CCTV cameras had caught her. She was a criminal selling faulty chips who had bribed Lionel so her gang could kill Alan Lee. She would run, Doll. If Sushila wanted to kill Lionel, she would hardly have used her credit card for his hotel stay.'

'Well, if it was murder, it wasn't premeditated. Sushila had no inkling Lionel was turning against the syndicate,' Dolly said. 'So, she treats him to a staycation, arrives to bribe him some more and then realizes he has become the enemy. And kills him. A decision made there and then.'

'Would she have been able to overpower him.' Lily looked sceptical. 'And why would she kill him? She hadn't ordered Alan Lee's murder. But yes, if he talked to the police, Lionel could finger her as a criminal, and she would go to jail. However, then it makes more sense to run than kill.'

Dolly told Lily they had to wait for more forensic evidence from the hotel balcony and CCTV footage of the mall before they could draw conclusions.

Dolly's face became reflective. 'Alan Lee had a premonition about his death so left the evidence with me. Why did he have to be a lone ranger and go after the syndicate? He should have left it to us.'

'Maybe he had a death wish.' Lily's romantic nature surfaced. 'We've heard how shattered he was when his girlfriend died, then his father died and his friend, the pilot, was implicated in the crash. He had nothing to live for except to nail the criminals he felt were responsible for his father's death. When Joy died, Doll, I lost the will to live, too. When you do, you take great risks, you don't care if you live or die.'

Dolly's mobile phone rang. She switched it on, listened intently, and switched it off. She gave a heavy sigh.

'That was Marty Sim from our Interpol branch. By the time our request to detain Sushila at Chennai Airport cleared India Interpol and reached the Chennai police officers, Sushila had cleared Immigration. We were too late. She could be on her way to a remote village in India. We won't be able to catch her. This is the problem involving Interpol and police from other countries on short notice in chasing a criminal. Too much red tape and bureaucracy to clear before we get help. Oh, Lily, this case keeps running away from me!'

'You always get there in the end, Doll,' Lily said, comfortingly. 'Slow and steady now.'

Dolly frowned as she drove back home. Could she detain any suspect at all? They were as slippery as eels, right from Bali. Dolly's face grew grim as she understood she faced a formidable foe.

Thursday, 23 May 2013

Singapore

19

At 10 a.m., Dolly and Charlie sat across the wide expanse of a desk from Sushila Iyer's supervisor, Peter Tan. Peter's round face was worried, and he kept tapping a pencil on his desk, nervously. He was scanning files on the computer from Alan Lee's hard disk and as he continued, his face grew increasingly pale.

Finally, he told the superintendent that South-East Asia Semiconductor Turnkey Solutions had many clients, Waferworld, being their biggest one in Singapore. The turnkey company did all the testing on their wafer chips and the only complaint so far had been from Alan Lee when Lexco returned some dies that had failed in the field.

Peter mopped the sweat from his forehead although the air-conditioner hummed steadily along. 'Alan Lee and I met in my office, and he asked whether we were applying the reliability test Waferworld devised for all dies before we pass or discard them. I called my testing supervisor in, and he swore all Waferworld dies had been subjected to the reliability test Waferworld wanted done. And only those passing this test were sent for packaging. The faulty dies were thrown away. We called in our electronic waste manager, Sushila Iyer, and she confirmed she had been getting rid of all faulty dies.'

Peter Tan peered into his computer and compressed his lips. He went on to say with an edge to his voice that Sushila had been lying in the light of the evidence on Alan Lee's hard disk. The disk contained an inventory of dies that were set aside by Sushila Iyer. Peter Tan said he respected the AI Sentry test findings, the dies had all been faulty.

He looked up at Dolly, his eyes bleak. 'Was Sushila selling these dies on the black market? There are reports of people doing that and that's how faulty dies enter a supply chain. Ms Iyer is missing, ASP Das. She did not report for work yesterday without any explanation and when we called her home, her mother said she had to fly urgently to Chennai to see to a sick relative. But it is company policy to apply for leave and she did not. Ms Iyer oversaw our electronic waste laboratory and handled the Waferworld account. Our liaison officer with Waferworld is an engineer called Toby Wong, he is waiting to talk to you in the conference room.'

Dolly nodded. 'Yes, we have reason to believe Ms Sushila Iyer was working for a counterfeit chip syndicate and stealing dies from here to sell on the black market.' She turned to her subordinate. 'Charlie, make a note of Ms Iyer's address and send a constable to see her mother in case she knows her daughter's whereabouts.'

Peter Tan leant forward, sweat pouring from his face. 'I can assure you I was unaware of Sushila's activities. She joined us five years ago with impeccable references. She was hardworking and I had no cause to suspect she was corrupt. Please believe me, ASP Das.'

Dolly narrowed her eyes. 'At present, we have no reason to believe any other employee was involved with the crime syndicate, but it's early days yet. May we talk to your engineer, Toby Wong, now?'

Toby Wong rose from a chair when Tan's secretary ushered Dolly and Charlie into a conference room. Dolly seated herself across from Toby, and Charlie took a seat next to her. Charlie whipped out his tablet from his briefcase and sat with fingers poised over it. Dolly looked with interest at the nervous and perspiring man in front of her.

'You worked for Ms Iyer?' Dolly asked, pleasantly, when Toby had sat down.

'Did Lionel take his own life or was he killed?' Toby Wong burst out, his hands gripping the edge of the table and his body tense. 'There was a snippet in the newspaper this morning about his death. It seems he fell from a high floor of a hotel in the business district.'

'Did you know Lionel Chu well?'

Toby looked around furtively although the doors were shut. He began to whisper, 'Lionel told me to keep an eye on Ms Sushila Iyer, he was on to her and now I fear for my life.' Toby's voice broke.

'Ms Iyer was your boss?'

'Yes, and I gave Lionel information on electronic waste and what happened to it here. Ms Iyer did not throw away all the partially functional dies. I know as I oversaw some of the work. I saw, say, 100 dies fail the reliability test, and she would tell me to discard only twenty of them.' Toby glanced at Charlie who was diligently typing away on his tablet, recording the interview.

'What happened to the other eighty dies?'

'I don't know but Lionel told me Ms Iyer was part of a syndicate that served the semiconductor black market, he had obtained this information from his boss, Alan Lee, the man who was murdered in Bali. Lionel told me Ms Iyer must be in contact with a chip broker who sold these dies to distributors on behalf of the syndicate. The dies were only partially functional but there are many distributors, especially in countries like China, India, Africa, Brazil, Indonesia, that would buy the semi-failed dies and sell them to retailers to place in products like phones that would malfunction with shorter than expected lifetimes. Since they were being sold in the Chinatowns and Little Indias of the world, there were no warrantee certificates involved. Then the syndicate would make profit from the original dies from respected companies like Waferworld. Lionel said he needed evidence and hired me to snoop through Ms Iyer's computer files.'

'*Hired* you? Did he pay you money?'

Toby Wong's face went red. 'He paid me around five hundred dollars a month for information. I think the money was given to him by Alan Lee since Lionel was by no means wealthy. Lionel asked me to give him some of the faulty dies Ms Iyer had set aside so Lee could send them for testing. Alan Lee was investigating the black market syndicate and he and Lionel were murdered. I am next,' Toby wailed dismally.

'We have no evidence yet that someone pushed Lionel Chu off the balcony of the Swiss Hotel. Anything else you can tell us?' Dolly asked.

'A couple of weeks before Alan was killed, I was snooping around outside Ms Iyer's office, and she was speaking on the phone. I eavesdropped on the conversation. She was talking to someone in Bali and was asking whether the factory there was recycling dies on schedule. I could not hear properly, but I heard her talk about a pub called Nightowl Bar. I reported this conversation to Lionel and the next thing I know Alan was killed in Bali.'

Dolly asked Toby Wong to accompany them to HQ to sign a statement as to what he knew about the crime syndicate. While clearly, Sushila Iyer was a member of the counterfeit chip syndicate and had probably been talking to Mark Latham on the phone, Dolly did not believe the manager, Peter Tan, and the rest of the turnkey company employees were corrupt. It was Toby's eavesdropping and his information about Bali and the Nightowl Bar that had rung Alan Lee's death knell.

The sky had darkened and there was the scent of rain in the air. The officers and Toby got into the squad car and Charlie drove to CID HQ.

* * *

After Toby Wong had signed a statement regarding his collaboration with Alan Lee and Lionel Chu to record Sushila Iyer's activities in the turnkey company, Dolly began writing her report. In the report, she noted Peter Tan's admission that from Alan Lee's evidence of faulty dies from his company, Ms Iyer was a likely criminal selling the dies on the black market. She then wrote an email to Supt Rachel Kelly of Interpol, appealing for her help locating Sushila Iyer in India. To the email, copied to DAC Nathan, Supt Sim and Supt Geraldine Ang, Dolly attached Toby Wong's signed statement regarding his surveillance of Ms Iyer and her own report detailing Peter Tan's view of what was going on in his company.

In half an hour, Dolly's phone rang and Rachel Kelly was on the line.

'ASP Das, I have read your report and Mr Wong's statement, and I concur with you that Sushila Iyer may have been a member of a counterfeit chip crime syndicate in Singapore. She was also the last person to see Lionel Chu alive. I understand the urgent need to arrest and question her. I am applying to HQ at Lyon for the issuance of a red notice for Sushila Iyer. As soon as the application is approved, I will let you and Supt Sim know. Supt Sim can then coordinate with NCB-Interpol, New Delhi to start the hunt for Sushila Iyer in India with the aim of an arrest. I'm still not recommending the search for Latham until you get me more evidence, ASP Das, on the chip recycling factory he headed in Bali or any connection with Sushila Iyer. I have read Mr Toby Wong's statement and while he says Ms Iyer may have been talking on the phone to someone in Bali, nowhere is Mark Latham's name mentioned. You will be happy to know that Interpol has issued a red notice for the arrest of Mohammed Hadyanto. Inspector Harjono of Bali CIA arrested Ali Khalil two days ago and he has confessed to murdering Mr Ramdin on Hadyanto's orders. NCB-Indonesia is coordinating with NCB-China in Beijing to hunt for Hadyanto.'

Dolly replaced the phone receiver in its cradle, her brow puckered. She bridled at the thought that lack of evidence on her part was stopping the investigation into Latham's whereabouts.

Her phone rang and it was Constable Petula Lee asking her to view some CCTV footage from the mall.

Dolly entered Techie Pet's office where Corporal Mok rose from a chair, his face excited. 'Madam,' he said, 'the other side of the hotel corridor leads to the mall via a second set of elevators. We have tracked Sushila Iyer taking that lift into the mall and having coffee at Coffee Club on the third floor of the mall. All by CCTV footage.'

'Good work,' Dolly said, enthusiastically. 'Let's see what you've got.' She seated herself next to Techie Pet and peered at the computer screen.

It showed the inside of a restaurant and Sushila Iyer sitting at a corner table having a tall glass of cold coffee and talking on her mobile phone. The time on the footage read 9.00 a.m.

'And when does she leave this restaurant?' Dolly asked.

Giving a nod, Techie Pet fast forwarded the tape. The time on the footage read 9.20 a.m. On the screen, the officers saw waiters huddled together, talking excitedly. Sushila had looked up from her coffee, she rose and went to the waiters, and talked to one of them. She returned to her table, gathered her handbag and left the restaurant. The time was 9.25 a.m. on the footage.

'We could track her going to the mall back entrance. There is no CCTV outside the mall,' Techie Pet said, 'but the disused lot at the back entrance of the mall is where Lionel Chu's body landed, Boss.'

Dolly gave a heavy sigh. 'Thanks, Techie, and you too, Mok. Good work. It seems to me Sushila Iyer went to have a coffee after her heated argument with Lionel. Then she heard about the suicide and went to look at the body. When she saw it was Lionel, she decided to flee. Yes, I am more inclined to believe in the suicide theory now. It's up to Interpol to find Sushila.'

Back at her office, Dolly called Charlie on the phone and reiterated her request to send a constable to speak to Sushila Iyer's mother at the address registered with the turnkey company. 'Charlie, send Constable Ranganathan and ask her to speak to the mother in Tamil, she may then open up about Sushila's whereabouts. The mother may know where Sushila has gone.'

She updated Charlie on Mok and Techie Pet's information and said, 'Joey did some sleuthing on Mark Latham. He only told me about it yesterday. It seems Latham worked in Singapore wafer fabs as an engineer and manager before switching to the job of a hotel manager. Interesting, eh?'

'Latham knows about chips and it's likely he is a crime syndicate member,' Charlie agreed.

20

Alice Lee had just met with her PI, Philip Wee. She now sat in her car as Samy drove her home, quietly processing the information her PI had fed her. Nelson had bought a new bungalow near Jelita, and his lady friend and her old mother were living with him there. Alice fumed, her lips setting in a thin line. She had to get the address of Nelson's new bungalow and see for herself who lived there. She had committed adultery for Nelson and while she had not pressed him in any way, she had dreamed of being the wife of Nelson Ong, Sauce King of Singapore. She knew Nelson had a roving eye, but they had been together for many years and now Nelson had become tired of her.

A dangerous light glimmered in Alice's eyes. Nelson had dared to cuckold her, and her father an ex-cabinet minister of Singapore. And where was all his money going? Why were his businesses being wound up? Was he going to declare himself bankrupt? According to the PI, most of his factories had closed or were going to shut down.

At 39, Primrose Crescent, Alice found her lawyer, Selvaraj, waiting for her. He had been contacted by Alan Lee's lawyer, Jonas Ellis, who, on the instructions of Lester Chong, was offering a million dollars from Alan Lee's estate for Alice to leave 39, Primrose Crescent quietly. Otherwise, there would be a court case with bad publicity which he was sure Alice wanted to avoid.

'I will have a word with Lester and let you know my decision next week, Selva.'

Alice climbed up the stairs and entered her bedroom. She suddenly felt tired of life, holding grudges, and clinging on to a house. She looked around her well-decorated room and allowed some tears to fall. She had hated so many people, her stepmother, her husband, her stepdaughter, but she had cared for Nelson. In her barren life, devoid of love and sympathy, she had mistaken his fling with her for the real thing and now she was left sitting on the ashes of her romance.

Alice wiped away her tears. She was not Justin Chua's daughter for nothing, she would hunt down Nelson's lover and make a scene whether she liked it or not. Alice removed her wig and went to the bathroom to soak in the hot tub.

* * *

Dolly looked up at a knock on her office door. Charlie was there with a laptop in his hands.

'Madam, we searched Lionel Chu's apartment and investigated his bank accounts. There are two bank accounts with $100,000 in each, paid from Sushila Iyer's bank account. Sushila Iyer has moved most of her money to Chennai banks, so it is likely she was poised to flee Singapore at some point in time.'

Dolly sighed. 'Okay, good work, Charlie. This is proof Lionel Chu was being bribed by the crime syndicate. What about his mobile phone?'

'He was in touch with Alan Lee frequently until Lee's murder and with Toby Wong. But there are no records of any calls from or to Sushila Iyer. It is likely he used a burner phone for those conversations. There is a phone number in Little India he called on the days before his death. We are looking into the owner of that number. I have some more information, madam. Mok was surfing through Lionel Chu's laptop we retrieved from the room at the Swiss Hotel. You must look at an email he received, which is in his Gmail Inbox, madam.'

Charlie plugged in Lionel's laptop and tapped keys to access the email inbox. He opened an email and nodded to Dolly, who began reading the message.

Dear Lionel,

Good work done on investigating the Bali angle. I must visit the Nightowl Bar to find out if the proprietor is mixed up in this racket. Thanks for suggesting the Beachcombers

Hotel where your parents celebrated their twentieth wedding anniversary. We need to find the masterminds before we go to the police. Sushila is working with someone, she must have a broker who sells the dies for her. Shadowing Sushila is an option you may want to explore. Sushila, the broker, are all small fries in this racket. Who are the masterminds? I may have to inform the police as they have better resources to sniff out the masterminds.

Once we have got to the bottom of this racket and inform the police, we will be free. I loved my father and cared about Rosvinder. I want to see justice done. When I met you and learnt that your grandmother's pacemaker had also malfunctioned due to faulty chips, I found my ally in you. Remember your grandmother, Lionel, she needs to be avenged. There is a thriving counterfeit chip syndicate in Singapore, and we must stop the racketeers from taking people's lives.

I have felt of late that money means a lot to you. You have so many dreams of doing a master's in engineering in America and settling with a job there. And you will. But you must be patient and earn the money that will open the gateway to the west. And you must help me avenge our relatives' deaths and see the syndicate masterminds behind bars. See you, soon.

Alan

Dolly was gazing at the message, frowning. She nodded, slowly.

'Alan says Lionel had become money minded. We have found out from Lionel's bank accounts Sushila bribed him $200,000. And Lionel went over to the enemy's side. He was impatient to be gone from Singapore to America and he needed money to do that. The syndicate got Lionel to recommend the Beachcombers Hotel to Alan because Mark Latham was the manager there and could arrange Lee's murder. When Alan was killed, Lionel probably realized he had aided the syndicate in the killing by recommending the hotel. It is possible he had not realized the syndicate was ruthless enough to kill people in cold blood. He was filled with remorse. When Sushila offered him more money in the hotel balcony, he not only rejected the offer, but told her he was ashamed of what he had done, and they quarrelled. We have the testimony of the Korean hotel guest. Anything from the forensic team, Charlie? They processed the hotel room yesterday.'

Charlie shook his head. 'I talked to Jason Teo from the forensic team and he told me that there were no marks on the wall underneath the balcony rail that implied a body was being pushed over. There are, however, two prints on the wall that could be from shoes. There are smudges of shoe polish and Teo is processing Lionel's shoes. If the polish is from his shoes, madam, then it could have got there when he climbed over the wall to jump off the balcony.

The preliminary forensic findings from the clothes Lionel wore show no traces from another person. No fibres, say, from Sushila's clothing. And you would expect that if they had a scuffle.'

Dolly nodded, appreciatively. 'Good thinking. No foreign DNA on either Lionel's clothes or Lionel?'

Charlie said, 'Not yet, madam. The forensic officers are still working on the clothing and shoes.'

Dolly sighed. 'It's pointing to a suicide, then. In my opinion, the Korean guest's testimony and Sushila's movements after she left Lionel's room support the fact that he probably took his own life. Those words he spoke to himself in the balcony. It's such a pity the Korean man did not notice the time. If it was after 8.35 a.m., Sushila had already left the room.'

'It's a tight window of time, though, madam,' Charlie said. 'Sushila leaves the room at 8.35 a.m. and Shamsher, the waiter, comes with the coffee at 8.45 a.m. So that gives Lionel ten minutes on the balcony before he jumps.'

'If people bent on taking their own lives think too much, they will back out of doing so, Charlie,' Dolly mused. 'Lionel was filled with regret at what he had done, he jumped from the balcony on the spur of the moment and based on his emotional state. You told me you found Lionel nervy and edgy when you interviewed him. He was badly affected by Alan's murder.'

'Lionel talking on the balcony to himself—how does that fit in with murder, madam?' Charlie was curious.

Dolly said, thoughtfully, 'Well, from the CCTV footage, Sushila arrives in the room at 8.05 a.m. Lionel and Sushila start arguing and take their argument outside into the balcony. At 8.15 a.m., the Korean guest comes into his balcony and overhears the argument. Lionel and Sushila probably go inside soon, say before 8.25 a.m.? The Korean guest has also gone inside and is dressing but he says he comes out into the balcony again. He could not tell us exactly when he came out on the balcony the second time. What if it was 8.30 a.m.? He hears Lionel talking to himself. Now, it could be Sushila is still inside the room and listening to Lionel. She's just not on the balcony. Then the phone in his room rings and the Korean guest goes inside. Sushila comes out and pushes Lionel over the balcony. And leaves at 8.35 a.m. You're right, Charlie. The window of time for the murder is even tighter than the suicide. And why would Sushila go to have a coffee right after killing Lionel? She would have gone straight to the airport and flown. But we'll gather evidence by the book. We'll wait for the full forensic report on the balcony and Lionel's clothes and shoes. If there's no forensic findings to indicate it's a murder, then Lionel took his own life. What about Sushila Iyer's Singapore home? Did you send a constable there?'

Charlie nodded, a glint in his eyes. 'Yes. Sushila lives in the same apartment complex as your family, madam, the Silver Springs Condo. I sent Constable Revathi Ranganathan there. But Sushila's mother was frightened and did not say anything of value. Just that she does not know the whereabouts of her daughter. She clammed up, madam, would not say anything more and shut the door in Constable Ranganathan's face.'

Dolly's eyes sparkled. 'Small world, Sushila living next door to my mother. Text me her unit number and I'll see if I can get the mother to talk when I visit my family there this evening. Good work, Charlie!'

* * *

Dolly and Superintendent Geraldine Ang entered DAC John Nathan's office. He motioned them to be seated and waited for Dolly's report.

Dolly gave her update, clearly and concisely. She was a good speaker. She talked about Alan Lee's letter to her from Bali, the contents of the hard disk, the interviews with the turnkey company personnel and suggestive evidence of Lionel being bribed by the crime syndicate and experiencing enough remorse for him to take his own life. She elaborated on the murder theory explaining the window of time to commit the murder was too tight, Sushila's movements after leaving Lionel's room did not suggest panic and a desire to flee, and the forensic team had failed to find any evidence of a struggle between Lionel and Sushila. According to the pathologist, there were no defensive wounds on Lionel supporting the idea of a struggle before he fell to his death. When she had finished talking, she saw her supervisor, Supt Ang give an appreciative smile.

'Good work, ASP Das,' Supt Ang said. 'Sushila Iyer probably heard of Lionel's suicide while drinking coffee in the mall and went to see the body. Then, knowing she would become part of a police inquiry, and being a criminal, she fled. Pending final results from the forensic team, we can conclude Lionel's death is a suicide. According to the guest next door, he was conscience-stricken, and Alan Lee suspected him of betrayal. He, therefore, did not give the hard disk to Lionel Chu and hid it in the airport locker and sent you a letter to retrieve it. This hard disk is incriminating for both Sushila Iyer and the syndicate, it is hard evidence they were selling faulty dies on the black market. Toby Wong will be an important witness in Sushila Iyer's trial.'

Dolly looked sad. 'If we find Sushila Iyer, ma'am. She has escaped to India. It will be difficult to find her in a country as large as India. The Chennai police officers will be searching for her as soon as the red notice is issued.'

Nathan sighed. 'Iyer's flight is unfortunate, but ASP Das, you and your team did a good job on the Lionel Chu death investigation. We can close the Lionel Chu case as soon as the final forensic results are in favour of a suicide.'

Dolly said, 'Sir, about the Alan Lee murder case. We need to question the Bali hotel manager, Mark Latham. He had a chip recycling factory near Ubud and has absconded. It is highly likely he was involved in Alan Lee's murder. He is probably a member of the criminal syndicate. Latham has escaped to Hong Kong and Interpol refuses to search for him. Supt Rachel Kelly says we don't have enough evidence to show Latham's complicity in Alan Lee's murder and that Latham has an impeccable record with no criminal history. She refuses to help. Sir, if you could talk to her superior?'

Nathan nodded. 'Okay, I will have a word with Chief Supt Derek Randall at IGCI. Ms Kelly talked to me as well. The problem is that the Pujung factory was just an empty shed, no evidence there of any chips whatsoever. I will see what I can do. You are dismissed, ASP Das. Supt Ang, I need to have some words with you about the Redhill case.'

After Dolly returned to her office, she set to work, drafting out an appeal to Chief Supt Derek Randall of Interpol to mount a search for Mark Latham in Hong Kong.

Friday, 24 May 2013

Singapore

21

The late afternoon sun streamed into her office as Dolly rifled through reports. Mok entered the office after a diffident knock and handed a report to Dolly.

'Madam, here is Techie's report on the hard disk retrieved from Mark Latham's bungalow. We looked at deleted emails and many were deleted from a Singapore IP address. The address is in Sushila Iyer's name, madam. Latham and Iyer knew each other. Techie also found evidence of Skype calls to a Singapore number. Again, that phone number is registered to Sushila Iyer.'

Dolly's face brightened. 'Good job, Adrian, and Techie, too. We can pressure Interpol to locate Latham in Hong Kong. There is now a connection between Sushila Iyer and Mark Latham. This is what Supt Kelly wanted to initiate the search for Latham. I will call her as soon as Techie writes up a report on what she found from Latham's hard disk.'

After Mok left, Dolly made some calls to Supt Ang and DAC Nathan updating them on the newest evidence and was happy to hear DAC Nathan assure her that he would put serious pressure on Interpol to locate Latham. Dolly also called Inspector Harjono and congratulated him on arresting Ali Khalil. As his merry laugh came on the line, Dolly smiled and promised to send him Latham's hard disk by courier. Dolly left CID HQ in a happy frame of mind.

* * *

Dolly decided to visit her mother at Silver Springs and drove there after work. She used Lily's spare key to enter her mother's Silver Springs Condominium apartment and since it was 9 p.m., did not expect Uma to be up. She was, therefore, surprised to see not only Uma awake and chattering away, but surrounded by a crowd of people in the comfortable living hall of her apartment. Through a door, she could see the dining room where the chandelier shone brightly on the dining table laid with a buffet supper.

Lily came forward, smiling. 'We're having a small party to celebrate Vernon and Angie's third wedding anniversary.'

Angie, a blonde-haired, Chinese girl with a nose ring, sat near Uma, her face pale, a tired smile on her face. Vernon strutted protectively near her, his squint prominent, his face worried.

'Congratulations, Vernon and Angie!' Dolly said, sincerely.

Frankie, Lily's husband, who had been ladling prawn curry on to his plate from the buffet table, came into the living hall. He smiled at Dolly. 'Joey overseas?'

Dolly's face darkened and a sad light burnt in her eyes. 'Joey was supposed to go to Malacca next week, but he got an urgent phone call and left this afternoon.' She glanced surreptitiously at her sister, who was looking speculatively at her. She gave a slight nod, a signal between the sisters that at some point they had to talk alone.

'Doll, you must be hungry.' Lily began fussing over her sister. 'I've made prawn in coconut curry, pea pulao rice, fish croquettes and chicken chettinad curry. Do tuck in.'

Dolly began helping herself from the buffet. When she returned to the living room, Vernon looked downcast, Angie was crying softly while Lily tried to comfort her assistant and his wife.

'What happened?' Dolly demanded. 'This is a happy occasion, why the tears?'

Vernon's face was pale. 'Angie is working as a housemaid and today was her first day at work. We need the money, madam. But employers work you hard, cleaning toilets, sweeping, and mopping floors. She doesn't know if she can carry on.'

Dolly sat down on a sofa and mixed her rice with the curry on her plate. She nodded. 'A maid's job is hard work.' She looked around. 'Where are the babies, Molly and Ben?'

'Silly Belly!' Uma cackled and everyone except Lily laughed.

'Stop it, Mummy! I'm warning you.' Lily glared at her mother before turning to her sister. 'They are asleep in one of the bedrooms. Girlie is minding them.' Lily turned to Angie. 'Give it another week, Angie. You can always come back to work for me at my café. In fact, Ashikin says you cook better Malay food than Vernon, and she misses you.'

Angie sniffed, dolefully. 'Your pay not enough, Mrs D, sorry. I must work hard and take Panadol later. Not easy to clean one home and make a lot of money from that. I got lucky, Mrs D. My agent get me job at millionaire Nelson Ong's house. I clean every day for 2K a month. Hard work to clean bungalow. But good money. Only one house so much money, leaves me free to do another house when I am done there. I see how, Mrs D. If my leg pain too much, I switch to waitressing in a coffeeshop.'

Dolly exclaimed, 'Nelson Ong! Why, he is Alice Lee's boyfriend. Alice is the stepmother of the man who was murdered in Bali.'

Angie frowned. 'Madam, not true. Mr Ong live-in with a Caucasian lady. Her mother lives with them, too. A maid takes care of the old lady, and I will clean. I had interview with Caucasian lady yesterday already. She seldom home, have high-power job somewhere.'

'Well, well. That is useful information. Keep your eyes open when you work there, Angie.' Dolly ate more of her pulao rice and then looked around. She told everyone of Lionel Chu's death and Sushila Iyer's flight to India.

'Sushila Iyer.' Vernon was frowning in concentration. 'A Sushila Iyer lives in a studio flat in Block A, I think on the tenth floor, Supt.'

Lily looked at Dolly. 'We live in a small world, Doll. Two families connected to your case live in our condo complex. Linda Lee and Sushila Iyer.' Her eyes fixed on Vernon, who was on the verge of bursting out with some news. 'What is it, V?'

'Sushila Iyer is Patrick Singh's lover. Patrick Singh is the husband of Linda Lee, sister of Alan Lee,' Vernon mumbled.

Dolly's breath came out in a hiss. 'We know Sushila lives here and I even went to talk to her mother last night. But how do you know about Patrick Singh, V?'

'Sushila Iyer is our good customer. She orders delivery and I take the food to her unit. Patrick Singh is nearly always there. They are cuddling and all. It's surprising his wife doesn't know, them staying in the same complex. Different blocks.'

'What happened when you talked to Sushila's mother?' Lily asked Dolly, curiously.

Dolly shook her head. 'No one answered the door last night. My constable had come to talk to her earlier. The mother was frightened and did not say much. Shut the door in my constable's face.'

'Scared of the police,' Uma observed.

'Maybe she will talk to me,' Lily mused. She turned to Vernon. 'If she orders our food, I will take it up to her, V.'

Dolly warned, 'Don't meddle, Lil. This is an international case. Interpol has issued a red notice for Sushila's arrest.' She continued, 'Sushila only moved here in the last year, she used to live on Balestier Road before. Maybe she moved to Silver Springs to be near her lover, Patrick. That was useful information, Vernon. Thanks.'

Dolly glanced at her watch, wiped her mouth with a napkin and rose from the sofa. 'That was a delicious dinner. I will push off now. I need to tidy our condo a bit, Ash and Amita make a mess every day.' Dolly smiled as Lily and Uma both opened their mouths. 'Yes, yes, Ash will pay you a short visit soon, don't worry. He is in love so no time for Dida and Mashi.' She giggled.

'We can have lunch together tomorrow?' Lily suggested, knowing her sister was eager to confide in her. She deduced rightly it had to do with Joey.

Dolly nodded, pecked her mother on the cheek and left the flat. Soon, she was on her way home with Joey on her mind.

Saturday, 25 May 2013

Singapore

22

Pradeep Chopra's eyes were red rimmed from lack of sleep. He looked at his watch, soon he had to go to the library to hunt for research journals he needed to look up for his lectures next week. Blearily, he fried omelettes in the kitchen. He could hear Rina and Nina quarrelling in the living hall. All they did was fight with each other nowadays, he thought morosely. Rina was following her sister into a rebellious phase. What could he do? He keenly felt a father's emotional inadequacy. If only Rosie were here.

At his call, the girls trooped into the dining hall, still bickering with each other. They seated themselves and began to eat.

'Teacher said I need physics tuition, or I will fail.' Sixteen-year-old Nina bit fiercely into her omelette and flinched. 'Papa, you've sprinkled sugar on the egg instead of salt.'

'It still tastes nicer than *your* omelettes,' Thirteen-year-old Rina cut in, her large eyes glaring at her sister.

'Look, sorry, okay?' Pradeep turned to his elder daughter. 'Sweetheart, I will tutor you as much as I can in physics. We cannot afford a private tutor.'

'Then I will fail,' Nina said, uncompromisingly. She bit into her toast and grimaced. It was half-burnt.

'What? You don't think I can improve your physics grade? I'm an electrical engineer, Nina.' Pradeep sighed as Nina shrugged.

Rina piped up. 'Teacher said I can take singing lessons. She said my voice is sweet. I think the lessons cost twenty dollars an hour, two days a week, one hour each day, Papa.'

Nina laughed out loud. 'You have a *sweet* voice? Your teacher must be tone deaf!'

'Girls finish your breakfast and get ready for school,' Pradeep said, sternly. 'And Nina, you're a big girl now. Start taking turns to make breakfast, okay?' His lips thinned as Nina glared at him.

He turned to his younger daughter. 'Rina, sorry, honey, we can't afford your singing lessons. Have you two finished? You'll be late for your co-curricular activities at school. You know you enjoy them, so get going. Nina, I've kept some money in your backpack. Take Rina with you and have lunch at McDonald's, okay? I'm meeting someone for lunch.'

When his daughters had noisily left to walk the few yards to the neighbouring school, Pradeep sat down on the sofa and buried his head in his hands. He had little money left in his savings account and his salary barely ran the house. He looked with hatred at the court summons lying on the low glass table.

His lips twisted and his eyes were on fire. But after some time, his eyes dulled, and his shoulders drooped. With Alan gone, who would save him from the wrath of Alice Lee?

He wondered whether the woman had one ounce of compassion in her. Would it be worthwhile to appeal to her about his young children and ask her to withdraw the case? He remembered Linda Lee's words, 'Our Steppie is a dragon with a capital D.' But what harm could it do to appeal to Alice's finer senses? It could not make matters worse.

Pradeep nodded to himself and rose from the sofa to go into the kitchen to eat his breakfast and then wash the dirty dishes. He was looking forward to his lunch date. At least, there was someone he could unburden his worries to.

* * *

Alice Lee felt nervous driving for the first time in two years. Her mission was secretive, and she could not allow Samy, her chauffeur, to know she was going to spy on her lover's newly bought bungalow. *The shame.* She had run some errands in the morning and then given Samy the day off.

An irate motorist honked at her, and Alice gave him a glare as he whizzed by. After all, she was quietly driving along the left lane, all the other motorists had to do was regard her as a new driver. Thank god the car is automatic, she thought, she had been trained on a stick-shift car and had hated driving from that time.

Alice took the turning from Holland Road into Jalan Jelita and then on to Jalan Istimewa, which was a beautiful tree-lined cul-de-sac. She parked some distance from the corner bungalow. Alice took out a binocular from her capacious handbag and focused on the house. It was a single-storied building with a red-tiled roof and a pretty garden blooming with flowers fronting a wide porch. Plants hung from the porch ceiling and a wicker chair and table stood in the veranda.

Alice hid behind the wheel even though she had donned dark glasses. A young Chinese woman with blonde hair and a nose-ring passed the car, looking at her curiously. Alice watched the blonde woman enter the gate of Nelson's bungalow and ring the front doorbell. Who was she? Maybe a cleaner, Alice mused, the girl wore dirty jeans and a soiled T-shirt.

Alice stiffened. A shapely dark-haired woman in a smart jacket and skirt, came out of the front door, letting in the cleaner at the same time. She paused to speak to someone inside before walking to the car parked in the porch. She put on sunglasses and as Alice watched through her binoculars, the woman's face came into focus. Why, she was Caucasian with brown hair and very fair skin. *Not Eurasian.* Alice noticed with a pang that the woman was strikingly beautiful. She began rummaging on the floor of the car as the Caucasian woman's car passed hers.

Then Alice started up her car, reversed clumsily in the narrow lane and began following the white Mazda the woman was driving. After twenty minutes of weaving in and out of traffic, the cars finally snaked into Holland Road. They passed the Gleneagles Hospital and then the Mazda slowed down and passed through the gates of an imposing building. Alice's eyes widened. Was this where Nelson's new mistress worked? Frowning ferociously, Alice Lee U-turned, and began to drive back along Holland Road towards Pandan Valley, her mind in chaos.

When she stopped at the gate of 39, Primrose Crescent, her mobile phone beeped and she looked at a text message from her PI, Phil Wee.

Nelson's plane just left Changi. He will be in China for two days.

Alice nodded grimly before honking impatiently for Yusuf to open the gate.

* * *

While waiting for Dolly to arrive, Lily sat in a small cosy booth of a restaurant called Saffron Kitchen in Jurong, munching papadum. Both sisters enjoyed eating the food at the North Indian restaurant and Dolly had agreed to meet Lily there.

Lily looked at her phone and began browsing the web. On hearing a familiar voice, she looked up. At the opposite end of the restaurant, at a corner table, a couple were rising to leave. Lily's eyes widened. The woman was Linda Lee and the way she glanced at the man holding on to her waist, left Lily in little doubt that he was her lover. Lily placed the menu card in front of her face and peered out from behind it. With an arm around her waist, the man guided Linda towards the door. Soon, they had left the restaurant. Lily laid the menu card down, her brows puckered. So, Linda Lee was being as unfaithful as her husband.

Dolly soon came in, perspiration beading her forehead, it was a hot day outside. She sank into the padded seat opposite Lily and smiled while wiping away the perspiration with a tissue.

'Shall we order?' Lily asked. 'I think I'll have the butter chicken thali.'

Dolly nodded. 'Same.'

When the waiter arrived, Lily said, 'Two butter chicken thalis and two teh tarik, thanks!'

The steaming tea soon arrived and sipping it, Lily looked at her older sister. 'What's up, Doll?'

Dolly took a sip of her tea and sighed. 'It's Joey. He goes to Malacca every month. He says it's clients, but every month, Lily?'

Lily sipped her tea and nodded. 'A bit suspicious for a PI to go to one place regularly. But surely, you don't suspect Joey of cheating on you? Having a mistress?' Lily laughed at the absurdity of the notion knowing her sister was happily married. On seeing Dolly's dark face, she amended, 'Or do you?'

The waiter came with the thalis and for a time the sisters concentrated on their food. Dolly dipped a piece of naan bread into the butter chicken gravy and ate it. She looked miserably around before she said, 'I don't know what to think, Lil. He has a shifty look when he mentions Malacca.'

'How is your love life?' Lily was practical. She doled the butter chicken on to the biryani and mixed it before beginning to eat.

Dolly started on the biryani rice on her plate and said, 'Good. He is loving and we have a healthy sex life.' She munched for a while before saying, 'He is thoughtful, buys me gifts and flowers whenever he can. But then, Pritam and I appeared to have a good relationship when he was carrying on with Cheryl. Maybe I am being paranoid. It's just that I don't think Joey goes to Malacca on business. Here, Lil, have the rest of my naan bread. This thali has too much carbohydrates, rice *and* bread. I've got to watch my weight.'

Lily pushed her plate towards her sister and when Dolly had put the piece of bread on it, pulled it back to her. She concentrated on finishing her biryani rice before starting on the naan bread. She said thoughtfully, 'Only one way to find out what's going on. Ask him.'

Dolly chewed a piece of chicken, swallowed it and said, '*He* says he is going on business. If I question that, he will think I'm suspicious of him. We'll quarrel.' She took a sip of her tea.

Lily sighed. 'Honesty between partners is important. Two years ago, I nearly lost Frankie. He had a crush on his client, Nancy, and it was Joey who alerted me. If I had not agreed to adopt Molly, I would have lost him to Nancy. His OCD is so much better now. We talk things out. I think you need to talk about Malacca with Joey.' Lily dipped a piece of the naan bread into the butter chicken gravy and began eating it.

Dolly nodded. 'Yes, I believe you're right. Even if he gets angry, I need to confront him. Do you think he has a mistress?'

Lily laughed. 'No! One just has to look at him to know how much he loves you. The *way* he looks at you.' When her sister smiled and looked happier, Lily told Dolly in an excited tone about Linda Lee and her mysterious beau.

'Interesting,' Dolly said. 'Chinese?'

'No, the man was Indian,' Lily replied. 'Short, dark with a receding hairline. He was holding on to her waist and all.' Lily took a sip of the tea.

'No wonder Singapore's divorce rates are going up. Every second person is having an affair,' Dolly commented while drinking her tea.

The sisters took ten more minutes to finish their food before Lily glanced around the restaurant and looked at her watch. 'Ashikin leaves the restaurant at 1.30 p.m., and I need to return, Doll. There's only V working at the café, and it can get crowded at lunchtime. Don't worry about Joey, Doll, but do try to talk to him.'

'You haven't even drunk half of your tea!' Dolly protested.

'Finish it for me, Doll.' Lily gathered up her handbag, gave a cheery wave and was gone out of the door.

Dolly sipped Lily's tea slowly as she mulled over Joey. After fifteen minutes, she paid the bill and was in her car driving to CID HQ.

* * *

Della Pang looked in her compact mirror and outlined her lips with lip-liner. She and Etienne were sitting outside a café in the business district sipping cappuccino. Once she had applied the finishing touches to her make-up, Della looked speculatively at Etienne.

'So, you had a family meeting with the lawyer. What did you learn, Tien?'

Etienne looked shifty. 'Bro's cousin, Lester Chong, was there. You know, the Junior Transport Minister. He is the will's executor. Bro wanted Lester to sell the Primrose Crescent bungalow and then divide the proceeds into three trust funds in the names of Duleep, Natasha, and myself. I get to access my trust fund when I turn thirty, but before that, if I need money for overseas studies or something like that, I can apply to Lester to advance me money from the trust.'

Della blinked her beautiful light eyes. 'You only get the money from the house when you're *thirty*?' Her voice had become a trifle shrill, and a diner glanced at her from the next table. 'What about Alan's money?' She took an agitated sip of her coffee.

'He left his money for a foundation and quite a lot to Emily Gan.' On seeing the incomprehension on Della's face, Etienne explained, 'Emily is our neighbour. Bro was engaged to be married to her older sister, Selena. But Selena and Emily were in a car crash and Selena died. Emily is paralysed from the waist down. Bro was taking care of Emily's future needs. He was good that way.'

'Lucky Emily!' Della's lips twisted.

'She's disabled, Della!' Etienne protested before noting his girlfriend's red face. He sipped his coffee before saying anxiously, 'My grandmother has left my mother money. I believe it is around ten million dollars.'

Della looked deceptively at Etienne. 'So, you have mentioned. But your mother is alive and will probably use the money to buy a house now that she will be evicted from her husband's bungalow.'

'I can ask her for some money.'

Della finished her coffee and laughed. 'For what? Our wedding?' She glanced at her watch. 'There goes the time, and I must be at Boat Quay for a photo-shoot. See to the bill will you, darling? I'll see you at Cam's party tonight, yeah? Then we'll have a long chat and cuddles.' She gave a tinkling laugh as she gathered her handbag and rose from her chair.

Etienne looked after Della's retreating figure, a sullen expression on his face. He slowly sipped his coffee. There was no pleasing Della, he thought. He began hatching schemes to persuade his mother to raise his monthly pocket allowance of two thousand dollars.

A cool wind whipped up and Etienne hurriedly paid the bill and stepped into the roadside to flag down a cab.

23

The stars were out in the dark sky and a soft breeze blew dead leaves down the walkways of Silver Springs Condominium. At Lily's Kitchen, Lily was talking to her restaurant partner, Ashikin Ali, about their children and what mischief they made. Ashikin, dressed in a dark blue tudung and a matching baju kurung, had increased Lily's profits at the café with her delicious Malay food. The café, though called Lily's Kitchen, sold both North Indian and Malay food.

Vernon rushed in from couriering some dinner specials, his face excited. 'I was passing in the corridor outside her unit and Sushila Iyer's mother called out to me, Mrs D. She said her daughter left for Chennai and her daughter's boyfriend stopped bringing her food. She ordered our veggie dinner special.'

Lily's face grew excited, and her large eyes snapped with conjecture. She yearned to help Dolly crack the counterfeit chip gang case and Sushila Iyer was the strongest lead so far. She decided to ignore her sister's advice of not to 'meddle' in her case. 'I'll take up her order, V. Pack it for me, please. I'll have a chat with her. Maybe she knows where Sushila is hiding in Chennai.' She turned to Ashikin, who smiled.

'You go on ahead, Lily. You are so clever. Helping your sister solve crimes. I am sure you crack this one, too.' Ashikin laughed, her double chins wobbling. 'I will look after the café, no worries.'

Lily smiled her thanks and headed out of her café with the courier bag Vernon had packed. She walked towards Block A, passing the crowded swimming pool, with sounds of laughter coming from children splashing in the wading pools. Lily took the lift in Block A to the tenth floor.

After repeated knocking, the door to a corner studio unit in Block A Silver Springs Condominium was opened cautiously by a wizened, bent old woman in a housecoat.

'Madam, your food delivery,' Lily said, cheerfully, 'from Lily's Kitchen. I am Lily Das.' Lily gave her most dazzling smile.

The old woman peered at her, myopically, before giving a toothless smile. 'Oh, so *you* cook those tasty dishes. Come in, come in.'

Lily entered the small studio and looked around. There was a sofa, which she assumed folded up as a double bed, a glass-topped table, a TV playing a Tamil serial, two padded chairs and the kitchenette at the back. There was a small dining table for two, near the kitchen, where Lily placed the delivery bag and began taking out the microwaveable boxes.

'Auntie, have you got a microwave oven? If you eat now, the food will be piping hot.'

The old woman nodded. 'Yes, yes, there is a microwave oven. I will eat later after I have prayed. How much do I owe you?'

'Twelve dollars, Auntie.' Lily smiled and spied in one corner incense sticks burning in front of photos and images of deities.

'Sit down, sit down,' ordered the old woman. 'I will get you the money.'

Later, after she had paid for the food, Mrs Iyer confided that she and her husband had followed their daughter, Sushila to Singapore. Her daughter excelled in her studies in Chennai and she wanted to study and work in Singapore and earn lots of money. Her father put up the money for her to study at a Singapore university and when she graduated and got a job, she paid back her dad. When Mr Iyer fell ill, said his wife, Sushila brought her parents to Singapore on long-term visit passes, she had obtained her permanent residency by then. Mrs Iyer added garrulously, 'Sushi took her dad to good doctors here and he was fine for a while. He died a year ago, and Sushila moved us to this unit. But she suddenly left for Chennai. Wouldn't say why. She has a boyfriend, you know, Patrick. I am hoping for a marriage soon.'

Lily did not have the heart to tell Mrs Iyer that Patrick Singh was a married man with two children. She asked instead, 'So your daughter is in Chennai? Do you have a house there?'

Mrs Iyer nodded. 'A flat in Besant Nagar in my name. It's near Elliott Beach, on the coast of the Bay of Bengal. It's a beautiful luxury flat. We own two properties. My late husband inherited land and a large house from his father in a village far from Chennai. That's our holiday home. We have a caretaker looking after that property. But you know, I keep calling my Besant Nagar home landline. No one answers. I don't know why Sushi is not taking my calls.'

'And your name is?' Lily asked, sweetly.

'Why, you *are* a busybody.' The old lady smiled, good-naturedly. 'My name is Vijayalakshmi Iyer, dear. My family call me Viji.'

She continued, 'Sushi suddenly said she had to leave for Chennai, and later she would send for me. It was very fishy. I try not to interfere in my daughter's life, but I know she was stressed at work. But she earned good money. She took Dad and me on a tour of Europe, her dad always wanted to see the Swiss mountains. Patrick was taking care of me for the last two days but today he did not come at all. So, when I saw Vernon pass down the corridor, I called out to him. I have not had anything much to eat the whole day. Sushi's boss at work was calling asking her whereabouts. I had to make up a story of a relative suddenly falling ill. And a policewoman came to ask about Sushi. I closed the door in her face. We don't like the police in Tamil Nadu, big bullies they are. I wonder why Sushi left in that way?'

'This condo rent must be around $3000 a month,' Lily said, conversationally, glancing around the room. She was eager to be gone and text Sushila's mother's name and the locality in Chennai where she owned a flat, to her sister.

'Yes, yes, my daughter earns good money,' the old woman mumbled.

Seeing the woman looking longingly at the food on the table, Lily got to her feet. 'Thank you, Auntie.' She gave a business card to Mrs Iyer. 'Any time you need a food delivery, just call the number. Good night, Auntie, enjoy your dinner.'

Lily smiled and exited the condo unit while Mrs Iyer shuffled to the prayer corner. Lily was deep in thought. Sushila Iyer indeed had a good income for Lily had recognized a landscape painting hanging on the wall painted by a famous Singaporean artist, it was easily priced at $50,000.

'A good profit from the counterfeit chip black market,' Lily muttered to herself as she walked along the corridor towards the lifts. Soon, she was texting Dolly Sushila's Chennai address and her mother's name. Sushila might be holed up there, Lily wrote on the phone. She smiled as her sister texted her thanks back.

Sunday, 26 May 2013

Singapore

24

Yusuf, the gardener at 39, Primrose Crescent, was busy stirring a pot of beef rendang on the small gas burner in his little kitchen on one side of the shed that served as his quarters. He blearily glanced at the clock near the window of the tin contraption. It read 7.45 p.m. Yusuf sighed. Alan would come to his humble quarters to share his dinner. He loved rendang with a vengeance. Now he was gone forever.

Yusuf's eyes teared up. Alan had promised to take care of him in his old age. Give him a pension and retire him to a room rental in Geylang. Now, everything had changed. He doubted Alice Lee, with her miserly ways, would give him a single cent. Yusuf wiped his perspiring face with a towel and stirred the rice on the second burner. It was when he sat down to eat that the shouting started. It was so loud that Yusuf flinched. Alice Lee and her son were going at it hammer and tongs.

In the dining room of the bungalow, Alice had pushed aside her dinner plate and was glaring at Etienne, sitting across from her with a plate of rice and curry. He was moving the rice around on his plate with a spoon, his face red with anger.

'I've told you I won't increase your allowance. Two thousand dollars a month is enough. Why do you keep harping on my mother's wealth? She left it to me, not you. It's *not* yours.' Alice's eyes were narrowed in anger.

Etienne raised a red face from his plate. 'Ma, I want to get married to Della. We need money. The sale of this house will give me a trust fund, but I can't access it till I'm thirty. Della is not going to wait so long. She has so many young men at her feet.'

'You're right about that!' Malice glinted from Alice's eyes. 'Your Della sleeps around. Did you know, Tien?'

Etienne's eyes widened and his lips trembled. 'Stop lying, Ma!' He shouted.

'Oh, I'm not.' Alice grinned at her son. 'I had my PI follow Della Pang. Ask her about James Ng, he is a hot TVcorp actor, I think. She sleeps with him most nights.'

Etienne said with a white face, 'Della will marry me. She said so.' He began sobbing.

'You'll marry Della Pang over my dead body, Etienne! Your papa would have been so ashamed of you. He hated gold-diggers and Della is first in line among those. Our family is wealthy so it's natural we'll attract gold-diggers, but one should have some sense, right. You are the same as your silly stepsister. Patrick Singh is a gold-digger and so is Della Pang.'

Etienne had recovered himself. 'I want to marry Della and that's it. I need money.'

Alice narrowed her eyes. 'Then get a job. No one is stopping you. Your father built his entire business from scratch, he worked day and night in the initial years. And look at you with a begging bowl in your hands. And doesn't your Della work? I'm sure her salary can keep you both.'

Etienne stood up, tears streaming down his face again. 'I'm not trained for a job! How can I get one? Who are you keeping all your money for, Ma? Nelson Ong?'

'Stop right there!' Alice screeched. 'If you're not trained for a job, you can go get trained. Go and speak to Grandad and Uncle Marvin. Learn the ropes in the biscuit factory and make something of yourself. And stop snivelling to me for handouts.'

Etienne looked at his mother, hatred blazing out of his eyes. 'If you don't increase my allowance and lend me money for marriage, I will leave this house and live somewhere else.'

A smile flitted across Alice's lips. 'Live where? With Della Pang? No one is going to cater to you, Etienne! You want to leave this house? Well, go ahead! Pack your suitcase.'

Etienne looked with surprise at his mother. 'I really mean it, Ma.'

'And I'm equally serious,' Alice said, pulling her dinner plate back on the place mat and looking with interest at the fried rice and sweet and sour chicken she had enthusiastically mixed up before Etienne started the fight. 'Go ahead and leave this house.' As Etienne stormed out of the dining room, Alice smiled and bent to her food. Fifteen minutes later, she heard the front door slam. She looked at the clock on the wall of the dining hall. It read 8.30 p.m.

Alice Lee peered at the rice pudding Joyce had prepared before she left for her off day. It looked creamy and appetizing. Nothing like a good dessert to finish a meal, she thought.

* * *

Pradeep Chopra's face was pale. He sat in the living room of 39, Primrose Crescent facing Alice Lee. The woman is made of stone, he thought. His pleas about his daughters fell on deaf ears. She sat across from him with a glass of wine in her hands (without offering him any refreshment), sipping it slowly while looking at him with narrowed eyes.

'My husband died before his time,' she said in a raspy voice. 'My son was left fatherless at a vulnerable age. Etienne has become wayward and it's all your wife's fault. She was probably inebriated before the flight.'

Colour rushed into Pradeep's face. In a shrill voice he could hardly recognize as his own, he cried, 'No, she wasn't drunk! How dare you say that. She only had a couple of drinks that one time in Hong Kong before boarding a flight. How long is she going to be punished for that one time? Madam Lee, you travelled on the plane with Uncle Ronnie many times when my wife was the pilot. Did you ever see her being under the influence?'

Alice sniffed. 'Who knows whether she took a tipple or two? This time, she must have been drunk. Well, Pradeep, I am not withdrawing my civil suit. I will see you in court.'

'Alan said there was a faulty computer chip in the flight display unit of the plane that made it malfunction. That was the cause of the crash!'

'Proof?' Alice raised one pencilled eyebrow.

Pradeep cried, 'And where is your proof that Rosie was drunk when the plane crashed?'

The telephone jangled in the hall and Alice rose from the sofa. She was dressed in a floral cheongsam and her lips were painted a dark red.

She's a vampire, who will suck the blood out of our family, Pradeep thought. He was at his wit's end. What should he do to stop his girls from becoming homeless?

Alice Lee was going out of the room, saying over her shoulder, 'I need to get the phone.'

Pradeep Chopra could hear her tinkling laugh from the hall and his eyes narrowed in anger. He had built a life for him, Rosie, and the children in Singapore. He had been a student from India, studying at Temasek University when he fell in love with Rosie, a Singaporean.

He teared up as he thought of his dead wife, her big, kind eyes. He had lost his Rosie, but she had applied for a citizenship for her husband even before the children were born and the government approved Rosie's sponsorship as soon as he obtained the lecturer's job in Pelangi U. Nina and Rina were Singapore citizens, well-adjusted to life here. If Alice Lee took away their home, he would have no choice but to return to India to the property his grandparents had left him, depriving Nina and Rina of their Singapore heritage. He could not let that happen.

* * *

Alice Lee heaved a sigh of relief when upset and emotional, Pradeep Chopra rushed out of the living hall. She heard the front door slam and through the window, she saw him running to the gate.

Their heated exchange had left her with a headache. Pradeep had called her cold and unfeeling. Alice shrugged. Anything not to take responsibility, she thought. Her lips thinned into a line. She would get the better of Ronnie Lee yet. He had disinherited her from claiming his property, she would use his death to make money by embroiling the pilot's estate in a wrongful death and negligence civil suit.

Alice's phone buzzed. She picked it up and looked at a message from her PI.

Then her brow furrowed, she got to her feet and walked out of the room after switching off the lights. She went into the passage leading to Alan's wing of the house. Switching lights on as she went along, she entered Alan's study and flicked on the light switch. Alice Lee seated herself at her stepson's computer terminal, her back to the window, and switched on the computer. As it blinked to life, Alice glanced again at her phone text message in puzzlement.

Nelson had a new factory in Shenzhen, China? He had never mentioned it. As the computer blinked encouragingly, Alice Lee tapped the keys and began her search. Beside her on the table was a notepad and pen. When she had found what she wanted, she noted the details down on the notepad.

There was a sound near the closed door. Alice frowned and glanced up. Joyce must have woken up and come to investigate. She swivelled her chair, turned her head to look outside and saw a square of light the window cast on the garden. She heard the door open and turned around in annoyance. She looked at the visitor in surprise.

'What are *you* doing here?' She asked.

WHO KILLED ALICE LEE?

Monday, 27 May 2013

Singapore

25

When Dolly came to work, she found Charlie waiting for her in her office to discuss the final forensic findings of the Lionel Chu case. The phone rang. Dolly picked up the receiver to find Interpol's Rachel Kelly on the line.

She had bad news. Alerted by Dolly's text regarding the location of Sushila's mother's flat in Chennai, Rachel had sent the details to the Chennai police via India Interpol. When the police raided the apartment, there was evidence Sushila had been living there and signs of a struggle in the study. When the police combed the surrounding areas, they found Sushila's dead body on a neighbouring train track.

Rachel continued, 'The lower part of her body was on the tracks, her face was untouched. The police suspect she had been drugged and left on the tracks. It's a murder case there. The Chennai police officers working on the case will share information on Iyer's autopsy, mobile phone, and laptop data with your officers. I'm sorry we could not find Sushila Iyer before someone killed her.'

'Well, that's that. Latham cannot be questioned, and Sushila Iyer has been murdered. We cannot retrieve any information from these individuals. Charlie, I don't think we can solve the counterfeit chip syndicate case!' Dolly gazed in dismay at Charlie after disconnecting the phone.

Corporal Mok appeared in the doorway. 'Madam, you, and the inspector are wanted immediately in DAC Nathan's office. It's an emergency!'

189

Inside Nathan's spacious office, at a secluded corner where there were comfortable sofas and chairs, sat former cabinet minister, Justin Chua, in his wheelchair. His face was worried, his small eyes behind the black-framed spectacles flicking over Nathan, sweat trickling down his face even with the air-conditioner humming away.

Nathan was frowning at a paper in front of him but looked up at the entry of his subordinates. His face was stern, and his moustache bristled with tension.

'Ah, ASP Das and Inspector Goh. Good.' He looked at Justin Chua. 'ASP Das is a capable police officer and in charge of the investigation into Alan Lee's murder. You can rest assured she will do her best to find your daughter.' He turned back to his subordinates. 'ASP Das, Alice Lee was scheduled to have breakfast with her father in his house at 8 a.m. When she did not turn up or answer her mobile phone, Justin called the house and the maid after searching the house, reported both Alice Lee and her son, Etienne, missing. Their beds had not been slept in. I have already sent out an alert.' Nathan turned ingratiatingly to Justin Chua. 'Don't worry, Justin, we will find Alice and Etienne.'

Justin Chua grunted. 'You've been my golfing buddy for years, John, I trust you more than most. I leave everything in your hands. Please make sure this is a priority case, John. First Alan and now Alice and Etienne.'

Beads of perspiration were clouding Justin Chua's forehead and he rummaged in his trouser pocket for a handkerchief. After he had wiped his forehead with it, he said in a rasping voice, 'I should let you know some of Alice's activities before her disappearance. Last week, she visited me and wanted to hire a private eye. I recommended a retired police inspector I used to know called Phil Wee, he works out of an office at People's Park.'

Dolly's reaction was immediate. 'Why did Madam Lee want to hire a private detective?'

'Her boyfriend, Nelson Ong, is rumoured to have taken a lover and Alice wanted the PI to spy on Nelson and find out the identity of the new woman in Nelson's life.' The former cabinet minister took a name card out of his wallet and handed it to Charlie. 'That has the address of Wee. Maybe you can have a word with him, Inspector Goh, in case he knows Alice's whereabouts.'

Dolly was thoughtful. Justin Chua's words corroborated Angie's assertion that Nelson Ong had a new girlfriend.

'Is there anywhere Etienne would go, maybe stay the night with a friend?' Charlie asked, tentatively.

Justin Chua's face went red. 'Alice said he is dating a model older than him. He may have spent the night with her. As far as I know, the model's name is Della Pang. You may want to talk to Etienne's stepsister, Linda. She may know more about Della Pang.'

Dolly said, 'Maybe Etienne went to stay with Linda?'

Justin Chua shook his head. 'I have called Linda and Etienne is not with her.'

After Charlie had wheeled Justin Chua out, Dolly told Nathan, 'We will go directly to 39, Primrose Crescent, sir, and look around in case there was foul play. We will question the maid and the gardener.'

Outside, the sky had darkened with rain clouds.

* * *

Charlie drove Dolly to 39, Primrose Crescent. The gate of the bungalow was closed, and the property looked deserted. Charlie pressed the bell at the side of the gate and waited. Dolly caught a movement through the corner of her eye and looked up to see a woman waving urgently from the window of a flat.

'That must be Emily Gan, the younger sister of the girl who was engaged to be married to Alan Lee. I'd better see what she has to say. Interview the gardener and the maid while I'm gone, Charlie.'

Dolly walked slowly towards the private apartment complex next door. Her sensible pumps had worn out and new high-heel shoes were causing her pain and discomfort. She was surprised to see no security guard in sight. Maybe it is not a gated community building, thought Dolly. She was even more surprised to find the sole lift out of order. Dolly cursed and trudged up the four flights of stairs and knocked on the door of the east side apartment. A Filipina maid opened the door and led Dolly to a corner room. A woman in her forties with a tousled head and big eyes sat expectantly in a wheelchair by the window.

She said crisply, 'Close the door after you, Louisa. Please do come in, Inspector. Have a seat.' The woman pointed to a padded chair. 'I am Emily Gan. Alan Lee was like a big brother to me.'

'I am ASP Das,' Dolly said. 'You wished to see me?'

Sudden tears clouded Emily's eyes and her thick lips trembled. 'Alan and Linda were my childhood buddies. I feel duty-bound to report what I saw last evening from my window. Joyce, Alice Lee's maid, told my maid that mother and son are missing. I was waiting for the police to arrive. Is it true? Alice is missing?'

When Dolly nodded, Emily continued, 'I work from home at the computer by the window and yes, I do look out a lot.' Quietly, she told Dolly of the accident that had killed her sister and left her legs paralysed. She continued, 'I was sad after hearing of Alan's death and was looking at the neighbouring house, reliving childhood memories. My window overlooks the west side, and I can see Alice Lee's bedroom windows from mine. She usually goes to bed around 11 p.m. and from around 10 p.m., the lights would be on in her bedroom. Last night, the bedroom was dark.'

'So, she did not return home from outside,' Dolly mused.

Emily's eyes gleamed. 'I never saw her go out. Yesterday was Sunday and Samy, the chauffeur's day off. Alice, though, drove out herself, but that was on Saturday. Of course, I was not looking out all the time. But yesterday being Sunday, most of the day I was at the window reading a book. There was a lot of activity next door last evening. Alice was in, then.'

'What do you mean?'

Emily Gan leant back in her chair. 'There was an argument around dinnertime between Etienne and his mother. There were raised voices coming from the dining room which my window also overlooks. I could not see in, but I could hear them quarrelling loudly. He was demanding money from her, and she was saying no.'

'Wait, you could hear clearly from three floors up?' Dolly raised her eyebrows, sceptically.

'Their voices carried, and I think the whole neighbourhood heard,' Emily said. She narrated that about half an hour later, Etienne left the house with a suitcase. Emily's window partially overlooked the porch of the house next door, and the porch light was on. She went on to say that a little later, Pradeep Chopra arrived. Emily knew him as she used to go for meals with Alan, Linda, Selena, Pradeep, and Rosvinder. 'We were all friends,' Emily added.

'Did you see Chopra leave?' Dolly asked, sharply.

'Yes. At around 9.45 p.m. He rushed out of the porch and gate. He seemed to be in a great hurry. I looked at Alice's bedroom window, but the lights did not come on. Yusuf locked the gates at around 10 p.m., his usual time.'

'And you never saw Alice Lee go out after Pradeep Chopra's visit?'

Emily shook her head. 'I was going to turn in at 10.30 p.m. and looked out of the window. I saw a dark figure near the porch. I couldn't make out if it was a man or a woman. I am not certain of this, ASP Das, it's just an impression I had. When I went to bed, Alice's bedroom was still dark.'

Dolly thanked Emily and thoughtfully, made her way to 39, Primrose Crescent. Alice Lee had been intent on financially ruining Pradeep Chopra. What had happened between them when Chopra visited Alice?

26

Charlie was inside the house waiting for her. He sat in the living room, making notes on his electronic tablet. Dolly seated herself on a sofa and briefly related the gist of Emily's information. 'What did you find out from the gardener?' She asked.

Charlie told Dolly Yusuf had locked the gate at 10 p.m., his usual time. Yusuf thought Alice was inside the house and reported that at 8 p.m., from his quarters, he had heard Etienne quarrelling loudly with his mother.

Charlie had interviewed Joyce, the maid. Yesterday had been her day off, she arrived home at 9.30 p.m. and heard voices from the drawing room and assumed Alice had a visitor. She went up to her room in the attic and went to bed.

Dolly nodded. 'Call the gardener here, Charlie.'

When Yusuf shuffled into the room with an apprehensive face, Dolly asked him, 'When you went to lock the gate, do you remember if there was a light on in any of the downstairs or upstairs windows? We are just wondering where Madam Lee was at 10 p.m.'

Yusuf's leathery face creased in concentration. Finally, a light dawned in his eyes. 'Mr Alan's study light was on. I think Master Etienne use Mr Alan's computer.'

Charlie exclaimed, 'You never said this before, man.' He rushed out of the room and bumped into Joyce outside, her face frightened. 'Show me Alan

Lee's study,' he ordered, following Joyce, as she hurried away in the direction of the other wing of the house.

Soon, he was back with a sombre face. 'We have found Alice Lee, madam. She was killed in Alan Lee's study. Strangled. I'm calling Benny and the forensic team.'

Dolly rushed out of the living room, past Joyce having hysterics in the hall, following Yusuf to Alan's wing of the house. At the entrance to the study, she waved the gardener back and entered.

The study was ransacked. Drawers were open with papers spilling out, books lay on the floor, flung from the bookcases, and a pair of legs were peeping out from behind the study desk, by the window. Dolly gingerly picked her way among the books and papers and went behind the desk.

Alice Lee was lying by the window, a cord tied tightly around her neck. Her face was purple, and her blood-red eyes stared out. Dolly, having seen many murdered victims, deduced she had been dead for some time. She quietly left the room.

'Yusuf, no one is to come into the study, it is a crime scene. Madam Alice Lee has been killed. My officers will soon come and seal off the room and do work there. I want to lock this room up till then. Do you have a key to this door?'

Dolly stood at the door until Yusuf returned with the key. Then she locked the door and shepherded a stunned Yusuf in the direction of the kitchen where Charlie had managed to calm Joyce enough for her to put the kettle on. Leaving the gardener and the maid in the kitchen, Dolly and Charlie went into the drawing room to wait for Benny Ong, the pathologist, and the forensic team to join them.

* * *

An hour later, Benny Ong straightened up from the body. 'She was strangled, ASP Das,' Benny said, pointing to the purple marks around the corpse's throat where the cord had bit in. He looked at the gold-coloured cord in his gloved hand that had been tied around the victim's neck and looked up at the window. 'I think the cord used to kill the victim is a curtain tieback. It has tassels at the ends.'

'Time of death?' Dolly asked, tersely. She and Charlie wore gloves and had changed into protective apparel as soon as the forensic team had given them suits.

'The body is cold. I would say sometime before midnight yesterday. I can be more precise after the autopsy, ASP Das.'

The forensic team leader straightened up from examining Alice's nails. 'The victim put up a fight. The bloody eyes prove that. When the victim is struggling with the attacker in a strangulation, there is bleeding in the eyes,' Jason Teo said. 'There is skin underneath her fingernails. The victim scratched her assailant when trying to remove the cord from her neck and we have bagged the skin. We hope to retrieve the murderer's DNA. We will process the sample right away. The cord used to strangle the victim may give us the killer's DNA and fingerprints, we will process it also.'

Jason took a bag from one of his assistants. 'There was a notepad and a ball point pen beside the computer. Someone had scribbled these words, "Ong Electronic Brokerage, Shenzhen, China" on the pad. We are dusting the paper and pen for fingerprints, but I thought you should know what was written in case it helps with your inquiries, ASP Das.'

'Hm, interesting,' Dolly said. 'Please take away the computer, too, Jason, and do computer forensics. If the search engine was used last night, I want to see a log of all items searched on the internet. Let's look at the note.'

Teo held it up for the officers to read and then asked his assistant to seal the bag.

Dolly said, 'It should be easy to compare the handwriting to see if Alice Lee wrote those words,' Dolly said. She turned to the forensic team head. 'Jason, is Alice Lee's mobile phone in this room?'

Jason Teo nodded and pointed at a bagged item on the table. 'The phone was on the floor, probably fell there during the struggle between the victim and the assailant. The phone was on.'

Mok came forward. 'I looked at the phone calls and texts, madam. There were some missed calls from Justin Chua this morning. The last text on the phone was from last night, from a Phil Wee. The text was informing Madam Lee of Nelson Ong's electronic brokerage firm in Shenzhen.'

'Phil Wee was Alice's PI. So, he fed the information about the Shenzhen brokerage firm to Alice,' Charlie mused.

'Which made Alice Lee look up this company on the internet from the computer in Alan's study,' finished Dolly. She nodded at Mok. 'Adrian, process the mobile phone and let us know if anything interesting pops up.'

In an hour, the forensic team was finished, and Dolly ordered the mortuary van to remove the body to the morgue. Alice Lee left the home she had loved with Emily Gan watching from her window. Alice's father, ex-cabinet minister, Justin Chua, was waiting at the morgue to identify his daughter's remains.

* * *

It had started to rain when Dolly and Charlie returned to CID HQ with grim faces. They could imagine the headlines in the next day's newspaper: 'Prominent Socialite and Daughter of Former Cabinet Minister Murdered, Days After Stepson Killed in Bali: Police Nowhere Near Finding Killer.' Dolly shuddered.

She needed to crack this case; her career depended on it. She instructed Charlie to set about looking for Etienne Lee through hotel registers and cabbies near Primrose Crescent who may have picked him up and taken him to his destination. 'And get Della Pang's address from TVcorp and send a constable to her house to see if he is holed up there.'

When Charlie was at the door, Dolly asked, 'You texted me Patrick Singh, Alan's brother-in-law, may be a member of the counterfeit chip syndicate? What's the evidence, Charlie?'

'Patrick has closed it down now, but he owned a chip brokerage business called Golden Enterprises. He operated out of a small office in Little India. Mok was going through Lionel Chu's list of mobile phone numbers and this company's phone number and address in Roberts Lane was written in his mobile. When our officers went to the address, they learnt the brokerage business had closed and learnt the name of the owner was Patrick Singh. As he was also Sushila Iyer's boyfriend, I think it's safe to conclude he is a member of the gang. He was Sushila's man who sold the faulty chips to distributors. Mok is trying to track him down. He is a co-owner of a condiments shop in Little India, but when Mok went there, the partner said Patrick had sold his share of the business to him. His girlfriend has been murdered. Where *is* Patrick?'

'And now we have three murders—Alan, Sushila and Alice. Who could have killed Alice Lee? The syndicate? We have found no connection between Alice Lee and the syndicate.' Dolly frowned and then her face brightened. '*Unless* the brokerage firm in Shenzhen she was looking up on the computer, belonging to Nelson Ong, is a part of the syndicate brokers! *Nelson Ong* is a member of the criminal syndicate?'

Charlie held up his hand. 'One thing at a time, madam. We first compare the handwritten note to Alice Lee's letters in the house, see if she wrote those words. We also look at fingerprint evidence on the notepad and pen. And the priority now is to find Etienne Lee.'

Dolly looked chagrined. 'You are right as usual, Charlie. His mother dies and Etienne disappears. Suspicious, to say the least. But Charlie, if the handwriting on the note is Alice Lee's, it's important for us to look up the Shenzhen company and Nelson Ong's connection to it. Send an officer to talk to Alice's PI about this and ask Jason to expedite forensic findings from the computer.'

When Charlie left her office, Dolly decided to visit Pradeep Chopra. He had come to see Alice Lee last night and was the chief suspect. Did he kill her because Alice was trying to bankrupt Pradeep?

27

Dolly parked in the visitor's carpark of Pelangi University and walked towards the low, white university building, feeling flustered. While she could understand Alan Lee being hunted down by a crime syndicate, a member of his family being murdered as well raised the question of a personal angle to the murders. Who gained by Alan and Alice's death? *Etienne*. Dolly shook her head and entered the university.

When Dolly knocked on Pradeep Chopra's office door, there was a mumbled, 'Come in,' and Dolly entered to find the academic slumped in his chair, his eyes red and his hair dishevelled. The computer blinked on. On seeing Dolly, he leapt to his feet. 'ASP Das!'

After being seated, Dolly said without preamble, 'Alice Lee was found murdered in the house on Primrose Crescent. You visited her there last night? You may have been the last person to see her alive.'

The colour drained from Chopra's face, and he looked frightened. 'Yes, I did visit her at around 9 p.m.'

'Why?'

Pradeep rubbed his eyes and in a subdued voice told Dolly he begged Alice to withdraw the civil suit for the sake of his children, but Alice Lee was immune to reason.

'So, you killed her?'

There was pin-drop silence in the office. The clock on the wall could be heard ticking loudly.

'My wife was accused of killing Ronnie Lee and now I am being blamed for Alice Lee's death. How much more of this can I take?' Pradeep Chopra buried his head in his hands, his body heaving with sobs.

'Dr Chopra,' Dolly said in a gentler tone, 'please control your emotions. Alice Lee was found strangled in Alan's study. We need answers.'

Pradeep Chopra raised his head and blinked back tears. His voice was shrill as he asked, 'Strangled? In *Alan's* study?' He looked bewildered. 'She was in the living room in the other wing of the house when I left her.'

'According to preliminary examination, our forensic pathologist says she died sometime late last night. In fact, she was not seen by anyone after you left the house. If you could outline your movements last night, sir, it would be of help.'

Pradeep nodded. 'Alan told me if the civil suit went ahead, he would get his lawyer, Jonas Ellis, to fight on my behalf and he would inform Jonas of the evidence he had gathered to raise doubt that Rosie was at fault for the crash. When I called Jonas, he was clueless, Alan had not talked to him. He was killed before he could show Jonas any evidence. Alan's evidence died with him, ASP Das. So, I had no choice but to try and reason with Alice Lee to withdraw the civil suit.'

Pradeep took a bottle of water from his desk, unscrewed the top and took a long drink. Fortified, he continued, 'I went to see Alice Lee at 9 p.m. I pressed the bell, and she opened the door. We talked in the drawing room, rather I pleaded with a statue. Her last words to me were that I had to pay two million dollars compensation from Rosie's estate. Distraught, I ran out of the room, the front door and gate. I hailed a cab on the main road. I looked at my watch, it was nearly 9.45 p.m. When I left her, Alice Lee was alive and she was seated in her drawing room.

'ASP Das, I hated Alice Lee for what she was doing to our family but I did not strangle her.'

'Did anyone see you at all in the house?'

'No one was there. But halfway through our meeting, I heard the main door slam and footsteps on the stairs, so someone had come in.'

'That would be the maid, Joyce.'

'So, maybe Joyce was the last person to see Alice Lee alive,' Chopra said, hopefully.

'Unfortunately, although she says she heard voices from the drawing room while going up the stairs, Joyce went straight to her bedroom in the attic and went to sleep. She did not see Alice Lee.'

Dolly looked keenly at Chopra. His face and hands bore no mark to indicate he had been scratched by Alice Lee while murdering her. Sighing, Dolly left Chopra's office.

* * *

After a hurried lunch at the canteen, Dolly sat in her office at HQ. There was a knock on her door and Charlie entered. His face was animated as he sat in the visitor's chair.

'Madam, a cabbie answered our alert. He had picked Etienne up from Primrose Crescent at around 10.15 p.m. and taken him to a hotel in the Orchard area. Our officers went to the hotel, picked him up and he is now in Interview Room 4.'

'Did our officers get in touch with Della Pang?'

Charlie nodded. 'Mok spoke to her on the phone. She claimed Etienne was not with her and she hasn't seen him of late. Mok got the impression she was lying, madam.'

Gathering up her mobile phone and tablet, Dolly followed Charlie out of her office.

In Interview Room 4, Etienne sat slumped in a chair, his face white and shocked. His eyes were furtive as they surveyed Dolly.

'We offer you our sincerest condolences on the death of your mother,' Dolly said formally, sitting down opposite him. She saw tears spring up in the youth's eyes. 'We need to know what happened last night, Etienne. Your mother was murdered.'

'First Alan, now Ma, what is going on?' Etienne looked thoroughly frightened. 'I want to go to Grandad.'

'Soon enough. We want to know what happened last night, Etienne. You left the house after packing a suitcase. Why?'

Etienne looked uncomfortable. 'Ma was going on about how Della is after our money. I had enough.'

'Yusuf and a neighbour heard you quarrelling at dinner.'

Etienne nodded in the affirmative. 'We had words. Della and I want to get married and we need money to buy a property in our name. I asked Ma to loan me some money. She had loads from Grandmama's inheritance. Bro left me money in a trust fund I can access at thirty. But I need money now and Lester will not loan me any money from my trust fund. So, I asked Ma. She went ballistic and said Della's character was not good and she slept around. Ma said her PI was following Della and that is what he found. I did not believe her. My mother lied a lot. I told her if she did not loan me the down payment of a private flat, I would leave our bungalow and live with Della.'

Etienne's eyes became round, and his lips trembled. 'And Ma told me to go ahead.' His voice held layers of wonder and indignation. He flicked a glance at Dolly. 'So, I went ahead. Packed my bags and left to stay at a hotel. I called Della this morning and she advised me to return to Primrose Crescent and reconcile with Ma. I was about to check out of the hotel when Inspector Goh met me at the lobby. I learnt Ma was dead.'

Now you will get the money you wanted. Dolly looked speculatively at the youth while Charlie took over the interview.

'You went straight from the bungalow to the hotel last night?'

Etienne's eyes were frightened. He swallowed convulsively. 'I went to a nearby park and sat there to clear my head. I also called Della from there. I wanted to crash at her pad, but she said no. She was at a party and could not talk for long. I sat in the park and when I felt calmer, I called a cab and decided to spend the night at a hotel.'

'You left your house at what time?'

Etienne pondered before saying, '9 p.m.'

'Someone saw you leave the house at 8.30 p.m. And when did you leave for the hotel?'

'10 p.m.,' this time the reply was prompt.

Charlie looked at some notes. 'The cabbie who picked you up says he did so at 10.15 p.m. So, you sat in the park for nearly two hours?' His voice was no longer pleasant but had an edge to it.

Etienne's square face had become bland. 'I wasn't looking at my watch all the time. I thought I left the house at about 9 p.m. and spent an hour at the park. Does it matter?'

'Yes, it does,' Dolly intervened. 'Your mother was murdered around that time.'

Etienne stood up, agitated. He shouted, 'I did not kill Ma, why should I? She would have come around with the money. I'm her only son! You're trying to frame me for murder. I want Grandpa! I demand you let me call Grandpa!'

'It's all right, Etienne, you can leave now. Inspector Goh will call you a cab and you can visit your grandpa. We will be in touch.'

When Charlie returned after seeing Etienne off, Dolly sighed. 'Etienne Lee is in the clutches of a leech, who may or may not have incited him to murder. I do not believe he sat in the park for two hours.'

'There were no marks on his face or hands.'

'Who knows where Alice Lee scratched her murderer. Etienne was wearing a long-sleeved shirt. What about Patrick Singh? You need to ask him in for an interview.'

Charlie nodded. 'Mok's on it, madam. He is not at home nor at his shop. We don't know Patrick's whereabouts, but I'm sure we will find him soon. Madam, the forensic team's report on the Lionel Chu case is in your in-tray. The shoe polish on the wall underneath the balcony belonged to Lionel's shoes. The forensic officer reports that the marks are consistent with someone climbing over the balcony. No traces of fibre or hair from Sushila was found on Lionel. The Chennai police faxed over Sushila's DNA profile. So, no evidence of a struggle between Lionel and Sushila, madam.'

Dolly sighed. 'We can close that case as suicide once we inform our superiors.'

There was a knock on the door and Mok entered. 'Madam, I talked to the PI, Phil Wee. Madam Alice requested him to investigate all of Nelson Ong's businesses, how they were faring. That is how Phil came across Nelson Ong acquiring an electronics brokerage business in Shenzhen last year. Shall I talk to the Chinese police about this company, madam?'

Dolly smiled appreciatively and Charlie beamed. 'Yes, and good work, Mok. We will soon see you as a sergeant.' Dolly smiled at Charlie after Mok had left the office, blushing furiously. 'Okay, Charlie, we carry on with the case tomorrow. Have a nice night.'

After Charlie had left, Dolly tidied her desk, gathered her handbag, and walked towards the carpark.

28

As the maid served them dinner, Linda Lee watched her husband, warily. He had come home from his spice shop in Little India, his face pale and tense, and gone straight to the bathroom. After a long shower, he had closeted himself in his study, only emerging from his den when Natasha knocked loudly on the door to call him to dinner.

During the meal, Patrick was silent, morose, and Linda could have sworn tears glistened in his eyes from time to time. They made awkward conversation over pratas, chicken curry and long beans. Patrick left the table halfway through the meal without a word. After a dessert of rice pudding, the children retreated to their rooms. Linda came into the living room to find her husband watching television.

Linda seated herself and smiled at Lestriani who came in with two cups of spiced tea. 'Natty's enrichment class is at 8 p.m. and Duleep's is at 7.30 p.m.,' she told the maid.

'Yes, ma'am.'

When the maid had left the house with the children, Linda tackled her husband.

'What is it, Pat? You did not eat your curry and you love chicken curry! And you did not come home last night. The police were looking for you.'

Patrick looked at his wife. 'The police? What did they want?'

'To ask about your business, though why they are interested in your condiments shop, I don't know.' Linda sipped her masala chai.

Patrick upped the volume of the TV and turned his back on his wife.

The ring of the landline sliced through the silence wedged between the couple.

Linda went to the alcove near the balcony where the phone was kept. It was Yusuf calling from Primrose Crescent with the terse message Alice Lee had been murdered and Joyce was threatening to leave and take shelter at the Philippines Consulate.

'*What?* Where is Tien?' Linda screeched into the phone and at last got her husband's attention. Patrick stood up and looked inquiringly at his wife, his face sad and unsmiling.

Linda listened for some time to Yusuf and then put down the phone and faced her husband, her eyes, wide. 'Alice was found in Alan's study, strangled.' She looked astounded when Patrick shrugged and began walking towards his den. 'I am going to Primrose Crescent. Joyce does not want to remain in the house. She is alone as Etienne is staying with his grandfather. I will go and calm Joyce and Yusuf down.'

Her husband stopped walking and stood still, his back to her.

'Why am I always told news late in the day? No one thinks of informing me beforehand, not even Etienne. Alice was found earlier in the day, for heaven's sake!' Linda said to her husband's back. 'The children will arrive from tuition at 9.30 p.m. Can you tell Lestriani to feed them some jam and biscuits before bed, Pat?'

Patrick nodded and slipped into his den and Linda could hear the key turning in the lock of the study door. She hurried into the bedroom and dressed herself in a black suit and came out. She was frowning—what was wrong with Patrick? Surely Alice's death would mean something to him? She was a relative, after all. A light dawned in her eyes. Had Patrick found out about her lover? Was that why he was distant? She glanced at her mobile phone from time to time, but there were no text messages from her lover.

* * *

At 10 p.m., Linda Lee returned home with Joyce. She had failed to persuade Joyce to continue living at 'a crime scene' (as Joyce dramatically said before having a bout of hysterics) and had seen no other option but to bring her to Silver Springs. Linda did her best to ignore Lestriani's glare as she settled

Joyce in the helper's bedroom, grateful she had bought a double bed for her helper. Leaving Lestriani and Joyce to break the ice, Linda entered the dark living hall.

She looked at the door of Patrick's den. It was shut but a sliver of light shone from underneath it. After checking her children were fast asleep in their respective rooms, Linda knocked on the door of the den. There was no answer and Linda tentatively pushed the door open.

The room was empty. The computer was switched off but light from the lamp on Patrick's desk fell on a white sheet of paper with words written in red ink. The window of the den was open, and a slight breeze was blowing in, ruffling the paper on the desk, a paperweight preventing the sheet from being blown away.

Linda snatched the paper up and read the letter. Her face went white with shock, and she uttered a small cry. A solitary tear made its way down her cheek and the hand that held the letter, trembled. What would she tell Duleep and Natasha in the morning? The letter was brief but to the point:

Dear Linda,

I am leaving you and the children. Forgive me.

I was in love with someone else for a long time. She died with my unborn baby.

We needed money to start our new life in India and were involved with a crime syndicate. They killed my love and now they are after me. I need to leave Singapore and go underground.

Linda, I am sorry our marriage did not work out. Please do not betray me to the police. Let me leave Singapore. From far away, I will bless my children.

I have sold my spice shop to Muthuswamy, and I have deposited the money from the sale in our joint account. Please use that money for Duleep and Natasha's education. Try not to poison our children against me, Linda. Let them remember my love for them.

Pat

With the letter in her hand, Linda left the den, banging the door shut, rushed into the master bedroom, and locked the door. She sat on the bed she had shared with her husband and wept quietly.

The knowledge he had a lover filled her with shock and anger. How dare he? He was a father of two children, and he had been on the way to being a father of an illegitimate child. And being involved in a crime syndicate? He had been so desperate to leave her and settle with his mistress and child in India that he had stooped to crime.

Linda's tears dried and only a sheen of sadness remained in her eyes. After all, she was having an extra-marital affair herself. Who was she to judge Patrick? It was true, they had both gone their separate ways. What should she do? Her eyes filled with instinctive vindictiveness, and she wanted to call Lily's sister, the superintendent, and rat on her husband. But it was better in the long run, she felt, not to attract police attention.

With tired steps, she went to the bathroom to have a shower and after that, lay on the bed and had a long chat with her lover on the phone.

* * *

Dolly hurriedly parked in the basement carpark of a Jurong shopping mall at 9 p.m. and rode the lift to the first floor. Her face shone with sweat, and she wiped the perspiration off with a white lace handkerchief. Joey had texted her some hours ago that he was back in Singapore, and they could meet for dinner.

Dolly sighed. Joey seemed to be commuting between Singapore and Malacca. She remembered Lily's advice and her mouth set with determination. She had to confront Joey on what took him so often to Malacca. She was late for her dinner date, the investigation simmering busily in the wake of the discovery of Alice Lee's body.

Dolly arrived in front of The Good Trio restaurant. She found Joey sitting in a booth. He waved at her and gave a smile.

Dolly slid into the opposite seat. 'I'm sorry I'm late, darling, there was another murder in the Alan Lee case, this time it was Alice Lee who was killed.'

Joey blinked behind his Ray-Ban designer spectacles. 'Wow. I wonder who killed her. Let's order some food before we talk, I'm famished.' Joey signalled to the waitress and briskly ordered chrysanthemum tea, a plate of fried rice, a bowl of seafood noodles, sweet and sour pork, and pickled cabbage.

Although tired, Dolly found she was ravenously hungry, and she knew she could think better on a full stomach. They talked about one of Joey's cases and Uma's health while waiting for their food to arrive. When the steaming plates and bowls arrived, Joey served the seafood noodles to Dolly before helping himself.

After eating for some time, Joey said tentatively, 'My work in Malacca finished abruptly. I thought I had to stay longer, but I didn't.'

Dolly gazed frankly into her husband's eyes. 'Whom do you visit in Malacca? I'm not dumb, Joey. You can't be having clients in one Malaysian city every month.'

She was afraid of what Joey might say and glanced at him only when the silence stretched on.

Joey's face had lost colour and his eyes were on his bowl. He had stopped eating.

'Joey?' Dolly's voice was gentle.

Slowly, Joey looked up and his eyes held a glint. 'You're right. I was going to tell you, soon.'

'Tell me what?'

Joey glanced around the restaurant. It was crowded and the babble of diners were in their ears. 'I promise to tell you, soon, what keeps me in Malacca. I don't want to have any secrets from you, sweetheart. This has nothing to do with our love for each other,' he added, earnestly.

Dolly smiled. 'I know *that*.' She pondered on Joey's words. If he was not having an affair, then what *was* it that kept him in one city every month? She sighed. She knew Joey would speak when he was ready. She said, 'Okay, Joe, once I wrap up this case, we'll talk.' She ladled some more sweet and sour pork on to her fried rice and began eating. After chewing a mouthful, she said, 'This case is getting to me.'

Joey looked up from his food. 'There is something you may want to know regarding the Interpol officer, Rachel Kelly. You told me she was blocking the hunt for Mark Latham. I've been investigating her. She joined Interpol HQ at Lyon only a few years ago, before that she was a disgraced police officer at Scotland Yard.'

'What do you mean by "disgraced"? How did you find all this out?'

'The Web has archives of sensational news. In 1995, a plane crashed at Gatwick because landing lights malfunctioned. Two passengers died, one was a famous archaeologist, Archie Miller. Rachel Kelly headed the investigation into the crash from Scotland Yard and concluded a power trip in the control tower had extinguished the landing lights and caused the crash. However, Miller's daughter, Charlotte, talked to airport officials and came up with an alternative theory that faulty computer chips in the landing lights caused the lights to go out just when the plane was about to land. She confronted Detective-Inspector Kelly and according to Charlotte's complaint to Scotland Yard, duly reported by the press, DI Rachel Kelly told her to butt out of the investigation. Charlotte, then, got a petition going, signed by all her father's famous friends and the petition was responsible for re-opening the case with another police officer in charge. The new officer agreed with Charlotte Miller that faulty computer chips in the landing lights were responsible for the crash.

Scotland Yard suspended Rachel Kelly, sent her for remedial training and then re-instated her a few years ago before she transferred to Interpol.'

'Faulty computer chips!' Dolly cried. 'Wait! Supt Kelly seems reluctant to hunt for Latham and she was removed from investigating a counterfeit computer chip case. Is that a coincidence?'

Joey shrugged his shoulders, expressively. 'Your Rachel Kelly certainly does have a link to faulty chips. But she could just have been incompetent investigating the counterfeit chip case in London and was removed from the investigation as a result.' He saw Dolly had finished her food. 'It's getting late, let's go.'

Dolly nodded and rose from her seat. 'Joey, do you mind if I visit Silver Springs? Mummy had a fever last night and I want to see how she's doing. I'll drive myself home, darling.'

While driving to Silver Springs Condominium, Dolly reflected on Joey's information. A light burned in her eyes. Could it be that Rachel Kelly was a member of the counterfeit computer chip gang? Was Kelly a corrupt police officer? That would explain why she was refusing to track down Mark Latham. Dolly frowned. Was she drawing hasty conclusions? She focused on the road.

29

When she entered her mother's apartment, Dolly saw a crowd in Uma's living room. Angie was sitting on a sofa with Vernon, eating ice-cream, and Ash and his girlfriend, Amita, were talking animatedly to Uma on the divan. Uma's cackles lent the scene an air of merriment.

Dolly asked, 'How are you, Mummy? Any fever?'

Girlie, hovering near the door, said, 'No more fever, ma'am. Go away already.'

Dolly nodded, smiled at her mother, sat down on a sofa, and told her family of Alice Lee's death. There were startled exclamations.

'It seems many hated her,' Lily observed after Dolly had told them about Emily Gan's information on Pradeep Chopra and Etienne Lee. 'Alice Lee's murder may have a personal angle. Pradeep Chopra had the best motive, in my opinion. He has two children and Alice was trying to bankrupt him. Etienne, hmm, it's suspicious he has no alibi for the time of the murder, but to kill his own mother!'

'Oh, I need to check something!' Dolly got up from the sofa and settled herself at the computer table in the far corner. She took her laptop out of her briefcase and plugged it in. Lily bustled curiously, looking over Dolly's shoulder.

Dolly googled 'Rachel Kelly' and photos of the Interpol officer came up on the screen.

'Who's that?' Lily asked.

'A person of interest,' Dolly said, tersely, before inserting 'counterfeit chips' in the search engine. Angie scurried over and gasped.

'I know this woman!'

Dolly swivelled around, startled. 'What? Where?'

'This is Sauce King, Nelson Ong's mistress. She lives with him and her old mother in his bungalow. I go to clean every day.' Angie's eyes were shining and Vernon standing next to her began squinting madly.

'Nelson Ong!' Dolly and Lily cried out in unison.

Angie animatedly informed Dolly that on her way to work a couple of days ago, she had seen Alice Lee watching Nelson Ong's bungalow through binoculars from her car parked on the road outside. She knew Alice Lee's face from photographs in women's magazines she occasionally flipped through.

'Could Nelson Ong have killed Alice Lee? Maybe she was going to create problems about his new love interest,' Lily opined.

Dolly looked thoughtfully at her sister. 'Supt Rachel Kelly, an Interpol officer, is blocking the search for Mark Latham, and she blocked an investigation in London on counterfeit chips. And Alice Lee was searching the internet when she was strangled. She had jotted down "Ong Electronic Brokerage" and an address in Shenzhen on a piece of paper. As far as I know, Nelson Ong sells sauces. If he owns this Shenzhen company and is Rachel Kelly's boyfriend, can it be that Rachel Kelly and Nelson Ong are members of the counterfeit chip syndicate? Or is it mere coincidence?'

'Maybe Alice Lee was on to them, and the syndicate killed her,' Lily said. 'It will be hard to collect evidence against them. Maybe you could start by finding out if Nelson Ong does own an electronics brokerage firm in Shenzhen.'

'Yes, yes, my officers are making inquiries,' Dolly said.

The doorbell rang. Girlie opened the door, letting Charlie in.

'Charlie?' Dolly looked at her subordinate in surprise. 'What's happened? Why are you here?'

'Madam, I saw your car when I parked at the carpark here. I came to Silver Springs to see Patrick Singh. But he has disappeared.'

'What do you mean? Send out an APB and alert the immigration checkpoints, Charlie. Sit down, sit down.' Dolly's face had flushed.

'I already sent out an APB, madam.' Charlie smiled his thanks as Girlie brought him a cool glass of lemonade. He sat down on a chair and said, 'I went to Singh's unit and Linda Lee opened the door. She had been crying.

She told me her husband has left her and the children. She would not say anything else.'

Dolly said, 'Patrick has learnt of Sushila's death and thinks he will be the syndicate's next target and has gone underground. Charlie, don't you think this is a logical conclusion?'

Charlie nodded, morosely. 'If I had come here even three hours earlier, I would have nabbed him.'

Uma said from the divan, 'Doll, this case of yours can be called "The Case of the Disappearing Suspects."' She gave a prolonged cackle. Her fever gone, Uma was her merry self, intent on riling her elder daughter.

Dolly glared at her mother. 'What is done is done. We now need to interview Nelson Ong, Rachel Kelly's boyfriend.'

Lily objected. 'Doll, you're always scolding me for jumping to conclusions. What about you? You have no *evidence* linking Rachel Kelly to the crime syndicate. Just because she is blocking Mark Latham's extradition. She may just be following Interpol protocol.'

When Charlie looked baffled, Dolly narrated to him what Joey had found out about Supt Kelly's work history at Scotland Yard and informed him of Angie's evidence of Kelly being Ong's mistress.

'Rachel Kelly is linked to two counterfeit chip cases then, madam.' Charlie's mind was whirring into action. 'I remember you telling me Supt Kelly volunteered to take on the Latham case at Interpol. She came forward to take on the case and promptly blocked the investigation. But Madam Lily is right. We need evidence linking a police officer to a crime syndicate. Need to be careful about this, madam.'

Dolly nodded. 'I know we need evidence. But Nelson Ong should be interviewed. He was romantically linked with Alice Lee, and she was killed.'

Lily nodded. 'Yes, you need to keep in mind, though, you may have two unlinked cases. Alice Lee could have been killed by someone in her close circle for personal gain or revenge.'

Charlie finished his lemonade and got up to leave.

Dolly told him, 'Charlie, get the team working tomorrow to find out if Nelson Ong is a registered owner of any electronics brokerage firm in Shenzhen, China. If Rachel Kelly is a bent police officer, her boyfriend could be involved in the counterfeit chip scam as well.'

Charlie nodded and made his way to the door. Angie and Vernon left with him followed by Ash and Amita who went to visit little Molly and Frankie in Lily's flat. Girlie helped Uma to bed. Dolly and Lily settled themselves on the sofa in the living room with cups of hot cocoa.

Lily sipped her cocoa and said, 'Does Etienne strike you as cold and calculating, Dolly? You told me he is due to inherit a lot of money from his mother. And he has a girlfriend interested in that money. But only someone who is *very* cold and unfeeling would murder his own mother.'

Dolly pondered. 'It's hard to make Etienne out. He is slow of intellect, but shifty at the same time, if you know what I mean. He doesn't appear to be particularly warm, and he is fixated with this model. What was he doing for two hours while his mother was being killed? The good news is Alice scratched her killer while being strangled, and the forensic team is working over-time on the killer's DNA pattern. That doesn't really help us unless we swab all the suspects for DNA samples.' She took a long sip of her cocoa.

'And Emily Gan saw someone in the porch of 39, Primrose Crescent at 10.30 p.m.? That could have been Etienne as Yusuf had closed and locked the gate. Etienne would have the key. You do need to find out more about Etienne Lee.' Lily summed it up. 'You may be dealing with two murder cases that are different rather than being part of the same investigation, Dolly. We already know Ramdin killed Alan Lee, so the Alan Lee case is about discovering the identities of the masterminds of the crime syndicate who were behind the murder. The Alice Lee murder case may have nothing to do with the syndicate and she was killed by someone in her circle who hated her. Let's not forget my classmate, Linda Lee. She hated her stepmother. Quite a few suspects, Dolly.'

Dolly nodded, appreciating Lily's clarity of thought. While there was still a long road ahead of her in solving the cases, the glimmerings of truth were becoming brighter.

'Joey returned from Malacca,' Dolly said, drinking the last of her cocoa. 'He agreed to explain the reason for his trips as soon as we are a bit free.'

Lily giggled. 'I'm sure Joey hasn't got a secret mistress stashed away in Malacca. He talks to Frankie and my husband has never mentioned Malacca. So many mysteries. The crime syndicate, Alice Lee's murder, and Joey's visits to Malacca. We are trying to solve three cases,' she said with a straight face.

Dolly burst into laughter and got up. 'It's good chatting with you, Lil. I need to get home now. Joey is waiting.'

'I'm going to visit Linda Lee tomorrow morning. To get her take on her stepmother's murder. She hated her so much,' Lily said.

Dolly nodded and let herself out of the door. As she walked down the path to the carpark, Dolly felt uneasy. Why did she still feel Alice Lee's murder had to do with the counterfeit chip gang?

Tuesday, 28 May 2013

Singapore

30

A sleepless Linda got up from her bed and drew back the window curtains. The bedroom wall clock read 7.30 a.m. Far away, she could see the shimmer of Little Guilin Lake. They once had a picnic at the lake, Natasha, Duleep, she, and Patrick in the days when the children were young, and Patrick was still a loving husband and father.

Her children's school holidays had started. They would pack and leave for the Primrose Crescent bungalow and stay there for the time being. Joyce needed to be back at the bungalow and take care of it. Once she reached the bungalow, she would call Etienne and ask him to return home. He would be good company for the children.

Linda also thought it was a good idea to establish her claims on 39, Primrose Crescent by ensconcing herself in it. Alice was now not there to deter her. She needed to think of her children's future. A slow smile spread across her face. She would broach the idea of living together as a family to her lover and with her owning a bungalow and a condo unit, her lover, who was financially unstable, would agree to her proposal. The Silver Springs condo unit was her father, Ronnie's gift to her and the house was in her name. Yes, now she was free, to enjoy the life of a millionaire's daughter. *Finally*.

Linda had a brisk shower, dressed in street clothes, and began to pack a suitcase. Lestriani knocked on her door and entered with her morning lemon tea.

Linda smiled at her maid. 'Lestriani, the children and I are going to stay for the June holidays at Primrose Crescent. The bungalow is empty, and Joyce needs to return there. You are welcome to come with us or you can stay here and take care of this apartment.'

'What about sir?' Lestriani asked in a small voice.

'He is on a business trip and will join us, later,' Linda lied.

Lestriani hung her head. 'My contract finishing, ma'am. Please not to renew contract. I wish to transfer to new employer.'

Linda flushed. 'Scared to stay with us, is it? We treat you well, Lestriani.'

Lestriani raised a red face. 'Yes, ma'am, no question about it. I love children too. But, yes, ma'am, I am scared and wish to transfer. Too many killings in family.'

'All right,' Linda said, stiffly, 'You don't need to come with us to Primrose Crescent. Take care of this apartment and find your new employer. Once you do that, I will sign the transfer papers.'

Linda held her head high and walked out of her bedroom and into her children's room.

'Duleep! Natasha! Wake up! We're going to stay at the bungalow for the holidays. Brush your teeth, have your showers, and go for breakfast.'

The front doorbell pealed and Linda walked towards the door and opened it. Lily Das was standing outside, a thermally insulated bag slung over her shoulder.

'I've brought some nasi lemak for breakfast, cooked by Ashikin. Duleep and Natasha love it. I heard about your stepma's death, so sorry, Linda.' Lily took in the dark circles under Linda's eyes and her nervous demeanour.

Linda frowned but stood aside to allow Lily entry. 'We're a bit busy now. We're leaving to stay at our bungalow for the school holidays, Lily.'

Lily nodded. 'No problem. I'll leave the bag here on the table.'

Linda came over to the table and began taking the microwaveable boxes out of the bag. 'Thanks, Lily. But I want to pay you for the meal. How much is it?'

Lily was staring at Linda's right wrist. *It was bandaged.*

'Lily!'

Lily looked up at Linda and smiled. 'Oh, no need to pay anything. This must be such a worrying time for you so this is the least I can do.'

Linda sighed. 'Yes, bad luck is dodging our footsteps. Our gardener, Yusuf, says it's because my father's ghost is not at peace.' She smiled, her eyes a trifle suspicious. 'I can't say I'm mourning Alice, but the way she died was tragic. Who would want to kill her?'

Lily gazed into Linda's eyes. 'Yes. Was there a family quarrel?'

Linda said, rudely, 'Well, not with me, though I had plenty to fight about. Lily, the children need to take their breakfast and we need to get going. Thank you so much for the meal.'

'You're welcome. You are locking up this unit then?'

Linda shook her head. 'Oh, no. Lestriani will stay and take care of it. Bye, Lily.'

After Lily had left, Linda cheered up. *39, Primrose Crescent.* The house she had grown up in and loved. It would be good to stay there. Linda's eyes filled with pleasant conjecture. She could rent out the Silver Springs unit and the rental would pay Yusuf's salary. She could even afford to keep Joyce and entrust her with the duty of taking care of her children with Lestriani gone. Patrick had left the car behind, and the Certificate of Entitlement was not slated to expire for another five years, the car loan had been paid up so she could drive Duleep and Natasha to school.

Linda dreamed. Her face was tinged with happiness. They would all live in the bungalow, her children, her lover and his family. The house was large enough. She quite forgot her husband was a criminal on the run.

* * *

Justin Chua, his eyes red-rimmed, looked piercingly at his grandson as they sat in the study. Etienne's face was bland though his eyes were reddish. Justin had spent a sleepless night thinking of his dead daughter, her childhood and all the good times they had together. He had also talked at length last night to Etienne, who had cried bitterly when talking of his mother but had been reticent about his girlfriend and an account of his movements Sunday night.

'You need to tell me where you were after you left the bungalow the night Alice died, Etienne. Before you know it, you will become a prime suspect in your mother's murder.' Justin Chua's voice was raspy.

Etienne looked up, his small eyes swivelling from his grandfather to Alice's photo in a frame on the table. 'I didn't kill Ma,' he mumbled.

'The police don't know that, boy. You need to convince them and for that, you need to tell them where you were from 8.30 to 10.30 p.m. on the night of Alice's murder. Witnesses have testified you left the house at the time stated and the cabbie who picked you up testified to the time you got into the cab. And don't give me bullshit, Etienne, about sitting on a park bench for two hours. Where *were* you?'

The colour drained from Etienne's face and a tic pulsed near his left eye. His hands on the table trembled. 'I can't tell the police where I was, it will involve another person.'

'Della Pang?' Justin Chua thundered.

Etienne blinked. 'I texted Della I had left the bungalow forever after a fight with Ma. She was partying at a pub nearby. I walked to the pub and talked to her. She was angry and we had a fight in the pub carpark. We spent an hour arguing there. She did not think it was a good idea to leave Ma and wanted me to return home. She refused to allow me to live with her at her pad. We had our first fight, Grandad.' Etienne burst into tears.

Justin Chua looked at his grandson with a mixture of pity and disgust. How had Etienne grown up to be so foolish, he thought. 'Now then,' he said, his voice gruff. 'Della Pang will tell the police you were with her for one hour?'

Etienne sniffed hard, wiping the tears from his eyes with a large white handkerchief. 'I don't think so, Grandad. She doesn't want to be involved in a murder inquiry and she broke up with me, anyway.' Etienne's phone beeped and he glanced at a text message. 'Linda and the children have arrived at the bungalow for the school holidays. Linda asked me to return and help look after the children.'

Justin Chua heaved a sigh of relief. He was old and did not know any more how to deal with young people and their love problems. Linda was more than capable of counselling Etienne. Tears filled his eyes. Alice had died before Etienne had truly grown up. How he missed his daughter and how much Etienne needed her!

'Go back to the bungalow, Etienne,' Justin said in a thick voice. 'I will talk to DAC Nathan and tell him about where you spent that one hour after you left the bungalow. What about the other hour, eh?'

Etienne said sullenly, 'I really was at the park for the other hour, crying my eyes out. Then I decided to spend the night at a hotel and think about my options.'

'Della Pang is not good for you, Tien,' Justin Chua admonished. 'You are young, eh? Time enough for romances and choosing a partner wisely. Go on then. Pack your bag and go back to Primrose Crescent.'

After Etienne left, Justin Chua heaved a heavy sigh before dialling DAC Nathan's number. Later, the former cabinet minister sat at his desk in his study thinking of his daughter. A fire of vengeance burned in his eyes. The police had to find her killer; he would not rest until they did. Slowly, he picked up the phone and dialled the funeral parlour to plan Alice's embalming and wake at his house once the police released her body.

* * *

The afternoon was cloudy and humid. Girlie was cooking Uma's vinegar chicken in the kitchen, humming a song while she went about her work. Occasionally, she glanced, puzzled, at Lily, who was walking around the kitchen, opening the lid of the sugar can, peering into a cupboard.

Girlie turned to Lily. 'Ma'am, you looking for something?'

Lily banged the lid down on the rice container and faced Girlie. 'Not really, Girlie. I've been thinking of the Alice Lee murder and my classmate, Linda. I visited her this morning with breakfast from the café and I noticed her right wrist was bandaged.'

Girlie looked puzzled. 'She hurt herself, maybe.'

Lily's nostrils were flared with excitement. 'Dolly said Alice Lee scratched her killer so the killer would wear a plaster or bandage where she was scratched.'

Girlie dropped the ladle and it fell with a clatter on the counter. 'Oh, ma'am, you think Linda Lee killed Alice?'

Lily nodded. 'She may have. Linda and her family have gone to the Primrose Crescent bungalow for the holidays and Lestriani is alone in the flat. It may be useful to question Lestriani. Can you come with me, Girlie?'

They pressed the bell of Linda's condo unit. After five minutes of repeated ringing, the door opened a crack and the maid, Lestriani's frightened face peeped out.

Girlie immediately stepped forward. 'Lestriani, it's okay. My ma'am want to ask you questions. Don't be scared.'

Lestriani nodded and opened the door and unlocked the grille gate. She ushered Lily and Girlie into the living room.

When they were all seated, Lily spoke. 'About Sunday night. The night your ma'am's stepmother was killed. Do you remember where ma'am and sir were on that night?'

Lestriani's brows puckered, she thought for some time and then nodded. 'I remember. Sir never come home. I go to bed at 10.30 p.m. and sir never come. Maybe he come in, later. When I sleep.'

'And ma'am?' Lily asked.

'Ma'am work in library, come back 9.30 p.m. I just bring children back from enrichment class. They all have dinner. Then children go to bed.'

'And ma'am?'

Lestriani looked furtive and gulped hard. She glanced at Girlie.

Girlie said sternly, 'Tell the truth, Lestriani. Don't lie for employer. It's no good.'

Lestriani nodded and in halting English told Lily that after dinner, Linda had gone to her bedroom, and she could hear her angrily shouting on her mobile phone. Lestriani paused and said, 'She shout, "Alice can't do this to you. She needs to be stopped." Yes, I think that is what she say. Then, I clean kitchen and hear door closing. I go to look. I open main door softly and see ma'am walk to the lifts. She go out.'

Lily sighed. 'What time was this?'

'After 10 p.m., ma'am.'

Lily asked, 'Do you know who was on the phone?'

Lestriani shook her head. 'But she say one word again and again. Pareep.'

'Pareep?' Girlie looked puzzled.

'Was it Pradeep?' Lily asked, her eyes shining brightly, her mind going to the restaurant and the man who was holding Linda so possessively.

'Yes, ma'am, I think so.'

'You noticed your ma'am's hand was bandaged? Do you remember from when it was bandaged?' Lily asked, eagerly.

Lestriani frowned. 'I see Monday morning, I think.'

'The day after your ma'am's stepmother was killed?' Lily gave a sigh when Lestriani nodded her head in acquiescence. She got to her feet. 'Lestriani, you have been helpful. Do you know what time ma'am came home Sunday night?'

Lestriani shook her head. 'I sleep at 10.30 p.m., ma'am.'

Back in her own flat, Lily called Dolly and when the phone went on to voice message, she called Charlie. When he was on the line, slowly and clearly, Lily told him what she had discovered.

* * *

Charlie sat in the large drawing room of the house in Primrose Crescent watching Duleep and Natasha playing a game of chess in the corner by the French windows. Linda fussed over a tea trolley Joyce had wheeled in.

Linda Lee offered him biscuits and a cup of tea. Charlie's eyes gleamed as he noted her bandaged wrist. Lily Das was sharp, Charlie mused, and chided himself for not noticing the bandage on Linda's wrist when he had gone to her condo unit on Monday night. He had been so upset at being unable to locate Patrick Singh that he had not paid attention to whether there was a bandage on Linda's wrist.

Charlie looked up now and smiled at Linda. 'We are checking the movements of people close to Alice Lee. Madam Linda, where were you last Sunday night from 8 p.m. to 12 a.m.?'

Linda's tea splashed on to the saucer and she said, waspishly, 'Why am I a suspect? I wasn't even close to Alice. Anyway, I was on duty at our regional library from 3 to 9 p.m. I am a library officer. I work a few days a week at the library. Then I returned home, joined my children for dinner and saw them to bed. I then had an early night.'

Charlie looked keenly at Linda. 'Do you have keys to this bungalow and the gate?'

Sweat sprung up on Linda's forehead and she stuttered, 'Keys? Yes, of course, I have keys to this house. It was my brother's house.'

'What about the gate, ma'am?'

Linda's voice was shrill. 'Yes, so what?'

Charlie said, 'Routine questions, ma'am. What about your husband? Where was he that night? Did he have keys to this house and gate?'

Linda lay down her cup with a clatter on the glass-topped table. The noise attracted the attention of her children, who looked up at their mother.

Linda said, 'Children, go to your bedroom and play. I will send Joyce up with some sandwiches. Go on.'

When the children had left, Linda nibbled at a biscuit, and said more calmly, 'Inspector, my husband did not have keys to this house. He had not returned from work on Sunday when I went to bed. He must have come home late. He has a shop in Little India, and they close at 11 p.m.'

Charlie now focused on her relationship with her stepmother.

Linda said, readily, 'I disliked my stepmother. Pa was having an affair with Alice when my mother was ill and married her very soon after Ma died. It would have been okay if Alice really loved Pa, but she married him for status. She was a bad mother as well, left Etienne with maids and nannies while she attended concerts and parties.

'While I disliked my stepmother, Inspector, I did not kill her,' Linda said emphatically. 'Why should I? Yes, she was living here, but I knew it was easy to evict her, she had no documents to prove she was the owner of this house. I had no cause to kill Alice.'

Charlie eyed the half-eaten biscuit on Linda's plate. He said, 'May I have a glass of water, ma'am? It's a hot day.'

Linda smiled, rose, and went out of the room. Charlie took an evidence bag out of his capacious pocket, bagged the biscuit on Linda's plate and returned the bag to his pocket. He quickly broke the biscuit on his plate into half and placed one half on Linda's empty plate. When Linda returned with the glass of water, Charlie was examining the paintings on the wall.

He thanked Linda, drank the water, and said, 'Nice paintings. Valuable too, I think. I will be on my way, ma'am. Please let me know if you hear from your husband.'

Charlie sailed out of the gate with the biscuit in his pocket. Linda Lee's DNA could be extracted from the dried saliva on the half-eaten biscuit. His admiration for Lily grew. Everyone knew Linda hated her stepmother, but Lily had found out she was having an affair with Pradeep Chopra and Alice Lee was intent on ruining Pradeep. If the DNA in the evidence bag matched that in the skin from under Alice's fingernails, Lily Das, an amateur, would have solved Alice Lee's murder.

31

Dolly drove down Holland Road and turned into Jalan Istimewa. Around her were affluent bungalows hiding behind tall shrubbery and beautiful gardens. Jalan Istimewa was home to the wealthy of Singapore.

Nelson Ong's house was a small white bungalow in a cul-de-sac. Dolly parked her car and made her way down the winding paved pathway to the blue main door. She pressed the bell outside and waited. Angie, in a green and white apron, opened the door and seated Dolly in the living room while she went to call Nelson Ong.

Dolly looked around the room. There was a huge chandelier and down lights fitted into the false ceiling. A mock fireplace stood inside one wall with knickknacks on the mantlepiece. The sofas were upholstered with floral printed covers, reminiscent of English homes. Some oil paintings of English landscapes hung on the walls but there were no photos in frames anywhere.

A burly man with a goatee beard and friendly eyes, wearing a dressing gown over his pyjama suit came in. 'ASP Das, sorry to keep you waiting. Please do sit down. I got back late last night from Shenzhen, and I woke up only an hour ago. I'm going to have some orange juice. Can I get you a glass?'

Dolly declined and Nelson went to the bar at one end of the room and busied himself pouring orange juice from a carafe. When he was seated sipping his juice, Dolly began her interview.

'You returned from Shenzhen, sir? Do you have a sauce factory there?'

Nelson looked surprised at Dolly's question and took a gulp of the orange juice. He cleared his throat and said, 'No. I have other business interests there.'

Dolly's eyes were sharp. She took in Nelson Ong's discomfiture and shot back, 'Do you own an electronic brokerage business there?'

Nelson's grimace reflected his struggle to maintain composure. He said in a faint voice, 'Why do you ask, ASP Das?'

Dolly explained about the note found beside Alice Lee's computer.

Nelson nodded. 'I see. Alice was spying on me, eh? Well, I co-own Ong Electronic Brokerage Services in Shenzhen. While my partner owned it for five years, I've only joined as co-partner a year ago.'

'The name of your partner?' Dolly asked, affably.

Nelson Ong lost his temper. 'Why do you want to know? Alice was snoopy and she may have been suspicious about my trips there. My partner is a secretive man, and he has managers running the company. He is seldom in China. I go over there more often to keep an eye on the company.'

Dolly's suspicions of Nelson Ong being a counterfeit chip syndicate member grew. Was Mark Latham his partner? Or was Hadyanto his partner? Since both were known to the police, Nelson had become reticent. Dolly changed the subject. 'I'm here in connection with Alice Lee's murder.'

The colour flooded back into Nelson's face. 'Poor Alice! What a shock I got when my secretary texted me the news. Who would want to kill Alice?' Nelson's eyes were more calculating than sad.

'When did you last see her, Mr Ong?'

Nelson screwed up his eyes. Then his brows cleared. 'Last week, Alice and I had lunch at Goodwood Park Hotel's Min Jiang Sichuan Restaurant. That was the last time I saw her. She was worried about being turned out of her home as Alan had been murdered and Linda and her never got along.' Nelson gave a rueful smile. 'It's strange her wanting to hang on to that house when she could easily buy a bungalow in any area of Singapore with the millions her mother left her. It's possible she never got over Ronnie disinheriting her.'

'Ronnie Lee was your friend?'

A frisson of sadness flitted through Nelson's face. 'We were golfing buddies and great friends. Then Alice and I fell in love. Ronnie was angry, and it was the end of our friendship. I don't blame him since I would react similarly. In revenge, he cut off Alice from his will.'

'Ronnie Lee's plane crashed due to faulty chips in the flight display unit.' Dolly was surprised to see sweat break out on Nelson Ong's forehead. He reached for the aircon remote and pushed buttons to further lower the room's temperature. His voice was on edge as he said, 'What do you mean? Someone engineered the crash? Tampered with the plane?'

Dolly said soothingly, 'No, I'm not saying that. There is a counterfeit chip syndicate operating out of Singapore. Alan Lee recovered the cockpit voice recorder of the plane and the pilot had screamed that the flight display unit had gone blank, seconds before the crash. A counterfeit chip in the unit could have caused it to malfunction.'

A mask had drawn down over Nelson's face. 'Have you got proof? The flight display unit, itself, can't give you leads. It was probably smashed up in the crash. The investigation revealed pilot error. At least, that's what Alice told me.'

Dolly was very interested. Why was the mention of counterfeit chips making Nelson Ong nervous? 'Madam Lee did not mention a counterfeit chip syndicate?'

For a moment, the mask slipped from Nelson's face to reveal burning eyes. Then the mask slipped back into place. 'No. We never discussed the plane crash.'

Dolly changed the subject. 'You live alone?'

Nelson relaxed and smiled. 'Yes. I like my own space. I remained a bachelor because of that.'

'You had no plans to marry Madam Alice Lee?' Dolly's voice held the right degree of surprise.

Nelson's smile grew broader, and he spread his hands out expressively. 'Alice wanted me to marry her, but I was stalling. You know, ASP Das, one really gets used to living alone. Alice was fine as a date but other than that ...' His voice tailed off.

Dolly wondered why Nelson Ong was lying about Rachel Kelly and her mother living with him.

'Madam Lee was murdered Sunday night. Where were you, Mr Ong?'

Nelson laughed. 'Oh, I'm a suspect, eh? Well, you can check with Singapore Immigration, and you will find I was out of Singapore for three days. As I told you, I was in Shenzhen. I received the news of Alice's death there through a text from my secretary. I immediately called Justin Chua and offered my condolences. I told him I would attend the funeral next week. I left Singapore on Saturday and returned last night.'

Nelson Ong could not have murdered Alice Lee and Dolly felt disappointed. She was certain the business magnate was telling the truth though Charlie would follow up with the Immigration and Checkpoints

Authority. She coughed discreetly. 'We have evidence Alice Lee was spying on this bungalow. She thought you were cheating on her. Are you telling the truth when you say no one else lives here, Mr Ong?'

Nelson Ong's face grew red. 'I live here *alone*. Alice had a nasty mind.'

'Were your relations with Madam Lee cordial of late?' There was a note of resignation in Dolly's voice, the interview was not proving fruitful in pointing out Alice Lee's murderer, but it was interesting Nelson Ong was denying the existence of Rachel Kelly, not to mention him declining to give the name of his partner in the Shenzhen enterprise.

Nelson recovered and gave a small smile. 'We'd not had a fight or anything, ASP Das. I was falling out of love with Alice. There was no other woman, but I felt Alice expected me to propose marriage and I liked my bachelor life and did not care to share my life with anyone yet. Is there anything else? I have a business meeting in an hour and need to get to the office.'

Dolly drove away from Jelita. She wondered if Charlie had contacted the Shenzhen police to know more about Nelson Ong's chip factory. It was strange a man who manufactured sauces was suddenly brokering computer chips. Dolly nodded to herself. Both Nelson Ong and Rachel Kelly were looking like good candidates for being members of the criminal syndicate packaging counterfeit chips. But Nelson Ong could not have killed Alice Lee. Alice Lee's murder had nothing to do with the syndicate. Lily was right. Then Dolly shook her head. Nelson Ong could have hired someone to kill Alice Lee and given himself an alibi by being out of the country. One could not rule that out.

Back at CID HQ, Dolly called her old friend at Singapore Interpol and asked him for the registered Singapore address of Supt Rachel Kelly. Marty Sim was surprised, but readily gave the information. Rachel Kelly's address was a two-bedroom condo unit on Orange Grove Road and Interpol HQ paid her rent. Once settled in Singapore, Supt Kelly had sponsored the long-term pass of her old mother and registered herself as her mother's caregiver.

Dolly was thoughtful after she had rung off. She had not seen Supt Kelly nor her mother at Nelson's house, could it be that Kelly sometimes stayed there and the rest of the time at her own flat?

There was a tap on her door and Charlie entered. He seated himself opposite Dolly and clearly and concisely told her what Lily had found out about Linda Lee. Dolly looked stunned.

After a few minutes, she found her voice. 'Yes, Lily saw Linda with a man at a restaurant and they appeared to be lovers. So, Linda was having an affair with Pradeep. Take Pradeep's photo to Lily and ask her to confirm that's the man she saw with Linda at the restaurant. We must tie loose ends. The man on the phone to Linda that night was probably Pradeep Chopra then. He was upset with Alice Lee, ran out of the Primrose Crescent bungalow and called Linda. And Linda was not at her house at the time of Alice's murder. She had gone to the bungalow to have it out with Alice. Why, if the DNA matches, Lily will have solved Alice Lee's murder!' Dolly sat back in her chair. Her eyes were wide with conjecture before they narrowed.

Surprised at the glint in Dolly's eyes, Charlie hastily left the office. He chided himself for thinking his boss was jealous of her sister.

* * *

Dolly was stiff and overly courteous to Lily that night at dinner at the Silver Springs Condo unit. After thanking her for her information about Linda Lee, Dolly became distant.

Lily hastened to say, 'You or Charlie would have seen the bandage on Linda's wrist sooner or later. I just visited Linda and saw it first. I did try to call you, Doll. When I couldn't get through, I called Charlie. And well, Lestriani stays just two doors away and I thought to ask her Linda's whereabouts the night of Alice's murder. Maids notice things. Lestriani told me about the phone call and Linda leaving the house late at night.'

Dolly said in a deceptively casual voice, 'Well, Charlie did meet Linda before you when he went to look for Patrick Singh. He failed to notice the bandage on Linda's wrist. You did well, Lily. Has Charlie shown you Pradeep Chopra's photo?' When Lily nodded, Dolly raised her eyebrows.

Lily said, 'Pradeep Chopra was the man with Linda at the restaurant the day we went there for lunch, Doll. I've identified him from the photo.'

Dolly nodded and said, her voice cold, 'Good. At least, one murder will be sewn up if the DNA matches. Though I will tell my bosses it was you who solved it.'

Lily looked thunderstruck. 'No, no, why would you do that?'

Dolly looked at the dismay on her sister's face and sighed. She said in a mollified tone, 'Well, you deserve the credit, Lil. You're a good amateur detective and thank you for the work you did.' Her smile was still cold. 'Word gets around, Lily. It's not good for Charlie's career prospects if our bosses learn that a trained officer like him failed to notice a suspect's bandaged wrist when a member of the public did. It's a good idea for us to solve our own cases. I would appreciate it if you didn't meddle, Lily. And I will stop discussing my cases with you.' She started on her roti and dal at the dining table.

Her sister was seated next to her with Vernon and Angie eating chicken curry and rice opposite them, looking apprehensive. The assistants liked both the sisters and they could sense Dolly's animosity.

Lily, taken aback by the rebuke, doled some dal on to her rice and said, 'Sorry, Dolly. I observed something and told Charlie, that's all I did.'

'Charlie would have interviewed Lestriani,' Dolly said, frigidly. 'There was no need for *you* to talk to her.'

Tears glistened in Lily's eyes. 'I was just trying to help.' She rose from her chair and left the dining room.

Dolly looked away from Angie's dismayed face, ate her food before saying, 'Angie, I didn't see Supt Kelly or her mother when I visited Nelson Ong today. Supt Kelly has another residence in Singapore. Does she and her mother stay only sometimes with Nelson Ong, not all the time?'

Angie shook her head and told Dolly Supt Kelly and her mother stayed at Nelson's bungalow all the time. Rachel Kelly's mother was sick and warded at Gleneagles Hospital and the maid went with her. 'And ma'am go to work. So you never see them, Madam Superintendent.'

Dolly nodded and added some chicken curry to her plate to have with the roti.

Lily returned to the dining room and sat down on the chair next to Dolly. Her eyes were red and she sniffed. It was apparent she had been crying. She began to eat her dal and rice. Dolly, hearing the sniffles, felt ashamed of her jealousy, stretched out a hand and patted Lily's arm.

'Sorry, Lil, I know you were trying to help,' she said.

Lily nodded and began finishing her meal. When she was more composed, she eyed the bowl of rice pudding Girlie had left by her plate. She looked up to say, 'If Linda's DNA doesn't match that of the killer's, we are back to scratch. Linda may have just gone to quarrel with her stepmother, not kill her. Then someone else killed Alice. Like Etienne Lee.'

Lily decided to forgive Dolly, but inside, she was desperately afraid her sister was serious about not confiding in her about her cases. Lily enjoyed the amateur detecting as well as helping her sister and hoped Dolly was just having a jealous moment. She initiated more talk on the case, hoping to add her input.

Dolly helped herself to some rice pudding while shaking her head. 'No, it's not Etienne. The forensic experts have analysed the killer's DNA pattern. Etienne is ruled out as his DNA would have matches with Alice's and the DNA found on the skin underneath Alice's nails does not have matches with Alice's DNA. Someone unrelated to Alice by blood, killed her.'

Dolly began eating her rice pudding and when she had finished the last of it, she leant back in her chair and sighed. 'Alice was on Nelson Ong's tail. It seems he owns a chip brokerage factory in Shenzhen. Why aren't you eating the rest of your kheer, Lily?'

Lily sighed. 'Dr Heng told me to cut back on sugar. But Girlie makes such delicious kheer. Like Mummy used to make.'

Dolly doled a second helping of kheer into her bowl and began eating. She looked up at Lily. 'I'm in my mid-fifties and if I don't solve such high-profile cases as the Alan Lee murder, there's no chance of getting promoted to the rank of superintendent. Many young officers are waiting to step into my shoes. I still need a salary. Ash hasn't finished schooling and Joey doesn't earn all that much. We won't have much saved for the future. Alice Lee's murder is the easier case to crack. How to get anything on the syndicate? Lester Chong asks for updates every day from DAC Nathan and he is really determined to know who hired a thug to kill his cousin.' When Lily beamed at her, glad to be included in her sister's cases and happy to discuss them with her, Dolly gave a smile.

Angie, who had relaxed after seeing the sisters friendly again, now frowned at the fried okra bowl on the dining table. 'I need to learn how to cook,' she muttered. 'At Mr Nelson Ong's house, Auntie ask me to cook food for money. The Indonesian maid no good at cooking. Auntie want English food. Baking and all. Auntie ask me to find a cook. Come in every afternoon, cook, and leave. Good money.' She looked at her husband and grinned. 'Sad V cannot make English food.'

Dolly said, 'By "Auntie", you mean Supt Kelly's mother?' When Angie nodded, Dolly looked at Lily and noticed her staring at Angie, transfixed. 'Lil, what's the matter?'

Lily blinked her eyes, looked innocently at her sister, smiled, and said, 'Nothing, Doll. Angie, are you home tomorrow? I want to have a chat with you.'

When Vernon and Angie had left, Lily said over coffee to Dolly in the living room, 'Don't worry, Doll. You usually do solve your cases. You will have a breakthrough in the crime syndicate case. Are you going home?' Lily finished the last of her coffee.

'Yes.' Dolly rose from the couch. 'I've hired a part-time maid. Ash and Amita make such a mess. She is a good *patri* for Ash, but she is untidy.'

'Patri? Prospective bride. You make it sound like it's going to be an arranged marriage. They are in love, Doll. They will move out, anyway, after marriage. Then you don't have to worry about the mess Amita makes.' Lily giggled. She glanced at Dolly's face and said, contritely, 'Sorry again for talking to Lestriani before Charlie could do so, Doll.' She grinned when Dolly smiled at her.

Late at night, lying on her four-poster bed, all Dolly could think of was that Lily may have solved one of her cases. While growing up, she had been fond of her sister and with the indulgence of older sisters, viewed her as a feather-brained busybody. That she failed some of her exams in school cemented Dolly's belief that Lily was a trifle empty-headed. And during the Silver Springs Condo murder case four years ago, she found out how wrong she had been. Her sister was astute, creative, and had a clarity of thought Dolly envied. She knew it was wrong to be jealous of her sister, but Dolly could not help it, she was human. Slowly, she fell into a fitful sleep and dreamt Lily had solved the crime syndicate case, too.

Monday, 3 June 2013

Singapore

32

Dolly was looking through some papers on her desk when Charlie, with a perfunctory knock, burst into her office. He had a faxed report in his hands and his eyes were shining with excitement. The wall clock read 10 a.m.

'Madam, the forensic technicians did an all-nighter and came up with Linda Lee's DNA pattern. It's a perfect match to the DNA found on the skin underneath Alice Lee's fingernails. Linda Lee strangled her stepmother!'

Dolly's eyes shone before her brows puckered. 'Let me see,' she said. She looked through the report Charlie handed her and returned it to him, saying, 'Yes, there is no doubt whatsoever. Please take this report to Supt Ang and DAC Nathan, Charlie. We need to bring Linda Lee in.'

When Dolly and Charlie were seated in DAC Nathan's spacious office along with Superintendent Ang, Nathan looked up from the DNA report. 'Linda Lee strangled her stepmother. What is the motive, ASP Das?'

Dolly said, crisply, 'My sister, Lily, did some detecting, sir. Linda Lee is her former classmate and she had seen Linda with a man in a restaurant. He was being intimate with her, so Linda had a lover. My sister went to see Linda last week and noticed her wrist was bandaged. After Linda left her condo, my sister talked to Linda's helper, who is her helper's friend. The maid said Linda left her home late the night Alice was murdered after talking loudly on the phone to someone called "Pradeep". Charlie showed a photo of Pradeep Chopra to my sister and she identifies him as the man with Linda at the

restaurant. Linda and Pradeep are lovers, sir. We know Pradeep visited Alice
Lee the night of her murder to plead with her to withdraw the civil suit. Alice
refused and being emotional and upset, Pradeep probably called Linda and
she went to confront her stepmother. And killed her.'

DAC Nathan's eyes were wide. 'Your sister noticed the bandage and
questioned Linda Lee's maid, all on her own? Very resourceful. Wait, didn't
your sister help you solve the Silver Springs case? Supt Siti Abdullah told
me you get help from your sister to solve your cases.' Noticing the flush on
Dolly's cheeks, he hastened to say, 'Well, sometimes, we, the police, do need
some help. Have your sister join the force, ASP Das. Then she can work for
us and not with us.' He grinned.

When Dolly gave a wan smile, Nathan continued, 'We need to bring
Linda Lee in for questioning. I will have the arrest warrant ready, but you
will have to get a confession out of Linda Lee, ASP Das. We have DNA
evidence, true, but for a case to come to trial, there must be a clear motive and
a confession. Grill her, ASP Das.'

Dolly nodded as Superintendent Ang said, 'Inform us of the time of the
interview, ASP Das. We will both watch via CCTV.'

In her office, Dolly collected her handbag. 'Okay, Charlie, let's go to
Primrose Crescent. Have a backup squad car follow us.'

While walking to the lift lobby, Charlie said, 'Madam, we contacted the
Shenzhen police. Nelson Ong owns an electronic brokerage firm in the Luohu
district. But his partner is not anyone we know. He is a Chinese businessman
named Ming Tao Chen, who went into partnership with Nelson Ong just a
year ago. The police have no records or convictions against Chen.'

'He may be a syndicate member we don't know about, or Nelson Ong
may be buying over this firm from Chen. Tell Marty Sim to ask the China
police to keep an eye on this firm.'

Dolly got into the squad car in some excitement. Her jealousy of her
sister dimmed in the excitement of catching a killer.

* * *

The gate of 39, Primrose Crescent was wide open with a black Mercedes-
Benz parked in the porch when the police arrived there late morning. Dolly
marched to the front door, Charlie on her heels, and pressed the bell. Joyce,
the maid, showed the officers into the drawing room where an argument
was going on.

Linda was seated on the sofa next to Lester Chong and speaking loudly to her cousin. 'Etienne and I don't want the house sold, Lester, whatever the terms of Alan's will say. We want to live here. Don't be such a stickler for duty, Lester. You know we love this house.' She stopped short when she spied Dolly at the door. 'ASP Das, this is not a good time to visit. We are in the middle of a family conference.'

Dolly entered the room and said, her face wooden, 'We need you to come with us to CID HQ for questioning, Ms Lee.'

Etienne, dressed in shorts and tee, stood up from his chair. 'Why? What's happened?'

Lester Chong, Singapore's Junior Minister of Transport, was a short, dapper man with a head of thick hair and even features. He looked at Dolly with narrowed eyes before rising from the sofa and coming forward.

'ASP Das, I have heard DAC Nathan sing your praises,' he said while shaking Dolly's hand. 'Why do you want to question my cousin?' He looked at Linda, who remained seated on the sofa, her eyes filled with dread. 'Linda, what's the matter?'

Dolly said in a hard voice, 'When Alice Lee was being strangled, she scratched her killer and as a result, we have the DNA of her murderer from the skin underneath Alice's fingernails. That DNA matches yours, Ms Linda Lee. Why did you murder your stepmother?'

Tears gathered in Linda's eyes, but she defiantly raised her chin, her cheeks red. 'How do you know it's my DNA? You never swabbed me.'

Charlie stepped forward. 'When I came to this house, I took the liberty of bagging your half-eaten biscuit. The laboratory was able to extract your DNA from the dried saliva on the biscuit.'

Linda's tears had dried, and her eyes were blazing as she stood up. 'Isn't it illegal to take my DNA without my permission?' She glanced at her cousin. 'Lester, do something!'

Lester Chong, who was looking thunderstruck, stuttered, 'The police are asking you to accompany them to the station for questioning. That's all.'

Linda's face was transformed into a white mask of fear. She looked at her stepbrother and her face softened. 'Tien,' she began.

Etienne was standing by his chair, listening to the police officers. When he turned to Linda, his face was white.

'*You* killed Ma?' Etienne's voice was horrified. He took a step towards Lester Chong, who patted him on the shoulder. But Etienne could not take his eyes away from his stepsister. In a trembling voice, he said, 'Sure, you didn't like her, but why would you *kill* her? We don't kill everybody we don't like. She was my *mother!*' As the full realization of what his stepsister had done, hit him, Etienne went over to the sofa, sat there and buried his head in his hands.

Linda moved towards her stepbrother, her eyes filled with tears, but stepped back when Lester Chong slowly shook his head.

'Are you refusing to come with us for questioning?' Dolly's voice lifted Linda out of her introspection. She brushed the tears away from her eyes and lifted her chin.

'I'll come,' Linda said, sullenly. Then she wailed, 'What will happen to my children? Who will take care of them? Their father has left me and I don't know his whereabouts.'

Etienne raised his head from his hands, brushed tears away from his eyes and said in a shaking voice, 'I'll look after them. What you did is not their fault. I'll see to it the kids never know you're a killer.' His eyes were filled with a vibrant dislike that made Linda Lee drop her eyes and look down at the floor. She slowly followed Dolly out of the room.

Linda walked out of 39, Primrose Crescent, her head held high. She ignored Yusuf's exclamations of distress, looked up at Emily Gan sitting at her window, gaping at her, lowered her head and walked out of the gate.

* * *

Linda Lee's interview took place at 2 p.m. in Interview Room 4 of CID Headquarters. DAC Nathan and Superintendent Ang watched the interview via CCTV.

Linda sat on a chair, her head bowed, her fingers drumming repeatedly on the table. She was under extreme stress. Charlie and Dolly sat opposite her while Mok sat beside Linda manning the tape recorder. When Mok switched on the recorder and announced the time and the names of the people present in the interview room, Linda finally looked up.

Her face, white and strained, she said, 'I already gave my statement to Inspector Goh. I was working at the library the night Alice died and came home at around 9.30 p.m. and had dinner with the kids. Then I had an early night. I have nothing to add to this statement.'

Charlie said, 'Your helper says you left the house after 10 p.m. and had not returned by the time she went to bed which was 10.30 p.m. You were also heard talking loudly on the phone before you went out. To whom were you speaking and where did you go?'

Linda glared at Charlie. 'No comment.'

Dolly intervened, 'Your helper was smart enough to catch the name of the person you were talking to on the phone. Pradeep. Pradeep Chopra, is it? Maybe, we should ask Mr Chopra in for an interview.'

Linda's face went as white as chalk and her eyes were dark pools of despair. Her hands trembled so much she tried to hide them in her lap. Finally, a tear trickled down her cheek. 'She wouldn't listen, at all. And she had the power to make Pradeep bankrupt. She had already seen to it he did not get tenure at the university. If she took him to court, he would have to sell his flat and even that would not pay for a lengthy court case. Pradeep had no choice. His grandparents left him property in India, he was going to leave for India with his children and settle there if Alice went ahead with the civil suit. I could not let that happen.'

Linda sobbed as grief wracked her frame. 'I love Pradeep. We were to live together and merge our families once I got a divorce from Patrick. I had it all planned out. I did try to reason with Alice. But she sat there in Alan's study, her face cold, a malicious smile on her lips, telling me she would not withdraw her case. She *mocked* me. Asked me if I could not find a better man than a down-and-out weak fellow like Pradeep Chopra. She said I always went for scoundrels and Pradeep, like Pat, was after me for my money. She said if my father was alive, he would see to it I didn't end up marrying a second leech. She cottoned on to the fact I was in love with Pradeep. It was her mocking that got to me, ASP Das. I looked at her grinning evilly at me, and something snapped.'

'How did you kill Madam Alice Lee?' Charlie asked.

Linda ran a hand through her dishevelled hair. 'She sat in Alan's chair, the curtains of the window behind her. I rushed to the curtains, tore down a tieback cord and pulled it around her neck. Oh, she fought all right. She was strong, but I was stronger. She soon went limp. I opened drawers and chucked items out to make it look like a robbery. I did that quietly so Joyce wouldn't wake up. Then I came away.' Linda looked down at the table, and a tear formed like a dewdrop at the corner of her left eye.

Dolly sighed and looked at the tape recorder faithfully recording Linda Lee's confession. She looked at the distraught woman in front of her, to whom it seemed a relief now to confess her sins. Linda's eyes glittered with the tears of unfulfilled dreams. Her face reflected a deep despair that made Dolly make up her mind to instruct the remand officers to keep her on suicide watch.

Dolly said, softly, 'You are in love with Pradeep Chopra?'

Linda Lee lifted hopeless eyes. 'Always. From when we were young,' she said in a shaking voice. 'Alan used to tell me to get over it. Pradeep and Rosvinder were already a couple, and you could see Pradeep doted on his wife. Rosie was nice, she never suspected I was in love with her husband. I know it sounds awful, but I sometimes wondered what would happen if Rosie died in a plane crash. When their children were born, I began seeing less and less of Pradeep. What was the use? Then Pat came into my life, and I began dreaming again of a husband and family. We married and I found a new lease of life with the children. ASP Das, what's going to happen to my *children?*' Linda Lee burst into tears and buried her head in her hands.

After she had recovered, Dolly asked, 'And then Rosvinder died. What happened then?'

Linda raised tear-stained eyes. 'All my forgotten dreams resurfaced. Pat and I had drifted apart, and I strongly suspected he was having an affair. I would get a whiff of a woman's perfume sometimes from his clothes. I began spending time with Pradeep, and we fell in love. We made plans to marry, merge our families. His children, Rina and Nina, like me, and they were becoming rebellious. Pradeep could not manage them. We thought if we were a family, the girls would bond with Duleep and Natasha and become the normal fun-loving girls they were before Rosie died. I was going to ask Pat for a divorce.

'And then came Alice's civil suit taking Pradeep to court, seeking compensation for Pa's death. Alice was the daughter of Justin Chua. We knew she would get her way and make Pradeep bankrupt. Alan told Pradeep he anticipated Alice taking Pradeep to court. He assured Pradeep he would find evidence to raise doubt about Rosie being responsible for the crash. He said he was gathering evidence and would soon talk to Jonas, his lawyer. He would ask Jonas to represent Pradeep in court and he was sure Jonas would win the case. But Alan died before any of that could happen and his evidence clearing Rosie died with him. Alice was vindictive and you would think a former cabinet minister would not be so blind to his daughter's faults. Pradeep was up for tenure, it was a certainty and then Justin Chua, influenced by his daughter's evil words, blocked the tenure. Pradeep was shattered. Alice was so *evil.* I told Pradeep to appeal to Alice, talk about his children's futures. Alice was a mother herself, surely, she could not take the roof away from his children's heads. So, Pradeep went to see Alice on that Sunday night. He called me as soon as he came out of the bungalow. He was crying, ASP Das. You don't know what that did to me. To hear a grown man cry as if his life was over. And then he said his grandparents had left him property in Pune in India and he would leave everything and take his children where Alice Lee could not get at them. He did not want to live in Singapore any more. I was so angry at Alice. I decided to confront her.' Linda hiccupped and looked around.

Dolly nodded at Mok who went out to get a glass of water. After Linda had drunk the water like a parched traveller in a desert, Dolly said, 'So you went to Primrose Crescent.'

Linda's eyes were tearless now. 'Yes, I left after 10 p.m., took a cab to Pandan Valley. I had a key to the gate, opened it and went in. To my surprise, I saw a lit window on the ground floor, and the light was coming from my brother's study. I crept to the window and saw Alice at the computer.'

Charlie interrupted. 'What time would this be, ma'am?'

Linda looked dazed. 'What? Oh, after 10.30 p.m. probably, or it could have been a bit earlier. I went to the main door, used my key to let myself in and went to my brother's study. Alice was surprised to see me. You know the rest.' Linda Lee sat in her chair with tears streaming down her face.

Dolly nodded to Mok to switch off the recorder. A constable quietly entered and handed a piece of paper to Dolly. DAC Nathan had signed the warrant for Linda's arrest. Dolly handed the warrant to Charlie and rose to her feet.

'Inspector Goh will type up your statement and you can sign it tomorrow, Ms Lee. We are arresting you for the murder of Alice Lee.' Dolly nodded at Charlie and walked to the door and quietly went out, leaving Charlie to formally arrest Linda Lee.

In the corridor outside, Dolly caught her breath. She shook her head. What a heartless, evil woman Alice Lee had been. She felt sorry for Duleep and Natasha. She entered the ladies' toilet, splashed cold water on her hot face and washed away the tension of the hour.

THE COUNTERFEIT CHIP SYNDICATE

Wednesday, 5 June 2013

Singapore

33

Lily, dressed in shorts and a tee, looked with interest at her prospective employer. Rachel Kelly was beautiful, she thought, with her piercing blue eyes and creamy complexion. She did not look a day over forty though Lily suspected Rachel was at least fifty years old from the crow's feet branching delicately, like filigree, from the corners of her eyes.

Angie and Lily were seated on a large sofa in the living hall of Nelson Ong's bungalow. Rachel Kelly, sipping a cappuccino, sat on a winged chair while her mother, Gertrude, peered at everyone from her wheelchair.

Rachel looked at Angie. 'So, Lily Das is your friend? You don't look close in age, though.' Her eyes probed into Lily and then she flicked a glance at Angie. 'It is hard to find hired help, but I need to be able to trust Lily. I go to work, and my mother is alone in the house with her helper.'

Angie said confidently and truthfully, 'Lily was my neighbour before my marriage. We stay in the same housing complex. She is a widow.' Angie looked at Rachel through artificial eyelashes as she became mendacious. 'Hard to earn money with no man in house.' Angie was glad Lily and her husband, Frankie, had bought a unit in the same condo complex where Uma Das lived. It was easier to lie about Lily, but truthfully give her right address, which Rachel Kelly was checking by looking at the back of Lily's identification card.

'Lily's mother in her eighties, already, ma'am.' Angie looked guilelessly at Gertrude, knowing Rachel's devotion to her mother. 'So sick all the time.

Medicines cost money. Lily work as cook in a restaurant in the housing block where she live,' Angie added, truthfully. 'But only at night. Not enough money for her Ma's medicines. No more family. Mother is only family Lily got.' Angie was warming up to her fictitious account of Lily's life, ignoring Lily's warning glances.

Gertrude Kelly quavered from the wheelchair, 'My Rach is the best daughter a Mum can have.'

Rachel's face softened, and she looked at Lily with a modicum of camaraderie.

Lily smiled. 'You can taste my cooking and then make up your mind on the hiring.'

A smile tugged at Rachel's lips. 'Sounds good, Lily. Our full-time maid cannot cook, and her time is taken up caring for my mother. Can you cook Indian curries? My mother is especially fond of them.'

'Not a problem,' Lily said, cheerfully. 'We can start tomorrow, if that is convenient, ma'am.'

Gertrude said, 'We need a cook, Rach. I remain hungry every day.'

Rachel Kelly made up her mind. 'All right, then, Lily. You can start tomorrow afternoon. Please make enough food for dinner and Mum's lunch the next day. She will tell you what she wants to eat. I am away the whole day as my work is very demanding. Mum and her maid are the only people in the house during the day. Thank you, Angie, for your referral.'

Outside the bungalow, while walking along the road towards the bus-stop, Angie asked in a scared voice, 'Mrs D, will you be safe? Ms Kelly like tiger when angry. This one is a new Indonesian helper. The old one left, crying. Ma'am shout so bad at her. Mrs D, does Mr Frankie know you are doing this dangerous job?'

'Of course not. Don't worry so much. And don't tell anybody, especially Dolly. If I tell my family, they will not allow me to look around Nelson Ong's bungalow and help Dolly with her case. But Angie, Dolly deserves a promotion to superintendent. She has worked hard for it. Nelson Ong and Rachel Kelly are not going to talk to the police and it's hard to get any evidence of their involvement in the crime syndicate.'

Angie sat down on a bench at the bus shelter. 'I come with you every day, Mrs D. And I call V if I hear Ma'am Kelly shout. She so fierce. You just look around only, Mrs D?'

Lily sat down on the bench next to Angie. 'I will plant a listening device in Rachel Kelly's bedroom, so we know what she and Nelson Ong talk about at night when they are alone. If they belong to the crime syndicate, we will know for sure. I'll go to the mall and buy the device. I'll connect it to my phone, and I can listen to conversations between Nelson Ong and Rachel Kelly. Now mind, not a word to Dolly or Mummy.'

Angie looked more scared than ever. 'All illegal, Mrs D. Sure you get into trouble. Ma'am Dolly shout at me. I bring you here. Ma'am Dolly already tell you not to meddle in her cases. She will fight with you, Mrs D, not nice to see sisters fight.' Her eyes began to glisten. She was surprised to see Lily waving.

Rachel Kelly's car had come out of the cul-de-sac and from the driver's seat, Rachel smiled at the two women at the bus shelter.

When her car was out of sight, Lily called a cab on her mobile phone. 'I wanted her to see we were waiting for the bus,' she explained to Angie. 'I'll go to the mall to buy that device. You want a lift, Angie, though I'm going the opposite way.'

'It's okay, Mrs D, I take bus.'

They talked fondly of Molly and Ben until the cab arrived.

* * *

Patrick Singh lay on the hotel bed, gazing out of the window at the sky littered with stars. His eyes were tearless though Sushila stayed in his heart and mind every minute of the day. He remembered her long black hair, her curly eyelashes, her eyes alive with desire, and the diamond stud on her nose. Her voice came lightly on the breeze fluttering in.

'Pat, we'll make a living selling mobile phones in Chennai. We'll have a grand retail shop in one of the busy shopping malls and a bungalow with a garden in a prestigious district of Chennai, near Marina Beach. Our child will grow up there and whenever he wants, he can run to the beach to play.'

She said this the weekend after Alan's murder. He had begged her not to hurt Alan and leave it to him to gauge whether his brother-in-law was a real danger to the syndicate. He had gone out with Alan to the pubs in the early days of his marriage. He knew Alan was decent and he had fought with Sushila over his fate.

When Lester Chong phoned Linda with the news of Alan's murder, she began wailing loudly. He shut the bedroom door, whispering to her the children would wake up, all the while a white anger burning inside him. *Sushila had not deterred their bosses from arranging Alan's murder.*

When Linda had recovered from her hysterics and was crying quietly, he had gone to the bathroom and dialled Sushila's number on his mobile and asked her to meet him near the swimming pool. He had decided to break off their affair. Alan's murder was too much for him to take.

They sat together, two figures on a bench near the swimming pool, merged into darkness, the pool's water alight with reflections from the lamps around the area. She wept bitterly when he broke off with her. She told him Alan had collected evidence against her through one of her engineers and she was frightened of the police arresting her. Reluctantly, she had, therefore, agreed to their bosses arranging Alan's murder in Bali. It was she who told Lionel Chu to recommend Alan the hotel where Mark was manager so it would be easy to kill Alan and cover it up as a robbery gone wrong.

Patrick had been adamant, he wanted to have nothing to do with her. It was then she cried again and told him she was carrying his child. She promised she would give up the syndicate and go away to India with him, to her house in the village and lie low until they could continue their lives in a big city.

The news of impending fatherhood jolted Patrick, but he had given in only when he saw the love and determination in Sushila's eyes. He had known Sushila cultivated him just as she had Lionel, to get close to Alan Lee, but he truly loved her and the money he made from the syndicate washed away the disappointment of Ronnie Lee not leaving Linda any money. He had been a willing syndicate broker, but he had drawn the line at harming Alan. He had tried to see Alan, visited the bungalow when he became sure the syndicate was preparing a hit on him, but Alan had not been in. It had been too late.

Sushila whispered, 'I know we did wrong and took risks. But it's all worth it when we have the money to lead the rest of our lives in India in luxury, have the means to give our child a good home and education. I need to tie one or two loose ends and then we will leave for India. I am already moving money there.'

Had it been worth it? Patrick shook his head. Sushila had been murdered and dumped on the railway track. And he knew very well who had ordered Sushila's murder and why.

He would confront the killer and take revenge if that was the last thing he did.

Thursday, 6 June 2013

Singapore

34

Angie and Lily, dressed in shorts and tees, pressed the bell of Nelson Ong's bungalow. The full-time caretaker of Gertrude Kelly opened the door and smiled at them. She had a broad forehead, a pock-marked face, and a nice smile. They followed her into the kitchen.

The room was large with natural sunlight streaming in through big windows. Angie made her way to a cupboard and opened the door. Inside, there was a vacuum cleaner, mops, pails, and cleaning fluids. Angie dragged out the vacuum cleaner, gave Lily a smile and walked away into the corridor leading to the living hall.

The Indonesian maid led Lily to a double door fridge and nodded, encouragingly. Lily smiled and opened the fridge door. It was well-stocked with vegetables in a compartment, red meat and white meat in separate compartments, and various condiments. The maid then pointed to a small larder opening from the kitchen which was stocked with herbs, spices, and other bottles.

In the kitchen, there was a counter designed as a chopping board and an inviting set of knives beside it. There were woks, Dutch-ovens, frying pans, either hanging from the ceiling or stacked neatly in a glass-fronted cupboard. Lily noted the double ovens and six gas burners.

When the maid began to leave the kitchen, Lily asked, 'May I speak with Madam Gertrude, please? I would like her to tell me what to cook.'

After looking a bit puzzled, the maid nodded and gestured Lily towards the inner sanctums of the house.

In a back parlour, resembling an English glass conservatory, Gertrude lay on a recliner, a book in her hand, enjoying the sunlight filtering through the glass. She glanced up when Lily entered.

'What would you like to eat, ma'am?'

The old lady's cornflower blue eyes lighted up. 'Can you roast chicken? I want to eat roast chicken and mashed potatoes today. We are British, you know, and I do miss our English fare. Make some vegetables as well, of course. Please prepare dinner for three people. And tomorrow's lunch, let's see, cream of chicken soup, boiled potatoes, and grilled fish. You will find sea bass in the freezer. My daughter bought that from Cold Storage last night.' Gertrude smiled toothlessly at Lily, who nodded and walked away. Somewhere from the bowels of the house came the whir of a vacuum cleaner. Angie was at work.

Lily took out an apron from her capacious bag and draped it around herself. Then she set to work. While defrosting the chicken and fish, she began chopping vegetables. Soon potatoes were boiling in a Dutch oven while Lily expertly chopped parsley, onions, carrots, and beans. She spied some mushrooms in the fridge and decided to make mushroom stuffing for the roast chicken.

There was a hiss from the door and Angie entered, stealthily. 'Mrs D, now is a good time to hide the bug in the master bedroom.'

Lily said in a low voice. 'Any suitable places in the bedroom to hide the listening device?'

'There is plastic plant near window with many leaves,' Angie said in a theatrical whisper. 'I can hide it there, Mrs D. I sure go to jail for this.'

Lily rolled her eyes, went to the chair at the corner, rummaged in her handbag, fishing out a small, slim black object. She handed it to Angie saying, 'Hide it in the potted plant and cover it with leaves. Thanks, Angie.'

Soon the bungalow was filled with the enticing aroma of roasting chicken and Lily set herself to grill the sea bass on the open-air grill, having marinated it well with lemon juice, herbs, spices, and a generous dollop of sambal she had found in the fridge.

It was when she was washing the dishes that Lily heard the whine of Gertrude's wheelchair. The Indonesian maid followed her charge in. The old lady looked animated, her blue eyes shining in anticipation, her hands sweeping back her snow-white hair.

'Your dinner is ready, ma'am,' Lily said, cheerfully, from the sink. She glanced at the kitchen clock. It read 6 p.m.

'Oh, the smell of the chicken is wonderful. I will have my dinner in the dining room, Lily. Please bring the food there.' Gertrude smiled. 'I am sure I will be giving a good verdict on your culinary abilities, Lily.'

Angie sidled in as soon as Gertrude had been wheeled to the dining room. She watched as Lily cut a generous piece from the roasted fowl and placed it on a bone china dish with a flowered pattern. Lily doled mash potatoes on to the plate along with vegetables au gratin.

'Well, I hope the old lady enjoys her dinner,' Lily said, taking the plate out to the dining hall.

Delighted laughter and squeals from the dining hall assured Angie the dinner was to Gertrude Kelly's satisfaction.

Lily returned to the kitchen and said, 'Well, I think I can keep my job. What about the device, Angie? Did you hide it carefully? Let's look.'

Angie and Lily made their way through a long corridor to the master suite. The bedroom was decorated in blue and gold with white furniture. Lily immediately went to the potted plant by the window and made sure the listening device was invisible and hidden behind leaves.

'What are you doing?' A pleasant male voice asked. Lily and Angie jumped.

A rotund short man with rimless spectacles and a goatee beard was standing at the door, looking quizzically at the two helpers. 'Angie, who is your friend? What is she doing here?'

Lily was the first to recover. 'I was hired by Ms Kelly, sir, for cooking Ma'am Gertrude's meals. Angie referred me for this job. She was showing me a spot of grease on the cabinet here, so I was telling her what cleaning liquid to use to get rid of the stain.' Lily smiled sweetly. 'I am Lily. If you would care to sample my roast chicken and give your verdict, sir?'

Nelson gave a booming laugh although his eyes remained a trifle suspicious. 'The whole house smells of roasted chicken and I am sure it's delicious.'

'Come, Angie, we will go and look for a suitable cleaning fluid.' Lily led the way out and Nelson Ong stood aside to let them pass. Angie looked back and could see Nelson peering at the bedside cabinet. She hoped he would not look inside the potted plant.

Nelson Ong soon joined them in the dining hall and his face was more friendly. Lily heaved a sigh of relief.

'Well, well, Gertrude, roast chicken at home after a long time, eh? I hope you don't feel too nostalgic for Manchester!' Nelson carved himself a piece of chicken and began munching it, using his hands.

'Why, this is delicious, Lily!' He enthused. 'You could be a restaurant chef!'

Lily smiled her thanks. 'I've left the chicken in the oven on low heat for when you and Ms Kelly have dinner, sir,' she said. 'The grilled fish should be cool soon and then may be placed in the fridge for tomorrow's lunch. I'll be leaving now. I've finished washing up. See you tomorrow, ma'am.' Lily directed a smile at an approving Gertrude.

In the bus shelter, Angie burst out, 'I could have died in there when Nelson Sir catch us. He has scary eyes. I think Nelson Ong see us look in the plant. If he finds the bug, I go to jail.'

'He won't find it! I can't wait to hear what Nelson Ong and Rachel Kelly talk about tonight in their bedroom.'

The bus arrived and as they boarded, Lily cautioned Angie. 'Don't tell anyone what we were up to. Okay?'

'I was scared, but excited too,' Angie admitted. She grinned. 'I feel I am in crime movie.'

They sat down on two empty seats. The bus rumbled on towards Holland Avenue.

* * *

Wan Chai District, Hong Kong

Mark Latham exited the MTR at the Lockhart Road exit and began walking along the road, making for The White Stag Bar. It was late evening in the red-light district and Mark blended in with the crowd. He had slept uneasily last night with recurring nightmares of his time in Bali and had woken up early in the tiny bedroom above the Chinese eatery he rented a few blocks away. He had tried to contact his friends, but they were elusive and hard to find.

The red-light district was a far cry from Summertown, Oxford, where he had grown up, the son of Oxford professors. After reading physics at Cambridge, he studied at Manchester Technical College before securing a job in an electronics firm in Scotland. In 1980, he took a break from his job to teach at a college in London and became friends with one of his Asian students. That had been a life-changing event. Mark's girlfriend of four years had broken up with him and Mark had, on a whim, taken a job at a wafer fab in Singapore. There, he had fallen in love with the tropics.

As he walked along the road, keeping to the shadows, occasionally jostled by drunk merrymakers, Mark reflected on his journey into crime. He thought about the British girl he had met in Singapore, their short engagement, before she had jilted him for a Chinese millionaire from Hong Kong.

At this vulnerable time, his Asian student in London, who was back in his native Singapore, approached him to join the counterfeit chip syndicate, he had worked in briefly before. Mark jumped right into the racket, his acumen quickly propelling him upwards to partially head operations. His romance woes were forgotten in the thrill of eluding the police.

He now entered 'The White Stag', and a wave of nostalgia swept through him recalling a similar pub in London called 'The Flying Horse'. He had gone there often with his mates in the sunny days of youth and a frisson of yearning passed across his bland face. He made for a table in a dark corner and ordered their popular ale and a chicken pot pie with chips in vinegar. Nothing like pub food, he thought fondly.

Sipping his ale, he remembered excitedly volunteering to head operations in Bali for the China, Vietnam, and Laos counterfeit computer chip black markets. But he had to have a cover. Mark had always fancied running a hotel and had eagerly taken up the manager position at Beachcombers. He was happily running his recycling counterfeit chip factory in Pujung, flying to sell the substandard remarked chips to distributors in Shenzhen, when like a black shadow, Alan Lee had suddenly appeared on the horizon. Yes, Lee had posed a threat to the entire black market operation.

Mark bit into his pot pie and burnt his tongue. It was piping hot. Allowing his pie to cool, he glanced around at the customers laughing in loud voices as they ate their food and drank their alcohol. Had there been a need to kill Alan Lee? He had questioned Boss and received a chilling reply that told him, yes, it had to be done.

Mark had planned the murder of Alan Lee so well, he thought. It was to be a robbery gone wrong. He noticed Alan's gold Rolex watch on his wrist when he checked in at the hotel and knew what to do. It was best for the killing to take place at night rather than in broad daylight. And where better than in the hotel he ran where he could mastermind the operation, get his man to bring in the killer, bribe a security guard in dire need of money. To the Bali police, he would emphasize it was a robbery gone wrong and cover his tracks and those of the killer.

Then it went horribly wrong. Mark was apprehensive from the time he saw Alan Lee chatting in the café with two women from Singapore. Next morning, when he understood one of them was a Singapore CID officer, he started planning his escape. Had Alan Lee told the police inspector about the syndicate? He did not know but he would not take any risks. He had thought it best to close the Pujung factory and go underground for the time being.

He sampled the pie cautiously. It was delicious and melted in his mouth. Boss had finally revealed the secret he had kept from him all these years. That they worked for ruthless killers who took half their profit and there was no turning back. This knowledge made it easier for Mark to plan Alan Lee's murder. Besides, despite the drawbacks, there were perks as well once he understood for whom he was working.

A Chinese girl was crooning a song on the stage and Mark liked the melody. He decided to order dessert.

Friday, 21 June 2013

Singapore

35

Rachel Kelly sat quietly behind her computer at her desk in her office. *The net was closing in. She could feel it.* Her supervisor, Chief Supt Derek Randall, had personally taken over the Mark Latham extradition case, asking her to return to her research duties at IGCI. Evidence from Mark's computer hard disk connected him to Sushila Iyer, and Derek had obtained the issuance of a red notice for Mark and was coordinating the search for Latham in Hong Kong with China law enforcement branches.

She was unable to shield Mark any more. Her face creased with a twinge of regret as she remembered their college days in Manchester when he had been her boyfriend. She mentally thanked him for saving her from drinks and drugs. The whirring air-con failed to remove the sheen of moisture from her short, tip-tilted nose and her blue eyes were clear and fearless. *She was prepared for an arrest.* Her thin lips parted in a sad smile as she thought of her mother.

Gertrude Kelly had been a mousy, quiet housewife, raising her child in a Manchester suburb when her husband, Andrew, left her for another woman. Untrained for office work, Gertrude earned a living as a charwoman, rented a council flat, and managed to send her little girl, Rachel, to school. When, at the age of thirty-two, severe arthritis, inherited from her own mother, curtailed Gertrude's career, she did what many others in her situation do all over the world. Blessed with a good figure and bosom, long legs, and a pleasant face, Gertrude left Manchester for the seedy alleys of London and resorted to prostitution.

To her surprise, Gertrude began earning more money than she had ever dreamed, allowing Rachel to go to a good boarding school and the Manchester Technical College. Unaware of her mother's trade, Rachel grew into an intelligent, fun-loving woman with dreams and aspirations. It all shattered when two policemen arrived at the doorstep of their modest house in St John's Wood and arrested her mother for prostitution. At the age of forty, Gertrude was sentenced to three years in prison. Rachel was twenty at the time.

Rachel's eyes filmed over as she relived the shock and agony she experienced on learning the truth about her mother. It seemed her whole life had been a lie. Rachel spiralled into depression and began taking drugs to overcome the misery of her existence. It was at this low point in her life that Mark Latham arrived and provided a sturdy shoulder to cry on and a weighty anchor to take her to safe harbours.

Slowly, Rachel recovered her equilibrium, but her mother's secret life had taken its toll leaving Rachel with a take-it-or-leave-it attitude to life. Mark's devil-may-care attitude inspired her and when in a dusky pub, a Chinese man had broached the idea of selling counterfeit computer chips on the black market, the idea appealed to Rachel. Her astute mind figured out that for the racket to be successful long-term, insiders were needed to squash or ferret out information. With that in mind, Rachel applied to study for a degree in criminology and later joined the Police Academy.

It had been hard to choose between Nelson and Mark. Her attraction to Mark made her many times refuse Nelson's advances but in the end the notion of being the mistress of a business tycoon won over being an engineer's girlfriend and Rachel broke off with Mark and started her relationship with Nelson. The syndicate was running smoothly, and money was flowing into her bank accounts when Charlotte Miller appeared on her horizon like an angry, vengeful hurricane. Rachel lost her job and livelihood but regained them with remedial training. She transferred to the job of a criminal intelligence officer at Interpol in Lyon, looking to head the department investigating the trade of illicit goods. The chip syndicate she formed with Nelson was harvesting electronic waste from Scottish fabs, recycling and remarking faulty airplane parts in a factory in Greece, the parts to be sold in Europe and the Middle-East. The syndicate needed her, an Interpol officer who investigated counterfeit and illegal goods, to easily squash and block investigations of their illicit operations. Then it took her seven years to get a transfer to the Singapore Interpol office, to be with Nelson.

Rachel had been at the prison gate when Gertrude Kelly, broken and destitute, emerged from behind the barbed wire fence of life in prison. Her health had deteriorated and most of the money Rachel made from the illicit counterfeit chip black market went to house her mother in one sanatorium after another. Switzerland had somewhat revived her before Gertrude took to alcohol and after that it was a steady decline towards oblivion. Rachel had firmly taken her mother in hand, spent a fortune on detox and rehabilitation, and finally Gertrude had been cured of her alcoholism. Rachel hired full-time help for her mother and took Gertrude with her to Singapore. By this time, the syndicate was operating out of South-East Asia.

Her fierce devotion to her mother was the shining star in an otherwise squalid life, Rachel thought, wryly. Her face clouded over. Gertrude had come down with pneumonia last week and three days ago, had been shifted to the hospice. There was little hope she would survive, but Rachel refused to believe the doctors. Her mother was her only reason for living, she *had* to survive.

Rachel sighed. She was practical, her greatest attribute. If arrested, she knew she would do jail time, but she also knew the police had no evidence Nelson had ordered the hit on Alan Lee and Sushila Iyer. Rachel smiled and for a moment the sun peeped into the shadows of her life.

She made up her mind to turn whistle-blower and give evidence for the prosecution in Nelson's trial. She had meticulously recorded their conversations regarding Alan Lee's murder and Sushila Iyer's killing. She had worn a microphone, she knew how, after all she was a policewoman, and Nelson had remained unaware she was taping him. In return, Rachel would negotiate a shortened jail sentence. It was she who had told Nelson about Sushila Iyer's mother's flat in Chennai when ASP Das had given her that information. And Nelson had sent his minions to butcher Sushila. He had even discussed with Rachel about leaving the body on the railway tracks. And this conversation Rachel had duly recorded.

Survival of the fittest, Rachel told herself. It would always have come to this situation, she thought. If they were caught, she knew they would rat on each other—Nelson, Mark, and her. It was the reason she had taken precautions and compiled evidence to nail Nelson for murder. Mark would not escape the Interpol search and hang or serve life sentence as it was on his direct orders and payment Ramdin had killed Alan Lee.

Rachel could have left. She owned a house in Switzerland and she could have fled there. But not with her ill mother left behind in Singapore. She figured if she did jail time in Singapore, she could still get to see her mother, transfer money from some of her British bank accounts into Singapore.

'You went through hell, Mum, to raise me. I will see to it your life is comfortable if that's the last thing I do,' Rachel murmured to herself.

The telephone jangled and Rachel snatched up the receiver. Her breath caught in a sob as she slowly replaced the receiver after hearing the news from the other end.

* * *

The blinds were drawn in the tiny hospice room assigned to Gertrude Kelly. A shaded lamp in one corner lit the bed and its occupant. The figure on the bed was shivering. Gertrude's pneumonia had taken a turn for the worse and there was no hope. She lay there, her face lined and wrinkled, her skin as white as parchment paper, her eyes closed, her breathing laboured. The end was near.

Lily sat in a chair by the bed, her hands stroking Gertrude's arm, her face sad. While she had not worked long at Nelson's bungalow, Lily had bonded with Gertrude, who had been a good cook in her youth. The Indonesian maid at the house had informed Lily that Gertrude was dying and Lily had come to the hospice to pay her respects. When a nurse whispered to Lily that Rachel was on her way and in the corridor, Lily got up from the chair and retreated to a dark corner and sat on a three-legged stool.

Rachel entered the room and rushed to her mother's bed, sat on the chair beside it, and began feverishly kneading her mother's cold hands.

'Mum! Can you hear me?' Rachel asked in a loud, trembling voice. 'It's me, Rach.'

The eyelids flickered and Gertrude half-opened her eyes. She opened her mouth, soundlessly.

'Mum, I'm here, right beside you,' Rachel said, desperately.

In a whisper, Gertrude said, 'I am leaving, Rach. It was a … sordid life, but you were the shining beacon. All the things I did, I did for you. When sweating, balding men grunted and screeched over my body … dumping poison in me … I would not be there, you know. My mind … would wander to you, my angel … to your boarding school … playing lacrosse … racing down to the stream you described in your beautiful letters. If I could … bring you up well, it was all worth it. The foul stench of the men … the twisted acts they made me perform. But prison was a horrible place … it broke my spirit … I reached for the bottle. But you took care of me, Rach. Remember our time … in Switzerland, at the sanatorium. That small Swiss village … we woke to the tolling of bells … outside the window were majestic mountain peaks … oh … to see that scene once more! It was our time, Rach. When I'm gone … keep that time alive in your mind and heart. Scatter my … ashes in that beautiful village of Wengen under the shadow of the great … Jungfraujoch.'

Gertrude's increasingly harsh breathing and Rachel Kelly's sobs were the only sounds to be heard in the room.

'Mum, I don't regret a single thing I've done in my life because it bought me time with you. The doctors gave up on you ten years ago, but the Swiss sanatorium saved your life, Mum. We had eight extra years together. I'm not sorry how I earned the money to keep you in that sanatorium, Mum. Now, I will be all alone. Oh, Mum, don't leave me!' Rachel howled.

Lily, her eyes teary, kept to the shadows and quietly left the room. She blinked in the bright sunlight outside. She called a cab and asked to be taken to Silver Springs. She wanted to be with her mother.

Wednesday, 26 June 2013

Singapore

36

Lily wandered into Nelson Ong's master suite to check on the listening device. It still lay in the same position she had placed it the day before after charging it in the kitchen. Rachel Kelly was none the wiser. Lily sighed with relief. She had turned on her mobile every night and accessed the device, but Nelson had been overseas and only returned home last night, so she heard no conversations between Rachel and Nelson. The bug remained in its place as Angie was the maid who dusted the rooms and she made sure it was hidden in the plant pot.

Now, Lily took the bug from the pot and with it in her hand, quickly went to the kitchen, where she plugged the device into a power point to charge it. She hoped Nelson and Rachel would talk soon. Lily was serving her three weeks' notice of the termination of her job and would soon not come to the bungalow any more. Without Gertrude, a cook was not needed in the household.

After making a chicken casserole, Lily returned to the master bedroom and placed the wireless listening device back in the potted plant. She failed to see the handbag on the bedside table and on her way out, bumped against it, sweeping it to the floor. The contents of the handbag spilled out. Lily quickly began gathering the articles to place them back into the handbag.

'What are you doing in my bedroom?' Rachel Kelly was standing at the door of the attached bathroom, her voice as cold as ice. Lily belatedly realized

Kelly had returned home from work early and it was her handbag she had knocked over.

'Oh!' Lily improvised wildly. 'There was a stain here yesterday on the bedside table and I was making sure it was gone.'

'You have been employed to cook in this household. You have no business in my bedroom. You were rifling through my handbag, you *thief!*'

Rachel Kelly advanced into the room, her eyes cold shards of blue ice. 'You'll accompany me to the police post.'

Angie, who had been mopping the living room, watched, scandalized, as Rachel Kelly marched Lily through the house and into her car parked in the driveway. As soon as the car revved up and sped away, Angie ran out of the door of the bungalow, leaving her mops and brooms all over the place, and hailed a taxi.

* * *

Dolly was busy reading a report from Derek Randall. While the Hong Kong police had raided a flat in the Wan Chai district where Mark Latham had been holed up, they had arrived too late. He had escaped and Interpol did not know his current whereabouts. He was proving to be a slippery eel to catch. There was a sharp knock on her door and Dolly looked up.

Techie Pet entered the room and for once, she looked ruffled. Charlie followed her in.

'Boss, your sister's assistant, Angie, is waiting in the lobby. It seems your sister is at a police post and may be arrested for burglary.'

'*What!*' Dolly shouted.

'Your sister requested the Holland Road Police Post to contact you and I took the call, Boss,' Techie Pet said. 'She was caught stealing in a bungalow at Jelita, belonging to Nelson Ong, and Supt Rachel Kelly brought her to the police post.'

'But, what, what … !' Dolly stuttered.

'Angie said your sister was working undercover as a cook in Nelson Ong's household.' There was a spark of admiration in Techie Pet's eyes.

'Lily is such a goose!' Dolly spluttered. 'It was dangerous for her to work in a suspected criminal's household. I guess Lily and Angie were hunting for clues. *Amateurs!* Lily's problem is she fancies herself a detective.'

Charlie intervened seeing Dolly's flashing eyes, a sure sign she was beginning to lose her temper. 'Madam, we should rescue Madam Lily.'

Leaving a smirking Petula, Dolly marched out with whatever dignity she could muster, Charlie trailing behind her.

* * *

'Doll, I *just* planted a listening device in Rachel Kelly's master bedroom. I knocked over Rachel's handbag accidentally and she thought I was stealing cash from her handbag. The police have checked, I have no cash on me.'

Dolly looked coldly at her sister in a small interview room of the police post. She was enraged to see Lily looking calm. Her voice was scathing as she said, 'You deserve to spend the night in jail, Lily. If it weren't for Mummy, I would let you do just that. How could you take on such a dangerous mission? These people may be criminals and murderers. They won't think twice about killing you. What were you *thinking*? That this was a page out of the murder mystery books you read? This is real life!'

Charlie completed the formalities with the duty officer who deigned to direct a smirk at Lily as she came out of the room with her sister. Grasping her sister firmly by the shoulder, Dolly led her to her car.

'So sorry about all this,' Dolly said over her shoulder to the officer.

Lily was unfazed. In the squad car, she said, 'Such a pity Nelson Ong was not in Singapore the past weeks. The device is working fine, and I can hear Rachel crystal clear, humming tunes, listening to the TV. I hoped at some point the device would record a conversation between Nelson and Rachel that would nail them.' Lily tried to look forlorn. 'I wanted you to have evidence. You deserve to be superintendent, Doll. Mummy says when you are, she will be so proud. She will then take a trip to India, visiting all the religious shrines to give thanks to the gods.'

On the act of scolding her sister, Dolly shut her mouth, tears sparkling in her eyes.

'They could have *killed* you,' was all she said.

* * *

That night, in their mother's house, Dolly convinced Lily to have Angie remove the listening device from Nelson Ong's bungalow the next day. It was too risky to leave it there. Lily nodded, sadly, but looked forward to one last night of listening to any conversations being recorded in Rachel's bedroom, now that Nelson was home.

Dolly was staying the night at her mother's house as her toilet was being painted and the smell of paint aggravated Dolly's allergic rhinitis. Reluctantly, she agreed to Lily's suggestion of listening to the device with her and grumpily climbed on to the twin bed in Lily's bedroom.

At 10 p.m., the sisters sat up on their beds. Lily switched on her mobile phone and clicked on the app that allowed her to access the bug in Rachel Kelly's bedroom. The sisters listened intently.

There was the sound of a man humming a tune and the TV in the bedroom was switched on. After about five minutes, the TV was switched off and there was the sound of a number being dialled on the bedside phone. The phone was switched to the speakerphone mode.

A man answered at the other end. *'Hello.'*

Nelson's voice said, *'Patrick, Rachel is attending an Interpol party at the Marchmont Hotel. Now is a good time, man. The hotel carpark is deserted and dark at this time of the night, it's the perfect time and place to eliminate her.'*

The voice at the other end said, *'Are you sure Rachel Kelly ordered Sushila's murder?'*

'Of course, I'm sure,' Nelson scoffed. *'I made her a partner two months ago, and this was her decision. She felt Sushila would rat on the lot of us if she was nabbed in India and it would be a matter of time till her arrest.'*

'Why? Rachel managed to block Latham's extradition, why couldn't she do the same with Sushi?'

'Don't you think that would attract attention? Too many blocked investigations. She could not do that. I'm sorry, Patrick, that your girlfriend died. She worked well for us. She misjudged Lionel Chu and she should never have gone to meet him at a hotel and used her credit card to check him in. The police are not fools and I thought Sushila had more intelligence.'

'Boss, she really thought Lionel was bent.'

'What's done is done, Pat. Rachel is the one who knew where Sushila was hiding in Chennai, the Singapore police told her, and she hired assassins over the phone to murder your girlfriend. Rachel oversees the counterfeit phone business in India, you know that. I am paying you well for this job and I have given you the locker number in the airport that has the money. It will see you through the rest of your life in India. Get rid of Rachel Kelly for me, Patrick! As soon as the job is done, get out of the country. There are ferries that will take you to Batam in the dead of night, no questions asked.'

'Okay.'

There was a click.

Dolly jumped down from the bed and rushed to the bathroom while Lily sat on the bed, stunned. Dolly came out in two minutes and was busy on the phone with Charlie while dressing in her outdoor clothes. When she clicked off the phone, she looked at Lily, sitting on the bed, her eyes as round as saucers.

'Nelson Ong is going to have Rachel Kelly *killed*?' Lily screeched. 'Did that sound right, Doll? And Patrick? That was Patrick Singh going to kill Rachel? An eye for an eye for Rachel ordering the hit on Sushila.'

Dolly gave her hair a quick brush and said, 'Yes, in a nutshell. I wouldn't bet on it, though, that Rachel Kelly ordered the hit. Nelson is cutting his losses, maybe he is scared Rachel Kelly has something on him and will rat to the police. I need to go, Lily! I must try to stop the murder. Charlie and two squad cars will follow me to the Marchmont Hotel. And there's an APB out for Nelson Ong in case he tries to leave Singapore.'

After Dolly left, Lily sat on her bed for a long time, gazing into space. The counterfeit chip crime syndicate was unravelling through infighting.

37

Patrick Singh sat on the motel bed, gazing through the window at the lights of a world he was escaping. After taking care of Rachel Kelly, he would slink away into the shadows of the docks, looking for a dark ferry with a boatman who would ask no questions once he saw the wad of dollars in his hands. In the dead of night, he would leave the land of his birth for an unknown future—did he have any regrets? Patrick sighed. While his parents were alive, life had been meaningful, he had run the condiments store in Serangoon with his father and even after his father's untimely death from a heart attack, he ran the store with his father's friend. Was it when he married Linda and realized he would never be a part of his wife's inherited wealth that the lust for money began?

Slowly, Patrick rose from the bed and entered the shower. When he had married Linda, he had been fond of her, but he had to admit he had been dazzled by her father's wealth and 39, Primrose Crescent. Linda had been vulnerable, angry, and irritable, the pain of her mother's death still fresh in her mind and her animosity to her stepmother reaching a boiling point. It had been easy to lend her his shoulder to weep on and they had married at the registrar's office after a whirlwind courtship.

But the wealth he had visualized would be his, eluded Patrick. Shrewd Ronnie Lee had tied up his money in trusts for his grandchildren and Alan had done likewise after his father's death. The pursuit of wealth became an obsession, and resentment towards Linda grew until he no longer loved her. He was a consummate actor, though, giving his wife no inkling of his true feelings for her.

It was when he was going through a bout of depression due to business woes that Sushila came into his life, and with her came new hope and dreams. He had fallen madly in love and had shared her dream of becoming wealthy enough to retire early in life to a mansion in a small corner of India. When he visited India with her, the peace of the countryside resonated with him, it was so different from the urban jungle in which he had been raised. When she had told him of her membership in the counterfeit chip syndicate, he too had eagerly wanted to join and had no qualms opening his internet brokerage firm, selling the malfunctioning chips Sushila recovered from electronic waste, on the internet chip black market.

How he missed Sushila. If only she had not plotted to kill Alan, that and the interaction with Lionel Chu had been her undoing. The rain shower's spray was a balm to his fevered skin and his tears mixed with the water.

Towelling himself dry, he spared a thought for his children. A frisson of sadness flitted through his face as he visualized Duleep's round face and merry twinkling eyes, full of fun, chasing his long-haired sister, Natasha with the innocent joy of childhood. He would miss his children. That paled in comparison to the legacy he would leave behind for them—their father a criminal. Patrick began dressing in black clothes.

In the darkness of his mind, a ray of sunlight lit the memory of the green paddy fields with little huts that had been Sushila's village in Chennai, that would have been his home if she were alive. He could see in his mind's eye the banyan trees in the village beneath which people sat in groups, segregated by age, chatting with each other, without a care in the world. They had decided to live in the village when they were not busy making money in the teeming city of Chennai. He would escape from Singapore and go there now. He would find Sushila's essence in the village of her birth.

Patrick did not know what propelled Sushila to join forces with the black market syndicate, she had been curiously reticent about her induction into the racket. Patrick had met her when she bought condiments at his shop. When he learnt she loved to cook at home, he had become friendly with her, and they spent many weekends cooking up a storm in the condo unit she rented at Balestier. Her father had been ailing and armed with a Singapore Permanent Residency, Sushila had brought her parents to Singapore to live with her.

Patrick, who had only passed his 'O' levels had been in awe of Sushila's capabilities, knowledge, and prowess as a successful turnkey operations manager. He never dreamt she would fall in love with him. On a sultry afternoon, after cooking biryani with a different set of condiments than they usually used and which unknown to them had contained an aphrodisiac, they had made violent love in her bedroom, accompanied by the sound of rain pounding down on the air-con compressor outside her window. He had taken it for granted it was a one-time event and had been pleasantly surprised when she asked him to stay the night on a weekend when Linda and the kids were away in Malacca attending the wedding of a cousin and Sushila's parents were away on a holiday in China.

There had been a wildness in Sushila that sometimes disturbed him, but it was a turn-on as well. She made love with an abandon that excited him beyond measure. Sushila was restless, always seeking out new avenues to calm herself like meditation and yoga. Not born a beauty, with a dusky complexion, a sharp, hooked nose too large for her face, bright eyes and a thin mouth, Sushila had readily told Patrick the reason she sought him out—lust. She loved his lithe body, his muscles, his handsome face, and noble bearing. It was enough for her, she said, brains were not everything. A flicker of pain had rippled through her face and Patrick wondered if Sushila had loved and lost someone.

He had only found out later that Sushila had cultivated him to get close to Alan and because she needed a chip broker. Nelson had probably told her that Patrick was money-hungry and would leap at an illicit broker's job. His lust for money was no secret in the Lee family to which Nelson was privy, being Alice's boyfriend, but by then Patrick was so in love with Sushila that he could not care less why she had sought him out.

After her father died, Sushila moved to Silver Springs Condominium, renting a unit there. She wanted to live closer to Patrick for both love and work. Patrick had been apprehensive of Linda discovering his affair, but they had been discreet, and he was sure Linda had been none the wiser. It had been a thrilling, forbidden love, he thought. Making love to his mistress with his wife next door, so to speak. Snatching hours of love-making when Sushila's mother visited the temple or went to Little India to do shopping.

Patrick brushed his hair at the mirror. *Sushila*. She had left this world, but she would never leave him. As desolate and barren his life had become, an ember of revenge sparked until it had become a roaring fire, blinding him to reason. He forgot he was a father, after all, he had been willing to leave his children, abandon them for a life with Sushila and their unborn child. Sushila's death had to be avenged, he had to take revenge for Sushila. She had been discarded like a rag on the railway tracks to be mowed down by a train, dashing forever their hopes of a life together. If Boss said Rachel Kelly had ordered the hit so as not to have too many blocked investigations at Interpol, Patrick believed him. Why would Boss lie? And Rachel was the one who had known where Sushila was hiding in Chennai.

He stuffed clothes into a backpack and took a cab to the airport to retrieve the money Nelson was paying him to kill Rachel Kelly before making his way to the Marchmont Hotel.

* * *

Rachel Kelly came out of the ballroom of the Marchmont Hotel where the Interpol party was still in full swing. Dressed in black mourning, she looked tired. She glanced at her watch. It was 11.30 p.m. In the wake of Gertrude's passing, a spark had been extinguished in Rachel. Only Mum had known the slow progression from a squalid life to one filled with amenities and the toll it had taken. Now Rachel had nothing to live for. When Nelson talked of the Cayman Island bank accounts filled with their ill-gotten gains, the beautiful villa they would share in Tenerife, Rachel gave a wan smile. Her life had included her mother always, without her, Rachel was bereft. For the first time in her life, Rachel understood the old adage—money cannot buy happiness.

Slowly she opened the door to the ill-lit stairwell and began to climb down to the floor where she had parked her car. A trained policewoman, she heard his footsteps long before he was near. What she was unprepared for was the silken rope tied across the bottom of the stairs. When she ran down, she tripped and fell, smashing her face on the concrete and soon felt a pain near her heart as the knife slid into her, smooth and seductive.

She lay there in a pool of blood, her eyes open. She saw two figures walking down the winding mountain path of Wengen as the sun beamed down, birds sang, and cowbells jingled. Switzerland lay written in her heart and mind as life oozed out of Supt Rachel Kelly.

* * *

Patrick Singh looked at the dead face of Rachel Kelly and tidied up after him. Why didn't he feel the exhilaration of victory? He had avenged Sushila's death by killing the woman who ordered it. All he felt was a curious detachment as he walked into the carpark towards Rachel Kelly's car, her car keys in his pocket. At least, he would have a ride to the ferry terminal.

The car came out of nowhere, smashing into him and pinning him to the ground. He lay there bleeding and blearily looking up, saw with wide eyes, the car reversing to run over him. The last sound he heard before losing consciousness was the distant wail of police sirens.

* * *

Dolly ran to the doctor as he came out of the ICU ward. 'Will Patrick Singh live?' She asked, tersely.

The doctor shook his head. 'It's touch and go. The car ran over him two times. But he is conscious now and I can't guarantee he will be conscious later. Ten minutes only, ASP Das. Then, we have to operate on him.'

Dolly nodded and with Charlie, entered the ICU ward and were directed to a bed in the corner. Corporal Mok followed them with a video camera. A man bandaged from head to toe lay on the bed. He was hooked to multiple monitoring machines which beeped and whistled. A pair of burning eyes and a red mouth peeping out of a bandaged face was all that was visible of Patrick Singh.

'Mr Singh, can you speak? Only a few words will do. And if it's a yes, give us a thumbs up sign,' Dolly said and nodded to Charlie who sat on a chair close to the bed with his tape recorder switched on. Corporal Mok was busy turning on his video camera to visually record the interview.

'Mr Singh, did you kill Rachel Kelly on the stairwell of the Marchmont Hotel tonight?'

Patrick gave a thumbs up sign, duly recorded visually by Corporal Mok.

'Did Nelson Ong order this hit?' When Patrick's thumb went up, Dolly asked, 'Why did you murder Ms Kelly?'

In a cracked whisper, Patrick said, 'Rachel Kelly ordered Sushila's murder.'

'Mr Singh, we have reason to believe you owned an online brokerage firm selling faulty computer chips on the black market. Your girlfriend, Sushila Iyer, supplied you with the faulty chips,' Dolly said. 'Is this true?'

Patrick gave a thumbs up sign.

'You and Ms Iyer were members of a counterfeit chip crime syndicate,' Dolly stated. 'Who headed this syndicate?'

Patrick said in a loud whisper, 'Nelson Ong ... and Mark Latham. Rachel Kelly looked after the India ... operations. Mark gave Sushi ... her orders.'

'Are you sure Nelson Ong heads this syndicate?' Charlie asked, softly.

Patrick gave a thumbs up sign. In a whisper, he told the police officers Nelson had employed Sushila to extract faulty chips from electronic waste at her turnkey factory and pass them on to Latham in Bali to remark and repackage them in his factory. The chips were then sent on to brokers who sold them cheap on the black market. Patrick had been one of the brokers.

'Who ordered the hit on Alan Lee in Bali?' Dolly asked.

Patrick gave a thumbs down sign.

'You may not know for sure, but can you guess?' Dolly insisted.

Patrick's whisper was weaker. 'Lionel Chu found out what Sushila was doing ... she told Nelson. Nelson asked Sushi to bribe Lionel ... we all surprised when Lionel took our money. Sushi told me Boss was plotting Alan's murder ... Nelson Ong. I asked Sushi not to take part in Alan's murder ... I broke off with Sushi. But she was pregnant with my child ... what to do? She agreed to give up the syndicate ... we ... go Chennai.' Patrick's voice died away in a crackle and a sob.

'What about Mark Latham?' Dolly asked, urgently. Patrick was soon going to lose consciousness.

Patrick took a deep breath and whispered into Charlie's microphone. He told the officers he believed Mark Latham executed the hit on Alan Lee. Latham had told Sushi to have Lionel recommend the Beachcombers Hotel to Alan. Then it was easy for Latham to arrange Alan's murder.

'And then Lionel Chu took his own life,' Dolly stated.

Patrick Singh's whisper was stronger. He told the officers the mistake the syndicate made was misjudging Lionel Chu. Nelson ordered the hit on Alan, he did not want too many murders, Patrick said, so he sent Sushila to the Swiss Hotel to bribe Lionel with more money. None of them guessed how intensely Lionel regretted betraying Alan. When Lionel took his own life, Sushila knew she was caught on the hotel CCTV tape and went underground in Chennai. Patrick added in a cracked whisper, 'She booked Lionel's stay ... police would be on to her.'

As the tape whirred, Patrick Singh continued whispering into Charlie's microphone. Even when life was seeping out of him, it seemed a relief to Patrick to unburden himself. He told the police officers of Sushila's flight to Chennai, her plan to lie low in her mother's flat before Patrick joined her. In a voice laden with tears, Patrick said that after he arrived, they were to relocate to the village of Sushila's birth and lead a simple life there until their child was born. His eyes flashed as Patrick said in a stronger voice that Rachel Kelly had Sushi killed, afraid she would turn informer when the police found her.

Patrick's voice was petering out. Then suddenly his eyes sharpened. 'ASP Das, where is my backpack, it has money ... Nelson paid ... for killing Rachel. Can this money go to ... to my kids?' A tear formed at the corner of Patrick's left eye. Slowly his eyes closed. One of the machines gave an alarming beep.

'Outside, officers, please. We need to operate on the patient.' The doctors and nurses entered, wheeling in a gurney.

The police officers went out of the ICU ward, leaving Patrick Singh to his fate. Charlie's mobile beeped urgently. He switched it on and listened carefully. Then he switched off his mobile and faced Dolly.

'My men, who are watching Nelson Ong's bungalow, report he has just left in his car with two suitcases. He is on the PIE, madam, heading for Changi Airport.'

'Are we set to intercept him there?'

'Yes, madam, our team is waiting there in case he absconded. I will bring the squad car to the front, madam.'

'Did our officers retrieve Patrick's backpack with the money?' Dolly asked.

Charlie shook his head. 'There was no backpack at the carpark. Patrick's killer probably ran off with the money. We'll nab him, madam.'

Dolly looked back and saw a gurney making its way out of the ICU ward and wondered whether Patrick Singh would make it out of the operating theatre alive. Those poor children, Dolly thought. *Both parents are criminals.* What sheer bad luck!

38

Nelson Ong stood in the queue for the Singapore Airlines night flight to Heathrow, a medium-sized suitcase, and a trolley bag at his feet. He was travelling light.

He frowned. His hit man informed him that he had run over Patrick Singh two times, but before he could finish him off, he heard police sirens and cleared off. It was then Nelson Ong decided to flee Singapore in case Patrick Singh talked. He had bought a villa in Tenerife facing the sea where he would spend the rest of his life with his ill-gotten gains. He had hoped Rachel would be loyal and would share that life, but he knew Rachel too well. He had seen a look in her eyes when she glanced at him that told him she would betray him and save herself. Would Mark do that, too? Hopefully, he did not have to find out.

He had known as soon as shrewd Alan Lee began snooping around that he would have to cut his losses and be content with the millions he had earned from the racket. He had begun closing his factories and consolidating his fortune, preparing for this very day.

Nelson inched forward in the queue, his eyes flicking nervously around him. Was he being watched? He was more afraid of the casino owners to whom he owed money than the police. He thought back to his youth and to the friend who had taken him to his first casino. Singapore did not have casinos then and they had travelled to Genting Highlands in Malaysia, two youths travelling on a bus intent on having fun. He had no inkling gambling would enter his blood like a strong narcotic, making him oblivious to his surroundings. He was only intent on ways and means of earning money to feed his habit.

His father refused to fund his hobby and Nelson had to wait until the old man died of a cerebral stroke to get his hands on big money. There was no stopping him then. He knew his business empire would collapse under the strain of his habit and saw a lucrative way of funding his habit in a dingy pub in London talking to Rachel and Mark.

Nelson smiled. The racket had been good while it lasted. Except for the incident of Charlotte Miller early on and the setback to Rachel's career, the operation had run smoothly. In the early days, it was a fledgling operation, harvesting electronic waste for plane parts from Scotland wafer fabs and reassembling them in factories in Greece. When the Greek police were on their tail, he transferred his factories to eastern Europe and the Middle East. Mark had left the syndicate after Rachel broke up with him, but he and Rachel had astutely masterminded operations until the debacle of the Gatwick crash.

Leaving Rachel to carry on low-key operations in England, Nelson, with Mark, had then started the black market operations in South-East Asia, working out of Singapore. Nelson had to admit that Mark's expertise and intelligence were behind the highly successful second phase of their operations. It was a pity that his gambling debts had resulted in the syndicate failing to keep all the profits it netted. That he had to share them with a third party. Otherwise, they would all have retired abroad two years ago—rich and contented.

He was so deep in thought that when a man spoke to him, Nelson jumped. A rotund man with rimless spectacles was speaking to him and with dismay, he saw ASP Dolly Das walking towards him.

'Mr Nelson Ong?' Charlie asked, politely. 'Please accompany us to CID HQ to help with inquiries on a counterfeit chip syndicate and the murders of Alan Lee, Sushila Iyer and Rachel Kelly.'

Nelson's eyes flicked around like that of a trapped bird, and he noticed uniformed policemen had formed an impenetrable cordon around him. Passengers behind him in the queue began murmuring apprehensively. Nelson Ong knew when the game was up and quietly, he left the queue to accompany the police to CID HQ.

* * *

Tin Shui Wai New Town, Hong Kong

Mark Latham was feeling pleased with life. He had connected with his friends who shifted him to a safe house away from the central business district. He escaped just in time. Two days after he left, the police raided the Wan Chai flat. Soon he would relocate to Macau and restart the syndicate. Without Nelson and Rachel, he would have a free hand in running the syndicate and making more money than he ever dreamed.

He still remembered that day when as a testing manager of wafer chips at an electronics firm in Scotland, he had marvelled at the amount of electronic waste he discarded each day and from that realization was born the dream of selling leaky wafer chips on the black market for profit. It was when they moved the syndicate to Singapore from where the black markets of Cambodia, Laos, India, China, and Indonesia were easily accessible, that the syndicate's profits skyrocketed.

Mark pulled the blind up at his window and noted with pleasure a sunny and mild day, reminding him of London in summer. It was there in 1980, on a day like this, that he had sat in a pub with Nelson Ong and Rachel Kelly, drinking lager and hatching a lucrative plan. Nelson had been doing his MBA at a London college where Mark taught on a part-time basis, and they had become friends. Rachel had been Mark's girlfriend, the woman he intended to marry. He could see that day in the pub as if it were yesterday. The dim interior, the raucous laughter, the smell of beer and cigarettes, the maudlin songs, and the three of them sitting in a booth dreaming of making money.

Mark had been talking of his years at the Scottish wafer fab, of electronic waste and the counterfeit chip black market and the millions that could be garnered from there, when Nelson's eyes sparkled and he broached the plan to run a syndicate, targeting the black markets of Europe and Asia. Mark agreed with alacrity, he had always had a penchant for taking risks, meandering towards situations and events possessing an element of thrill.

He had revelled in the notion of outsmarting the police even when he had been young, living with his parents in Oxford, and racing cars for the thrill in Blackbird Leys, keeping one step ahead of the traffic police. His parents, both Oxford dons, expressed a mild surprise when he declined to follow in their footsteps, not for the lack of brains but for the fact that he found academics as dull as ditch water. He moved to Manchester and joined a technical college to obtain his engineering degree and applied to a Scotland wafer fab for a job. He met Rachel while at college, and they had started dating.

Mark smiled wryly. That meeting in the pub years ago had been more of a catalyst than a business venture. Nelson had fallen head over heels in love with Rachel and she with his money. Mark became a bystander, helplessly watching, as Rachel spent more and more time with Nelson. He had done the right thing by them—bowed out by relocating to Singapore to join an electronics firm there, exotic locales had always appealed to him. He temporarily left the crime syndicate and concentrated on working at Waferworld in Singapore, the second largest foundry in Asia.

And one day in 1996, Nelson had showed up at his door in Singapore and they had shaken hands and become serious partners in the counterfeit chip syndicate once again, headquartered in Singapore this time. He experienced pure joy when the syndicate continued to evade the police and money poured into his Cayman Islands bank account.

He remembered the day Nelson informed him of the identity of their silent partner and why Alan Lee had to be killed. Nelson's tone was fearful, he would do their partner's bidding, or they would all be killed. Mark was more pragmatic. Unknown to Nelson, he contacted the Mountain Master through his minions and pledged his support, asking for protection. Now he was reaping the promise of that protection.

There was a heavy knock on his door. A member of the triad stood outside, ready to take him to the triad head.

Soon he entered a seedy building near the docks, walked through a maze of corridors to a door guarded by two Chinese men. He entered and coughed. The room was smoky with burning incense, and he could barely make out the figure seated behind a desk. A man emerged out of the smoke and came forward to shake Mark's hand. He was a clean-shaven man dressed in a smart suit.

'My name is Ming Tao Chen,' the man said. 'Pleased to meet you, Latham. I ran the electronic brokerage firm in Shenzhen with Nelson Ong. Mountain Master has some words of advice. I will translate for you.'

Mark nodded, glad to have met someone speaking fluent English.

The figure behind the desk spoke rapid Cantonese in a guttural voice. Mark could not make out his face at all, the incense smoke was too thick.

Chen translated the words. 'Welcome to the Tong Gang, Mark Latham. You are a chip expert, unlike your bloodthirsty friend, the gambler, Nelson Ong, and we are pleased to leave the past behind and do business with you. Some terms have changed due to the risk involved for us. Instead of taking 50 per cent of your profits, we will take 60 per cent. And instead of leaving decisions to you, we elect you second in command, you will report to Ming Tao Chen. You will run the business together and share the 40 per cent in profits. That is all, Latham.'

Chen stepped towards the door. 'It is time to go. I will see you out. The car will take you to a private aircraft that will fly you to Macau. Everything is ready there. Your office, your apartment, and your staff. We will commence operations in two weeks.'

Mark Latham followed Chen out into the bright sunlight and blinked. Being a puppet on a chain was better than rotting in jail. Or was it?

Friday, 28 June 2013

Singapore

39

Corporal Mok knocked on Dolly's door on a bright, sunny morning and told her DAC Nathan wanted to see her at his office. Dolly nodded and made her way to the elevator to ride up to her boss's office. She was in a happy frame of mind. She had caught the mastermind of a nebulous crime syndicate, a task she had told herself was near-impossible. All they had to do now was grill the prisoner until he confessed to his crimes. She was glad to have put behind bars a man who murdered innocent people for greed. As for Latham, Dolly believed it was a matter of time before Interpol found and arrested him.

Dolly entered Nathan's office to find Supt Geraldine Ang already seated there. Both her superior officers were smiling at her, and Dolly tentatively smiled back. She noted Geraldine Ang's eyes were red and wondered at the cause.

DAC John Nathan boomed out, 'Sit down, sit down, ASP Das. We have some good news and some bad news. The bad news is that Supt Ang's husband recently suffered a stroke and needs rehabilitative care and bypass surgery. Supt Ang needs to care for him and feels she cannot continue as a senior officer in Major Crime. The AC has transferred her to Cyber Crime, where she can partially work from home. I am sure she will excel in her job and at the same time take care of her husband.'

Dolly turned to Supt Ang in distress. 'Oh, ma'am, I'm so sorry. How is your husband now?'

Geraldine Ang's lips lifted in a tired smile. 'His left side is paralysed, but the doctors say it is temporary. With rehabilitation and surgery, he should get much better. Thank you for your concern, ASP Das.'

'I wish him a speedy recovery, ma'am,' Dolly said, sincerely.

DAC Nathan coughed. 'Now for the good news, ASP Das. The position of superintendent in the Special Investigation Section of Major Crime will become vacant when Supt Ang leaves our division. At the same time, you and Charlie Goh have excelled in solving four murders and two cases. Not only did you put Linda Lee, Alice Lee's killer, behind bars, but you have also exposed a crime syndicate and caught the man who planned the murders of Alan Lee, Sushila Iyer, and Rachel Kelly. Excellent work! It's my pleasure to inform you of your promotion to the rank of superintendent in the Special Investigation Section of the Major Crime Division of Singapore CID, ASP Das. You will take over from Supt Ang and I am positive you will do the division proud. Congratulations, Supt Das.'

'Congratulations, Supt Das,' Supt Ang echoed, smiling warmly. 'You are an astute police officer, and this promotion is well-deserved. The syndicate was hard to nose out, but you and your team did it!'

Dolly was grinning from ear to ear. 'Thank you so much, sir.' She turned to Supt Ang. 'Thank you, ma'am.'

DAC Nathan coughed. 'What about Patrick Singh's condition? And have we nabbed the crook who ran him over?'

Dolly said, 'Patrick Singh is on a ventilator. The end is near, sir. But his verbal and visual testimonies will stand up in court and convict Nelson Ong of murder. Our officers are combing the city's car dealer workshops and we have a strong lead to a small-time crook, Chee See Tong. His car was in a workshop and the dealer notified our men. There is blood on the car and our forensic team is at the workshop giving the car a once-over. If the blood found on the car's bumper matches that of Patrick Singh, we have the man whom Nelson Ong hired to kill Patrick. And he can give evidence against Nelson in court.'

'Excellent, excellent. I have another piece of good news for you, Supt Das. Please come with me to the conference room.'

Supt Ang remained in the office while Dolly followed DAC Nathan to the next room. As they entered, a tall man with thick white hair and blue eyes rose from his chair at the conference table.

DAC Nathan beamed. 'Supt Das, this is Chief Supt Randall from IGCI and he has some evidence for you.'

After shaking hands, everyone sat around the small conference table. Derek Randall took an envelope out of his pocket and extricated a small mobile hard disk. Pointing to it, he said, 'Supt Das, we were clearing out Rachel Kelly's locker at IGCI and found the disk and a letter in this envelope.'

Dolly glanced at the letter and began to read it. It was short and to the point.

Dear Derek,

If you are opening my locker, I am either dead or in jail. I am sorry to say I broke the law and I will take what is coming to me. I belonged to a counterfeit chip syndicate that sold substandard chips on the black market. Unfortunately, lately, the boss of the syndicate has begun eliminating people who could harm our operations. The boss is my boyfriend, Nelson Ong, and the mobile disk contains taped conversations where he discusses with me how he will kill Alan Lee and Sushila Iyer. Alan Lee posed a threat to our operations and Sushila was a syndicate member who made mistakes and could have potentially betrayed the syndicate if caught by the police. This tape is my 'get out of jail free' card. I wish to use it if I am ever brought to trial. I will be a witness for the prosecution in Nelson's trial. In return, I want a lighter sentence because I did not order anyone to be killed. If I am dead when you find this disk, use it as you see fit.

Sincerely,

Rachel Kelly

Dolly looked up after she had finished reading and gave a long sigh. 'Patrick Singh's testimony and this tape will convict Nelson Ong of murder.'

Derek Randall nodded. 'I'm sorry one of our officers was corrupt. We had no idea. We are still seeking Latham and there have been leads. We raided a flat in Hong Kong where he had been holed up and our intelligence reports he may be headed for Macau. The Interpol bureau there is on it. Mr Hadyanto has been located in China and the Interpol branches of China and Indonesia are conferring on his extradition. He will stand trial in Bali for the murder of Mr Ramdin.'

Back in her office, Dolly dialled Charlie's number and when he lumbered in, she told him the good news. After warm felicitations from her subordinate, Dolly said, 'It's my pleasure, Charlie, as soon as I assume my new rank, to promote you to a senior inspector. More money, Charlie! And you fully deserve the new rank.'

Charlie mopped his face with his handkerchief and couldn't stop grinning. 'Thank you, madam. Congratulations, madam!'

'Congratulations to you, too, Charlie! We'll celebrate with a meal at my mother's place, do bring Meena along. I will also be looking into promoting Adrian Mok.'

After Charlie rushed out of her office to call his wife with the good news, Dolly picked up her phone to call Joey. The unease in her mind about why he kept going to Malacca clouded her happiness at the promotion. She really had to get to the bottom of this.

Sunday, 30 June 2013

Singapore

40

Ash and Amita had gone out for breakfast and Dolly perspired as she vacuumed their room. Really, she thought, disapprovingly, young people nowadays were untidy and lazy. So much mess and no thought or desire to clean up after them. She remembered how she and Lily had to keep their bedrooms tidy in their childhood or no dinner that night. Uma had been strict in their upbringing. The part-time maid she had hired had left and Dolly was back doing household chores. She sighed. She had always found it difficult to take Ash to task, always tentative in her approach and it had been easy for Ash to ignore her half-hearted disciplining.

After taking a brisk shower, Dolly entered her dining room in a better frame of mind. The kitchen smelt of fried bacon and eggs, and Dolly smiled at Joey busy at the stove cooking an English fry-up, a luxury they indulged in on a lazy Sunday.

When they were seated at the dining table, Joey looked at Dolly. She was surprised to see his eyes were teary and his smile, tentative.

Cutting up her omelette into bite-sized pieces, Dolly said, 'What's up, Joey?'

Joey finished chewing a piece of toast and said, 'Are you finished with the case?' When Dolly nodded, he continued, 'We can talk about my visits to Malacca.'

Dolly sat up, her eyes apprehensive and curious. 'I'm listening,' she said, softly.

Joey set aside his plate and placed his hands in a steeple on the placemat. 'When we were courting, I wasn't honest with you. I said I hadn't found love in my young days, but I did love a Malaysian girl, only the relationship did not work out.'

Dolly's eyes rounded. 'Why didn't it work out?'

Joey sighed. 'We were both twenty-one and young. We were in love, but Mei Ching was always casual about our relationship. And one day she went back to Malaysia and did not return. We were classmates at the university. She broke my heart, and I was so affected, I dropped out of college. When my dad died, I enlisted in the Police Academy and became a traffic policeman. I did not hear from Mei Ching again until a year ago, when a woman called Rebecca wrote to me claiming she was my daughter.'

'*What?*' Dolly dropped her fork on her plate with a clatter and choked on her toast. She looked up at Joey after she had overcome a bout of coughing.

'Yes, I was as shocked as you are. Rebecca claimed in her letter her mother told her of her paternity on her deathbed. Mei Ching died of stomach cancer two years ago. It seems Mei Ching was pregnant with my child when she left for Malaysia all those years ago. Her parents worked in the tea gardens of Cameron Highlands and while she was there on a visit, there was a fire that gutted the house. Her parents lost all their savings. The family relocated to Ipoh and Mei Ching helped her father run a hawker stall. Her father's assistant fell in love with her and agreed to marry her knowing she was carrying another man's child. It seems Rebecca's stepfather was kind and caring and Mei Ching erased her past. Two years before Mei Ching's death, her husband died of a heart attack. So, when Mei Ching was dying, she did not want Rebecca to feel lonely and told her about me. It took some time for Rebecca to find my address and send me a letter.'

Dolly's face had lost some colour, but she attacked the bacon on her plate with determination. After eating for some time, she said, 'I wonder why Mei Ching never informed you she was carrying your child. You would have married her, right?'

Joey looked sad. 'Yes, of course. Maybe she did not love me,' he said in a small voice. 'It was a fling for her, nothing more.'

Dolly had lost her appetite and set aside her plate. 'There's more to this, right? If Mei Ching did not tell you about your daughter before, why would she speak on her deathbed? Just so her daughter wouldn't feel lonely?' Dolly looked sceptical.

Joey's brown eyes were misty. 'Rebecca was diagnosed with breast cancer two weeks before her mother died of stomach cancer. Maybe, Mei Ching thought Rebecca could use some support.'

Dolly's eyes rounded with concern. 'Oh, I'm so sorry, Joey. Rebecca is single?'

'Yes, though she is thirty-four.'

Dolly asked tentatively, 'You're sure she's your daughter?'

Joey gave an enormous sigh. 'Yes, we did a paternity test on one of my visits. The thing is, sweetheart, Rebecca's cancer is aggressive, and she would benefit from care at a Singapore hospital. I've been visiting her more often because of her illness and she is sinking.'

Dolly looked at her plate. 'Singapore healthcare is expensive if one does not have insurance.'

'I will dig into my savings and try to enrol Rebecca in a clinical trial of one of the promising drugs for breast cancer. She's already had a mastectomy and chemo.'

Dolly looked up at Joey, her eyes thoughtful. 'It's natural you would want to take care of your biological daughter, Joey. Do you want her to stay at our house during her treatment?' When Joey nodded, mutely, she said, 'Okay, though the mess Ash and Amita make, and Amita never cleans up after.'

A smile flitted across Joey's lips. 'You seem to blame Amita for the mess and expect her to clean up. Because she's a girl? You're turning into a dragon mother-in-law even before their marriage.'

Dolly was thinking hard. She looked up and smiled. 'No, I'm not. Ash has mentioned it would be fun living at the university dorm, this is the time we say yes. Then they will be out of the house. I'm not worried after they're married. They will have their own flat and they can clutter that up as much as they like. I won't care.'

'I say, it's decent of you to host Rebecca, sweetheart.' Joey began to take an interest in his omelette again.

Dolly said blithely, 'Well, we have a son and now we have a sick daughter. Sick daughter takes priority.'

Joey rose from his chair, came around the table and put his arms around his wife and lovingly kissed her. 'Thank you, my love,' he murmured into her hair.

41

Twilight had fallen and lights blazed from Uma's flat in Silver Springs Condominium. Family and friends gathered in the drawing room to celebrate Dolly's promotion to superintendent of police. Girlie had placed plates of appetizers on the low glass tables and everyone helped themselves to the delicious tidbits. After the chorus of felicitations had died down, Charlie talked briefly of the counterfeit chip murder case.

'Nelson Ong is all lawyered up and so far, he has mumbled "no comment" when we asked whether he ordered the hit on Alan Lee,' Charlie said after munching on a chicken tikka. 'But the public prosecutor's office has accepted Rachel Kelly's tape of Nelson arranging the murder of Alan Lee and Sushila Iyer and accepted Patrick Singh's deathbed visual and audio interviews.' Next to him, his wife, Meena, was enjoying the potato tikkis on her plate. Delicious aromas wafted in from the kitchen where Vernon prepared a quick supper of fish fry, fried rice, and sweet and sour chicken.

Dolly looked drained. The revelation that Joey was the father of an adult daughter was taking an emotional toll on her. That, too, a daughter needing medical treatment to save her life.

She roused herself, saying, 'Yes, Rachel Kelly had tape-recorded Nelson's conversations where he discusses ways and means of murdering Alan Lee. He says on the tape he will ask Mark Latham to identify a hatchet man to do the job and we know Latham paid Ramdin to kill Alan Lee.'

A rasping voice interrupted. 'Nelson Ong is a millionaire. Why would he be involved in this black market racket?'

Dolly looked at Uma and a tired smile flitted across her face. 'Nelson Ong was a compulsive gambler from a young age. We have been talking to some of his friends. All the millions he made from his businesses went to feed his gambling habit. He had to have an illicit side-business to make more money. He liquidated all his assets and we caught him in time. He was escaping to the hideout where he has stashed away his money.'

'What a case this has been,' Charlie mused, enthusiastically helping himself to fish tikkas. 'Out of five deaths, one turned out to be a suicide. Plenty of twists and turns.'

Lily looked up from the potato tikkis on her plate and asked, 'Will Patrick Singh survive?' She looked down at her plate when Dolly shook her head.

'Those poor kids,' Girlie moaned, sitting on the floor near Uma's divan. 'Father and mother both killers.'

'We had two cases, really. Alice Lee's murder had nothing to do with the syndicate.' Dolly began eating a vegetable pakora. She smiled thinly at her sister, a spurt of jealousy again rearing its ugly head. She swallowed a mouthful and said, 'Lily solved Alice Lee's murder. She noticed Linda's hand was bandaged, the helper told her Linda was not at home the night Alice was murdered and Lily identified Pradeep Chopra as Linda's lover.'

Charlie's smile held genuine warmth. 'Madam Lily, you should consider joining the CID.'

Uma noted the glint in her older daughter's eyes and quickly said from the divan, 'I shiver every time I think of that chit of a girl, Linda. She came to Lily's birthday parties when they were young. And to learn she is a cold-blooded killer. So, she was in love with Pradeep Chopra? Anyone talk to this man yet?'

Dolly nodded. 'Yes, we went to interview him. He is in shock but readily admitted Linda and he were seeing each other. He also confirmed he called Linda on the phone after Alice Lee refused to withdraw her suit on the night of her murder. He told us Linda was angry on the phone, but she never told him she would go and talk to Alice. Who knows? Pradeep is trying his best to distance himself from Linda Lee now.'

'At least those two girls of his will have a roof over their heads,' Lily said. 'Alice Lee was evil.' She glanced at Girlie, pointed to the fish tikka on her plate and gave a thumbs up sign. Girlie beamed.

'But Alice did not deserve to die. At last, Justin Chua has done the right thing by Pradeep Chopra and influenced the appeals committee at the university to rule in Pradeep's favour. Pradeep Chopra will be granted tenure and a full professorship at Pelangi U. This case has been very harrowing and made worse by your doings, Lily, and Angie!' Dolly scolded. Her latent jealousy of Lily and the news that Joey had an ill biological daughter were making Dolly crabby and malicious.

Uma pricked up her ears. 'What did they do?'

Lily was gesticulating wildly to Dolly not to tell their mother about her moonlighting as a cook in Nelson's bungalow, but Dolly was in the mood for taking out her bad temper on Lily. She looked at Joey, who returned her gaze, sadly. He knew his wife was still digesting his news of fatherhood. 'I want Mummy to know, Lily, so she can stop you from doing foolish things the next time.'

Dolly turned to Uma. 'Mummy, we were lacking evidence of Nelson and Rachel's involvement in the racket and the conspiracy to murder Alan Lee. So, Lily went to work undercover as a cook at Nelson Ong's bungalow. Angie referred her to Rachel Kelly, of course. They planted a listening device in the bedroom and collected evidence. What they did not know was that the evidence would not be admissible in court. They placed themselves in danger. Nelson and Rachel were murderers. Rachel Kelly took Lily to the police post and asked the officers to arrest her for thieving.'

Uma was goggling at her younger daughter. 'What were you stealing?'

'Nothing,' Lily said, hurriedly. 'I knocked Rachel's handbag to the ground by accident and she came and saw me with my hands in her bag. She thought I was stealing her money.'

Dolly was looking quizzically at her mother. 'Mummy, why aren't you scolding Lily?'

Uma gave a cackle. 'I'm trying to imagine her as a cook in that house. What daring! What enterprise!'

'She could have been *murdered*!' Dolly yelled.

Joey intervened. 'Dolly, you look tired. You should have an early night.'

Uma made amends. She nodded at her older daughter and said, 'I will speak to Lily about this tonight, don't you worry, Dolly.'

Dolly said sharply, 'And while we are at it, from now on, Lily, I will never discuss my cases with you and you are not to meddle in my cases. You make a lot of trouble!'

Lily's eyes flashed. 'It's because of the listening device in Nelson's bedroom that you heard him ask Patrick Singh to murder Rachel Kelly.

And while you were not there in time to save Rachel's life, you do have Patrick's testimony that will likely hang Nelson Ong. You are good at taking help without giving credit.' Lily was upset enough to storm out of the room.

Dolly sighed. 'But I *really* don't want her to meddle in my cases any more.'

Joey felt sorry for his sister-in-law and said tentatively, 'Lily has a sharp brain. I could always ask her to join my detective agency. She can be a partner.' He averted his face from Dolly's glare.

'Your cases involve getting the dirt on spouses who want to get divorced, Joey. That's how you met Dolly.' Lily had been just outside the door and now sidled in and seated herself.

Dolly rose to her husband's defence. 'Joey's research put us on the trail of Rachel Kelly.' Dolly smiled at her husband, wanting him to know she supported his desire to help his daughter. Dolly's bad temper was always short-lasting. She reached out to the small glass-topped table near her sofa and helped herself to a samosa. 'We were wondering why she would not search for Mark Latham and Joey looked her up on the net and researched newspaper articles.'

Joey smiled cheerily at everyone, his brown eyes twinkling. 'No big deal, it's my job as a PI.' He enthusiastically helped himself to some fish tikkas.

Girlie had a sad look on her face. She burst out, 'Poor Lionel Chu and Alan Lee. One friend stab the other in the back.'

Angie, who had finished a generous helping of appetizers, now nodded. 'And so, Lionel killed himself. He could not live with what he had done to Alan. It *is* tragic.'

'And Ronnie Lee's plane crashed because of one of these faulty computer chips?' Uma asked.

'We'll never know for sure,' Dolly said. 'There's the pilot's words, and the plane was refurbished at low cost where there's more chance of it being fitted with counterfeit parts. There was no real evidence, the plane was smashed up.'

Lily said, 'Sushila Iyer's mother flew off to Chennai, last night. She asked me to make some roti and lentils she could take on the flight. I feel so sorry for her.'

'Greed,' Angie opined. She flung back her blonde hair. 'Sushila was full of it. I'm glad I don't have to go back to work at Nelson Ong's bungalow.'

'It's so stuffy in here,' Lily said. She went and opened the windows, letting the night air in.

'They all rat on each other. Rachel Kelly tape Nelson and Nelson order his girlfriend's killing. Did Nelson know his girlfriend tape him?' Vernon had come in from the kitchen and seated himself near the air-conditioner.

'Maybe he suspected she would betray him. I'm just surprised Patrick Singh believed Rachel ordered the hit on Sushila. He killed the wrong person. Nelson Ong ordered the hit on Sushila. He manipulated Patrick to make him kill Kelly. I guess Patrick was so overcome with grief at Sushila's death, he became gullible, wanting revenge.' Dolly finished eating a samosa.

'Nelson Ong is not the only one running a counterfeit chip racket,' Joey observed. 'There are others.' He began to eat another fish tikka.

'Oh, Brendan Gan is welcome to crack the other cases,' Dolly said, smiling. 'I have had enough of criminal syndicates. I went for a holiday to Bali and then this dangerous case fell into my lap. It was such a difficult case to solve. People kept getting murdered and suspects kept disappearing. And for the first time, we had a corrupt police officer.'

'Who loved her mother very much.' Lily remembered the visit to the hospice days ago. 'Even criminals have one saving grace. For Rachel Kelly, it was love for her mother. Well, mother and daughter are together now.'

Angie asked, 'Rachel Kelly cremated, Ma'am Dolly?'

Dolly nodded. 'Her next-of-kin was a distant cousin. It seems Rachel Kelly instructed her cousin to scatter her ashes in the Swiss village where she owned a house and where she had lived with her mother for some years. The cousin came and took both urns back with her to England. She told us she will scatter both Rachel and her mother's ashes in the Swiss village.'

Lily said, 'And for Patrick Singh, it was his love for Sushila Iyer that made him become a criminal.'

'I don't see any saving grace in Nelson Ong or Mark Latham,' Dolly opined. 'Both were cold-blooded and ruthless. One was a gambler and needed money and the other, well, we have yet to discover what drove Mark Latham to do what he did. Oh, I could do with a holiday.' Dolly looked wistful.

Uma said in a surprisingly strong voice, 'Come with me, Doll. I promised Ma Durga that if you were promoted to superintendent, I will go on a religious pilgrimage to all the holy shrines in India. There is a special train in India that takes devotees to all the shrines and Lily has looked up the information. They serve good vegetarian fare throughout the journey. Come with me, Dolly. Lily has already agreed to be my companion. It would be lovely to have both my daughters with me.'

Dolly's eyes rounded. 'And who will look after little Molly?'

Girlie was grinning from ear to ear. 'I will, Ma'am Supt. She will be coming with us on the train. Ben, too. Angie and Vernon say they never take honeymoon, so Ma'am Lily is going to give them one. In India! They are coming, too, ma'am.'

'Well, quite a party. Oh, I don't know if I can go.'

Dolly looked at Joey, who said, 'Sweetheart, please do go. I can manage everything here.'

Dolly smiled tremulously at her husband.

'Will Linda Lee hang?' Lily asked. Her mind was on Linda's two young children.

Dolly sighed. 'Yes. She killed Alice Lee in cold blood.'

Uma quavered, 'Those poor children. What will happen to them?'

Dolly said, 'Our Junior Minister of Transport has been speaking with DAC Nathan. Despite Linda killing his daughter, Justin Chua is taking in Duleep and Natasha. Etienne is going to stay with them and help take care of them. The maid, Joyce, will stay with them. The Primrose Crescent bungalow and Linda Lee's flat here in Silver Springs will both be sold to supply money for the children's needs. It seems Etienne has turned over a new leaf, according to Lester Chong. He is going to work at his uncle's biscuit factory and he is determined to provide emotional support to Duleep and Natasha.' She smiled as everyone nodded, approvingly.

Lily was thoughtful. 'Linda was always hot-headed as a child. But she never thought of what would happen to the children if she became a killer? As far as I know, she is a good mother.'

Dolly said, 'Her hatred for Alice Lee was simmering for many years. When her stepmother stood in the way of her future with Pradeep Chopra, the hatred reached a boiling point and she was enraged enough to strangle Alice. It was an unpremeditated murder. A killing done in the heat of the moment.'

'It's called "temporary insanity".' Vernon nodded, knowingly. He had become addicted to crime thrillers from the time he began helping solve Dolly's cases.

Charlie looked approvingly at Vernon. 'Yes, you're right. And that's exactly what Linda Lee's lawyer will use to help her escape the gallows.'

'With Emily Gan's evidence, we suspected Pradeep Chopra or even Etienne of murdering Alice Lee,' Dolly said. 'In a way, we were right. Linda killed for Pradeep.'

Vernon suddenly jumped up. 'All the food will get cold. Girlie and Angie, I need your help to set the table.'

After the three of them had gone to the kitchen, Dolly observed, 'I thought Frankie would join the party, Lil.'

'He is babysitting Silly Belly and Ben,' Uma giggled.

Lily cried, 'Mummy stop calling Molly that!' She looked at her sister. 'He will join us as soon as Girlie can take over the babysitting.'

Vernon stood at the door and gave a bow, urging everyone to enter the dining hall to sample the Chinese meal he had painstakingly prepared. Girlie wheeled Uma's chair to her and helped her into it.

Soon the living hall was empty, and the sound of laughter came from the dining hall along with the tinkle of cutlery.

After dinner, Charlie and Meena went home. Girlie served everyone hot beverages in the living room and went to babysit Molly and Ben in Lily's flat, allowing Frankie to come and have his dinner.

Seeing Lily and Joey huddled together, deep in discussion over their coffees, Dolly asked, 'Hey Joey! What's up?'

Joey turned to his wife, smiling widely. 'Lily was terrific solving Alice Lee's murder. I've formally offered her a partnership in my PI agency.' He took a sip of his coffee.

Dolly nodded. 'Well, now that I've thought about it, I support this idea wholeheartedly! At least, Lily will have some legitimacy to her detecting, and now she can get into as many scrapes as she likes. We'll all blame you, Joey. I won't be responsible.' She sipped her tea and smiled.

Lily looked sad. 'But your cases are tough to solve and challenging, Dolly. I loved sleuthing with you. I can't help you any more?'

Dolly shook her head. 'You need to think of me, Lil. I am a full superintendent and when you upstage me in front of my subordinates, how do you think that makes me feel?'

Lily's eyes rounded. 'I *didn't*. Charlie or you would have seen the bandage on Linda's wrist soon enough and drawn the same conclusion. And yes, well, I did go overboard with planting the bug in Rachel Kelly's bedroom but that's how a ruthless killer was caught.' She drank her coffee, burnt her tongue and grimaced.

'No, Lily.' Dolly's voice was firm. 'Do your detecting with Joey. You'll enjoy it and you'll receive a salary as well.'

Uma looked at the storm brewing on her younger daughter's face and chimed in, 'Lily, let Dolly do her job and you do yours. I am confused. If you become a PI, what's going to happen to Lily's Kitchen?' She took a sip of the hot Milo Girlie had placed on the table next to the divan.

'Oh, my feet are killing me doing housework, Mrs D. I know how to cook all the dishes. I take over, Mrs D, and you pay me a good salary. Then no need to work as maid any more.' Angie's eyes were shining as she sat on a sofa with Vernon.

'Wait!' Uma cried. 'I already have a police superintendent daughter and now the other one is going to be a detective as well! I am tired of hearing about killers and criminals all day long. The only saving grace was Lily's chatter about all the delicious food she cooked in her café. In old age, food is my only solace. Even if I can't eat some of the food, hearing about them makes me dream about them at night. Now, what am I going to do?'

Amidst laughter, Lily said, 'We will all sleep on these new ideas.' She glanced apologetically at her sister. 'Sorry I caused trouble for you, Doll.'

Dolly smiled with genuine warmth and said, 'No worries. Let's go for lunch next weekend to one of the hotel buffets, Lil. Just you and me. And have a long chat.' She glanced at Joey and turned back to Lily, giving a nod. 'I have plenty to tell you.' Dolly began finishing her tea.

Lily immediately understood Joey and Dolly had talked about his visits to Malacca and nodded. 'Looking forward to a good natter, Doll.' Lily's tentative smile widened when she saw the love and warmth in her sister's eyes.

Uma said, 'Lily got a brochure about that train in India, Doll. Here, Lily, show the brochure to your sister.' She continued sipping her Milo.

The two sisters sat on the love couch poring over the brochure, bonding over the holiday they would take in India with their mother and friends. Uma looked at her two daughters, glanced at Joey and gave a wink, bringing a smile to Joey's face.

One Month Later

Singapore

Epilogue

Etienne walked out of his uncle's biscuit factory and flagged down a cab. When he emerged from the cab and on to the pavement in front of the National Gallery, he was enveloped in a warm embrace.

'Oh, Tien, it's *so* good to see you!' Della Pang fawned all over her boyfriend. 'Sorry about Linda. I was so shocked, babe. You must've gone through hell. You're my rich boy now, aren't you, sweetie?'

Etienne blushed, looking overwhelmed. 'Shall we go to the restaurant inside the gallery for dinner?'

'Why, you should take me to a posh restaurant, my darling. You've inherited millions, haven't you, baby? And then we'll go to my place. You're welcome to stay the night, sweetie,' Della said, expansively.

Etienne nodded and began to walk together with Della along the pavement towards one of the fancy restaurants on the road.

Phil Wee, PI, walked behind them, his eyes honed on the couple, his mind pleasurably fixed on the money Justin Chua was paying him to spy on his grandson. His gambling debts would soon be paid off, Phil thought contentedly.

* * *

Nelson Ong sat in his stark prison cell at Changi, brooding on the irony of his situation. Painted as a criminal mastermind, little did the police know he was a mere puppet of the triad, after he got into their debt by his gambling. The only way out had been the syndicate and the triad collected half the money they made. He decided to ask his lawyer to plea bargain for him, sell out the triad to escape the death penalty. He felt relieved after he had made up his mind.

He hungrily ate his dinner when it arrived. Suddenly, his head swam, and he slumped to the floor. Just before he lost consciousness, he noticed a piece of paper tucked into the food tray. It read:

It is not personal. It is just business.
489

Tong Gang

Acknowledgements

My sincere thanks to my husband, Dr Royston Hogan, a thirty-year veteran working in the semiconductor industry, for acting as consultant for this work of fiction and helping me understand the technical details of integrated circuit chip manufacturing. My thanks to my Penguin Random House SEA publisher, Nora Nazerene Abu Bakar, for her support and for allowing my creativity free reign. My sincere thanks to my editor, Thatchaayanie Renganathan, whose detailed and critical feedback have made all my murder mystery books better. Many thanks to the entire Penguin Random House SEA publishing team, including the publicists, for their interactions and help in getting the books noticed. Last but not the least, I want to say a word of appreciation to the cover designer for all three detective novels featuring the Das sisters, Parag Chitale, who wove each book's motif into a murder framework on the cover of the books.